Praises for *Solomon's Porch*

Solomon's Porch brings home an important message to those led astray by the shallow materialism of contemporary society and is an accurate portrayal of life for those seeking Christ in American prisons.
—David Patton MA., Mdiv., Publisher, Dynamis,
St. George Orthodox Cathedral

One would hope that many a sermon in our churches could be as powerful, informative, and effective as *Solomon's Porch*—a potent message—fully consistent with Orthodox Christian teachings.
—Helen Tzima Otto, Phd., researcher and publisher
for The Verenikia Press

Phenomenal. *Solomon's Porch* is a unique yet powerful book filled with truth. It will keep you rivited and will give you much to ponder.
—Ruth Magan, author of *Laughing With Angels,*
My Angel, My Friend, and *Visions of Earth Beyond* 2012

Solomon's Porch is a must read for anyone who enjoys reading christian fiction. Wid Bastian provides the reader with great character development and a riveting plot line that highlights good versus evil. This book is for all who wish to see a positive alternative to life's hardships.
—Fr. Dominic Briese, O.P.

Solomon's
PORCH

Christian Suspense

Solomon's
PORCH

Wid Bastian

TATE PUBLISHING & Enterprises

Published by Tate Publishing & Enterprises, LLC
127 E. Trade Center Terrace | Mustang, Oklahoma 73064 USA
1.888.361.9473 | www.tatepublishing.com

Tate Publishing is committed to excellence in the publishing industry. The company reflects the philosophy established by the founders, based on Psalm 68:11,
"The Lord gave the word and great was the company of those who published it."

Book design copyright © 2010 by Tate Publishing, LLC. All rights reserved.
Cover design by Amber Gulilat
Interior design by Lindsay B. Behrens

Published in the United States of America

ISBN: 978-1-61566-423-8
1. Fiction / Religious   2. Fiction / Christian / Suspense
10.01.05

Dedication

For Deacon Harry, who taught me that
the Bible was just the beginning.

"And through the hands of the apostles many signs and wonders were done among the people. And they were all with one accord on Solomon's Porch."

Acts, Chapter Five,
Verse Twelve

Author's Foreword

We were created in the image and likeness of God. Our souls are eternal, but for a brief time the immortal is hidden within flesh, the timeless joined to the temporary. Trapped in this imperfect state, we strive to find ourselves and our Creator, our souls desperately seeking to become reunited with the Immortal One.

The characters in Solomon's Porch struggle between the conflicting calls of world and spirit, they reach out for God's mercy in the darkness. Through my imagination, they do battle with themselves and against evil, stumbling down the path of life making mistakes, sometimes horrific ones.

They ask, as we all do, why are we here? Is there a God and, if so, what does He want from us? What is our destiny? What is happiness? What is love? What is truth? Is it possible to make sense of a world that exalts the most violent, profane, and merciless among us?

The Son of God touched me, reached out to a very determined sinner and atheist, and by His grace is leading me toward salvation. While I by no means have all the answers, I no longer need them. Faith has replaced cynicism. Knowledge of Christ, who He is, and what He has called each of us to become, now lights my way as I patiently await the Lord's mercy.

Let all who read Solomon's Porch see if they can find their own road home through the One who assured us that He, and He alone, is "the way, the truth, and the life."

One

Of all of the places in all of the world, this was the last one Peter Carson ever expected to call home. He came from a good family, and had been blessed with a privileged upbringing and a pampered lifestyle, but all that was history. Now he was stuck here in this purgatory, in the sweltering July heat of South Carolina, methodically mowing the grass at a federal prison camp. Once he traded futures and options and managed millions of dollars. Now all he had to exchange was his pint of milk for an extra cookie at chow. It was nearly as depressing as it was humiliating.

The misfiring two stroke engine had a calming effect on Peter's fragile nerves. The rusty machine was a convenient distraction, focusing on the whirs and clangs of the old motor took Peter's mind off of his all too dismal reality. Mowing had become Peter's favorite escape, and he lost himself in the simple and repetitive task of cutting the grass whenever he got the chance.

But, without fail, within an hour or so of starting, Peter Carson would simply run out of lawn to mow. It was then that the demons returned with a vengeance and continued their attacks. Peter's life had become a living hell.

Three hundred miles away in Atlanta was the world Peter had been forced to leave behind. There was an ex-wife, who he considered to be the nexus of his misery, and a young son, barely ten, who desperately missed his father. Kevin Carson spent his days wondering why his dad left him, why his mother remarried a jerk like Walter, and why God was so cruel. Once a curious and playful child, Kevin was now anything but these things. Kev didn't seem to care anymore and, as kids are apt to do, he somehow believed the mess his life had become was all his fault.

Peter's calls and letters to his son were increasingly being met with hostility from both Kev and his ex, Julie. He was learning the hard way that when you're in prison, in many ways it's like you're dead. You can offer little comfort to those on the outside, and even less support.

So, on this day, Peter decided to skip his weekly call to his son. This would not be the first time he had opted out. He wondered, would he be missed, or rather, would Julie and Kevin be grateful not to have to deal with him? Slowly, but inexorably, Peter Carson was removing himself from his family's life. He was pursuing self-destruction, unknowingly serving a false god who offered only lies and pain.

Although he was permanently barred from the securities industry after his conviction, Peter Carson still charted his favorite stocks like a hunter who could no longer kill, but now only stalk his prey. Carefully and methodically he plotted price and volume numbers, kept abreast of the latest economic trends, and tracked the major stock indexes. He kept detailed notes, whole files even. Why he couldn't really say, but like mowing the grass going though the motions of being a stockbroker seemed to dull his pain.

But, on this day, by the time Peter put the mower away and sat down with his outdated copy of a less-than-adequate small town paper's financial page, his misery was peaking. The waste of it all, the seeming finality of his failure as a husband, a father, and especially, as a man hit home like never before. Peter had reached the stage where he despised his own soul without mercy. On this day he would stare into the abyss and see only blackness.

Finding a semi-private corner of the small library at the Parkersboro Federal Prison Camp, Peter rolled himself up into a ball and started to cry. His heart was breaking from the weight of his unforgiven sin. His mind was on fire, his spirit groaned, and he wished for the peace of death.

Mr. Peter Carson, the golden child, the MBA, the former owner of a fine home and a Porsche, husband of the beauty queen, the perpetual winner and success story, was now nothing more than an empty shell, a broken vessel. Everything Peter valued had been taken from him. Only a pitiful pool of pain and sorrow remained from the tidal wave generated by his prosecution and conviction.

In other words, God basically had Peter right where He wanted him.

"Panos Kallistos," a voice from behind Peter softly called. "Turn and face me and be of good courage. The angel of the Lord encamps all around those who fear Him, and delivers them."

Panos Kallistos. That was a name Peter Carson had not heard spoken, or even thought of, since he was a child. It was in fact his proper Christian name given to him at baptism long ago. After Peter's parents, Nicholas and Neitha Kallistos, died together in an automobile crash when Peter was two, he was adopted by his first cousin on his mother's side and her husband, Marie and Thomas Carson. His name was legally changed to Carson before he was old enough to speak it, yet someone now standing behind him knew him by this name.

Peter gathered himself, turned, and looked up at the striking face of a man who he was sure had to be a new arrival at the camp. With only two hundred or so inmates on the compound, everyone knew most of the faces, even if they didn't always remember the names.

"What did you call me?" Peter asked, at the same time using his sleeves to wipe away the last of his tears.

"Your name, of course. Panos Kallistos, son of Nicholas and Neitha. Do you object to being called by your proper name? Do not be offended by what is holy."

Do not be offended by what is holy? Peter's wits were rapidly returning to him and his first thought was that some psycho had gotten a hold of his Bureau of Prisons file and was now playing games with him.

"Who are you?" Peter asked.

"Gabriel," was the reply.

"Well, Gabriel, I don't know who you are or how you know my birth name, but don't screw with me. You are new here, obviously. F****with people in here and you could get hurt, pal."

"There is that word again. I hear it everywhere I go on earth these days. So crude and ugly an expression for such a beautiful act of love. Why do you use such coarse language, Panos?"

Okay, Peter thought to himself, *whoever this fool is, or thinks he is, it's time that I get away from him.* A year and a half in prison had taught Peter Carson that every inmate was a potential threat. He underestimated no one, and because he was white, forty years old, and had only minimal fighting skills, this was a wise policy.

"Where are you going, Panos?" Gabriel asked.

"Back out on the yard, Gabe. I'm going through some heavy sh. ., ah stuff, right now and I need some space. I'll catch you later."

"Panos, please, sit down."

With that Peter headed for the door. As he did so he thought, *weren't there two other guys in the library when I came in?* The place was empty now, except for Peter and the mystery man.

Looking out of the window at the yard, Peter did a double take. What he saw could not be real. Everyone, inmates, staff and visitors, were all on the compound as they should be, but no one was moving. People appeared to be frozen in place.

Peter closed his eyes and opened them again. This made no difference; there still was no change to the now paused world. It was as if someone had taken a snapshot and inserted it in place of the full motion of life.

Terror gripped him. Peter's legs got rubbery; he felt the urge to vomit and began shaking uncontrollably. Somehow he managed to fall into a chair.

"Now that I have your attention, why don't we start again? As I said, my name is Gabriel."

All Peter could do at that moment was stare, grunt, and nod. He felt himself being held captive, but by what he was not sure. An invisible force of some kind? Even if he could, which he couldn't, he no longer wished to run. At least part of him didn't anyway.

"Do you believe, Panos?" Gabriel asked.

"Believe in what?" came the weak reply.

"God the creator, His son Jesus Christ, and the Holy Spirit," was the response.

Of course, I believe, Peter thought, but did not say. *I have always believed. Obedience, that was another story.*

"Belief alone does not make one a humble servant of God, Panos, but you are stronger than you know, and more valuable to the Lord than you could possibly imagine. The time has come for you to begin your service to Christ."

Peter realized Gabriel was reading his mind, answering his unspoken thoughts. He trembled at the idea of being in the presence of such power.

"My God," Peter cried out. "Who are you and what do you want from me?"

"As for me, St. Luke and Daniel can tell you enough. As for you, Panos, that is why I am here. For you. The Lord, your God wants to reveal Himself, to convey His message."

Then Gabriel raised his right arm and passed it over Peter Carson, like a priest giving a blessing. Instantly Peter was transported to another realm, to a place unlike anywhere on earth. He became the reluctant recipient of a direct communication from the Immortal One.

Peter was completely surrounded by this new reality and given a three hundred and sixty degree view of what the Lord wanted him to see.

Out of the swirling darkness he heard a Voice, one with an authority unlike any other, call out, "Feed My Children!" As these words were spoken, Peter was set upon by people on every side, most barely alive, all starving and emaciated. As they touched him, Peter felt their hunger, their intense misery. He experienced himself dying with them, suffering along with each one of them individually.

He looked down and saw that he too was now nothing more than a decaying bag of flesh and bones. An all encompassing malaise came over him. The agony of his hunger was very real and acute. Peter was starving to death.

Peter thought, all of these souls, mostly people with brown or black skins, where did they come from? Why are they all trying to touch me? What do they want from me? How can I possibly help them?

Then, as quickly as it came, the scene vanished. For a second, the whirlwind of the vision ceased and Peter looked at his body. He was back to his previous self once more, healthy and well fed.

But before he had the chance to catch his breath (was he still breathing?), the Voice was speaking again.

This time He said, "Heal My Children!" Suddenly, again on all sides, Peter found himself within another sea of suffering humanity. This group was just as wretched as the first. Everyone here was sick, dying of one malady or another: AIDS, cancer, heart disease, dysentery, malaria, hepatitis, the list was endless. As they touched him, somehow he knew what was killing each and every one of them, and he felt their agony.

Peter's body became a ravaged open sore, wracked with pain beyond description. The spirits before him now were male, female, young, old, white, Asian, black; they were indeed everyone.

When he was sure that he too was dead (and wished that he was), the vision once again terminated and serenity was restored. Peter Carson's body reverted back to "normal," although he was now persuaded that normal would never be the same for him again.

As he heard the Voice speak for a third time, Peter was resigned to the experience. He knew that whatever was coming next, he had no choice but to endure.

The command now was, "Stop My Children!" A tangled and bloody mass of wounded bodies reached out for Peter, all of them injured by the instruments of violence: some were stabbed, others shot, and many had been beaten. All were hurting and dying, and as in the other visions, so was Peter. He felt the trauma of a bullet ripping through his gut, the horror of a blade being stuck in his back, the ghastly sensation of having his head bashed in by a brick.

These encounters were very real and also, blessedly, brief. However impossible, he was experiencing what each of these people were experiencing, both their physical and emotional anguish.

Once again, the torment ended. Peter was still in one piece. He wondered how much more of this he could stand before he went insane. Was he already insane? He thought he must be.

For a fourth time the Divine Voice spoke and said, "Change My Children!" The suffering mass of flesh returned, but their torment now was different.

Peter saw children being cursed, abused, and neglected; people condemning, judging, and berating one another; blacks being called niggers, women being called bitches and whores, Asians and Africans treated as slaves, ministers of God preaching hate. This exposure to man's inhumanity seemed to have no end, and it sickened him to the very center of his soul.

Peter realized that this last vision was by far the most horrible of them all. God let Peter see, let him feel, just how cruel and hateful man can be toward his brother and how little love and mercy is shown to so many in need.

As the last message closed it was Peter's heart, rather than his body, that was broken and this wound did not heal at the vision's end. God had gone to a great deal of trouble to teach Peter Carson that man's free will decision to be disobedient, unmerciful, and unforgiving was the root cause of all his suffering.

The Lord made it known to Peter that if man would truly love his brother, as Christ commanded him to do, nothing would be impossible for him.

Still existing in this other place that God had taken him, Peter was now bathed in an intense white light. A milder, kinder, but still authoritative Voice asked, "How much longer must My children suffer, Panos?"

As he stood waiting in the brightness, it became clear to Peter that this question was not rhetorical.

"What can I do, God? I am only a man and not a very good one."

The Voice then said, "Do not be afraid, Panos, only believe. Watch and pray. Others are coming to help. Teach them as I have taught you, and be obedient to My Word."

It was one p.m. when Peter Carson entered the library. At three p.m. some inmates found Peter, unconscious and curled up underneath a bench on the cement floor of the outdoor library patio.

This patio would soon become known by another name, Solomon's Porch.

Two

Peter's head didn't clear until later that evening. While the memory of his vision was vivid, his recollection of being carried from the patio to the infirmary, then being examined and released was vague. It took several hours for Peter to gather himself, to regain the full use of his mind and senses, and to put in some order what he had experienced.

Although he could not explain why, Peter Carson was absolutely sure that his vision was real. "Real" being defined as having come from God. Peter knew that what he had felt and saw were pure truth. Further, he knew that he knew that he knew. This certainty defied rational reasoning; it went far beyond any worldly standard of proof.

As soon as he was fully revived, Panos Kallistos did something he hadn't done since he was in grade school. He prayed.

As he did, he really didn't know what to expect. He surely didn't know what to say, much less how to say it. Was God going to put him through another ordeal every time he spoke to Him? He wondered if he could survive another vision, given his weakened condition.

Peter Carson's first prayer was for three things; strength, wisdom, and peace of mind. He wasn't sure why he was praying for these specific blessings. It was almost as if someone else inside him was doing the praying.

There were no more visions, for which Peter was very thankful, but after offering his simple prayer, Peter began to feel better, much better.

For the first time in what seemed like forever, Peter noticed that his anxiety was gone. That dull anguish, that gnawing erosion of his soul, had ceased. Instantly. *When was the last time I felt this good?* he silently asked himself. *Has it really been three years since my arrest? Since the day my world fell apart?*

Peter's mind had begun the process of renewal. Old ideas and values, judgments, and self-images; views of right and wrong, everything was being rewired.

A new man was emerging. A child of God was replacing an unfaithful soul.

While Peter genuinely regretted stealing his client's funds, down deep, in the center of his being, what Peter regretted most was getting caught. Part of him had known this all along, but for some reason he had never admitted it to himself. At his sentencing, Peter Carson said all the right things. He delivered his lawyer's prefabricated and hollow apology speech to the court perfectly.

But, until this moment, the true nature of his sin, the heavy weight and blatant filth of it, had never been fully revealed to him. Peter had always tried to justify his evil using excuses such as "inordinate financial pressures," "lack of criminal intent," and even "clinical depression." While the world had held him accountable, Peter had never repented.

"S*** happens," he used to say. "No it doesn't," God told Peter, "you (and everyone else) allow it to happen." Seen through

God's eyes, Peter Carson's life was very different, far removed from his own previous conception of what it meant to be alive.

For the second time in two days, Peter wept; but these tears were healing, not condemning. He was truly sorry that he had allowed his weaknesses to overcome his soul, to take control, to make him an unwitting servant of the evil one.

He felt compelled to open his Bible, a book that had been given to him when he arrived at prison, but had so far seen no use. Without effort or conscious thought, he turned to the book of Job, the twenty-eighth chapter and the twenty-eighth verse. It reads, "And to man He said, 'Behold, the fear of the Lord that is wisdom, And to depart from evil is understanding.'"

It turns out that life was simpler to understand, and much more difficult to correctly live than Peter had ever imagined. He, like everyone else, could choose to obey or to ignore God. Striving to be truly obedient to the will of the Father, Peter now knew, was the toughest challenge any man could possibly face.

Through the power of the Holy Spirit, the far reaching impact of Peter's sin was made fully apparent to him. There was the pain and suffering he had caused his immediate family, the harm he'd done to his clients, both financially and emotionally, and the disgrace he brought upon his firm and his friends. He mourned over the encouragement his sin might have given others to steal. Worst of all, Peter realized, he had deeply offended God.

His fingers flipped though the pages of his Bible once more, until again, without deliberate selection, they reached the one hundredth and third psalm, twelfth verse. It reads, "As far as the east is from the west, so far has He removed our transgressions from us."

Peter knew that this was a message specifically directed to him. All of his sins, pain, regrets, sorrow, anxiety, guilt, and shame were suddenly not his anymore. He had been liberated. Another now bore his burdens for him.

Peter closed his Bible, flipped off his reading light, and shut his eyes. With a clean heart and a peaceful mind, Panos Kallistos then slept for the better part of the next three days, waking only occasionally to eat and to be counted by the guards.

Soon after Peter was up and around again, he committed himself to the study of the Scriptures and prayer. He did these things as discreetly as possible; making no mention of his vision or his new found spirituality to anyone. He felt compelled by this new and powerful Inner Voice of his to wait before taking action. The command he received was to "watch and pray." He took it literally and seriously.

Over the past eighteen months at Parkersboro, Peter had made a few casual friends, but none of them so close as to make much of a fuss when he now politely avoided them. Chaplains came and went at the camp, conducting Bible studies and services for the men. Most meant well, but few had any real insights into God's true nature or His word. Peter respected their efforts, but did not participate in their meetings or discussions.

He read all day long, making notes and asking questions through prayer, and then receiving answers through understanding. His mind and soul were a sponge and he was soaking up information and gaining knowledge at a fantastic pace.

From the time of the Apostles it was believed, although the Protestant reformation to a degree tries to deny this truth, that the Bible must be interpreted if it is to be properly understood. Through interpretation, many supposed contradictions are resolved, messages and prophecy become plain, and God's unchanging voice is made more apparent and consistent. When the books of the Bible are synchronized into the harmony of God's purpose it flows, and the same universal truths are revealed from beginning to end.

St Luke's Gospel says that for His Apostles, Jesus "opened their understanding that they might comprehend the Scriptures." God now did the same for Peter Carson. It was a gift that would enable him to fulfill God's purpose for his life. It would also make him unique, and set him apart from other men, with all of the blessings and trials that such a privileged status endows.

With each passing day, Peter was changing, further evolving into a "new creature," as St. Paul testifies. He didn't seem to get angry anymore and began to feel compassion for those he used to despise. The petty things in life that formerly irritated Peter to no end no longer mattered. Patience, a virtue almost unknown to the old Peter Carson, was becoming the core of his new character. The world's influence on Panos Kallistos was diminishing, and love, God's perfect and unconditional love, was replacing it.

Before his vision, if Peter dreamed at all about the future, it was of him having survived his ordeal and then living the "good life" once again with a new career, a new wife, and plenty of money. He now understood, with clarity and certainty so intense it frightened him, that if he had continued down this old road, his particular weaknesses, dishonesty, and greed being chief, would inevitably have gotten the best of him. Without a doubt, he would have ended up back in prison, and worse, in hell.

Money meant little to Peter's "new man," beyond what was required to survive and to care for his son. Status and worldly glory, all of the "stuff" that this fleshly existence holds to be so valuable, had become worthless to him.

Peter began to realize, to believe by faith, that he had been snatched from the jaws of the evil one not for his own glory, pleasure, or comfort, but to fulfill God's purpose. Exactly what he was supposed to do he didn't know, but he trusted that Christ would reveal this to him in His time.

Meditating often on his vision, Peter could not help but wonder what it all meant, for him specifically and for everyone else. Who were these "others" God spoke about who were coming to help him? How would he know who they were? What were they supposed to do once they arrived?

Yet, even in the face of all this uncertainty, Peter was not anxious. He worried for nothing, wanted for nothing. Even though the United States government held his body captive, Peter was now truly free. He had asked God for the forgiveness of his sins and had received it. He was at peace with the Lord and with himself.

He did still enjoy mowing the lawn, maybe even more so now. One bright September morning, while he was happily cutting away, engrossed in some thoughts about the prophet Isaiah, two men came walking toward him. Both were unfamiliar.

One was black, maybe thirty, and he was large, muscular, and menacing. The other was much older, slender, and white, and had the look of someone who had gotten the worst of one too many bar fights. They stood directly in his path, obviously intent on making Peter stop and pay attention to whatever it was they had to say.

Peter pulled back on his machine and turned it off. He removed his earplugs and watched as both of them looked him over, silently but very thoroughly. After a minute or so, it was the skinny white man who spoke first.

"Is your name Panos, Panos Chrismos, or something like that?"

"Yes, yes it is," Peter responded, startled by being addressed by his birth name once again by another total stranger.

"Good. We need to talk to you, man. Are you the one Gabriel sent us to find? What do you know about our dreams?"

Three

Peter needed a few minutes to prepare himself, so after brief introductions he asked the two new men to meet him in the library in half an hour. Peter's mind was racing, he could sense the Spirit telling him that whatever God was planning was starting right here, right now. It was a holy mission that could not be stopped or delayed, something both magnificent and perilous.

Their names were Malik and Saul. Evidently they rode in together on the Federal Bureau of Prisons (BOP) bus from Atlanta, but had come from separate institutions. Saul, the thin white guy, mumbled something about being "drawn" to Malik, but he did not elaborate further.

It was also certain that both of them had seen Gabriel. Dreams, they'd also mentioned dreams. Peter wondered if God had put them through the same tortuous series of sufferings he had endured.

Walking toward the library, Peter saw Malik sitting alone on the patio. They greeted each other and shook hands, which with Malik Graham was like grabbing a bear. Even restrained, Malik's physical strength was impressive. As were his tattoos, which consisted of various women's names, assorted firearms, drug paraphernalia, barbed wire, and snakes. His two front teeth had gold caps and his left forearm bore a surgery scar from elbow to wrist. Anyone with eyes and common sense could see that Malik Graham had a violent past and that he was not someone to be disrespected.

Before his vision, Peter Carson would never have come near a man like Malik Graham unless he had been forced to by circumstance. If that happened, outwardly Peter would have remained calm, but on the inside he would have been panicky.

But as they sat down together on one of the hard wooden benches on the outdoor library patio, Peter wasn't afraid. Malik's body was saying, "I'm a dangerous man," but his eyes were those of a frightened child. Peter understood the source of this fear immediately, God must have recently touched Malik. No matter how big and bad you are in this world, you are as helpless as a fly in a hurricane before the Almighty.

"Should I be callin' you Panos or Peter?" Malik asked.

"Peter is good, it doesn't matter."

"Are you some sort of prophet? Do you have any idea of the weird s***, sorry, crap, that's been happenin' to me bro?"

"Can't seem to curse much anymore, can you," Peter said, laughing.

"No, and it's a pain. I thought God's last name was damn until real recent. I was a mothereffing, straight up gangsta, Mr. Pete. No one badder'n me. Genuine thorough hoodlum. Now look at me, sitting here in this punk a** prison conversating with a crazy old white dude. Oh, no offense there, Mr. Pete. Damn! What's happenin' to me?"

"Why don't you tell me about it," Peter asked, trying his best not to smile.

Using the broken syntax of sixth grade level English mixed with a unique southern variety of Eubonics, Malik began telling his life story, condensed and summarized to the best of his ability.

Like so many other black, violent, and incarcerated men, Malik Graham came from a poor home with no father. Born and raised on the north side of Charlotte, North Carolina, Malik learned his lessons early.

Lesson one was that he was bigger and meaner than almost anyone else his own age. Once he hit sixteen or so, this comparison then also applied to the population as a whole. Being large and tough in the projects meant that you were respected and feared. Malik's self-image was built entirely around his ability to be the "baddest mothereffer on the block."

Lesson two was that the way to get ahead in this world is to deal drugs and steal. None of Malik Graham's peers were anything but antisocial and criminally inclined. The guys that drove the Beamers or the classic cars with the three thousand dollar rims, the homies who passed around benjamins like they were candy, the gangsters who had a stable of bitches and whores, these were Malik's role models. Who else, what else, could he possibly want to be?

Only one person in his whole life ever saw Malik Graham as anything other than a career criminal and a violent felon, his grandmother Josie.

Josie Arnold was Malik's maternal grandmother. When her daughter abandoned her only child at the age of twelve because her coke dealer boyfriend didn't want him around, Josie took Malik in. But by then it was already well past too late. Malik's heart was hardened, his life's course set.

Granny Arnold was the only person Malik truly loved. While she wasn't nearly a strong enough influence on him to keep him away from the streets, drugs, violence, and "the life," Granny Arnold was able to get his attention when no one else could.

In and out of juvenile facilities on charges ranging from assault to grand theft, Malik left a swath of destruction from an early age. During those rare short periods when Malik slowed down for awhile to appease a judge or a probation officer, Josie Arnold got him to read the Bible and go to church.

The Arnolds had been Pentecostals always, which meant church services included copious amounts of "spirit-filled" worship, like prophesying and speaking in tongues.

One Sunday night, when Malik was fifteen, Josie was able to cajole him into going to a particularly raucous service. Men were "on fire with the Spirit" that night, many were "slain," demons were "exorcised," "miraculous healings" were achieved, new and unique "heavenly languages" were spoken.

Malik told Peter that during all of this commotion, a man appeared out of nowhere. A white man about thirty or so, with light brown, curly hair. This man's presence at once made Malik uneasy or, as he put it, "scart to death." Why? For one thing, white people didn't go to Granny's church, so at first Malik thought he might be a cop or a social worker that had come to take him away. For another, this person, in Malik's words, threw off a "righteous power" he could readily sense if not easily relate.

Before Malik even said it, Peter knew he was describing Gabriel.

Young Malik sat there petrified as Gabriel held his hand and said to him, "Say of the Lord, He is my refuge and my fortress; My God, in Him I will trust." Gabriel repeated this short verse from the Psalms three times.

Then he said, "Be ready when you are called, Malik. The Lord will protect you always and make you honored among men."

Malik remembered that at that moment a blanket of peace swept over him. It was unlike anything he had ever experienced before. He described it as "pure joy," a calmness, a passive, positive feeling of acceptance and love both "intense" and "comfortin'." Malik remembered thinking that this has to be "what heaven is like."

Malik told Peter that he turned his head to get Granny Arnold's attention and to show her this unusual white man. Josie was evidently completely engrossed in the service and in the thirty seconds or so that it took him to get her awareness, Gabriel disappeared.

On the ride home, Malik told Granny Arnold everything Gabriel had said to him. Almost anyone else would have dismissed Malik's statements as the rantings of a disturbed and impressionable teenager, overcome by an intensely dramatic Pentecostal service, but Josie Arnold wasn't anybody else.

"That was your angel, Malik," she told him. "We all have 'em. Always remember what he told you, boy. God must have somethin' real special planned for you." She said this with such assurance that Malik believed it without question. He didn't understand it, but he did believe it.

"Scary thing is, Mr. Pete," Malik said, catching his breath after telling the Gabriel portion of his story, "now I think I do understand."

From the age of fifteen on (he was thirty now), Malik Graham lived the gangster life. His encounter with Gabriel did not change that. By eighteen he had killed his first man. There would be several more.

Malik sold "rocks," crack cocaine. He robbed other drug dealers, pimped whores, fenced stolen property, and set up a counterfeit money ring. Every few months or so, he would get arrested.

Since he had plenty of money for lawyers and "business expenses," like bail and bribes, Malik was never in jail for very long. Clever at his craft, the local authorities could never stick Malik with anything serious enough to put him behind bars for any length of time. This would change when Malik turned twenty-four. It was then that a federal drug task force zeroed in on his operation. The FBI set up wires and surveillance, paid informants, and tracked all of Malik's criminal activities for six months. Then they nailed him.

Malik woke up one morning to the sight of ten U.S. Marshals, all pointing shotguns at his head. They seized everything; cash, cars, motorcycles, boats, jewelry. The Feds also found twenty kilos of crack cocaine, enough to put Malik away for the rest of his life.

You cannot easily buy or talk your way out of major federal drug trafficking charges, Malik found out. He spent the last fifty thousand he had stashed on a top-notch defense attorney.

What did it get him? Rather than life in prison, he signed a plea for a sentence of three hundred months. Thirty years. Even with good time, that meant Malik Graham wouldn't see the world again until he was fifty something.

They sent Malik to the United States Penitentiary (USP) in Atlanta. He fit right in. Malik knew four or five of the inmates there, because he once ran with them in Charlotte. They quickly became his crew and did Malik's bidding.

Always the dominant one, Malik Graham ruled his block with harsh discipline and cruelty. What privileges and luxuries that existed in a bleak place like a USP, Malik made sure he had plenty of, like drugs, liquor, and dirty magazines. Actually, his life was little changed from the one he lived on the streets, the only real differences being he couldn't move around freely, and his "hos" were now punks.

So should have ended the saga of Malik Graham. Over and done, a menace to society, put away and left to rot during the best years of his life. Granny Arnold died just before the Feds arrested Malik. Despite the fact that he had at least ten children by six different "baby mamas," after Josie Arnold passed on, there was no one left in the world who really gave a damn about Malik Graham.

As it turns out, this world is not what it seems.

About six months ago, Malik told Peter, he started having "crazy dreams." The first set of these were not dreams at all, but rather lucid nighttime recollections of several near death experiences he'd survived during his thug life.

Malik relived the shotgun blast from ten feet away that somehow completely missed him, the time he rolled his new Corvette, totaled it, yet amazingly walked away without a scratch, and the night when his ex-best friend Tyrone blasted away at him with a pistol from across his living room and only managed to graze him.

Malik awoke from all of these dreams with the same thoughts. *Why am I still alive? Just to sit in this human zoo for twenty plus years? I should be dead.* Malik had questions, but no answers.

Then one afternoon, about a month before this day on which Malik Graham sat pouring out his heart and soul to a complete stranger at Parkersboro, a new inmate arrived on his block at the USP. He was white, about thirty or so with light brown, curly hair. Malik recognized him immediately, even though he had not seen him in fifteen years.

At the time he didn't recall Gabriel's prophecy because he was so taken aback by watching this "angel" stow his gear in a cell and then walk out on to the recreation yard. Without prompting, Malik followed him.

"Hello, Malik," Gabriel said, extending his hand. "Do you know who I am? Do you remember that Sunday some years ago when we first met?"

"Yes sir," Malik answered.

"Your time has come, Malik. The Lord requires your service. He shall make you honored among men."

Then Gabriel touched him and said some words in a language Malik did not understand.

Malik felt a surge of power hit him. It was a force far greater than anything of this world. It took control of his body. It froze him physically and mentally.

"And that's how I found out about you, Mr. Pete. Gabriel shows me you and this place and Saul and four other guys. God wants us to work for Him, Mr. Pete, and I don't think we best say no."

"Tell me what happened when Gabriel touched you," Peter asked.

"Like I said, Mr. Pete, God shows me all seven of us standin' in a circle on this porch prayin'. White lights so bright it'd blind ya if ya stared at it shootin' off our heads like bolts of lightnin'."

"You're the leader, Mr. Pete. Gabriel his self told me. He says, 'Find Panos Kallistos and he will help you to fulfill your purpose. He is God's instrument and you are his servant.'"That's what he said, Mr. Pete. On my life, on Granny Arnold's soul. I'm here to do what you tell me. I won't disobey anymore, Mr. Pete. I know how rotten, violent, and sinful I always been, but you gots to believe me, ever since Gabriel touched me, I can't hurt a fly. I'm not the same man that I was, Mr. Pete."

Peter was trying to absorb all of this when Saul appeared and joined them on the porch.

"I guess by now you've heard Mr. Graham's story," Saul said, nervously finding a seat on the bench next to Malik. "Since he and I had the same dream, and believe me, we did, let me lay it all out for you, Mr. Carson."

Saul Cohen had none of the language handicaps of Malik Graham. It became immediately obvious to Peter that Saul was well-educated and articulate.

"It's frighteningly simple. In our dreams, we are brought here, and by "here" I mean right here, Mr. Carson, to this porch. It's so fuc…, sorry, bloody real, it's not like you're just seeing it, you are actually there."

"He's tellin' you true, Mr. Pete. Swear he is," Malik confirmed.

"We are all standing around in a circle, holding hands and praying. I know that we're praying, because I figured out after my visit with Gabriel that we are all saying the Lord's Prayer in unison."

"We keep repeating this prayer, over and over, until this intense white light, brighter than the sun, suddenly shoots out from the tops of our heads. Then I wake up."

"That's how we knew who you were, Mr. Carson. We've both seen you before, many, many times." Malik nodded his head in agreement.

"You also spoke to Gabriel, Saul, is that right?" Peter asked.

"Same man, different uniform. Gabriel came to me as an FBI agent, but he told me the same thing he told Malik. Essentially, anyway."

"Essentially?" Peter repeated. "Exactly what does that mean?"

While Malik Graham's lack of verbal skills limited the type and breadth of his expressions, they did not limit their length. Malik loved to talk. Saul Cohen was just the opposite when it came to communication. He had the ability to explain and expound, but not the desire.

All he would tell Peter about himself (for the moment) was that he was fifty-eight years old, Jewish, from New York City, and in the middle of a fifteen year sentence for bank robbery. He also caught the BOP bus to Atlanta, but his journey began at the Federal Correctional Institution in Lexington, Kentucky, a "low custody" facility. This type of prison is one step up from a camp, but nowhere near as onerous as a penitentiary.

The moment Saul stepped on the bus to Parkersboro, he said he recognized Malik from his dreams. Without stopping to think, because if he had he would have realized how stupid and potentially suicidal it was, he pushed his way into a seat next to Malik. But before the other black inmates sitting nearby could react and beat down the skinny old white dude for his insolence, Malik said, "He's with me."

They spent the next three hours trying to figure out why God wanted anything to do with the likes of them, and how in the world they ended up on this bus together.

Under Federal Bureau of Prisons guidelines, neither Saul Cohen nor Malik Graham had any business being designated to a Federal prison camp. Camps are for people like Peter Carson, non-violent offenders with sentences under ten years.

While someone like Saul might see a camp near the end of his sentence, it was unheard of for a man to go from a maximum security USP straight to a camp. Malik told Saul that the BOP people in Atlanta checked and rechecked his paperwork several times before they put him on the bus, even going so far as to call Washington for confirmation.

A man like Malik Graham, such as he was before God through Gabriel touched him, doing time in a prison camp, would be like turning loose a tiger on a herd of trapped deer. In the few hours or days he would spend there, since there was no fence, a man like Malik Graham would be gone almost instantly, he would intimidate, rob, and beat the other prisoners at will.

Yet, as Peter sat looking at his new friends, he was struck by how unthreatening they both now were. Malik had become a lamb in a lion's body, and Saul, who Peter rightly surmised had been every bit as evil if not as violent as Malik, looked like a chastened schoolboy ready to obey his Daddy and get straight.

"Well, brothers, if what you say is right, and believe me I do not doubt anything that you've told me, we've got work to do. I guess we should be expecting four more to join us shortly," Peter said, contemplating exactly what his next move should be. "I'm new at this business of being God's servant, but let me assure you, He won't leave any doubt about what we are to do next."

"Do either of you have a Bible?" Peter asked. Two heads shook no. "We will solve that problem quickly. For now let me quote to you from a book in the Bible called James, the first chapter and the fifth verse. It describes our current situation. James says, "If any of you lack wisdom, let him ask God, who gives to all liberally and without reproach, and it will be given to him.""

With that Peter stood and motioned for Saul and Malik to do the same. They held hands and formed a small circle. Peter led them in prayer.

Several inmates who had been milling around the porch watched this happen and wondered why Peter Carson was praying at all, much less with two new guys he couldn't possibly know.

It was the first time men were seen praying on the porch, but what now seemed odd would soon become a regular part of life at Parkersboro.

Four

"Daddy?"

"Kevin, how are you, son?"

"Okay, I guess. I miss you so much, dad. I've been reading the children's Bible you sent to me. It's neat. You help me to understand it better too. It's just that mom…"

Kevin Carson hesitated. He was so happy that his father was calling him regularly again, saying how much he loved him, and promising that God was going to help them both. He didn't want anything to mess that up.

"It's alright, Kev. You can tell me the truth. Don't be afraid."

"Mommy says you are a phony. I don't know what that means, but it can't be very nice. She and Walter were talking last night in the kitchen and I heard what they said. I wasn't trying to spy, dad, honest. I was just coming downstairs for a glass of milk."

"What did they say, son?"

"Walter said you're a thief and a liar and that you should be in jail "until you drop," whatever that means. Mommy says you are a phony, trying to use God and me to get something you want."

"What did you say, Kev?"

"Nothing. I walked back upstairs and made a bunch of noise before I came back down so they could hear me coming. I kinda frowned at mommy, got my glass of milk and went to my room."

"Daddy?"

"Yes, son."

"Are you a phony?"

Out of the mouths of babes. The old Peter Carson would have used his son like Julie was trying to, as a tool to hurt the other parent. In the past, not so long ago in fact, Peter had done just that, passing on thinly veiled insults for Kev to hurl at his mother on his behalf.

"Remember Moses, Kev? What did he do bad before he became a servant of God?"

"He killed the Egyptian who killed the Jew."

"Right. Now a couple of weeks back we talked about King David. What did he do wrong, do you remember, Kev?"

"He sent a guy to die in war so he could steal his wife."

"You are so smart. One more. What did St. Paul do before Jesus appeared to him on the Damascus road?"

"St. Paul hurt and per-se-cutted Christians."

"Now, what did daddy do wrong to get sent to prison?"

"You stole money from people."

Over the past few weeks Peter Carson had been doing his best to explain the divine mechanics of sin and repentance to his son. He wanted Kev to understand, even at the young age of ten, that we all sin, but we need not be conquered by it. Most importantly, Kevin needed to know, down deep in his soul, that his father was now a new man, someone whom he could both love and trust, without fear or reservation.

This was a delicate task. Peter's goal was to make Kevin safer, happier, and more content, not to make things worse for him at home.

"Now, Kev. Do you think I'm a phony? A phony is a person who says he's going to do something, or is something, when he knows that's not true."

"No, daddy. I don't think so."

"Why not?"

"Because you told me you were sorry, and that if you got do-overs you wouldn't steal anymore. Because you love me. You never talked to me like this before, daddy. Now you 'splain things to me so I know what they mean. I'm going to tell mommy you're not a phony, she shouldn't say that!"

"No, Kev, don't. I've got a better idea. Let's pray for her."

So they did, asking God to help Julie Morgan, to protect and prosper her. Peter made sure Kevin understood that his mother was simply making a mistake, and since we all make mistakes, he should be nice about it, not mean. "God," Peter Carson told his son, "is love and is not mean."

They spent awhile going over how the Lord uses our weaknesses to show His strength, to glorify His name. Peter explained how God often times picks men and women who "people think are bad" to show how merciful and powerful He is. Heavy stuff, whether you're forty or in the fourth grade.

"Is God using you like that, daddy? Are you like Moses?"

"Yes, son, God is using me to help you and I hope some other people, and also no, Kev, I'm not Moses or anybody special. I'm just your dad."

"I love you, daddy."

"Love you too, Kev."

Peter was beginning to see the fruits of his labors with his son. Kev was happier, more active, and alert. His schoolwork had improved. He was hoping that Julie might bring him to the camp for a visit, something she had never done during Peter's incarceration.

Julie. Julie "Morgan." Peter still couldn't adjust to calling her "Morgan." Mrs. Walter Morgan.

Unreal, Peter often thought, my wife is married to another man. He wondered, would Julie always be his wife, down deep in his soul where it really counts? He prayed not, but there was a connection between the two of them that could not be broken, not by prison, and not by Walter. As far as Peter was concerned that wasn't necessarily the good news. He didn't consciously want Julie back, but he was still unable to rid himself of her influence, her presence in his daily thought life.

But now he trusted God, and that meant Peter had given Him this problem to solve. Sooner or later, whether she admitted it to herself or not, or even recognized it at the time as a choice, Julie Morgan would have to pick a side. Peter prayed it would be the Lord's.

"The toughest thing for me, Peter, is the whole Christ as God, Lord, and Savior business," Saul explained. "I've never been religious, until now I guess, but I have always been Jewish. Tough to go back on my entire family's beliefs and traditions. I feel almost, well, disloyal."

"Do you know now that Christ is who He claimed to be?" Peter asked.

"Yes."

"How do you know?"

"Same way I know that you're a man of God. The Voice inside me leaves little to doubt."

"Don't ever forget that Christ was a Jew, Saul. He never stopped being a Jew. In fact, he fulfilled the law, the Old Covenant, perfectly since he was without sin."

"I hear you."

"Then remember, you're still a Jew. Difference being now you know the truth, your ancestors rejected the Chosen One. Don't even ask me why, Saul. I don't have a clue. We'll ask Christ about this someday, you and me."

"Do you have any idea, even a little bit, how weird this all is, Peter? I mean me sitting with you and Malik on this porch and talking about God?"

"I do."

"I'm not sure you do, man."

"Try me."

Peter had been coaxing Saul Cohen along for a couple of weeks now, doing his best to get his new friend to open up. With Malik Graham it was like trying to control a fire hose when it came to him sharing his history, which had now become a powerful testimony. All Peter had to do with Malik was to be sure that the water was aimed at the flames and then get out of the way. But Saul, he was altogether different. Finally, Saul began to share himself with his brothers.

Saul Cohen, in his words, had been a "disappointment" all his life. His two younger brothers were both lawyers, but he was quick to add that neither one would speak to him anymore, much less help him. His father had been an accountant, and Saul, being the oldest son, was expected to follow in his father's footsteps. Seymour Cohen told Saul literally from birth that the family's two room, modestly successful accounting practice in the Bronx would someday say "Cohen and Son" on the door.

Saul remembered thinking that he would rather be dead than live to see that day.

Coming of age at the end of the Vietnam era in the early seventies, Saul managed to stay in school through 1974, earning a degree in accounting from Cornell almost by default.

"I hated accounting, always have," Saul told Peter, "but I hated the idea of dying in some Southeast Asian jungle even more."

As soon as his student draft deferment was no longer required, Saul quit his pursuit of a master's degree. He had always played his cards close to his vest with his father, not wanting to risk getting his financial support cut off. Seymour Cohen believed that Saul was dropping out of graduate school in order to return to New York City and set up shop with him.

Saul told Peter that all he could think about at this stage of his life was, "I'm free!" No more threat of Vietnam hanging over his head, no more stupid, boring accounting classes to suffer through, and no longer any need to placate his overbearing father.

Saul recalled going home, getting really loaded on pills and whiskey, and telling his dad just what he could do with the dreary life he had planned for him. It was an ugly scene, filled with petty name calling and sharp tongues. It left scars that were not healed by the time of Seymour Cohen's death fifteen years later.

It wasn't as if Saul Cohen didn't have other plans. He had found a much more enjoyable and profitable way to make a buck than doing tax returns, growing and selling marijuana. So rather than becoming what he called "one of the living dead" with Mr. Cohen, Sr. in the Bronx, Saul and two of his college buddies moved to Albany, set up shop in an old warehouse, and proceeded to become the reefer kings of the upstate.

Life was sweet until 1980. The money was great and the perks were better. It was then that the New York State police moved in and shut down their operation. Saul caught three years prison time, an incredibly short sentence if you consider that someone convicted in the twenty-first century of conspiring to sell five thousand pounds of marijuana would be lucky to get a term of only twenty years.

"Peter, you know what stands out most to me when I think back on those days?" Saul said, reflecting on his former life.

"What?"

"How incredibly selfish I was. Didn't give a damn if my folks suffered, which they did. Women were nothing but disposable objects of pleasure to me. I got mine and thought the hell with everyone else."

"Been there, done that, Saul."

"But prison didn't even slow me down, man. I just learned a new trade."

During his sixteen month stay at a New York State prison (three years minus good time), Saul Cohen earned an advanced degree in the art of bank robbery, courtesy of Mr. Dan Weber, a.k.a. the "Happy Bandit."

Weber gained limited fame in the Northeast during the late seventies for his ability to walk into a bank with a big grin on his face, wave a gun around almost nonchalantly, and demand cash in such a polite manner that Emily Post would have been proud. Many people robbed by Weber described him as a "nice guy" or a "gentleman." He always left the bank laughing, hence the nickname the "Happy Bandit."

Dan Weber was doing state time for a bad check scheme he had also "happily" run when Saul became his cellmate.

"Danny taught me to be truly amoral," Saul explained. "The world to him was nothing more than an opportunity for gain, at whose expense it mattered not. Laws, he always said, were written by fools and obeyed by suckers. "Get some while you can" was his philosophy on life. It became mine."

So Saul Cohen gave up growing reefer to pursue a career in armed robbery. He managed to hold up some fifty plus banks in the mid-eighties before getting caught. He told Peter that he "pissed away" all of this money, well over a million dollars. The FBI was able to tie Saul to ten bank heists. He was sentenced to twelve years. He did the better part of ten.

"You might think," Saul testified, "that after getting caught and being punished for dealing dope and robbing banks I might have slowed down. Wrong."

The very day he was released from federal prison in 1997, Saul Cohen robbed another bank. Amazingly, and as a testament to his considerable talents at disguise and target selection, the feds didn't catch up with Saul again for years.

Who finally busted Saul? An FBI agent who was a white man, about thirty, with light brown, curly hair.

"This agent, Gabriel, of course, appears out of the blue in a parking garage at my car door and says, 'You're under arrest.' I swear he popped up out of nowhere. Believe me, I know what I'm doing, Peter. I wasn't followed from the scene. There was no doubt that I'd gotten away clean."

Saul said that he had never been arrested so "gently." In fact, once he got to jail and was booked he thought back and couldn't remember if "Agent" Gabriel had brandished a gun or even handcuffed him.

"I never thought to run or resist," Saul told Peter. "For some reason I just obeyed. Bizarre, to say the least. I knew that if I got caught again it was over for me. But now it all makes sense."

Gabriel made the arrest solo, which should have made Saul Cohen suspicious. FBI agents don't go out for coffee unless their partner is with them, much less make an arrest.

"On the way to the jail, he said the strangest things to me," Saul recalled. "I thought I'd been popped by a preacher or something."

"Gabriel starts off by telling me that God loves me despite my sins, and that He has given me a 'sound mind,' which I have seen fit to 'misuse.' What kind of cop talks like that? Then he starts chanting in Hebrew. I knew it was Hebrew because I remember hearing the language as a kid."

At this point in his narrative Saul pulled up. The expression on his face changed from someone who was matter-of-factly describing events to a boxer who was getting ready for a fight. Peter read equal doses of fear and intensity.

"Well, don't leave me hanging. What happened after Gabriel spoke to you in Hebrew?"

"He gave me a gift."

"Sounds wonderful, what was it?"

"An ability."

Peter wondered why getting Saul Cohen to offer complete thoughts was like pulling teeth. Rather than ask him "what ability?" Peter flashed Saul a "get on with it" look.

"I can see demons."

"Come again?"

"I can see demons. They are everywhere, Peter. Believe me, you have no idea how much I hate the little bastards and how much they hate me."

"Is there one on me, Saul?"

"No. They're afraid of you, man."

"What about Malik?"

"Nope. Clean as a whistle."

"What about that guy over there. Sam Harris. Decent enough person, got caught embezzling from his boss. As criminals go, he's bush league. Gets released next week."

Saul shifted his focus on to Mr. Harris. He was fifty feet away, busily engaged in an animated discussion with another inmate about last weekend's stock car race. He seemed oblivious to the world. However, after a few seconds of Saul's attentions, Sam Harris stopped talking, glared over at Saul and Peter and flipped them off.

"If you were to go ask Sam why he just gave us the bird he'd look at you like you're crazy," Saul explained. "He was very likely unaware that he did it."

"Wow. He has a demon on him then?"

"Three, no wait. Four."

"Lord have mercy!"

"Exactly."

Saul Cohen then explained what life had been like for him since receiving Gabriel's "gift." It hadn't been easy.

He told Peter what happened the first time he washed his face in his jail cell after Gabriel arrested him.

"It was hideous. In the mirror I saw some nasty devil creature and twenty odd of his imps. They were all over me, taunting me."

"To think for all those years I was stupid and prideful enough to believe that I was in control of my life, robbing and lying and blaspheming at will. The truth is it was me who was being played for the sucker. The evil one was controlling me through my weaknesses like a puppet on a string."

"What did you do, Saul?"

"I dropped to my knees and said God, my God, save me! Have mercy on me Lord! By His grace I remembered the twenty-third psalm from my childhood. You know, Peter, the one with "Yea, though I walk through the valley of the shadow of death, I shall fear no evil," in it? I focused my conscious mind on the psalm all the while another part of me, my soul, was praying for deliverance."

Saul stopped. Tears cascaded down his cheeks; he turned pale and began to shake. Clearly any recollection of the events in that jail terrified him.

"Steady, brother, I'm here. You have nothing to fear now."

"Peter, you are so smart, yet still so green. Of course, I have something to fear. So do you. Let me tell you what those rotten sons of hell did to me."

"For the next three days they kept at it, trying to get me to curse God. If I would do that, they promised, they'd go away and leave me alone. Somehow I held on, but it was the most difficult and horrible thing I've ever been through."

"When they could see that I wasn't going to break, then they really turned up the heat. For awhile they threw me around my cell like a ping pong ball. Then they made me scream and foam at the mouth. It took eight guards to get me strapped down. One of them is minus an ear, another a finger. I bit them off."

Peter tried to visualize this battle, to experience it through Saul. He knew as an absolute spiritual principle that his only enemy was Satan, but like a genius who believes he can read a blueprint once and then be able to build a house, he really can't, because there is simply no substitute for learning how to use a hammer to drive in a nail. Peter would have to learn how to beat the devil simply by doing it, but Saul's insights added much to his already considerable knowledge and strength.

"My strap down chair, you ever see one? They put people all strung out on dope or poor sots suffering through the Delirium Tremens in them. You're sitting there slightly tilted back and tied down tight enough to where Samson himself couldn't break free."

"Well, my strap down chair floated four feet off the ground, Peter. People freaked. I'm sure they considered shooting me. Thanks to that little demonstration, many of those guards are God fearing men today, let me assure you."

"But you won, Saul. You're here now, alive and well and free of them."

"True, by the grace of God. But know this, Peter, they are relentless. You see how they are from the Bible, and nothing has changed since those times. Demons delight in torturing humans, because Satan hates man. He will never understand why God loves us primitive, imperfect mortals more than he does His angels. The evil one fears he's ultimately doomed, but he's going to get his by hurting us before he's through."

"Can you get demons off of people, Saul? Exorcise them I guess is the right term."

"Sometimes."

"How often is sometimes?"

"Maybe just over half the time. But some of them, Peter … let me say this. I'm glad I'm here with you."

"Why do you say that?"

"Because some demons are much, much stronger than others, and while none of them are more powerful than our Lord, it's faith and grace that beats them, drives them away."

"You have faith, Saul. I know you do."

"True, but not like you do. The Holy Spirit is exceptionally strong in you, Peter."

"Well, Saul, if you see one of these super strong devils headed my way, be sure to give me a heads up, okay?" Peter said, chuckling, trying to lighten things up a bit.

"How much notice do you want?" Saul replied.

"How much can I get?" Peter asked, still smirking.

"In this case about thirty seconds. See that guy coming toward us from across the yard? It's the same son-of-perdition who beat me up in jail, and he looks like he's ready to try you."

Five

Peter shut his eyes and silently prayed for strength. When he opened them he was looking right into the face of evil.

It was a very pleasant face, actually.

The unfamiliar man wore a utility workman's uniform and appeared benign. At five foot ten inches, and maybe one hundred and sixty pounds, his stature inspired no fear. Styled hair, a slight build, and small, round gold-rimmed glasses gave him the look of a banker, not Beelzebub.

This was the ultimate proof that looks can be deceiving.

"Been dying to meet you, Mr. Kallistos," the man said, extending his hand. "You're a very special person. Between my buddy Saul over there and that meddling Gabriel, I'll bet you've heard enough lies about me and my kind to where you're sh***ing your pants about now."

Peter kept his arms at his side. He looked his enemy straight in the eye, did not flinch, and did not waiver.

"I'm not afraid of you. As for lies, your master is the father of them all."

"Come on, Pete! Who are you kidding? You're scared to death. Afraid I might hurt you. But you've always been a coward, haven't you, Panos. Afraid your precious Julie wouldn't love you if you didn't get her that big house you couldn't afford, afraid of being a loser, scared of being locked up. We both know that short list is just for starters. Truth is your nothing but a bundle of fear. It drives you, it's what you really are."

"I'm not in the least bit interested in what you think about me. What do you want here? Say what you will before I toss you aside like a piece of garbage."

Saul shot Peter a look that screamed, "Are you out of your mind?" Peter squeezed Saul's arm to reassure him.

"Brave man, brave man, well done!" The demon taunted, clapping his hands sarcastically. "You don't have a clue, do you? Your precious God has put you in danger, Mr. Kallistos. Don't believe all of His public relations. You're the one who is helpless before the superior power. Don't become another useless martyr for the Nazarene. He lets you all die such horrible and needless deaths. I mean think about it, Panos, what kind of God allows himself to be nailed to a tree and spat on? Weak, pathetic. Humility my a**, your marvelous Christ was just a wimp."

No sooner had this blasphemy come out of his mouth than Malik Graham's fist entered it. Five more blows delivered in rapid succession sent the "utility man" to the ground, face first.

"Malik, no!" Peter shouted.

"What? Why? C'mon, Mr. Pete, he's a bad man. Hell, he ain't even a man. Let me send him back to the devil! No one calls my Lord and Savior a wimp."

"Listen to me, Malik. You just played right into his hands. We are not men of violence, we belong to God. You will never attack anyone again unless I tell you to. Do you understand me?"

"Yes sir. Sorry, Mr. Pete. Damn! I did wrong, but I was tryin' to be right. I got angry hearing all that foul talk and lies, that's all."

"You've got to chill, brother. I understand your feelings, but you must control your passions. Satan will use your anger against you."

"Got that right."

When they turned to put a face with the voice, they saw Charley O standing behind them. He was an inmate well known for two things, his ability to score heroin at will and to pay for his habit with homosexual favors. He was loathed by all, except for those reprobates who kept punks.

Only he wasn't Charley O anymore, at least not for the moment.

"That's impressive," Peter said, as calmly as he could manage. "What happened to . . ." In mid-sentence Peter looked over to where the "utility man" was laid out. Only now he wasn't there, he had vanished.

"Nice trick."

"I've got more."

"Bet you do."

"You're on the wrong side, Panos. You've been fooled by propaganda and spiritual arrogance. Let me show you the real power on this earth. Come with me."

"No."

"What do you mean, no? Who do you think you are anyway? Do you imagine that you and your friends are anything but a waste of space? You're a useless, weak little bag of bones and water. Piece of s*** is the phrase that best describes you."

"Thought you said I was a special person."

Saul laughed. He shouldn't have.

Charlie O reached out and touched him. As soon as he did Saul began screaming in agony. He appeared to be having a heart attack.

All of this commotion was drawing a crowd. By this point, about twenty men were gathered around watching the spectacle.

Peter reached down and helped his friend to his feet. When he did, Saul's torture ended.

"You'll have to do better than that, Charley. But you aren't Charley. What is your name anyway? Or do you sons of hell even merit a name?"

The demon was not expecting this level of resistance and confidence. Peter's faith and power was stronger than any human's he had encountered since the time of the Apostles.

"What did I tell your Lord back in Judea? Yes, I remember. My name is Legion, for we are many. Want to see if you can do what Christ did? Don't see any pigs around here, but give it a try monkey boy, come on!"

"He doesn't have to, I will."

Out from among the growing group of curious onlookers stepped an old friend. He was a white man, about thirty, with light brown, curly hair.

"Nice to see you, Gabriel. Come to save the day? Afraid that your little friends here might get hurt?"

"No, I don't want them to hurt you. It's not time yet. Now leave that poor soul alone and be on your way."

As Gabriel spoke, Charley O fell to the ground and flopped around for a minute like a beached fish. He looked up at Peter, smiled and then puked all over Saul's feet. Legion left Charley O writhing hysterically in pools of his own vomit.

By this time the guards had been alerted to a disturbance on the compound. Two of them rushed in expecting to break up a fight, hopefully before it became a riot.

All they found was a gay junkie who had gotten sick in front of an audience. Gabriel was gone. Peter, Malik, and Saul had quietly slipped away.

When asked, all that the inmates in the crowd could remember was that Charley O had run onto the porch ranting and raving about being "attacked by spiders." The only people who knew what really happened weren't talking, they were busy walking the yard together trying to figure out what might be coming at them next.

During the weeks after "Charley's meltdown", as the inmates called it, Peter focused his attention on the preparation and education of Malik and Saul.

Peter Carson knew that each of the seven (with four still to come) would bring with them their own unique spiritual gifts. Saul's was all too obvious, the discernment of evil. This talent had already come in handy in dealing with Legion. Peter now worked on Saul's ability to refine and control his gift.

Through prayer, fasting, and faith, Saul Cohen was able to self-install an "off button." No longer would he be subjected, twenty-four seven, to seeing demons all around him.

This did wonders for Saul's attitude. He was happy, truly happy for the first time in his life. He was maturing rapidly and given his extraordinary raw intelligence, soon he was quoting Scripture almost as quickly and accurately as Peter.

Malik too was moving forward. His gift, his most obvious gift that is, was his physical strength. Peter worked on Malik's "inner man" to build his self-control. Properly harnessed, Malik Graham's ability to physically defend the disciples could prove invaluable, perhaps lifesaving.

But Malik Graham had another far more powerful spiritual gift, the ability to evangelize, especially with black inmates.

Young black men at Parkersboro thought Malik was a god. His reputation as being one of the toughest men around carried over with him to his new prison home. There was a group of about forty or so young African-American inmates at the camp. Most of them had less than five years left to go before release; all were in for drug related charges. None had graduated high school. Most were barely literate.

With a degree of respect that they granted no one else, these young men daily lined up to gape in awe as Malik Graham smoothly bench pressed four hundred pounds, performed hundreds of one handed push-ups, and made a heavy bag whimper from the force of his fists. However, demonstrations of Malik's physical prowess came with a price; if you wanted to see the show you had to stay for the sermon.

This all began without the prompting of Peter Carson. The work-out room was Malik's territory, and as always, he ruled his domain with stern discipline. The difference was this time, Malik's authority came from God, and his discipline was righteousness.

The results were impressive. After a few short weeks, half of the forty, twenty now former drug dealing street thugs, were on their way to becoming soldiers for Christ. Malik proudly displayed his new brood, who called themselves "Reverend Graham's Army," to Peter Carson one Sunday morning.

Sundays at Parkersboro had begun to take on a life of their own. Peter was a magnet for anyone seeking the Lord. Because of the specific nature of his calling, Peter always put the needs of Malik and Saul above all others, even his own, but there was still plenty of time left over to minister to all who came searching.

Solomon's Porch

59

Without formal announcement or any official sanction, men began gathering on the outdoor library porch at nine a.m. for Sunday services. The number of the curious and the faithful grew each week.

One Sabbath day in the early fall, Malik presented his "army" to Peter with a hymn and some fanfare. The twenty sang Amazing Grace accappella, and then each of them took a minute to publicly proclaim their newfound salvation. Peter spoke on the universal love of God, who makes no distinction between Jew or Greek, black or white, male or female. He focused on the twelfth chapter of Romans, exhorting each of his new found flock to "abhor what is evil" and "cling to what is good." Men who had previously known only disappointment and hate were getting a taste of love and joy. Spirits ran high.

Into the midst of this celebration rolled Alan Audry. Paralyzed from the waist down by multiple gunshot wounds, he was known to one and all at Parkersboro as "awful Alan," due to his unrelentingly negative attitude. Audry was a bitter man, and he wasn't shy about telling you just how much you, and the rest of the world, really sucked.

In its infinite mercy, the United States government does not cut you a break for a minor issue like the loss of your mobility. Despite being shot six times, having ten surgeries, and suffering paralysis, the U.S. Attorney in Georgia refused to reduce Audry's sentence or even recommend that he be placed in a medical facility.

Audry's crime? He was a minor player in a fairly large cocaine distribution conspiracy, but that wasn't really the issue.

The problem was Alan Audry refused to snitch. The Feds reserve their harshest treatment for those who will not tell on their brother. In this case the head of the dope ring in question literally was Alan's brother, Maurice Audry.

Rather than send his best friend and only sibling to prison for the rest of his life, Alan took the hit and got ten years for his trouble. While he never regretted his decision, unlike his accusers, he knew the difference between right and wrong, he did come to view the world as one giant pig sty. No one blamed him, but then again, no one wanted to hear about it constantly, either. Whiners are ignored in prison, if not preyed upon.

"I've come to be healed," Alan declared, as matter-of-factly as if he was ordering a burger at a drive-thru. "Had a dream you guys fixed my legs, and that I walked right off this porch. Which one of you fellas is Kallistos?"

It took everyone a moment to get over the astonishment of "awful Alan" saying anything other than "f*** you!" to a group of inmates. The boldness of his claim that he'd "walk right off this porch" drew quiet murmurs of disbelief from the congregation.

All eyes focused on Peter. No one knew what to do. Was this a joke? A set up for a con maybe?

Peter looked around, first getting Malik's attention and then Saul's. Non-verbally he shot them each a stare that said, "Did you tell him my birth name?" Without a word being spoken they understood and shook their heads sideways for "no."

Peter had given his two new disciples strict instructions not to discuss any aspect of their common dreams or angelic encounters with any of the inmates. He had no doubt that his men had been obedient. Whatever this was, it was not the result of hearing about miracles and hoping for another one.

"Do you believe that we can heal you?" Peter asked.

"Yes, you and the two new guys. I don't know how, but I do believe it," Audry responded.

"Then claim your victory."

One of the men rolled Alan over to where Peter was standing. Malik and Saul, looking unsure of what was happening, but unafraid, linked hands with Peter and formed a circle around the wheelchair.

"Lord," Peter began, "Your servant James taught us 'the prayer of faith will save the sick, and the Lord will raise him up.' We present ourselves to You Christ, our Lord, our Savior, and our Redeemer as righteous men who, as Your humble servants, ask You to heal this brother, Alan Audry. Lord, return to him the use of his legs, but also Lord, we ask You to return to him his joy. Give him faith in You, Lord. Give him faith in Your life, death, resurrection, and second coming. Do all this for Your mercies' sake. In the name of the Father, Son, and the Holy Spirit, amen."

No one said a word. Peter, Malik and Saul remained surrounding Alan, all on one accord and silently praying. More than five minutes passed filled only with an eerie hush. Then Peter opened his eyes and loosed his grip on the hands of his friends. Attention shifted totally to the man being blessed.

Audry's face was covered with tears, but he wore a smile that no earthly emotion could ever produce. Peter looked down and noticed Alan's toes protruding through his prison issue shower sandals.

They were wiggling.

Malik stepped back and extended his hand to help Alan up. For the first time in five years, Alan Demetrius Audry, Jr. took one step, then another. He let go of Malik and walked on his own from one end of the porch to the other.

Two men fainted, most looked on silently and in wonder, not knowing what to think. A good number dropped to their knees and started praying.

Some were sure they had witnessed a miracle. Others were skeptical from the outset. Scams are a routine part of prison life.

"Did you feel that surge, that pulse, when Peter finished his prayer? Tell me it wasn't just me," Saul asked.

"I felt it, Saul. Sure enough, it was like someone jolted me with a live wire," Malik confirmed.

Peter Carson dragged himself over to the nearest wooden bench and collapsed onto it. His first healing had taken all of his strength. While he would not admit it to either Malik or Saul, Peter's prayer was not made in total faith. He doubted his ability to perform the miracle, but he never doubted the possibility that it could happen. He knew God's power was limitless, but would He act?

He wondered if this was how it was "supposed" to be done. Did this mean that he and Malik and Saul had power over the material world like the prophets and the Apostles did? Could this really be true? The concept was too staggering to contemplate.

The answer to Peter's question was now standing right in front of him.

"Thank you, God bless you," Alan said, trying his best to control his adrenaline surge long enough to speak coherently. "I knew you could do it, I absolutely did. Never a doubt! That guy in my dream was so convincing. I don't know…"

Peter cut him off. "What did this guy look like?"

"He's a white dude. Imagine me dreaming about a white man, and he wasn't arresting me or calling me a nigger. I guess he might have been thirty or thirty-five. Had brown locks, kinda curly."

"Thought so," Peter responded.

"You know this guy? Guess I shoulda figured that. He must be real close to God. Can I meet him, say thanks?"

"Maybe someday, Alan, who knows. God bless you brother, go in faith and peace."

With that the crowd, which by now had swelled in size and constituted three quarters of the camp, could no longer be contained. They mobbed Alan, touching him, hoping to reap a small leftover of the Power that had restored his crippled body. Thoughts of possible miracles and healings of all kinds filled their heads. No place needs miracles more than a prison, yet sadly, not many places see less of them.

Somehow in this chaos Malik and Saul rounded up Peter and the three of them headed for the now vacant and locked chow hall. Malik worked mess duty and knew how to sneak in. They were hoping for a few moments alone before the mob finished with Alan and came hunting for them.

"Talk to me, Peter," Saul begged.

"Yes, Mr. Pete, tell me too," Malik added.

"Was it real?" they both asked, nearly in unison.

It turns out Peter Carson wasn't the only one who had prayed with some doubts.

"I'm sure of this, our prayers were answered. Audry couldn't walk, we all know that. Remember that time he cussed Jenkins and got knocked off his chair? Alan sat in the mud for two hours before someone found him and pulled him out. Alan Audry was healed here today, but we had little to do with it."

"I don't quite understand," Saul said.

"It was Alan's total faith and no doubt the mercy he'd shown his brother that brought forth God's healing. We were merely the obedient vessels who carried out His will."

"Never forget that, my friends. We are nothing but servants of the Most High God. Any good that comes from our efforts and prayers cannot be of our own doing. Humility, brothers, we must always remain humble."

Peter's admonition was a timely one, because an instant after it was delivered, the crowd discovered their hiding place and burst in. They were in a frenzy, one half sure they'd seen a miracle, the other half positive it was all an act. Each side was looking for validation.

Parkersboro would never be the same again.

Six

"Why me?" Gail asked herself. Transferred to Parkersboro six months earlier, Warden Gail McCorkle had hoped for, and until now had received, a peaceful and routine assignment. Coming from a medium security prison where she was an assistant warden, "Miss Mac" expected to lay back and cruise at her new duty station. No more fights with shanks and clubs to break up. No more bloody gang battles on the compound. Inmates at mediums are serious, hard core felons, who, in some cases, may never go home again. On the other side of the spectrum are the "campers," the cream of the crop when it comes to federal prisoners. They are non-violent and pretty much trouble free. At least that's the theory.

"So, why am I here on a Saturday morning sitting around with you three gentlemen when I should be home polishing my bowling ball, drinking beer, and kicking my dog?"

Peter, Malik, and Saul could only shrug sheepishly in response to Gail's question. They didn't want to be in her office that morning anymore than Warden McCorkle did.

The news that a man who, by all appearances, could not possibly have been faking his paralysis simply got up and walked away after being prayed over in a federal prison spread quickly to the outside world. The media were asking questions, requesting interviews. The Justice Department demanded a report, but none of this really troubled the warden.

"My concerns, gentlemen, are not with your desire to avoid publicity. Your reluctance to speak out only makes my job easier. My problem is the impact that your little "miracle" is having on the men under my care. You've made a mess of a very neat and tidy situation. I must tell you this does not make me happy."

The residents of Parkersboro knew from experience that when "Miss Mac" was unhappy they were all made to suffer right along with her.

In the three weeks since Audry's healing, the camp had split into two factions, those who believed Alan Audry's miracle was genuine and those who thought it was an elaborate snow job.

Warden McCorkle, being a realist and a seasoned corrections officer, put her money down squarely on the scam side. Over the past couple of weeks she had expected to see a slew of new "miracles," followed inevitably by the solicitation of more "healing prayers" for money by the men now sitting in front of her.

Not only had this not happened, neither the additional miracles nor the shake down of the inmates, she had on her desk reports from three separate physicians all documenting a surprising truth; without question Alan Audry had been paralyzed, his spine was shot nearly clean through by a nine millimeter shell.

All of this served to make the already cynical Gail McCorkle even more suspicious, because she knew that the best schemes are so clean anyone can be fooled, for a time anyway.

"I'm only going to ask you gentlemen this once. Please take me at my word. What's going on here? No bull**** now, don't make it any worse."

"Do you believe in God, Warden McCorkle?" Peter asked as humbly and politely as he could.

"Oh please, don't start in on that crap with me fellas. Who do you think you're talking to? I've had more smoke blown up my a** than Santa Claus on Christmas Eve."

"I need you to answer my question if you want us to answer yours."

"Alright, Mr. Carson, I'll play. Sure, I believe in God. She's a two hundred and fifty pound black lady that sits in the sky throwing gas balls around the cosmos for all I know."

Warden McCorkle thought her bit of blasphemy was cute, but when she stopped smirking long enough to look over at the inmates parked across from her, it became clear that no one else in the room was amused.

"If you believe in God, Miss McCorkle, why do you automatically assume that He didn't heal Alan?" Saul asked.

"Well, let's see, Mr. Cohen," Gail answered, opening all three of the files on her desk. "First, because you're a drug dealer and a bank robber. As for Mr. Graham, let's just say if it's violent and illegal he's done it. How in the hell you two characters ended up in my camp is still a mystery to me.

"And last, but far from least, there's Mr. Carson. You're obviously the brains behind this operation. Your ability to tell convincing lies is well documented."

"So, what is it boys? Where's the other shoe? Did you manage to fake Audry's medical records, switch them up somehow? C'mon now, speak up! Believe me I haven't got all day for this nonsense. I'll ship you all out of here within twenty four hours if that's the only option you leave me."

"You can do nothing to us unless God allows you to, Miss McCorkle," Peter said, knowing his presumption would generate a harsh response.

"Boy, oh boy! Playing it for all its worth are we?" Warden McCorkle was getting angrier by the minute. "Mr. Carson, how would you like to visit a medium for awhile? Ask Mr. Graham about how it works up there with the big boys. Let's put it this way, ever see *Deliverance?* You'll be playing Ned Beatty's part."

All three men knew Warden McCorkle could easily make good on her threats and that she was right, Parkersboro had become unsettled and tense since the healing. Half a dozen fights, minor scrapes but still violence, had broken out between the two factions. Unchecked, even these little incidents were a danger to everyone. Today's busted lip can be the catalyst for tomorrow's melee.

Regardless of the consequences, Peter had instructed his disciples to "wait on the Lord" and, for a short time, that meant doing nothing in spite of the temptation to take action on their own and get ahead of God.

They were learning to be disciplined. It was not easy, but it was essential if God's plan for their lives was to succeed.

Peter ignored Warden McCorkle's crude threat of male-on-male rape and changed the subject entirely. "You have a niece, don't you Miss McCorkle? Carrie Lynn Johnson of Montgomery, Alabama. She's ten, I think. Been disabled since birth, something to do with being oxygen deprived during the course of delivery. Am I right?"

"How did you know all that? Why, you miserable son of a..."

Peter cut her off and continued.

"You adore little Carrie, your only sister's only child. You go to see her as often as you can, spend every extra dime you have on things for her. The child loves you perhaps even more than her own mother. You call her "Care Bear" and no one else refers to her by that name."

It takes a great deal to stun a hardened prison veteran like Gail McCorkle. Nothing in her life had ever shocked her so much as to render her speechless. Until now, that is.

How could he possibly know these things? Gail silently asked herself. Only Bernice, her sister, knew about the name "Care Bear." Gail did not use it except in private when she wanted to express her ultimate affection for the child. She did love Carrie more than anything else on earth, certainly more than herself.

Peter didn't wait for a response, he simply moved on.

"There isn't anything you wouldn't sacrifice if it meant that your niece could be healed. You have asked God hundreds of times to have mercy on Carrie, I know. Didn't think He heard you, did you?"

Gail McCorkle, unflappable woman of the world and tough as nails, was now reduced to a quivering bowl of jello.

At that moment, Gail had a vision, so strong and pure it was as if it was superimposed on her view of the world. She saw her beautiful little niece as she had never seen her before; healthy, happy, running, talking, laughing. It was so real she knew she could reach out and touch her. Then, as quickly as it came, it vanished.

"Would you like God to make what you just saw a reality?" Peter asked.

Somehow Gail managed to move her head up and down signifying yes. It did not occur to her at the time that Peter Carson must also have seen her vision in order to ask this question. There was no opportunity now for Gail to think through anything, reality itself was being redefined.

"Then the Lord your God says this to you, 'Leave My servants alone.' Do you understand Him, Miss McCorkle? You are not to limit or hinder us in any way as we work for Him at this camp. Christ wants to bless you, Warden, but He needs your cooperation."

Gail eked out another nod.

During this exchange Malik and Saul remained silent. They were engrossed in the unfolding events, but by now, after Legion and Audry, they had seen too much to be thunderstruck.

Peter rose, joined hands with Malik and Saul and began to pray. Little Carrie Lynn Johnson was lifted up to the Most High God in a short, but eloquent, plea.

This time Panos Kallistos was praying with total faith. The Holy Spirit had told him what to say to Gail McCorkle. Peter had complete trust that He would now finish the job.

"Call your sister, Gail," Peter instructed, as the three men returned to their seats.

"What do I say? I mean really, Mr. Carson, I can't just…"

"Call you sister, Gail. Use the speaker phone, please."

Warden McCorkle dialed her sister's number, not sure if she had completely lost her mind or finally found it.

When the call was answered all they could hear at first were outbursts of emotion, but not the type made from panic or fear.

Gail had dialed into a celebration.

"Bernice! Bernice! It's Gail. Is that you, girl? What's going on down there?"

"Gail? Is that you? My God, honey! I can't believe you called. Do you know what's happened? Lord in heaven, sister!" In her excitement Bernice dropped the phone.

Gail listened to the voices and tried to make out what was going on. She heard her sister saying, "It's Gail! Can you believe it?" Larry, Bernice's husband, was having an excited, but undistinguishable, conversation on a cell phone or on another land line. Charlene and Diane, Larry's sisters, were carrying on as if they'd just won the lottery.

There was another voice, mild, soft, and sweet, that Gail could not place, but was nonetheless very familiar. It was speaking to her sister and she could tell by its increasing volume that whoever it belonged to was about to pick up the phone.

"Auntie Gail, it's Care Bear."

Gail McCorkle let out a scream that could literally be heard a hundred yards away through concrete walls.

Carrie Johnson had never spoken, never walked, never so much as fed herself. Care Bear understood some words, recognized a few faces, but those minutes without oxygen had decimated her mind and body. The doctors said she was strong enough physically to survive for many years, but that she would never develop much beyond her "current capabilities."

Gail McCorkle was the only person who, from Carrie's birth, had somehow seen beyond the damage and into the child's soul. Care Bear would smile when Gail entered the room, even though the doctors said she probably didn't know how to "deliberately" smile. More than once Gail would notice little Carrie looking at her and swore there was more going on behind those beautiful brown eyes than anyone imagined.

What Gail McCorkle didn't know until today was that God works with what we've got, and Gail certainly had a special love for her broken and helpless niece who couldn't walk or talk, but had somehow just said hello to her beloved aunt.

"Carrie?"

"Hi auntie. I love you."

"My God." Gail could hear her sister crying in the background.

"It's okay, auntie Gail. I woke up now. It's okay."

"You woke up?"

"I woke up now. I saw you when I was asleep, auntie. I heard you talking to God for me. I love you, auntie Gail."

"You know about God, Carrie?"

"Sure, auntie, just like you do. God's friend Gabriel told me not to be scared. Told me when I woke up to tell you I love you. Oh, yea, and he told me to say, 'I love you, Peter.' Peter is my friend too."

Gail McCorkle looked over at Peter and totally lost it. She began to blubber, then to wail. In all her forty-eight years, Gail had only cried twice that she could remember, once as a child when she broke her arm, and then again at her mother's funeral. Now the tears were coming in rushes as the evil-created dam that had blocked her from loving God, and indeed everyone else in the world except little Carrie, finally burst.

Peter picked up the phone, prayed with Carrie, and told her that her auntie would call her back in a little while.

Forgetting their roles as jailer and convict, Gail fell into Peter's arms. He calmed her, reassured her that what was happening was very real. Neither of them cared what it would look like if someone came into Gail's office and saw an inmate holding the warden as she wept. Appearances and man-made rules are trivial when compared to God's awesome power and grace.

Half an hour passed before Gail was composed enough to begin facing the wonderful and dramatic changes God had made in her life.

"You know I can't force the BOP to release you three, but I'll do anything you ask, delay my escape notice and feed them false information, whatever. I have twenty thousand saved, it's all yours. I can have it here in cash tomorrow, maybe get you a car, fake id's perhaps…"

"Gail, Gail, slow down. We're not going anywhere," Peter said. "Remember what you promised God?"

"Yes, okay, I know. I'm not to hinder your work at this camp. Sorry, I should have known you weren't leaving."

"More than that Warden, you are our protector here. Powerful forces, both of man and of evil, are going to try and stop us, hurt us. You must do your best not to let them succeed. God will help you, Gail."

"What does that mean exactly, Peter? Who is coming after you? How can I protect you properly?"

"Your questions will be answered in due time. Watch and pray, Gail McCorkle."

"I need to know now, Peter. What should I do? I mean I could…"

"Gail."

"What! I'm trying to think here!"

"What you need to do is call your niece. We can talk later."

Gail let that thought register for a moment. *I can call my niece and talk to her.* It was so overwhelming, yet utterly simple, God had acted.

"Peter, I don't quite know how to say this. I've never said it to a man other than my father. I love you."

"God loves you too, Gail, and so do we. Now call Carrie. We are leaving."

As he closed the door behind them, Peter saw his warden, the once bitter, isolated and arrogant Miss Mac, humbly on her knees in front of her desk giving thanks to the Lord for His mercy and His messengers.

Between late October and Christmas, the environment mellowed at Parkersboro. Petty fighting ended and tempers cooled. The farther away in time "Alan's miracle" became, the less prominent it was on the minds of the men. Camp gossip moved on to other topics. The press lost what little interest they had in the story.

For some reason, Gail McCorkle made an effort to meet with every inmate one-on-one, she granted requests for furloughs and other privileges, asked about families, checked on medical problems, made sure the food was top notch for the holidays, and generally behaved more like a mother hen than a prison warden.

Rumor had it Miss Mac snagged herself a boyfriend and that his tender mercies were the source of her newfound qualities of kindness and concern. Peter, Malik, and Saul knew better, but they weren't talking. Neither was Gail, but she was participating in a private prayer service and Bible study every other night in her office with her newfound spiritual advisors.

Attendance at the "Service on the Porch" was increasing every Sunday morning. By mid-December most of the camp was showing up, although many were more motivated by curiosity than by a genuine hunger for the Word. Peter preached, everyone listened, a few souls were awakened. Those in the camp who considered all this "fuss over a con man" nothing but manure simply stayed away, but were no longer openly hostile.

Over the course of the fall, Peter continued to work on his relationship with his son. As an obedient servant of the Lord, he rejoiced and gave thanks for the miracles he had been privileged to be a part of, but God's benevolence also served to increase his desire to have Christ so bless his own family.

By December, Peter's twice weekly phone calls to Kev were going unanswered more than half the time, no doubt thanks to the technology of caller i.d. He wrote letters almost every other day to try and compensate, but when he finally did get the chance to speak to Kevin he found out that most of them had not reached his boy.

Peter knew all too well what the problem was. Actually there were two problems, interrelated yet distinct.

Julie Morgan had a legitimate right not to trust her ex-husband. The Peter Carson she knew would say anything to anyone, however untrue, to further his own selfish aims. Why should Julie believe he'd changed now? Jesus? Because he'd found Jesus?

Julie believed in God, but there was no substance to her faith. She knew that religion was often a convenient refuge for scoundrels. As a Southern woman, Julie had plenty of bad examples to choose from when it came to false teachers. A few years back a prominent televangelist conned her mother out of thirty grand before she and Peter caught on and put a stop to it. "Bible thumpers," a label she pinned on any outspoken Christian, were all phonies as far as she was concerned.

In Julie's mind, Peter's "jailhouse religion" was almost certainly part of some new scheme. To what exact end she wasn't sure, and didn't feel she had to be. As she told Walter, "If it walks like a duck and quacks like a duck, it has to be a duck."

While understandable, Julie's skepticism was also self-serving, which led, Peter knew, to the second problem.

Through the process of his spiritual growth, God confirmed a truth Peter felt like, on some level, he had always known; no one succeeds alone, and no one fails alone. God sews all of us together in a great fabric of life. While ultimately we are judged by what we do (by our own works), we are also held accountable to be our brother's keeper. In addition to showing kindness and love to his fellow man, a Christian must also never actively participate in another's sin.

Peter Carson had a wife who pressured him into feeling inadequate if he didn't have a "million in the bank by forty," made him feel small when he didn't measure up to her standards of what a "man" should be, and in very subtle, effective, and ingenious ways constantly sent and reinforced the message, "If you want to be worthy of me, you've got to be the best."

Peter bought into this trap, one of the devil's biggest lies. The evil one wants us to measure ourselves by our worldly status, or by what others think of us, rather than by our good works, love, and obedience to God. This is idolatry and it is a mortal sin.

The second problem was that Julie Morgan still worshipped this evil, hollow idol.

Walter Morgan was the oldest son of Lewis Morgan. Back in the mid-1800's Walter's great-great-great granddaddy started making high quality bourbon in Kentucky. By the end of the twentieth century P.R. Morgan Distillers had a net worth of over $400 million dollars. When Lewis died, Walter was in line to inherit half the company.

Julie stepped right into Walter's world, beyond grateful for the second chance at marrying the "right man." That Walter was a boring, spoiled, childish trust-fund kid who at forty-five still acted fifteen mattered not. She didn't give a damn that Walter couldn't turn on a light bulb in the bedroom, or that he looked like a toad sucking on a lemon.

That Walter ignored Kevin and resented him was a problem, but she did the best she could with the situation. Kevin would be given the pick of everything, from clothes and cars, to friends and schools. In her mind, this more than compensated him for having a distant and uncaring step-father.

None of this was Julie's first choice.

What Julie really wanted was to live the life Peter Carson had promised her. Together they were going to set the world on fire. Their strong sexual attraction and intimate friendship only intensified all their other desires. She loved Peter, always would, but he was a failure. Worse, he was a criminal and a disgrace. Her god made no allowances for such foolishness and neither did she.

In order for her to overcome, to not be denied at least part of the dream that was rightfully hers, to atone to her gods of materialism and pride, Julie "captured" Walter Morgan.

The ugly spectacle of Peter's arrest and conviction drug Julie through the sewage along with her ex-husband. While the affair was by no means a sensation by Atlanta standards, it got more than a little public attention. All of Julie's family and friends were caught up in the soap opera of it all; some had even lost money at the brokerage.

Although she never bluntly declared it to herself, or to the world, Julie knew she had to make a choice. She could either be a victim or an accomplice. She had to tread that fine line between abandoning her husband at his most critical hour, which no "proper" wife could do, and being dragged down with him.

Julie played the game superbly. From the time of the initial exposure of Peter's embezzlement, she knew that they were through as husband and wife, but she didn't tell him that. Keeping her distance from both him and the situation from that moment on, she kept up appearances until Peter was convicted and sentenced. A week before he self-surrendered at Parkersboro, their divorce was made final.

Julie was devastated, but by no means destroyed. An old college friend introduced her to Walter Morgan a couple of months after Peter began doing his time.

Theirs was not a romance. They didn't fall in love. Walter loved only his money, but he was enchanted beyond measure by his future bride. Julie became adept at the art of having sex with a man she found physically repulsive, while at the same time making him feel like he was the most exciting and accomplished lover on the planet. She fed Walter's ego, played the Madonna and the whore to perfection, and charmed his friends. Julie knew she would never be heir to Walter's fortune, because he had two ex-wives and a grown daughter. She would have to "make do" with a cash settlement of five million dollars upon any divorce.

This was a downside Julie could live with.

In little over a year, Julie went from being a broken, divorced ex-wife of a criminal to a player in the Atlanta area upper crust social milieu. She was proud of herself, for what she had accomplished required planning, hard work, and sacrifice.

Now Peter was trying to get back in her life through Kevin, to set her up for God knows what, to bring more embarrassment upon her, just as she had finally risen above his last disaster. This, Julie could not tolerate. She wanted Peter Carson to completely disappear, to never again be around to remind her of their failure.

So, on Christmas Eve morning, Mrs. Walter Morgan hopped in her Benz and made the five hour drive from Atlanta to Parkersboro to see her ex and rid herself of a problem once and for all.

Seven

Peter's heart leapt when he got the call that he had a visit. His first thought was that God was answering his prayers and had brought Kevin to see him. God always responds, but sometimes the answer even to the most righteous of men is "no."

Julie wore a dated outfit she knew Peter liked, a somewhat conservative white dress that fit snugly, highlighting her voluptuous curves. If everything went according to plan, her attitude would be friendly, consoling, even loving in the manner of a dear old friend. All of her conflicting emotions about her ex-husband, the love she still felt for him and yet resented, the anger over the shame he had brought upon her, and, most of all, the sense of betrayal she felt at not being given the life she deserved because Peter Carson wasn't "man enough" to make it happen were all put away, not to be displayed. Today was strictly business.

Peter's heart sank from the moment he opened up the visiting room door. There stood Julie, but not Kevin. Then his spirit quickened. He sensed danger, an evil presence. Even without his demonic blood hound Saul around to confirm it, Peter knew he was about to be tested. As they walked outside, he bolstered himself with a silent prayer of protection, knowing that he needed all the strength God could give him to repulse whatever assault Julie had come to deliver.

Peter hadn't seen Julie in almost two years, but none of her powers had diminished over time. Despite his closeness with God and knowledge of the truth, he sensed his "old self" rising to the surface, just at the sight of her. He felt that all too familiar ache, that longing to be with her physically, and to share emotionally. Her proximity began to unravel him. By the time they reached the south lawn, a place where they could speak in private, Peter was fighting an almost irresistible urge to run, to get anywhere but where Julie was, as quickly as possible.

Just before he was about to give into his fear and flee, into his mind flashed a Scripture, "My grace is sufficient for you, for My strength is made perfect in weakness." A smile came across Peter's face as he sat down on the grass. God had not forsaken him; He was with him all the time. He reminded himself that the Lord was in control, not Julie. His anxiety began to fade.

"Peter? Hello, Peter. Did you hear me?"

"Sorry, yes. I, uh, mean no. Sorry Jules, I was distracted for a moment. Forgive me."

There was definitely something different about Peter. Julie picked up on it the minute she laid eyes on him. She wondered if maybe Peter's "God garbage" (as she called his faith) and this new calmness she was perceiving were the result of some psychotropic medication.

Putting on her best phony front of concern, Julie jumped right in.

"I said, how are you? Are you doing okay here? It doesn't seem so bad, Peter. No guns or fences, it's not like any prison I've ever heard of."

"Trust me, Jules, it's still very much a prison. Where's Kevin? Why didn't you bring him with you?"

"Can we just talk, you and I, for a minute before we bring Kevin into this? Please, Peter, I'm here to help you."

"Lord have mercy," Peter mumbled under his breath. He knew the devil never came to help, but only to steal, kill, or destroy.

"Sure, Jules. Say what you need to say, please."

Julie had rehearsed and perfected her game plan in detail over the past two weeks. She had no doubt that she could execute it flawlessly and was quite certain it would be successful. After all, when had Peter Carson ever denied her anything? Despite his many faults, Julie was sure that the man sitting across from her now was the same one who had always been willing to walk through hell barefooted in order to please her.

"Peter, I want you to know that I love you. Always have, always will. I'm so sorry everything came down like it did. I know you're really not that kind of man. I don't hate you, I do want you to be happy, and I also want you to have a life when you get out of here."

The best lies are always laced with some truth. No one knew this better than Julie Morgan. She was a master at the art of manipulating men.

"I'm married to Walter now, Peter. Maybe that's right, maybe that's wrong, but it is reality." She thought this little touch of humility might soften him up. "Being married to Walter means things have to change, Peter. My husband's needs must be considered, not just mine and not just Kevin's."

"Jules, if you've got something to say, just say it. Going the long way around the barn won't make it any easier for either of us."

"That's good, I can respect that. Plain and simple, Walter wants you gone from my life and from Kevin's life. Regardless of how you and I feel about it, I can understand where he's coming from, Peter.

"The fact that you're a convicted swindler," she used this term because she knew how much it hurt Peter to be called it, "is making things tough on your son. The kids at school tease him. Walter has to explain away where Kevin's father is over and over again to his family and friends. In Walter's circles, appearances aren't just a big deal, they can be everything."

"Your calls and letters and all this God talk is really putting a strain on my marriage and on Kevin. He already resents Walter enough as it is. Before, when you only called once in a while, it was fine, but now, Peter, this situation is getting seriously out of hand."

"Jules, Kevin is my son. God put him in my care as well as yours. I will not go away simply because Walter doesn't like either me or my past. As for your marriage, that's your business."

Peter's tone was all wrong. Where was the "Geez Jules, can't we work this out?" weak-kneed attitude she knew so well. Based on this unexpected resistance, Julie skipped ahead in her pre-programmed attack, figuring that trying to placate Peter at this point with further fluff might be counter-productive.

"Would a million dollars perhaps make you change your mind?"

The offer hit Peter like a slap on the face. His "old man" kicked up for a second, begging him to consider the offer. Temptation comes in many forms, and the devil was using two of Peter's biggest weaknesses, Julie and money, to try and defeat him.

But the hot flash of his former self was not nearly enough to shake Peter's faith. He decided to play the game out with Jules, to see exactly what she was up to.

"Who do I have to kill for the million?" Peter said, displaying a slightly snide attitude, hoping to disarm her a bit.

That's my boy, Julie thought. She was happy to see some evidence of her old ex-husband re-emerging.

"No one, Peter. All you have to do is give up your parental rights and agree never to contact either me or Kevin again. It's simple, you sign and I wire the money wherever you say. It's legal, it's binding, and it's final."

"I can never see Kevin again? That's what you want, Jules?"

Time for the clincher.

"It's not what I want, Peter. It's what's best for Kevin, for me, and for you," Julie said, trying to sound as pained and sincere as possible.

Peter Carson closed his eyes and tried to gather his thoughts. The first thing that occurred to him was how foolish he was to ever fall in love with such a vain and shallow woman. How stupid he had been to ruin himself over her, to feel compelled to do anything to please her, to forsake his own life for her selfish desires. The true love he felt for Julie she could not return because she was still trapped in her sin.

Then the Holy Spirit took over.

"Walter doesn't even know you're here, does he, Jules?"

"I have no idea what you're talking about. How dare you accuse me of..."

"Oh, let me just say it. You're a liar."

"You, of all people, calling me a liar. Well isn't that rich? You wouldn't know the truth if it jumped up and bit you on the a**."

"My, my, Jules! Getting testy, aren't we? What did you expect, you could march right in here and buy me off? I can understand that, I truly can. The old Peter would have taken the money or probably bargained for more, but the old Peter Carson is dead, Jules. Believe it or not, accept it or not, it's still true."

None of this was making sense from Julie's perspective. The former patterns of her relationship with Peter were no longer valid. Regrouping, she quickly moved on to hostile tactics.

"Peter, I came here in goodwill to try and make your life better, and to help Kevin. You're still a damn fool, you know that? Why I ever married you, well, it's just beyond me."

Ouch. Rejection from Julie had always cut Peter to the quick. When he felt small, and Lord knows no one could do that to him like Julie could, he was pliable and vulnerable. She waited to see what reaction this emotion bomb would bring.

"Funny, I was just thinking the same thing. I'll pray for you, Jules, I want you to know that. My plea to God for you is that He not hold this sin against you. How I wish you could see what I see, feel what I feel! Jules, God is very real. We were so vain, shallow, and full of greed. You still are. Turn away from all this sin, Jules. Turn away before it's too late."

Right about then Julie Morgan's game plan got tossed out the window.

"Amazing. Very good. What's next, Peter? A TV show? Live from federal prison it's Reverend Carson? You're so full of crap. I know you better than anyone else. Don't you ever forget that!"

Peter pressed on. "Why do you want me to go away? It's not Walter, it's you, isn't it? That man could care less about me, and I'm sure he doesn't think much of Kevin. It's you he wants. You've used all your tools and skills and now he's fully under your control, just like I was. So come on, tell me. Even for a rich person, a million is big money. Why?"

"I don't know what you're talking about."

"Alright, I'll tell you. There is a part of you, deep in your soul, that nags at you. Wakes you up at night, brings you down out of the blue, reminds you of what you did. My coming back into Kevin's life is like pouring salt into that wound. You don't want me around because you don't want to deal with your own sin. You are a manipulative, greedy, liar, Jules. What's the matter honey, looking in the mirror getting tougher these days?"

While she wasn't expecting to be hit so squarely on the head, Julie Morgan prided herself on always being ready for anything. Even a rebuke so on point it was tearing her guts out did not alter her settled and indignant façade. It would take more than a few choice words to break her concentration.

"Who is the criminal here, Peter? I could swear you're the one with "Property of the U.S.A." stamped on your back, not me."

"Julie. Please honey, listen to me. That voice that haunts you, tells you something's desperately wrong, that's God trying to get your attention. Listen to Him! He will forgive you, I have forgiven you, and eventually you'll be able to forgive yourself. But you must submit, Julie. You must come to Him and repent."

"For hell's sake, Peter! I'll bite if it will make you happy. Repent for what? I never stole a dime. You did, remember? All I did was to be a loving and supportive wife and where did it get me? Broke, alone, and disgraced, that's where."

"You know better, Jules. I know better. One of the reasons you married me, perhaps the main reason, was you knew I'd do anything for you. I didn't have much, but I did have drive and ambition. I lived to make myself worthy of you. Now, no doubt once I got rolling my own greed and vanity kicked in right behind yours. My sin is my own, but it's on you too."

"That's what I've been trying to tell you, Peter."

"Come again?"

"I don't want your sin, your face, your voice, or anything about you on me anymore. The Feds took out my trash and for that I'm grateful. You are a pathetic loser and a con man, Peter Carson. I don't care what you do as long as you stay away from me and my son."

"I thought this was about Walter's needs."

"F*** you."

"No, I won't do that, but I will pray for you."

Part of Julie Morgan was actually very impressed. Never before had Peter stood up to her. They had fought during their marriage, particularly toward the end, and occasionally she'd given in a bit, but eventually Peter had always acquiesced to her plans and did what she wanted him to do. The one thing Julie didn't have the patience for was a man she couldn't control. It was time to play her trump card and move on.

"Peter, this is a copy of a restraining order," Julie said, handing him the document. "It says you cannot call Kevin or me pending the outcome of a hearing in Georgia Superior Court to determine if your parental rights should be terminated."

"Judge Grove is an old family friend of the Morgans, Peter. He owes us a favor, lots of favors. You are a sleazebag federal inmate. You do the math, Einstein."

Peter said nothing. He took the one page order, slipped it in his shirt, stood, and started to walk away. Julie watched, and when she saw Peter wasn't turning around, she got up to follow him.

They walked back to the camp offices in the most awkward of silences. Two people who once swore a lifetime of unconditional allegiance to one another, now shared only the pain of their mistakes.

As they approached the main lobby, Peter stopped and gently grabbed his ex-wife by the arm. He leaned over and whispered in her ear.

"Jules, God will not allow this to happen. Kevin is not a toy, and your demons aren't going away even if I do. Please, Jules, for the last time I'm begging you not to do this. I don't know what God might have to do to stop you. Don't play with Christ. The wrath of the Living God can be a terrible thing."

By this point Julie Morgan had heard more than enough. She took the gloves completely off.

"Tell your phony God to kiss my a**, and if you ever touch me or come near me again I won't stop at a court order, I'll see you get hurt. Now get your filthy hands off of me."

Having gotten in the last word, with a confident flair and her head held high, Mrs. Julie Morgan turned and walked away. Every man in the place was watching her, trying to visualize just how perfect that body really was under that tight dress. Every man but one, that is.

Peter had already started back to the south lawn to be alone and to pray for his ex-wife and his son.

Christmas in prison can be the most depressing day of the year. More so than at perhaps any other time an incarcerated man's thoughts focus on the family and friends he may no longer have and on the good times past. Joy is often in short supply.

Peter was by no means immune to this problem. His heart and mind were not on the miracle of Christ's birth, but rather on his son, and the fact that he could neither talk to him nor see him. He wondered what Kevin had been told, but he really had no doubt; right now his mother was probably consoling him by saying, "I know your father was supposed to call. I'm so sorry, Kevin, but Walter and I love you."

The men were expecting a rousing Christmas service, one full of hope and the promise of "life more abundantly" in Christ. Miss Mac set up a hundred chairs around the porch (brought them in special, raising more than a few eyebrows) in anticipation of a large crowd.

"Pastor Pete," as most of the men now called him, wasn't polishing his sermon or making the rounds with Malik and Saul this Christmas morning. Despite his best intentions, he still hadn't gotten out of bed.

All night long he was haunted by his visit from Julie. It wasn't self-pity or rejection or anything to do with him that was troubling his soul. It was Kevin. Why must he suffer for my sins? He'd asked God this a thousand times since midnight. Despite knowing how crazy it was, Peter found himself seriously fantasizing about walking into town, stealing a car, driving to Atlanta and taking Kevin away forever.

Peter did believe, despite his fleshly urge to run out and save his son, in St. Paul's admonition that, as Christians, we must, "walk by faith and not by sight." What appears to be an insurmountable problem, everything from an illness to a divorce to a prison term, is often simply a vehicle for God to use to implement His perfect plan for our lives.

While Peter was nowhere near one hundred percent, a few hours of silent prayer sufficiently recharged him to be able to get on with the day. "Whether in season or out of season" (regardless of one's emotional state) it was his duty to care for his flock. Peter reminded himself that many of the men would also not get to see their children today.

Dressing quickly and gulping down a cup of coffee, Peter made his way out of the dorm and toward the compound. An inmate intercepted him and asked for a brief prayer for his mother, who was gravely ill.

Just as he was about to say "amen" and open his eyes, he heard a child's voice calling to him.

"Hi, Mr. Peter."

Although he had never seen her, he knew who it was. Peter turned and standing behind him was little Carrie Johnson, all four and a half beautiful feet of her.

"Mr. Peter, auntie Gail brought me to your Christmas church. I wanted to come and give you a kiss."

With a sudden surge of joy, Peter reached down and lifted the little girl into his arms. Seeing and feeling the flesh and blood of a miracle made his spirit soar and his own problems seem less daunting.

"Isn't she the most adorable child God ever made?" Gail McCorkle said, as Peter put Carrie down. "There are no words that could possibly express the incredible happiness and peace my family feels this Christmas, Peter. All of us thank God for you everyday."

At times the Lord reminds us of what He will do by showing us what He's already done. Peter knew that his anxiety over Kevin was unwarranted. If God healed this precious child, surely He would take care of his son too.

Peter picked up Carrie and carried her to the cafeteria where inmates and family members were gathering for Christmas dinner. They talked along the way.

"You look better in person than you did in my dreams, Mr. Peter."

"Yes? You knew what I looked like before you got here?"

"Of course, Mr. Peter. You came to me and told me to wake up, don't you remember? You and Gabriel."

Amazing. Peter hadn't realized that Carrie had actually seen him in her mind. Gabriel's involvement was no surprise.

"Oh, I almost forgot. Gabriel was in my dream last night too. He told me to tell you God will always protect Kevin. Who is Kevin?"

Peter didn't answer the question. He just smiled, kissed Carrie on the cheek and told her to thank Gabriel for him the next time she saw him.

After an excellent meal, not just by prison, but by any standards, Peter delivered a passionate Christmas message. Working primarily from the Gospel of Luke, he did his best to bring his audience to the events, to imagine with them what it must have been like to see God enfleshed, born of a virgin in a manger, to witness angels proclaiming the coming of the King, to see a new star rising in the east and shining down upon the Holy One. It was a vivid, personal sermon from a man who knew that what he was proclaiming was pure truth, that the events described in the Gospels surrounding the birth of Christ literally took place.

God sent Gabriel to give the Virgin Mary a vision, a divine purpose she freely chose to fulfill; because of her love and obedience, the world received its Savior.

Only a few in attendance at Parkersboro on that mild, almost balmy, Christmas day in South Carolina knew that in order to fulfill His purpose in modern times, God was intervening once more, sending forth His messenger angel to call the faithful to His service.

But it wouldn't be long before the whole world would be asked again to believe, to turn away from the darkness, and toward the Light. Would the answer be any different this time? Was the twenty-first century ready to embrace its anointed prophets, or would it reject them as the Jews of old had always done?

The answers to these questions, like so many others, were not given to Peter Carson. Like Mary, John, Samuel, Elijah, Moses, and all of the messengers of God who had come before him, he was called to proclaim the Kingdom and to leave the rest to Him.

Eight

"That still kinda freaks me out just a little," Saul said, eyeing the two men casually strolling into Parkersboro to be processed and imprisoned by the BOP.

"What's that, brother?" Malik asked.

"How a man can just come right up to the front gates of a prison, even one as laid back as our dear old camp cupcake here, and say, 'Honey, I'm home!' and waltz right in. Tell you what, the Feds never got me so easy."

"How would you handle it today, Saul, if you were free and told to surrender yourself to the government?" Peter asked, as he walked up from behind his two friends who were sitting outside the camp barber shop taking in the morning view.

Saul knew it was a loaded question. Pausing to think for a moment, he then confidently offered his response.

"I'd pray about it and then do what God told me to do."

"That's exactly right. Guess you have been paying attention after all. And to think Malik and I were considering trading you in for another felon. Trouble is you've got skills. Hard to find another Saul Cohen."

"You are both so lucky I'm still here. Especially you, big fella. Who would protect Malik if someone jumped him and I wasn't around?"

The absurdity of Saul's joke made them all laugh and carry on even more. Barbs were traded back and forth until eventually both Saul and Peter ended up in a Malik Graham headlock and were forced to "apologize" before he would release them.

On a level impossible to achieve even in the closest of worldly relationships, Peter, Malik, and Saul were now bound together as if they were one. They knew that their lives were no longer their own, that they belonged completely to Christ.

Formerly each had lived a selfish existence, seeking only to satisfy their passions. In their ignorance, they believed sin was liberating, but after they were called, they discovered that total surrender to God is, paradoxically, the ultimate form of human freedom. What happened in this world no longer controlled them as it once did. Now they had no need to impress anyone, to be anywhere, or to do anything. No more egos, no more vain lusts. They had been set free in a way unimaginable to natural men. They remained incarcerated of their own free will. God wanted them at Parkersboro, so they stayed. The minute He told them to go, they'd be gone. That the United States Government still believed they were prisoners was a detail of little importance to them.

"I know those guys," Saul said, looking down the corridor as the two newcomers emerged from the camp offices.

"Yep, me too, Mr. Pete," Malik agreed.

"Let me guess, these two gentlemen are part of the prayer circle you both saw standing on the porch in your dreams, two more of the seven?"

"Yes," they answered in unison.

"'Bout time," Peter replied.

December had casually strolled into April. Winter had passed by uneventfully, or at least without extremes, but now the men were ready for action, primed to respond to a call to duty.

About an hour later, roughly the time it takes to go through a Parkersboro initiation tour, one of the new inmates walked onto the porch.

He carried himself confidently, almost cocky, and acted as if he were greeting old friends, which in a very real way he was.

"No doubt about it, you must be Panos Kallistos," the man said while extending his hand. "And I don't know either of your names, but I know that you both belong here."

"You have me at a loss, sir," Peter acknowledged. "You know my name, but I didn't catch yours."

"Kenneth Robert Simpson. My friends call me Kenny. The Justice Department calls me a 'leach,' a pariah that 'feeds off of society and steals from his friends.' How did they put it exactly in my pre-sentence report? I remember, 'Mr. Simpson has no concern for anyone but himself and flaunts the law at every opportunity.'"

"Sounds like you'll fit right in," Peter said, amused by the banter. "We don't care what the Feds have to say about you, but who do you say that you are?"

"Me, well, I have been crucified with Christ, so it is no longer I who live, but Christ who lives in me; and the life which I now live in the flesh I live by faith in the Son of God, who loved me and gave Himself for me."

"That's not very original, Mr. Simpson," Peter said, happy to play along.

"Damn! Caught again! I confess, it was St. Paul who first said that in a letter to the church in Galatia. Chapter two, verse twenty, if I'm not mistaken."

"You're not."

Peter would soon learn that when it came to quoting scripture from memory, Kenny Simpson was in a class by himself.

"Had any interesting dreams lately?" Saul asked Kenny.

"Oh, a few. Keep having one staring you three, Larry and two guys I don't see here yet. We pray a lot and tend to emit flames from the tops of our skulls. Sound familiar?"

"Ever met a man named Gabriel?" Peter asked.

"Funny you should mention him," Kenny answered. "Saw him last night. Told me to tell you that he remembers the prisoners as if chained with them."

"Hebrews chapter thirteen, verse three," Peter replied.

"I can see that I have a rival to my title as the 'One most knowledgeable in the Word.' Everything is true! Gabriel was right, you surely are God's anointed messenger. I need to sit down, please."

Looking a bit peaked, Kenny managed to stumble into a seat on the bench.

"Forgive me, gentlemen. This is all more than a little overwhelming. You men need to know that I've spent most of the last thirty years of my life preaching God's Word, yet not truly believing. I thought it was all a game. To me the Gospel was nothing more than a 'means of gain,' if I may be allowed to quote St. Paul again. I'm afraid, my friends, that you have fallen in with the worst of sinners, a con man who used God's name to exploit people."

Malik brought Kenny a cola from the vending machine. The caffeine burst seemed to pick him back up, and after a few minutes of small talk Kenny was ready to share his testimony with his brothers.

"Back in the early seventies I graduated from Duke with a degree in business. Truth be told, my sheepskin should have read, 'Bachelor of Science in Partying.' Man, those were the days, a bag of weed, a keg of beer, and fifty of your best friends. Life was good, worries few. My flat feet and severe myopia, along with my student deferments, kept me out of the running for a body bag."

"That sounds vaguely familiar," Saul said, thinking of his own history. "I remember those days well."

"Trouble was in '73 it all ended," Kenny explained. "Went through this little drama called graduation. Evidently after this blessed event, I was expected to go out into the world and make something of myself. For some reason I never saw that one coming." Kenny's smart aleck delivery was laced with self-deprecating humor and presented with panache. His style was disarming, amiable.

Before Kenny had the chance to detail his dance with the devil, Peter could already see how powerful the man's charisma was, and how easily it could be used for evil.

"So, surprise, a girl enters the picture. Sheila and I are busy having bong hits for breakfast one morning, this is right after I graduated, and she says to me, 'Kenny, you should be a preacher.' Right out of the blue, just as matter-of-fact as can be.

"I say, you need another hit darlin', maybe three, if you're saying crazy s*** like that."

Catching himself, Kenny apologized.

"My toilet mouth isn't quite where it should be yet, men," he said. "I'm working on it. Forgive me."

"We understand, brother. We'll pray about it later. Don't let it slow you down. Continue, please." Peter was never one to let form impede substance.

"I'll never forget what happened next. Over the following four weeks, every Sunday, Sheila and I made the rounds in the Piedmont Triangle. We hit a charismatic in Raleigh, a fire breather in Durham, a holy roller in High Point. She's taking notes like we are still in class. I'm laughing my a** off, getting loaded, and aping each pastor for Sheila in the car on the way to our next service."

"You know what she says to me at the end of that first month, July '73?" Kenny asked.

"Haven't a clue," Saul answered, assuming the role of the straight man.

"She says to me, 'Kenny, you have no idea how good you are. You're a better preacher right now than any of these bums we've been studying.'"

"Truth be told, God forgive me, from a purely stylistic point of view, my old gal was right. I have the gift. Always will. Wait until you guys hear me preach. If you like straight up, old fashioned, in your face, step on your toes, fire and brimstone laced, born-again booming there aren't many better than me."

"Bet you put on quite the show," Peter acknowledged, "but we don't do shows here, Kenny. This is the real deal."

"Don't I know it, Peter. Between Gabriel and the Lord I've been convicted not only of my own sin, but of the absolute reality of the Living God. Thought I might do a number or two just for you guys sometime, you know, show you how I used to knock 'em dead."

"We'll pass on that one, Kenny," Peter said, wanting it to be clear what was expected. "Our mission is all substance, very little style. Please don't go off and preach on your own. Our message must always be consistent. We act on one accord at all times, or we do not act at all."

"You know what, Peter, I understand, I really do. Gabriel told me to be obedient to God's messenger and that's you. Don't worry about me."

Softly, so that no one else could hear, Saul leaned over and whispered in Peter's ear, "Do worry about him."

Peter looked anxiously at Saul, who answered the unspoken question.

"No, but they are all around. I think they sense weakness, an undisciplined spirit perhaps."

"What was that? Didn't catch that," Kenny asked, clearly annoyed by the private whispering during his recitation.

"Nothing, Kenny, nothing. What happened after 1973?" Peter didn't know yet exactly where Kenneth Simpson was spiritually. Until he was comfortable with Kenny's abilities and stability he would be kept on a short leash for his, and everyone else's, protection.

"Probably best if I give you fellas the condensed version. I enroll at the *Way of the Cross Seminary* in Winston-Salem. Learn the Scriptures, the moves, the whole act. Takes me one year to finish a two year program. Sheila and I support ourselves by selling grass and running a liquor house."

"I'm ready to rock and roll by '74. We find a small time revival preacher with tents and trucks and team up, travel all over the South. 'Healing the well, saving the staff, and banking the cash.' That was our modus operandi. Old Otto, that was his name, Otto Meeks. Have never had a better partner. Good God Almighty, he knew how to make the mullah! Otto was a money magnet."

"Lord have mercy," Peter prayed aloud, nauseated by the crass vulgarity of using God to victimize other souls.

"Oh, it gets worse, Peter. Much, much worse," Kenny confessed. "God should have killed me long ago and sent me to hell. That I live and breathe today is a testimony to His grace."

"Luke chapter seven, verses thirty six through fifty," Peter offered.

"You couldn't be more right, Peter. I am the same as that sinful woman whose sins, which were many, were forgiven. I too love much in return. I know what the Lord has done for me. To have mocked Him as callously as I have, for as long as I did, and now to be called by God's holy angel to carry His message, to fight His battles? Who but God would be so merciful?"

"Who indeed," Peter agreed.

Kenny moved on, undeterred by the interruption.

"So, we bounce around for a few years. We make some decent money, but we blow it all on fast living. Sheila gets pregnant twice; both times she gets an abortion. Found out later one of those babies was Otto's."

"Ah, but all good things must come to an end. Our little troop gets run out of Jackson, Mississippi in '78. After a few complaints, one night the local sheriff decided to pay close attention to the act. He gets a hold of one of our plants, the people we set up to be "healed," but were really paid lackeys, and makes the poor kid sign a statement saying that we're all a bunch of criminals. When the police raided us a few days later the hidden microphones, phony blood, pills, twenty pounds of weed, and the porno tapes didn't exactly make us look like children of God."

Saul, who no longer had the power to resist, burst out laughing. It became contagious and soon enough everyone was enjoying the joke. However outrageous, Kenny's antics were amusing and he told his story very well.

"Why isn't it hard for me to visualize you in a tent with a p.a. system and a choir, slaying people in the Spirit and laying on the hands," Saul said, still chuckling. "You are quite the character, Kenny."

"Know what? It is funny. I see the humor, but we did a great deal of real harm. Most of our marks were poor people and desperate for help. They believed, we took advantage. Remember how much righteous anger Christ showed toward the Pharisees? Abusing the trust people give you when you hold yourself out to be a man of God is no small sin."

"I couldn't agree with you more, Kenny," Peter added, "but remember that you are forgiven. You can't be anything like that old person now, not if Gabriel and God have put you here with us. I've also found that it is tough to take advantage of someone who doesn't open themselves up to it, consciously or unconsciously, at least to some degree. That in no way excuses your sin, but in the con game it often takes 'two to tango,' if you will."

"Sounds like you speak from experience, sir."

"I do. You are not the worst sinner amongst us, Kenny. Believe that."

"I'll have to take your word for it on that one, Peter," Kenny said, seemingly reluctant to accept Peter's assessment. After taking another sip of cola he returned to his saga.

"Anyway, they threw us in the county jail. Not a good place to be in the late '70's, a Mississippi lockup, especially if you're white. Otto and I got out four days later after a few beatings and a bail reduction hearing. Sheila wasn't so lucky."

"What do you mean?" Saul asked.

"She was raped in the lockup by three guards who took turns on her for over twelve hours. Poor girl was never the same after that. Lord in heaven forgive us! She died ten years later in an asylum back in Carolina, broken and alone."

The reminder that sin can have very ugly, physical consequences sobered the men back up. Suddenly there was nothing funny about Kenny's past anymore.

"Okay, then Otto and I split up. Sheila disappears, I go back to Raleigh. My parents were still living so I moved home. Never did go back to Jackson to answer those charges. Someone told me years later they were dropped. I have no idea why."

"Now mom is real pleased and impressed that her son has become a man of God. As I told the story, it was that terrible ogre Otto who lured me into his sordid scheme. I played the young innocent, a lamb led to the slaughter. After a few months of pious living and cosmetic repentance, I landed a job as an associate pastor at the First Calvary Baptist Church."

"The pay was a joke, something like fifteen grand a year if I remember right, but the fringe benefits were enormous. Right quick I was doing five or six of the church hotties, all married, I might add, and skimming the collection plate for an extra grand or so a month. Got back together with a couple of my old college pals and soon I was moving grass again too."

"Talk about your double life. How long before it all collapsed on you?" Peter marveled at Kenny's ability to live in two worlds at the same time without obvious anguish. He recalled the mental torment he endured while trying to hide his lies and embezzling from his clients and his family. Such detachment is a gift. For evil this talent is abused and those, like Kenny, who are very good at it, are often labeled sociopaths and said to be devoid of a conscience. For good this same gift has enabled the exceptionally devout for two thousand years to be tortured, burned alive, or eaten by wild animals without fear or complaint for the sake and glory of Christ. All talent is a gift from God, thus the villain and the saint can be seen as two sides of the same coin, one using his gift for evil, the other for good.

"Til '83. Yep, I had almost five full years of bliss there, in Raleigh. Right about the same time Pastor Henderson caught on to my skimming, my little 'surtax' as I liked to call it, one of the good ladies in the church came up pregnant and claimed I was the father. The fact that I drove her to the clinic and paid for the abortion and then dropped her off back home drunker than a skunk didn't exactly make me look innocent."

"Man, oh man. Mr. Pete, I swear. Never knew you white boys could do so much damage. Yes sir, Mr. Simpson, you left quite a trail, I can see that." Malik, who never said much when the brothers were all together, was clearly impressed by Kenny's matter-of-fact attitude and brazenness. Before he came to Parkersboro and interacted with Peter and Saul, Malik knew little about the world outside of the hood and the prison yard. Much to his surprise, the so-called "good people" could be every bit as mean and ugly as the rough crowd in the projects.

"Since this is a confession of sorts, Malik, I must tell you that yes, I did leave quite the 'trail,' as you put it, and it only got worse as the years rolled by."

"About '85 or so I ended up in Nashville. This time I figured I might as well skip the middleman, so I started my own church. Called it the Covenant of the Blood Ministries. I had a covenant alright, but it wasn't with the blood of Christ. For ten years I milked that situation for all it was worth. I was slicker by then, more experienced. Never got too big, didn't want the attention. Attracted some wealthy folks into my flock. Did "deals" with them on the side, told them I was making "investments for the church." The denouement came in '96. Stole three hundred grand from the building fund, in cash. Changed my name, moved to Florida, bought a sailboat. Nobody looked for me for very long or very hard. When you embarrass rich people, sometimes they're much happier when you just go away."

"As you might imagine, three hundred G's doesn't last that long, especially when you're putting coke up your nose an ounce at a time, living large, and whoring. By '98 I needed a new gig. That's when we met."

"I'm sorry, have we met before today?" Peter was sure they hadn't. He would never forget a man like Kenny.

"No, not you, Peter. Gabriel. That's when I met Gabriel."

"It was March 1998. I'd been up all night in Key West partying like a madman. Keep in mind, gentlemen, I'm fifty years old by this time, still trying to be seventeen, but nonetheless fifty. Drunker than a skunk and strung out on coke, I'm sitting in this funky little bar at three in the morning and in walks this dude."

"A white guy about thirty with light brown, curly hair," Saul interjected.

"That's him. Never changes, does he? I'm sure you guys know him as well, or better, than I do."

"We're all very well acquainted," Peter confirmed.

"Gabriel sits down next to me and starts shaking his head back and forth with this incredible look of disgust on his face. Makes it very apparent that he is not at all pleased with me."

"Being an idiot, and being wasted, I take exception. Say something real slick like, 'Why don't you go bother someone else, a***hole.' Yeah, that's exactly what I said.

"Gabriel, what's the best way to put it? He's less than impressed. Starts speaking in Aramaic. I recognized the tongue from my time in the Seminary. Now I have no idea what he's saying, but it's unnerving me. I get up to leave. Let me rephrase.

I try to get up to leave. Can't move a muscle, like my butt is a piece of iron and the chair is a magnet."

"Uh oh," Peter said.

"Oh yeah. Next thing I know he waves his hand over me and I pass out. Or do I? I've never really been sure. I don't know how, but while my body remained in that bar, my soul was taken somewhere else."

"Let me guess, he made you listen to one of your sermons over and over again," Saul said, smirking.

"Nope. He took me to hell."

For Saul Cohen this was a very serious subject because he knew a few things about the residents of that principality.

"Took you to hell? You mean literally where Satan lives? Good Lord in heaven! That's my worst nightmare."

"Let me say this, Saul. I didn't see a sign saying, "Welcome to Eternal Damnation." Didn't have to. Did I see a side show or the main play? Couldn't tell you that either, and I sure as he…, sorry, heck don't want to know if there is someplace worse."

Kenny's tone and body language now abruptly changed. Gone was the swagger, the cheekiness that only a moment ago seemed an inseparable part of who he was. This transition did not go by unnoticed.

"Kenny, take a minute. Don't feel like you have to tell us anything more if you don't want to. We're here for you, we will listen. You are among brothers now."

Peter's heart was filled with compassion for his new friend, because he knew from first hand experience just how intense and life-altering one of Gabriel's visions could be.

For a few minutes, neither Kenny nor anyone else said a word. They just sat there watching the parade of the camp pass by, people going about their business on a normal afternoon completely oblivious to what was happening on the porch.

Then Kenny slowly raised his head and Peter removed the arm he'd placed around his shoulder.

"I need to tell you guys what I saw. As God is my witness, what I'm about to share with you men is the truth. In the many years since this happened I have told no one, and I mean no one, about this. It's about time that I did."

Once again, Saul whispered to Peter. "Keep your guard up. The nasties are watching. I don't think they want you to hear this, or maybe they're just scared. I know I am."

"Anything coming at us?" Peter asked.

"No, not yet. But they are in a snit. Buzzing around the porch like a bunch of pissed off bees."

Before he began, Kenny made the sign of the cross and said the Lord's Prayer. Peter, Malik, and Saul laid hands on him and offered a confirming prayer of protection.

"First thing I remember is being carried away by some force, invisible yet very tangible. The hand of God? Maybe that best describes it. For a moment out of the corner of my eye I could still see myself sitting in the bar looking completely at ease and normal. Gabriel was there too and he was talking to me. Yet I wasn't really there anymore, and I was getting farther away every moment."

Kenny paused and nervously looked around.

"You guys think I'm nuts, don't you. Crazy old Kenny, the drugs have finally destroyed his mind. That's what you're all thinking, isn't it."

"Actually, that could not be farther from the truth, Kenny. Your testimony is in fact being validated at this very moment." Saul offered this analysis and then stood, turned around, and took in a three hundred and sixty degree view of the immediate area.

"They are all around us now, Peter. Doesn't look good. No sir, not too good at all." Saul was close to panic. He realized that whenever evil congregated in such large numbers, very bad things could happen, usually to him.

"Steady. Hang on, Saul. If they're not attacking yet, maybe they just want to watch. Faith, brother, have faith." Peter knew he was the glue that held his men together. Regardless of his own fears, it was his job to be strong and confident, to be their anchor in the storm.

Kenny, thrilled to be accepted and not to be considered delusional, ignored Saul and Peter's exchange and continued.

"I start to feel, how best can I describe it? Like a corpse. My skin went not just clammy, but ice cold. My heart stopped beating. I had the sensation of being drawn downward, but I could make out nothing by sight. A whirlwind of grays and blacks surrounded me. It was like being in the middle of a blender filled with ashes and muddy ice.

"Each moment that passed brought me deeper and deeper into a state of depression, a hopelessness beyond all hopelessness. All the while this force, the hand of God as I choose to call it, has me firmly in its grip. I pray that He won't drop me and leave me here."

"Then all at once it hits me. I must be dead. I'm not back in some bar in Florida, I'm dead and going to hell to pay for my sins.

"You cannot possibly imagine what that feels like. Trying to come to grips with the concept of being damned for all time. It's beyond all pain, fear, remorse, sadness, or anything human. God have mercy! Pray for the souls who suffer in hell!"

Kenny needed another minute.

Saul, on the other hand, couldn't be more anxious for Kenny to get on with it.

"Saul, talk to me," Peter said, himself hyper alert and anxious, knowing that the enemy was close by and menacing.

"You don't want to know," Saul replied, his voice and body both wobbling. "I don't think anyone is left in hell, they're all here."

"Peter, what is he talking about?" Kenny was now paying close attention to what was being said around him.

Peter dodged the question and instead gave an instruction. "Kenny, please. Don't stop. Tell us the rest, brother. Our time might be running short."

Kenny set his curiosity aside for the moment and did what he was told.

"I start to slow down, or the world around me does, I'm not sure which, and I see a landscape below me. It's dark and desolate. It looks like something out of an old war movie; a bombed out city of nothing but ruins, only far more final, if you will. I had the sense that no one would ever rebuild this city; as it was, so it shall always be.

"Then the hand takes me closer to the ground. I start to see people everywhere moving amidst the rocks, the broken walls, and other chunks of rubble. *What are they doing?* I ask myself.

"After a bit it becomes apparent. They're hiding. They scatter like cockroaches as I pass by, clearly terrified. But they're not afraid of me. Soon enough I found out what was going on.

"The hand takes me to a spot on the ground and sets me down. I want you to grasp how horrible this place is. It is completely devoid of goodness, of anything worthy. The dirt, the rocks, the debris, everything is gray or dull black. A sadness, a palpable despair, permeates everything there."

"Peter, please, tell Kenny to hurry up," Saul begged, sounding every bit like a man staring into the lights of an oncoming train.

"I look down and what do I see? I see me. Twenty years younger, but me. My eyes are bloodshot. I'm shaking, rail thin, and ghostly white. Tormented."

"As I'm trying to come to grips with the idea of being present along with my damned self, I hear screaming and the sound of a million souls scurrying for cover. In the distance I see it coming, a black, putrid mist enveloping everything in sight.

"The mist surrounds me and the other me. To say that it carried the stench of death does not do it justice. It was the foulest of foul things. Imagine the smell of decaying bodies and excrement rotting for days in the jungle heat. Words do not exist, I mean ..."

"Peter, do something now, for the love of Christ!" Saul was in agony and he wasn't alone. Across from the porch are the bocce ball courts and the horseshoe pits. Ten inmates, who moments earlier were casually amusing themselves, were doubled over in pain and heaving their guts out. From the library they heard three men screaming about being attacked by "purple snakes." One poor inmate, who happened to stray too close to the action, was flopping around like a carp on an anthill not fifteen feet away from the porch.

"What in the name of our Lord?" Kenny said, not believing his own eyes.

"Brother, finish! We will never be intimidated by the servants of hell. Greater is He that is in you than he who is in the world. Remember that. Hold fast to that truth."

Kenny didn't hesitate. He too now figured the sooner he was through, the better.

"The stench and the oppression brought by the black mist had a purpose. Somehow it carried with it visions. I believe that these visions are unique to each soul that endures them, but they have a common theme.

"In my case I saw a wife, the girl of my dreams in every way, and four children. We had a nice, but modest home and lived productive lives. I'm given glimpses of things; birthdays, baptisms, ball games, homework. A rather fast but full sampling of many years of experiences. I'm brought to a church, clearly my church, and I see a well-cared for group of a couple of hundred families. A momentary feeling of peace and settledness lessens my agony. I knew that I was seeing things as they could have been, as they should have been, had I chosen to live an obedient, godly life.

"Then, as quick as it came, bliss vanishes. Now I see the woman of my dreams being beaten by an ugly brute of a man. She has needle tracks on her arms, weighs maybe ninety pounds. My kids, two of them anyway, are watching on in horror.

"I'm moved away from that nightmare and forced to endure a rapid succession of others; children being abused, a suicide, a murder, a rape. All of these tragedies are happening to people who could have been in my church, who would have been safe under my care.

"Somehow I understand that these second visions of pain and tragedy are in fact reality. I'm being shown a 'spiritual movie,' for lack of a better term, of the damage caused by my sin, by my willful rejection of God.

"The mist passes. The visions end. Looking down I see myself. I look up and say, 'It's never the same when the black mist comes. Different every time. I'm not alive, but I cannot die. God will not come to this place. Please help me, oh dear God, please help me!'

"My soul, if I still have one, because at that point I wasn't sure of anything, cries out for mercy. But I know that He is not coming. It is in fact the absence of God that creates damnation. There can be nothing more condemning than the unchangeable reality of hell.

"Before I have a chance to say anything else to my other self, I'm back in the blender again. This time I feel like I'm going "up," although, like I said, up and down seem like ridiculous concepts in that universe. With each passing second I'm feeling better, hope is returning in stages. I realize that I am not yet sentenced. Don't ask me how, but I know that what I have seen is both real and imaginary, but definitely not complete."

"I wake up, reappear, whatever, back in the bar with Gabriel. Everyone and everything is exactly as it was the instant I 'left.' If I ever left, that is. Gabriel is looking at me with this menacing kind of scowl.

'Kenneth,' he says, 'you have openly mocked God. Used His name to do great evil. You have no excuse. If God were to see fit to take you right now, you know where you would go, don't you?'

I ask him, 'Where I just was?' All he does is nod his head. By the clock on the wall I've only been in the bar for less than five minutes."

"How are we doing, Saul?" Peter asked, half expecting the ground to open up and frogs to start raining down at any moment.

"Believe it or not, holding steady," Saul answered, sounding much calmer. "The ghoulies aren't in attack mode, or at least not yet. Who knows, maybe they like hearing about home. But as far as I'm concerned, the sooner we're done here the easier I'll breathe."

"I never doubted that my vision was authentic, from that moment until this one. Sitting there at that table for the first time in my life I prayed honestly, earnestly, and simply, 'Lord Jesus, have mercy on me a sinner. Give me the wisdom and strength to do Your will.'

"Led by the Spirit, I went to work as an interpreter for a group of free legal aid lawyers down in Miami. Spent my days and nights trying to help people in need, both at work and in my free time. While I know that I cannot possibly atone for my sins through good works, as we are all saved by grace, I wanted God to know how serious I was about doing things His way, about being His obedient bondservant."

"How did you end up here then?" Peter asked.

"About a year ago, a U.S. Marshal shows up at my office. I recognized him immediately."

"Gabriel?"

"In the flesh. Do angels have flesh? Have to ask him that sometime. Anyway, he says the Lord needs me to work for him at a Federal prison. My time has come, he says. He asks if I'm ready. I say yes.

"I'm then served by an angel of the Lord with a two count indictment for marijuana distribution. For once in my life I'm innocent. Isn't that cute? Evidently one of our firm's clients claimed I was part of his drug ring."

"Knowing this is the will of God for my life, I accept a plea agreement, and in no way fight my conviction. This morning I self-surrendered, now I'm here with you gentlemen."

"Thank God," Saul said.

"Amen, brother. We are blessed to have Kenny with us," Peter agreed.

"I'll give that an amen too, but what I'm really thankful for is that the story is over. Our friends seem to be losing interest rapidly."

"Peter, will you please explain to me what Saul is talking about?" Kenny felt like the only kid in the room who wasn't in on the gossip.

"Later. There are still a couple of things that aren't quite clear to me, Kenny. You said you saw Gabriel last night, is that right?"

"Yep. At a motel in Georgetown. Brought me an extra large pepperoni pizza, twenty hot wings, and a huge soda. Didn't even have to tip him."

"And?"

"And he wanted me to be sure to tell you that all is well, God is pleased. As I said, he remembers you always. His message for me was a bit different. I am to be cautious, to go slow, and rely on you, Peter. Now, I've had the same dreams all of you have, I get the general picture as to why we are here. Gabriel said he wanted me to be aware that I am vulnerable and that I will be attacked. I'm not completely sure what that means, but it has to be true."

"We will take the good angel's advice and watch you closely, Kenny," Peter said, already fully intending to do just that regardless of Gabriel's instructions. "One more question. You said that you worked as an interpreter in Miami. What languages do you speak other than English?"

"All of them."

"Excuse me?"

"You heard right, all of them."

"Brother," Peter was trying to be as open and as positive as possible, "how can that be? No one on earth can speak every language."

"Wrong. I can. After I came back to life in that bar in Key West I soon realized I had been given this gift. Over the years I'd picked up some Spanish, French, Aramaic, and Hebrew, clearly I had an aptitude for it, but I never studied any of them seriously. Now? Well, as best as I can describe it, the Lord has turned me into sort of a 'universal translator.' Ever see *Star Trek?* I'm a human form of that little machine they carried around so they could talk to the aliens."

"What about reading and writing? How many lang…"

"All of them."

"Should have guessed."

Before they had any more time to explore this latest twist, an out of breath and freaked out Gail McCorkle ran up to the porch.

"What in the world are you boys doing out here?" Gail asked, managing to speak in between gulps of air. "Do you have any idea what's going on inside? In the kitchen, the deep fryer exploded. Then every knife in the place starts flying around, thirty of them are now stuck in the ceiling. Black slime is oozing out from all the toilets, and I just had a man tell me his name was Artemus and he asked me where his legion was encamped."

"Saul?" Peter asked, needing an evaluation quickly from his expert.

"Well, you didn't think they came here just for the view, did you? Trouble follows them, that's what they do. I'd say we're very lucky no one's been killed."

"Then don't say we're lucky," Gail interjected.

"Good Lord! Who? Let me go to him." Peter felt a stirring in his soul, the Power was awakening.

"It's the new guy, the other new guy. Lawrence Coleman. He said he was tired after his orientation. He took a shower and went to bed. Some inmates found him lying on the floor in his cube. He's dead. Was he one of yours, Peter?"

"Kenny? You know this man, right?" Peter asked.

"Can't be, Peter. Can't be," Kenny said, shaking his head. "He is definitely one of us, one of the circle. We met last night at the motel. He is, he was, an extraordinary person. I haven't even had the chance to tell you about him. How can he be dead? What does that mean?"

Malik and Saul were wondering the same thing. Coleman's death definitely didn't fit.

"What's up with the demons, Saul? Are they still in the area?"

"No, Peter. They are gone. I don't think anyone else is in immediate danger."

"Good, then take me to Coleman. Quickly, we may not have much time."

Nine

Dorm number one at Parkersboro houses a hundred men whose living quarters are arranged in cubicles that hold three inmates each. It's very much like a standard white collar open office arrangement, difference being in a federal prison camp this area is not where you work, it's where you sleep. Inside each cube are three beds, a small desk, and three lockers.

At the front of the dorm, near its only general entrance and bathroom, is an area the inmates call "the beach." Unlike its counterpart in the free world, the beach at Parkersboro is anything but desirable real estate, because all of the dorm's foot traffic is, by design, forced to travel through it. The beach is the noisiest and least peaceful place to live. Its beds are reserved for newcomers, and for those few prisoners who refuse to pay their court-ordered restitution.

The former Mr. Lawrence Coleman was lying motionless on the floor four rows back in the 'beach sand,' his eyes wide open and mouth agape as if something had taken him by surprise. As the warden and her entourage approached, the small crowd that had gathered around the body moved slightly aside.

"We called the Georgetown EMTs, Peter," Gail explained. "They are en route, but I'm afraid there isn't anything they can do. Listen to me. I know dead when I see it. This man has been gone for a while, at least half an hour. I'm very sorry."

Peter closed his eyes, but said nothing at first. He tried to empty his mind, to rid himself of any conscious thoughts. He was preparing his spirit and his body to become a pure conduit for God's Uncreated Energy.

"Everyone, please, give us some room here." That Peter, and not the warden, was barking orders struck no one in the dorm as odd other than Kenny.

"Peter, what are you going to do?" Gail asked this question so that she might offer some assistance to her friend, not to try and restrain an inmate.

"Clear the dorm, Warden. No one should be in here except you, me, Malik, Saul, and Kenny. Please, do it now."

Without hesitation Warden McCorkle did as she was asked. By the time everyone had been removed, they could hear the approaching ambulance's siren wailing in the distance.

As Peter knelt over Lawrence Coleman and began to pray, a strange sensation was felt by all present. Later Gail McCorkle described it as "a surge, an energy pulse passing through my body."

Everyone blessed to be present in dorm number one that afternoon also saw the same thing. A white light, more of a "glow" according to the witnesses, surrounded Peter Carson as he began to minister to Larry.

Peter's prayers were silent for a couple of minutes. Then he spoke. "My friends, do you believe that Christ is the resurrection and the life, and that he who believes in Him though he may die, he shall live?"

On one accord they all answered "yes." Kenny recognized the close parallel between Peter's question and Christ's words as recorded in the eleventh chapter of Luke. *Fitting*, he thought, since in that passage Lazarus is raised. Was Peter Carson about to do what only Christ, His Apostles, and a few saints have been able to do? Restore life to the dead?

Despite the miracles that each of the witnesses had already seen and experienced, bringing back the dead seemed extreme, perhaps impossible. Yet they did believe, using the measure of faith God had given them, a measure that was being increased by the second.

The white glow that had formed around Peter suddenly extended itself from his person upward, opening a hole in the roof with its brilliance. As it did, a sound erupted like a hundred cathedral bells, all being rung simultaneously. It was both stunning and deafening, like being hit directly by a thunder clap. No one could remain standing, the witnesses all dropped to their knees. The Power was so intense it enveloped the small group, temporarily rendering each of them unable to speak or move. That they could still hear and see what was happening was one of the greatest gifts God could ever give them.

Then Peter began to speak again, but now with an authority and eloquence beyond his human capabilities.

"Lord, I know that you always hear me, but because of the people who are standing by, I say thank you Father, thank you for loving us, protecting us, and allowing us always to be Your servants.

"Lawrence, get up."

As placidly as if he was waking from a casual afternoon nap Larry Coleman sat up, stretched out his arms and yawned. He seemed oblivious to the fact that he had been dead. While saying nothing at first, the look on his face was telling enough;

without a doubt he had no idea why all these people were on their knees surrounding him.

The white glow now began to dissipate, melting away first from around Peter and then moving upward. When it reached the ceiling, the "hole" in the roof disappeared and a sound like two giant steel doors slamming shut reverberated throughout the dorm.

When the Power was completely gone, Peter collapsed. Gail and Saul rushed to his side. Quickly they determined that Peter was breathing regularly and that both his pulse and his color were normal. Peter was simply asleep and would remain so for almost the next twenty-four hours.

"He is exhausted, nothing more. Saul, why don't you and Malik take him to his bed? Do not be afraid, all is well. Panos has been touched in a way few men ever have, by the very essence of the living God. In a short time he will recover."

Coming up from behind them, the Georgetown EMT crew had finally arrived. The one speaking was a white man, about thirty or so, with light brown, curly hair.

The other two EMTs stood by and looked at each other as if they had been listening to gibberish. They had no idea who this mystery medic was or what he was doing there. This mattered not, because a second later, after Gabriel passed his hand over them and spoke a few words in Aramaic, they had forgotten all of the events of the past fifteen minutes and busied themselves attending to a still quite confused Larry Coleman.

"They won't remember a thing, will they Gabriel?" Saul asked, already knowing the answer.

"No, Saul, they will not. It is not time yet for the world to know."

"When will it be, Gabriel? I mean, I'm not tryin' to speedball the Lord or nothin', but it don't seem like we're doin' a whole lotta good for Him stuck here in this play pen. If the Good Lord will pardon me for axin'." Malik was only verbalizing what everyone else was also thinking.

"Kenneth, what does it say in Ecclesiastes, chapter eight verses five and six?" Gabriel asked.

"You mean specifically about Malik's question?"

"Yes."

"Let me see. Okay, I think I get it. 'A wise man's heart discerns both time and judgment, because for every matter there is a time and judgment.'"

"Exactly. That is your answer. Trust in the Lord. Watch and pray. He will never leave you or forsake you."

Having done what he came to do, the angel of the Lord then turned and began to walk away.

"Wait!" Gail shouted. She had been patiently watching with both fascination and awe, but now she was desperate to speak with Gabriel.

"Gail McCorkle, dear and faithful woman. You want to ask something of me?"

"Yes sir, I mean Gabriel. Forgive me, I …"

"I cannot forgive anyone. Remember, it is men who will judge the angels."

"I'm sorry. Oh my. Second time in my life I've been tongue tied," Gail admitted, doing her best to gather her thoughts in a storm of emotion. "I need to say thank you, Gabriel. Thank you for helping Carrie."

"Dear woman, I go where I am needed and do as I am commanded. Your niece is very special, she has many gifts. It's God you should thank, not his messenger."

"I did that."

"I know."

"Gabriel, I'm not sure what to do anymore. Do I set these men free? I mean, I feel like such a bad person keeping them in prison. Peter says he'll tell me when it's time to act, and God knows how much I love and trust that man. I just, just tell me Gabriel, am I doing right? Is God pleased with me?"

"Are you doing what Peter asks, always and without question?"

"Always."

"Then God is pleased. There will come a time, dear woman, when God will ask you to do much more. Are you ready to serve?"

"Yes, Gabriel. I am ready."

"I believe that you are. Ask Kenneth what Christ said in the book of John, fifteenth chapter, thirteenth verse. Be ready for that, Gail McCorkle, and God will be pleased."

For a second Gail turned her head to try and get Kenny's attention, but seeing that he was still attending to Larry she switched back to Gabriel.

But Gabriel was gone.

The two Georgetown EMTs finished checking out Lawrence Coleman who they pronounced to be in perfect health. They left wondering why they were called.

A few minutes later, once the situation had sufficiently settled down, Gail took Kenny aside.

"Mr. Simpson, would you please tell me what it says in the book of John, fifteenth chapter, thirteenth verse?"

"Hmm," Kenny mumbled, not sure how he should respond. "Why, if I may ask, ma'am, do you want to know that particular verse?"

"Gabriel said it would tell me what to do, what I need to do to please God and protect Peter."

Kenny Simpson had been a prisoner of the United States for less than twelve hours. In that time he'd witnessed things many prophets and saints had yearned to, or feared, but had never seen. Head spinning stuff, both fantastic and inspiring. That he was unsure of himself at the moment was understandable.

Now his jailor, who treated him more like a brother, was asking him a very delicate question. His first instinct was to put her off and talk to Peter about it when he woke up.

"Maybe we should wait on that one, Warden, until..."

"Mr. Simpson, you tell me what that verse says this very instant!" This was an order, not a suggestion.

"Yes ma'am. It says, 'Greater love has no one than this, than to lay down one's life for his friends.'"

The first word Peter spoke when he awoke was "no." While he was asleep, God ministered to his spirit with lucid dreams. He desperately wanted to stay in that world. Compared to where he'd been, the earth was hell.

"That's a fine way to say good afternoon to your warden, Mr. Carson," Gail said, a broad smile beaming across her face. "But I can relate. If I were waking up after what you'd been through, the last thing I would want to see is my old, ugly mug."

Actually, seeing Gail McCorkle was marvelous. *Nothing could be better if I have to be stuck in this world*, Peter thought to himself. He managed a smile that rivaled hers.

"Larry, is he okay?" Peter asked.

"Fit as a fiddle. He's an interesting one, that Coleman. Quiet as a mouse. Ought to hang a sign around his neck saying, 'Beware: Extreme Humility Present.' Know what else?"

"What?"

"The man is innocent. I don't mean innocent by the Blood, servant of Christ innocent, I mean literally not guilty. The poor guy was railroaded."

"That so. How'd you find out so fast?"

"We wardens, you know, have this clandestine network. Every other Wednesday a few of us secretly get together to decide the fate of prisoners everywhere."

"And they call me crazy."

"An old friend of mine is tight with Coleman's attorney up in Maryland. One phone call later and I get the lecture of my life from this guy swearing that if I let anything happen to that "sweet, gentle man" before he can spring him on appeal he would, well, let's just say non-voluntarily rearrange my anatomy."

"In other words, kick your butt."

"Basically."

"Can't wait to meet him, let me get up and…" Peter's head felt like it was filled with wet cement, and he was certain that two guys with paddles were whacking his skull enthusiastically. Gingerly, he laid back down.

"What's it going to take for you to slow down, Mr. Carson?" Gail asked, placing some aspirin in Peter's hand. "The world can wait a few minutes while you get your bearings back."

"Guess you're right, my head…"

"Feels like you've been kicked by a mule, I'll bet."

"Something like that."

Gail McCorkle was looking at Peter differently now. He could sense the change. Their relationship had rapidly evolved from jailer-prisoner to spiritual siblings and now, Peter perceived, to something more.

"Gail, if you don't quit doting over me people will talk."

"And what would they say, Mr. Carson?"

"That the Warden is in love with one of her inmates."

"So? You know that I love you. Don't get nervous now, it's not a physical love. Although you are a little stud muffin, got to admit that. What I feel for you is far more real and permanent. You are a very special man, Peter, perhaps the most special man to grace our little globe in a couple of thousand years."

"Gail, please. Stop that kind of talk right now. I am only a vessel, an obedient servant. Nothing more."

"If you say so, you wouldn't be who you are if you had an ego. But I know the truth and that is sufficient."

"Are you trying to tell me something, Miss McCorkle? What happened while I was asleep?"

"Nothing, Peter, nothing. It's just that I, well, for the first time in my until recently useless life I know what my purpose is, what God really wants from me. I know that you know what I'm talking about. Once you find your purpose, life becomes much easier. Peace sets in."

Peace. Peter did know exactly what Gail was talking about. Despite the trials he was enduring (or was it because of them?), he did know a peace that went "beyond all understanding." As long as he walked in God's will, he knew that he could face any challenge, conquer any foe. Such confidence can only come from Above, and no earthly thing can shake it.

"Okay, Gail. Don't keep me in suspense. What's your purpose?"

"Hold on there mister! Who said I have to tell you? Mighty presumptuous aren't we?"

Peter thought she was kidding, but he was still taken aback. "Of course, Gail. Forgive me. I should not have assumed ..."

"Oh, will you stop it," she said, gently kissing his forehead. "You are my purpose, Panos. I'm to be your protector here, as you said, but I guess I never really knew exactly what that meant until yesterday."

Peter felt no need to delve further into Gail's comment. It was powerful enough standing on its own.

"That's pretty heavy stuff, Miss McCorkle. You don't give a fella much of a choice, now do you?"

"No sir. You have no choice and neither do I. Isn't that wonderful! Praise God!"

"Praise Him indeed."

Standing off in the corner of the cube, so quiet and unobtrusive he almost seemed invisible, was Lawrence Coleman. When Peter saw him and made eye contact Larry looked down at his shoes and gave a sheepish shrug as if to say, "Ah shucks, maybe I should come back later."

"Mr. Coleman. Warden McCorkle was telling me all about you. Come over here so I can shake your hand."

Without saying a word, Larry did as he was told.

"Well, don't keep us in suspense, Mr. Coleman. For heaven's sake speak up! It isn't everyday we get the opportunity to talk to someone who has crossed over and returned." Peter hoped by being upbeat and a bit boisterous he might make Larry more comfortable, draw him out some.

"Yes sir. If you say so, Mr. Kallistos. I'm afraid I can't tell you much about what happened, but I will do my best." When Larry spoke it was always in a soft, even fashion. If you didn't listen closely to what he was saying, you'd miss it. The volume and cadence of his speech were indicative of a man who was far more adept at listening than he was talking.

"Miss McCorkle and a couple of the guards gave me a tour of the camp. I saw Kenneth over talking to you guys and I was going to join you, but suddenly I got sick to my stomach and very tired. My plan was to shower, take a nap and then catch up with you."

"Saul's little friends?" Gail asked.

"Don't ever let him hear you calling them his friends, but yes, Larry was attacked," Peter explained.

"Yes sir, I'm sure you're right. I was attacked. Once I got in my bunk, I felt like someone had strapped me down and I couldn't move or speak. Next thing I remember is waking up on the floor and you were kneeling over me with that white glow all around you."

"That's it? What happened after you passed out?"

"I don't remember anything. Sorry I can't be of much help. Kenny says I was dead. Is that true, sir?"

"Yes, Larry, it's true. You had probably been dead for awhile before I arrived."

"Then the proper thing for me to do is to thank you, Panos. My, My."

"Larry?"

"For many years, sir, I have waited patiently for this day, for the time when God would send his heavenly messenger back to earth and show His mighty hand to His people. I knew this would happen, but actually living it is a joy beyond description. You are blessed, Saint Peter, as am I to be in your presence." Larry dropped to one knee, took Peter's right hand and kissed it.

"And you thought I was going too far," Gail said, barely able to control her laughter.

"Larry, Larry. My friend, we need to talk." Peter was getting more uncomfortable with each passing moment. "First of all, I'm not a saint. As I understand it, you don't get to be one of those until long after your dead, and I'm still very much alive. Please, don't ever call me that again."

"But Panos, I was …"

"Larry."

"Yes sir. I only called you that because Gabriel does. I meant no offense."

"Ha, ha. Got you on that one. You're gonna love this." Gail was obviously amused by knowing what Larry was going to say next, he having already told her and the brothers his story earlier in the day.

"Lord have mercy." Peter positioned his head on the pillow where it throbbed the least and settled in as Larry began to share his testimony.

"For many years, Peter, I've run missions in Baltimore and D.C. for the homeless, the Open Arms Ministries. We feed and clothe who we can as God provides, help the poor get services and shelter, and spread the Gospel."

"Tell Peter what you did before you ran Open Arms, Larry." Gail wanted to be sure every detail was covered.

"Since I was sixteen, when I dropped out of high school, I've been working with the homeless in one way or another. Started volunteering in a soup kitchen, now I run ten of them. Oh, sorry. I used to run ten of them."

"Why am I not surprised?" Peter said.

"Oh, it gets better. Believe me," Gail added.

"One day, I guess it's been nearly twenty years ago, a homeless man sought me out after dinner. He was a Caucasian, about

Solomon's Porch

127

thirty, with light brown, curly hair. Had the most captivating quality about him, he radiated goodness."

"This will blow your mind, Peter." Gail was as giddy as a little girl on Christmas morning.

"Gail, please. Let the man speak."

"He tells me his name is Gabriel and that he is an angel. Now I know everyone thinks I'm the easiest mark around but, honestly, I thought the guy was probably mentally ill. I see so much of that. Still, like I said, he had this aura that's really hard to describe in words. It has to be felt, it can't be explained.

"This man tells me Christ is very proud of me. Says I 'shall see God.' Now I know what that means Biblically. It was a very nice thing to say. In my mind, I'm thinking, this is really a good man, how can I help him? I swear to you I didn't take him seriously. That is until he touched me."

"It's a good thing you're lying down, Peter. Stay there." Gail held Peter's hand, as if to offer him support against some immanent shock.

"The moment he does, touches me that is, I get transported far away. Not physically mind you, I somehow knew that I was still standing in the dining hall, but I was gone nevertheless. You want to know where I came first? Right here, right now. I saw you, Kenny, Malik, Saul, even Miss McCorkle as you all look today. I knew where I was and when it was.

"My visions came in a series of short bursts, portions rather than complete events. I've talked to the other guys and I can tell you, I too saw all of us praying in a circle on the porch, tongues of fire shooting from our heads.

"But my visions didn't stop there. I saw you, Peter, speaking to what seemed like a hundred thousand people in some enormous stadium. Your picture and your words were being broadcast all over the earth. We, well some of us, were there with you."

"After you were done, many of the people were angry with you, started calling you names like traitor and even demon. They wanted to kill you, Peter. There was so much love in that arena, and also so much hate. Like two worlds colliding, two armies at war."

"I don't know what happened next, because I got transported somewhere else. I was in the midst of thousands of people, all of them asking about you. Is Peter alright, when will he be here, will he bless us, and so on. Why they were asking me in particular these questions I never knew. Until now, I guess."

"Then a flash of light bursts right in front of my eyes and I'm back in the mission. Gabriel is standing right in front of me."

He says, "Lawrence, you are worried and troubled about many things, but one thing is needed. Choose that good part and it will not be taken from you."

"Sounds like the story of Mary and Martha, but I don't get the connection," Peter said.

"Yes, Panos, that's it exactly. I knew what Gabriel meant. Martha was 'distracted with much serving' and she wanted Jesus to order her sister Mary to help her take care of the guests. Christ said no, because Mary was sitting at His feet hearing His Word, and this was a greater duty than serving others. Simply put, God's will must always be our first and only priority."

"Don't you see? Gabriel didn't want me to miss it, to pass on my calling of being your disciple because I was busy serving others, running my missions. Since then I have always known that when you called, I must go. God has taken care of my missions anyway; they no longer need me around to get things done."

"Tell him why you're locked up, Larry. This is nuts, Peter. I think God does have a sense of humor after all," Gail said, shaking her head in disbelief.

"Tax evasion."

In between snorts of laughter Peter managed to get out a, "You've got to be kidding."

"No sir," Larry answered. "What happened was I made some people in D.C. very mad when I refused to move two of my missions. They wanted to build condos or something on the properties. I publicly chastised them, said they should be ashamed of themselves for trying to take away what few things the poor had, when they had been blessed with so much.

"Rich people don't like being called names or challenged, I know that, but I felt strongly something had to be done. So I spoke out and the city council backed me and the missions stayed."

"A couple of months later, two federal agents, IRS men, came looking for me. They asked me about two parcels the mission owned on Jones Street down by the RFK. I said we sold those lots two years back and used the money to support the ministry. Then they said they knew that, but they wanted to know why I never declared the income."

"A sweet old woman named Eunice Pine left the ministry that land when she died. I remember seeing the deeds. Everything was in the name of the Open Arms Ministries, Inc., our non-profit corporation. The two IRS men said to me 'no sir,' and claimed those properties were given to Lawrence T. Coleman, Jr. personally, and were sold by me for five hundred thousand dollars. They said the United States wants its tax money on the sale.

"I laughed at them, I really did. What a joke, I mean me, Larry T., who drives a 1985 Chevy Malibu, lives in a gifted one bedroom flat in the worst part of the District, and takes home a whopping twelve thousand a year in salary is a tax cheat? 'Come on,' I said, 'is this for real?'

"Well, it wasn't very funny when they pulled out a bunch of documents showing that I had sold the land in my name and pocketed two hundred thousand dollars of the proceeds. They were phonies, all of these papers. I had no idea how they concocted this whole thing until my new lawyer showed up a few days later, a gift from my friends over at Legal Aid."

"Do I even have to ask?" Peter said, rolling his eyes.

All Gail McCorkle could do was shrug her shoulders and fight the nearly irresistible urge to spill out the details before Larry did.

"You're right, yes sir, it was Gabriel. Although it had been almost twenty years since I'd last seen him, I recognized him instantly. Hadn't changed a bit. I guess angels don't age, do they Panos?"

"No, I guess not Larry."

"To make the story short from here, he tells me, of course I hadn't cheated on my taxes, but God needs me to go to prison. He and I discuss my visions of twenty years ago. He says the time has come for me to serve. Everything fits. I say God's will be done.

"Now, the U.S. Attorney offered me a no jail time plea bargain, but I turned it down. I said I plead guilty, so sentence me. Those guys never wanted to send me to prison, Panos. How could they know they were being used by Him? God set it all up, so here I am."

Larry then abruptly stopped talking. He looked like a man who had just ran the marathon and was completely spent.

"Well, St. Peter, what do you think?" Gail wondered if Peter found Larry to be as uniquely captivating as she did. "I'll say this much, things are really getting interesting now."

"I think God is getting everything ready, Gail," Peter responded, ignoring the "St. Peter" comment. "And when He acts, we must be prepared. Much will be expected of all of us. I don't know exactly what's coming, but if what Larry says is true we are about to be sent out as lambs amidst the wolves."

Ten

As Peter surveyed the life outside the window of Gail McCorkle's government issued sedan, he thought about how different it was to see God's creation through new eyes. Nothing was the same.

Passing by a roadside pecan stand on the way into Charleston, the Spirit moved Peter and led him in unexpected directions. He was reminded of his mom, and how much he used to love the warm nuts she served during the holidays. He remembered her gentle voice and reassuring touch. Peter understood now how seriously Marie Carson took her duties as a mother, and how much effort and care she put into the role. That he hadn't shown either of his parents the amount of love and respect they deserved before they passed on was shameful, a wasted opportunity that could not be retrieved. *One of my many regrets,* Peter thought to himself.

When he looked back now at the mistakes he'd made during the course of his life, Peter was not depressed. The last time he'd traveled down this highway, going north instead of south, he was trapped in his sin, dying of guilt and shame. Now he knew the truth and his godly sorrow had produced repentance, not despair. This knowledge brought Peter closer to Christ and increased the mercy he felt toward his fellow human beings. Peter Carson had become a man truly thankful for his trials. He understood and appreciated the inestimable value of being chastened by God.

The pecan stand on the road to Charleston was operated by black folks, an extended family by the looks of them. Their old clothes, dilapidated nut cases and racks, and the twenty-year-old Ford parked behind the stand testified to their poverty. Before, Peter never gave a second thought to the fate of the poor, especially poor people of color. Now his heart went out to them and he hoped they knew that God loved them every bit as much as the man in the mansion. Did they know that if they lived lives seeking Him, their poverty in this world would be replaced by riches beyond measure in the one to come? He took a moment to pray for the family, to ask God to send them a reassuring and loving message.

Peter felt in many ways like a child, a newcomer to life for whom the simplest of things were fascinating. No doubt, he thought to himself, some of what he was experiencing was the natural result of going for a long drive after being locked up for two plus years, but only the presence of Christ in his heart could fully explain the difference in his attitude and the changes in his spirit.

"Quiet today, aren't we, Mr. Carson?" Gail McCorkle had also said little since they left Parkersboro.

"Sorry, I'm not being very good company, I know," Peter apologized. "I guess I just have a lot on my mind. I think I'd forgotten how nice it is simply to be out amongst the living."

"You know, Peter, we can just keep on going. Grab Kevin at the courthouse and disappear. Don't think I wouldn't do that for you." Gail constantly reminded Peter how guilty she felt about keeping him in prison, and how anxious she was to change his address.

"Gail, my dear sweet friend, Gail. God bless you honey, but you know we can't do that. We're both slaves, remember? Try not to think of Parkersboro as a prison. In our case it's really more of a sanctuary. God is using our little penal colony as a staging area. Soon enough, I fear we'll all be moving on, but that's His call to make, not mine and not yours."

"Peter?"

"Yes, Gail."

"Doesn't all this frighten you? I mean, if I were you I think I'd be scared to death. I'd be afraid of what all the idiots in this world would want to do to me, and I'd be even more worried about not living up to God's expectations."

As Gail said this they were entering the outskirts of Mt. Pleasant, a few miles north of Charleston and the freeway connection they needed to catch to drive to Atlanta. They stopped for a red light next to a row of restaurants and shops.

"See that place over there, Baron's Barbeque and Steak House? That's where I ate my last meal as a free man, Gail. Good Lord in heaven, that seems like yesterday and a thousand years ago both at the same time."

Peter was thinking about Gail's question, he wasn't trying to dodge it, but the answer was anything but simple.

"I remember sitting in a booth right by that window, thinking about what I'm sure everyone who is about to self-surrender thinks about, should I or shouldn't I? To tell you the truth, by that point I was so emotionally drained that it really didn't matter to me one way or another. I probably didn't have the strength or the courage to be a fugitive."

Gail brought to mind her first impressions of Peter when she arrived at the camp.

"I thought you were just another sorry a** rich boy mad at the world because you got caught slinging 'white crack.' One more log for the pile."

"What in the heck is 'white crack?'"

"Haven't heard that one? I'm surprised Malik never said something about it. 'White crack' is non-violent crime; fraud, counterfeiting, and the like. White boys can't go hustle a kilo of rock on the street to score, so they have to sling 'white crack.'"

Peter smiled, acknowledging the truth in the analogy. If there was one thing God had taught Peter about crime and punishment, it was that no man's sin is any worse or better than another's. Selling a fellow human being poison or stealing from him were equally ungodly.

"You want to know what I'm really afraid of Gail?" Peter asked, still staring out the window engrossed in the passing parade of routine human activity.

"From where I sit, you don't seem to be afraid of anything."

"You're so wrong. What wakes me up at night in a cold sweat isn't the demons or the idea of dying or pain. I'm scared to death that somehow I might end up like the stupid fool I once was, stuck in the misery of this world."

"I don't see how that's even remotely possible, Peter."

"Think again. Even Christ had a human side. His flesh didn't want to go to that cross, but He was also fully God, so He went, joyfully."

"You mean you still think about all that old junk? What you did and all?"

"Not like that exactly. I have no desire to lie, cheat, and steal. But running away and hiding? Let me put it to you this way; if it were up to me, you and I could just pick up Kevin and keep on going. Every time you say something like that to me, Gail, it hits a nerve. I would like nothing more than to just go somewhere quiet and live in peace, but I know that's not going to happen."

"You mean what Larry said about you speaking in that stadium and it being broadcast everywhere?"

"I knew before then, Gail, but yes, I believe Larry," Peter explained. "What I'm trying to tell you is that flesh is weak, even and especially my own. Don't ever believe otherwise, sister. Let your guard down for a minute and Saul's little buddies will be all over you."

That was something else Gail McCorkle hadn't really come to grips with yet, the reality of evil being ever present in the world.

"I can remember growing up and going to church and hearing all about the devil," Gail said, as she turned their vehicle onto the bridge that would connect them to the interstate. "I guess I never knew how real he was. Maybe I didn't believe, or didn't want to, I don't know. But now, seeing what I've seen? It's a wonder we all aren't trying to kill each other twenty-four seven."

"What do you think would happen if, even for an instant, God were to lift his hand of protection from our planet, Gail?"

"I never really thought about it like that before, you know, like two forces vying for control. I sure do now."

"It's a war, Gail McCorkle, and we are His soldiers. Our enemy may not be flesh and blood, but spiritual evil is very real."

"I know you're right, Peter. Still, it's so hard to believe the unbelievable, to make real the invisible. What we believe, what we know, really makes no sense at all, yet it is the only thing that explains everything."

"That's one reason why Christ taught in parables. Not only are human beings by our very nature limited in our ability to understand spiritual truths, we think with what little knowledge we have of God's ways we can answer all the questions."

"I'm confused again, but that's nothing new."

Peter took a sip of his tea and gathered his thoughts. Despite the challenge that lay ahead at the end of their drive, for now Peter was relaxed and peaceful and wanted to make the most of his time with Gail.

"Christ taught that He was both the creator of the world, and not of this world. What does that mean? It means that physical laws, which He created, have no effect upon Him unless He allows them to."

"I think I understand. Certainly I've seen you do things no scientist could explain."

"When we get back I'll point out some Scriptures on this for you; how Christ passed 'through the midst' of hostile crowds, walked on water, calmed storms with a simple command."

"I know where to find those passages."

"The learned men of this age, all the scientists, mathematicians, and physicists, assume that the universe is one big riddle that can eventually be solved through the application of human reason alone. They are mistaken."

"What, you're saying science is a waste of time? That doesn't sound like you, Peter."

"Not at all, Gail, not at all. Who gave us our brain, our ability to learn and discover, and make sense of the world? God. God's gifts aren't evil, knowledge isn't evil.

"The problem comes when we take God out of the equation. Modern man has discovered that the parables God used to teach the Jews about His nature, the creation, and flood stories in Genesis immediately come to mind, are not literally true. This really should surprise no one, especially anyone who has a relationship with Christ and knowledge of His ways."

"I remember you talking about this in a service last month, Peter," Gail said. "I guess I need to hear it again."

"All Scripture was written to teach human beings about the nature of God, and to explain what He expects from His people. This has always been so, from the time God called Abraham out of Ur until now. The creation parable teaches us one critically important lesson, that it was God who made the earth and everything on it and we are to worship Him and not His creation."

"If that's so, why do so many Christian preachers insist that every word of the Bible must be interpreted literally? Are they blind to the truth?"

"What makes us blind, Gail? Our own flesh, our lusts, our pride. The enemy uses our flesh to keep us from the knowledge of God. Basically, we get in our own way."

"Those pastors who insist that the Bible, especially the Old Testament, must be interpreted literally, meaning that it does not contain spiritual truths presented as parables, well, they just miss it, they miss God's message. Christ made the absolutes of the Scriptures very clear; love the Lord your God with all your heart, mind, and soul, and love your fellow man as Christ loves you. All Scripture must be interpreted looking through this 'lens of love' or we end up confused and off course."

"I'm learning, Peter, I am. Love is at the heart of the Gospel. What did St. Paul say, 'Love covers a multitude of sins?'"

"Yes, that's right. But relating this back to our discussion of evil in the world, we have to always keep in mind that love is our only real weapon against Satan. As Paul told the Ephesians, we must stand after having 'girded' ourselves with truth and 'shod our feet' with the Gospel. Our faith is our 'shield' and our salvation is our 'helmet.'"

Gail nodded her head, signaling that at least the heart of the message was getting through. She didn't know how all the puzzle pieces fit together, but by faith she knew that they were all in the box.

They let the next fifty miles of South Carolina countryside pass by in silence. Peter's eyes never left the landscape, every detail of the lowland farms and forest seemed to interest him.

"Peter, what's going to happen today? I mean, do you already know what the judge will do?" Gail asked, as they drove past the exit for Orangeburg.

"I believe that Julie is going to receive a lesson in humility today, Gail. That has been impressed upon me. Exactly how, I don't know. I pray that God will be merciful to her, and that He takes care of Kevin."

"You know, you never told me who you got to represent you. Some old friend in Atlanta owe you a favor or something?"

"Not exactly."

"What does that mean, 'not exactly'?"

"Well, Gail, I got down on my knees and asked God to take care of it. Next thing you know I have an attorney."

"Why is it I have less than no trouble believing that. Did you go over your case with him on the phone? I don't remember anyone coming to see you recently." Gail McCorkle made it her business to know where Peter Carson was, and who was with him, at all times.

"Not exactly."

"Enough already! Who is your lawyer?"

Peter opened the manila envelope that contained the restraining order Julie had given him (which was set to expire today), a copy of his divorce decree, two pencils, and a legal pad. A business card was also inside. He handed it to her.

"Good God Almighty!" Gail shouted. "You and the Lord don't play fair, you know that, Peter! I actually feel sorry for the woman."

They both laughed about it, agreeing that at times God could indeed be the ultimate comedian.

"What's the 'A.A.' stand for anyway?" Gail asked, doing her best to keep their car between the white lines as she enjoyed the humor.

"You know what, I asked Larry the same thing. He looked at me like, *I can't believe you don't know that,* and said 'Archangel.'"

They decided to pull over in a rest area for a few minutes so that Gail could take a short break, and they could finish their early lunch. No one watching Gail McCorkle and Peter Carson would ever have guessed that one was a warden, and the other a prisoner. They ate, talked, smiled, and hugged, both overjoyed simply to be in each other's company on a beautiful April morning in Carolina.

For the second half of the ride to Judge Grove's courtroom, Peter decided to sleep. They had left Parkersboro at five a.m. so they could make it to Atlanta by noon. He needed the extra rest.

In her exuberance, Gail dropped Peter's lawyer's business card. Before he pushed the seat back and settled in for a nap, Peter returned it to the envelope.

"Yes sir," Peter said, as he stretched out and yawned. "A.A. Gabriel, Esq. This could be amusing."

Eleven

Harmon Duke Grove, Jr. was born to be a judge, predestined to continue on in the family tradition. Since before the Confederacy, a Duke or a Grove had sat in judgment of his fellow man in one Georgia courtroom or another. The bench was Harry Grove's legacy, his virtual birthright.

The latest incarnation of the "Honorable Groves" played his role to near perfection. Harry was a rigid disciplinarian when it came to law and order, particularly concerning street crime, and especially if the defendant before him was black. H.D. Grove was known to throw not only the book at repeat offenders of color, but the whole library.

On the other hand, the average Caucasian defendant entering Judge Grove's domain was usually treated more mercifully. Especially if he was a local white guy with only a few priors, unequivocally if he was connected to one of the many "old money" Atlanta families.

Regarding civil matters, Harry tried to be fair, to administer justice evenhandedly. That is if both parties were white and had Southern roots. Let a black man or a Yankee seek equitable redress in his courtroom against "one of our own," well, that was a different matter altogether.

Justice, like beauty, is largely in the eyes of the beholder. To the men and women of the predominantly white, upscale, suburban Atlanta district where Harmon Grove presided, he did things just fine.

Judge Grove was intelligent and subtle enough to mask his prejudices, which largely mirrored those of the community he served, and to find excuses to obscure his true motivations. On the bench, he would even get preachy at times about the "new south." Privately, in chambers, the same Judge Grove regularly threw back a bourbon or three with his "good old boy" buddies and shared a laugh with them about those "stupid niggers" or bemoaned the fact that Atlanta was being overrun by "grease balls" from Mexico.

Despite appearances, like many people forced into their place in this world through circumstances beyond their control, Harmon Duke Grove, Jr. was not a happy man. Miserable was more like it.

The truth was he hated both the law generally, and being a judge particularly. Harry felt as incarcerated in his prison as the many that he'd sent to the penitentiary were in theirs. Of course, he told no one about his true feelings, he didn't dare. He most certainly shared nothing with his wife, the former Miss Sally Anderson Hill, a direct descendant of the famed C.S.A. General A.P. Hill. Miss Sally had long ago given up sex for scotch, and intimacy for barbiturates. Some time back, she and Harry agreed to loathe each other congenially. Neither desired the scandal of a divorce. The Grove's marriage was a hollow, cruel joke, much like the rest of their lives.

Those unfortunates like Harry who are stuck in one of life's ugly ruts invariably seek compensations, distractions from the mind-numbing dullness of their dictated existence. H.D. Grove was certainly no exception to this, in fact he was rather like the rule.

One of Harry's favorite amusements was to enjoy the company of various young women, little girls actually, who were provided to him on demand by a small and trusted network of extremely discrete, specialty pimps in the Atlanta area. H.D. preferred his girls to be petite, five-foot-four or shorter, and if they hadn't reached the ninth grade yet, that was even better. That his sexual partners were nothing more than enslaved children, owing their lives, and usually those of their families, to illegal immigrant gangsters did not trouble Judge Grove in the least. He got his, so what else mattered? They were only 'trivial little urchins' anyway, 'gooks, spooks, and spics' as he called them. No one gave a damn about what happened to them, so why should he?

A few years back, Harry also developed a taste for cocaine. Not that he had sworn off his beloved bourbon, P.R. Morgan Black Label being his favorite, it was just that things seemed to go so much better with coke. Another very small cadre of men supplied his drug habit. Harry never wanted for blow or for anything else that his sordid imagination desired, for that matter.

The Judge's partying habits were substantial, but they remained undetected by anyone outside his small and trusted inner circle. Harry would never allow himself to be seen intoxicated in public, and since he came from at least a degree of wealth, no one found it odd that Judge Grove had a full-time limo and a driver. His chauffer was "Little D," a three time loser in his mid thirties. Donovan Duncan brutally raped more than a few women before he came into Judge Grove's employ. Despite being a sexual predator of the worst kind, Little D's most recent transgressions were overlooked by the good Judge in exchange for his driver's absolute obedience and discretion. Harry kept a file cabinet full of evidence against Donovan in a safe place at the ready, just in case blackmail was required to ensure silence.

Although he knew full well that Judge Grove thought of him as nothing more than a pimple on the backside of humanity, Little D actually liked his boss, and considered him to be a kindred spirit. Once in a while Harry would let Little D have some fun with one of his girls.

In contrast to the depravity of his secret life, superficially Harmon Grove was a pillar of the local community. He regularly attended service club meetings, charity fund raisers, and supported worthy causes. Judge Grove even went to church at least twice a month, but he was so busy serving a different god, that none of the Gospel was able to penetrate into his diseased mind. Christ told the world all about Harry Grove in Matthew chapter seven, verse six, although calling Superior Court Judge Harmon Grove a swine is undoubtedly an insult to decent pigs everywhere.

While social status and sexual gratification were crucial to Harry, money was paramount. Not only did he live beyond his means, but not in such a way as to draw undue attention to himself, H.D. Grove also had serious long-term ambitions. He did not intend to sit on the bench for thirty plus years like his father did, and then retire to a life of golf, afternoon bridge, and the eventual fatal heart attack. Harry Grove's plans for the future centered on Southeast Asia, a part of the world he visited as often as the need for discretion and his schedule would allow. In Thailand, both the young girls and the coke were abundant; with the right connections and a few bucks, Harry could live like a perverted king down there for a very long time. This is why the Morgan family was important to him.

Judge Grove's father had a genuine, long-standing friendship with Walter Morgan's father, Lewis Morgan. This relationship created a bond of trust and cooperation between the two families. While P.R. Morgan's distillery had always been, and would forever remain, in Kentucky, the firm's corporate headquarters were in Atlanta. This meant that any serious litigation filed against the company would likely be adjudicated in Georgia, in a courtroom with a Grove on the bench.

Walter Morgan and Harry Grove were about the same age and grew up together in the 1960's and 70's in Atlanta. They had always despised each other. That they needed to set aside their mutual hatred and cooperate for business reasons was another matter entirely. Both men were smart enough not to let their personal animosity get in the way of their wallets.

Harry made it clear to Walter that he would be "honored" to continue on in the family tradition of protecting the best interests of P.R. Morgan Distillers, but not out of friendship or loyalty alone as his father had done. When he took over the judgeship from his dad, the new Judge Grove demanded cold, hard cash in exchange for his goodwill and protection.

Knowing Harry as well as he did, Walter was neither surprised nor insulted by this request. Given the state of litigation crazed America, even one large lawsuit be it for product liability, sexual harassment, or whatever could cost P.R. Morgan millions. In addition to himself, Harry brought along a U.S. District Judge in Atlanta who was also interested in being accommodating for a price. The total cost for both judges was four hundred thousand a year, of which Harry kept three hundred grand for himself.

Twice during the previous five years Judge Grove squashed serious litigation against P.R. Morgan and did it in such a way that his decision stood on appeal. Even Walter had to admit that, as much as he despised the greedy little dirt bag, Harmon Grove was damn good at his job.

Today all Harry had to do was deal with the routine matter of terminating the parental rights of a convict. The no-brainer of no-brainers. He hadn't even bothered to read the file, relying instead on Walter's assurance that the soon to be ex-father of Kevin Carson wouldn't be showing up in court, much less contesting the action.

As the time for the hearing drew near, Julie, Walter, and Kevin arrived first, along with their two attorneys. Harry couldn't help but notice Julie's dark red dress, which accentuated both her marvelous hips and breasts without being inappropriately revealing. Unlike the other men in the room who were also ogling her, Harry was the only one fantasizing about what Julie must have looked like as an eighth grader. With a casual nod, he acknowledged the two Morgan family lawyers, both overpaid hacks in his opinion.

As decorum dictated, Judge Grove was cordial to Walter, all the while thinking that a woman like Julie would have nothing to do with a dweeb like Wally if it wasn't for his bank account. But, he reasoned, that wasn't Walter's fault. All women were really like that; whores, one way or another.

The hearing was set to convene at one p.m. and, to be sure, the Judge's gavel would come down precisely at that time. Despite the fact that Peter Carson had not offered a written response to Julie's accusations and arguments, and no one could imagine how a South Carolina housed Federal prisoner could possibly make it to a Georgia courtroom to answer a civil suit, Judge Grove was still required to hold the hearing, go through the motions and note the respondent's absence.

With two minutes to spare, Peter, Gail, and Mr. A.A. Gabriel, Esq. arrived, walked in and took their seats. When they did, a barely audible groan could be heard, expressing both the surprise and the dismay of those present. The hearing now was something more than a brief formality.

"Mr. Carson, Mr. Peter Carson?" the Judge inquired.

"Yes, your Honor," Peter answered.

"And who might you be, sir? I don't believe you've practiced in my courtroom before today," Harry asked, trying to size up the impeccably dressed, thirty something white attorney with light brown, curly hair.

"My name is Gabriel, your Honor. You are correct, sir, we have not met, but I have noticed your works from afar, Judge Grove."

H.D. Grove immediately shifted from kick back to fully alert mode. Several internal alarm bells were ringing frantically, although he hadn't a clue as to why. At nothing more than the sound of Gabriel's voice, Harry began to sweat and squirm. His first inclination, a very strong one, was to call off the hearing, feigning illness if necessary. Judge Grove was about to do just that when he looked over at Walter who shot him a *who the hell knows but get on with it* look.

Harmon Grove was an arrogant man. While he hated being a judge, he took great pride in the fact that if he had to sit on this stupid bench, then he'd be damned if anyone would ever intimidate or otherwise get the best of him in his courtroom. Summoning what courage he had, he fought back his fears and pressed on; believing that he could handle anything this Gabriel fellow could throw at him.

This was the biggest mistake Harmon Duke Grove ever made, and in Harry's case, that was really saying something.

From the moment he arrived, Peter's eyes never left his son's. Kevin looked at his father and smiled, in sharp contrast to the morose expression he wore walking into court with Julie and Walter. They had told Kevin that his father didn't care about him anymore, and that's why they were severing him from his life. Kevin Carson now knew that was a lie, and that his mother had deliberately deceived him.

Quickly gathering himself, Harry was not only brilliant but also very fast on his feet, the Judge gave two forceful raps with his gavel and opened the proceedings.

"Before we get started I have a question," the Judge said. "It's my understanding, Mr. Carson, that you are incarcerated at Parkersboro under federal authority. Is that true, sir, or has the court been misled?"

Peter looked away from Kevin for a moment and rose to his feet. "That's true, sir. You are not misinformed."

"Might I inquire then as to how it is you managed to appear today, Mr. Carson?"

"I'll answer that." Gail McCorkle stood directly behind Peter's table. "I am the warden at Parkersboro, and I personally escorted Mr. Carson to this hearing. I have the requisite paperwork to prove that, if the court is interested."

"It is, ma'am. Please bring your documentation to the bench." Harry was using every spare second to try and get his head together. *Why am I so nervous?* he kept asking himself.

It only took a minute to see that Gail McCorkle was exactly who she said she was. Harry hadn't really doubted that, but still, a prison warden drives an inmate hundreds of miles on her own time to attend a family law hearing? What gives?

Had Harmon Grove been blessed with Saul Cohen's gift, he would have been able to see exactly what was going on. The most powerful of the many demons that tortured poor Harry was going berserk, trying to warn his faithful servant that the power of the Living God was about to be visited upon him. But Judge Grove had backed the wrong team for far too long, and now there was really nothing the servants of hell could do to help him.

"It appears all is in order, so let's proceed. Mr. Kemp, it's your motion I believe."

For the next hour Julie's co-counsel, Mr. Kemp and Mr. Palmer, laid out the case against Peter Carson. They did so with the help of a small time Atlanta private investigator, a no account lush named Oliver Conroy, who introduced all of the evidence against Peter under the guise of a "background investigation." Dredging up Peter's past was easy enough, and through Mr. Conroy they established that Peter Carson had indeed lied, cheated, and stolen from those closest to him, family and friends alike. Gabriel let all of this go, challenging none of the testimony, although he clearly could have kept a great deal of it out on nothing more than relevancy. But past criminal acts were not enough on their own to terminate Peter's parental rights. They just set the stage for the main show.

When Mr. Palmer dismissed Conroy and called her to the stand, Julie Morgan squeezed her son's shoulder and gave him a kiss on the cheek. She whispered to him, "It'll be alright, honey," just loud enough so everyone could hear. Kevin did not respond; his attention remained fully focused on his father, who mouthed "pray for her" as she approached the witness stand and sat down.

Julie was fighting off a large dose of anger and indignation. This was not supposed to happen. *Who was this Gail McCorkle bitch, anyway?* she wondered. Was Peter doing her, is that why she was helping him? Quickly she forced all these thoughts to the back of her mind. Like Harry Grove, Julie Morgan was both intelligent and agile, and they had prepared for this contingency. Business must be attended to; she would figure out who was responsible for this fiasco and punish them later.

With the appropriate amount of dramatic pauses, tears, and contrived humility, Mrs. Walter Morgan methodically went through her testimony. Peter had always been a distant father, she said. She wasn't at all sure if he even loved Kevin. Her ex-husband had "thrown away his family for the sake of greed" and inflicted wounds upon "Little Kev" that might never heal. There was enough truth in what Julie was saying that anyone neutral sitting in judgment would have taken her seriously. Add to this Julie's beauty and charm and she seemed to all the world to be a woman victimized by an evil ex-husband who wanted nothing more now than for her son to be free of him once and for all.

The final scene of Mrs. Morgan's well rehearsed play was to be the clincher. She explained how Peter claimed to have "found Jesus Christ" in prison, and that this religious conversion had renewed his desire to be a good parent. After a few months of more frequent contact between father and son, Julie said, she was "overjoyed" at the prospect of having Peter back in Kevin's life as his father, despite all the past problems. For effect she added, "I thought God was answering my prayers."

Carefully and slowly Julie then described for the court how she decided to go and visit Peter at Parkersboro on Christmas Eve last, to see for herself this "new man" and welcome him "back into the family." But rather than finding a father anxious to be a part of his son's life, what she found was the "same old jerk who had hurt us so much before."

Julie's story was that Peter demanded one million dollars in cash from her, or else he would "continue to harass me and play with Kevin's emotions until Kingdom come." A rather elaborate blackmail accusation then unfolded, with Peter threatening to embarrass Julie with claims of "drug use and sex parties." Peter vowed to "ruin my relationship with my husband by any means possible," Julie claimed, pretending to fight back the tears. She let her hands shake ever so slightly to demonstrate her frailty and anxiety.

After she returned from seeing Peter, Julie went on, she "broke down in front of Walter" and told him everything. They decided right then and there that "enough was enough" and swore to do whatever was necessary to remove the "cancer" of Peter Carson from their lives.

"Very impressive," Judge Grove whispered softly to himself. It was tough to get anything by Harry. He sized up the situation in short order and came to the rapid conclusion that not only was this woman lying through her teeth, but also that whatever crimes Peter Carson committed could probably also, one way or another, be laid at her door. Poor schmuck, he thought, but of course it didn't matter. He was here to earn his three hundred Gs, and right or wrong had nothing to do with it.

Mr. A.A. Gabriel said nothing during the entire plaintiff's presentation, made not one objection, asked no questions. He seemed to not even be paying attention. When Julie's direct examination concluded, everyone assumed Mr. Gabriel was going to continue to be a passive observer.

Just as Harry was about to dismiss the witness, Gabriel stood and said, "I have a few questions for Mrs. Morgan, your Honor." The knot in Harmon Grove's gut instantly tightened.

As Gabriel spoke, a bailiff opened the courtroom doors and wheeled in a large video monitor.

"Hold up there, Mr. Bell," Harry barked from the bench. "I didn't order you to bring that machine into my courtroom."

"Sir?" the puzzled bailiff responded.

"I said, what's that television set doing in my courtroom, Mr. Bell? I didn't ask you to bring it in."

The young bailiff was obviously confused. He unfolded a piece of paper as he approached the bench.

"Judge Grove, sir, yesterday you gave me this. Don't you remember? You told me to bring this TV in at two p.m. sharp. Look, you even signed the note yourself. You were very insistent, your Honor."

Harry examined the note. It was his handwriting, no doubt about it. He knew that Greg Bell, the pissant little nerd who was his deputy bailiff, would never have the guts to lie to him about anything.

Think, Harry, think, he urged himself. He felt out-of-control, which made him both jumpy and angry.

Rather than look like an idiot, Harry nodded as if he'd just remembered something and instructed Mr. Bell to wheel the video unit in and set it up in front of the currently unused jury box. He did so without further explanation, and with no knowledge as to who would be using the display or what would be shown.

"Thank you, your Honor," Gabriel said, as he stood and approached the witness chair. "My client and I appreciate your granting our request to use this picture transmission device."

"Picture transmission device?" Harry muttered under his breath. *Who talks like that? Where's this guy from anyway, Mars?*

The Honorable Judge Grove was desperately trying to get a handle on an increasingly unpredictable situation.

"Mr. Gabriel, remind me again why we need this video unit in here today? I'm still not totally clear on its purpose." Despite being so keyed up he wanted to leap out from behind his bench and choke this impudent new lawyer and his loser client, Harry dialed it down and kept his cool.

"Certainly, your Honor. If you recall, I phoned Mr. Bell and inquired of him about the rules concerning video playbacks. He told me there was no rule per se, they were permitted, but of course any evidence introduced was admitted at the court's discretion. I suppose it was sometime after that Mr. Bell informed you of our desire to introduce such evidence, with your permission, of course, your Honor."

Greg Bell looked over at Harry and rapidly moved his head up and down in agreement.

"Well, sir, then I have a question."

"Yes, your Honor."

"How do you intend to play your tapes or disks? I see only a television set over there, Mr. Gabriel. Where's the VCR or DVD player?"

The skittish Mr. Bell was noticeably anxious to answer this question too, but Gabriel quickly responded before that was necessary.

"As I told Mr. Bell, we have some new technology we'll be using today, your Honor. We can show our pictures without using one of your playback devices."

This comment drew a few chuckles from Mr. Kemp and Mr. Palmer, who thus far had let the video discussion go by unchallenged.

"Your Honor, if you please," Mr. Palmer said as he stood, adjusting his vest and tie. "This is a family law hearing. Videos, new technology, we have been told nothing of this. We obj..."

The moment the smug Mr. Palmer began his argument Gabriel closed his eyes, whispered something in Aramaic and passed his hand over his body from left to right. The move was so quick and subtle no one in the courtroom caught it. No one except Harry, that is. Everything Gabriel did was now the sole focus of his attention.

For some reason Mr. Palmer did not finish his statement to the court.

"Yes, Mr. Palmer, you object. What is it you object to, sir?" Harry desperately wanted Julie's lawyer to give him an out, to provide him with any reasonable excuse to put an end to the hearing or at least get rid of the video equipment.

"Nothing, your Honor, I have no objection. Plaintiff does not object to the introduction of accurate video evidence at this proceeding." Mr. Palmer had no idea why he was saying this, but he sure felt better once he said it and sat down.

Judge Grove glared over at the Plaintiff's table. What the hell was going on? Walter was clearly bored with all the courtroom chatter, the dimwitted sot. He kept checking his watch and fidgeting, obviously annoyed that the hearing was now well into its third hour. As for the crack legal team of Palmer and Kemp, they were sitting expressionless, as if someone had injected each of them with a heavy dose of Thorazine.

Harry recognized the box he was being forced into. The Morgan's lawyers had no objection to any "accurate" video evidence, and by some magic he had authorized its introduction into the hearing.

"Alright, Mr. Gabriel. It's your witness, but I warn you, sir. Keep this brief and relevant. This is a court, not a circus. I am a judge, not a ringmaster."

"Yes, your Honor, of course. I can assure you that everything done here today will be proper."

Julie patiently endured these exchanges from her vantage point in the witness chair, doing her best to seem detached and to remain confident. But like Harry, she knew that none of this was any good and never should have happened. She made a mental note to have Walter fire the two incompetents she had for attorneys.

"Mrs. Morgan," Gabriel said, "before I begin I want to give you the opportunity to change your testimony. Would you like the chance to tell the court what really happened last Christmas Eve?"

Julie felt Gabriel's eyes penetrating into her soul. She was used to men staring at her, but this was something else. What was it about this guy? Then it hit her. *He can prove I'm lying. Somehow, someway, oh God, he can prove I'm lying.*

Trying her best to demonstrate indifference, even Julie's considerable skills at deception were being pushed to the limit, she swallowed hard and answered, "I have no idea what you are talking about, sir. I told this court the truth about what happened."

"I'm so sorry, Mrs. Morgan. As the Lord once said to Saul of Tarsus, 'You must find it hard to kick against the goads.'"

As if on cue, the lights dimmed in the courtroom and the monitor turned itself on. On the screen were Julie and Peter sitting on the lawn at Parkersboro. The camera angle was so close, and the picture so sharp it seemed certain that whoever shot the video must have only been a few feet away. How Peter managed to film them together was beyond her, but based on the first thirty seconds of chit chat from the "tape," Julie knew it was the real deal. She had to put a stop to this. But how?

The first thing that occurred to her was her lawyers needed to do something, but when she looked over at her counsel table, Mr.'s Palmer and Kemp were mesmerized, totally captivated by what they were seeing. No help there.

Time for plan B. I'll faint, Julie thought. They can't ignore me if I fall out of this witness chair and tumble on to the floor.

It was then Julie Morgan realized that Peter had been telling her the truth. God had indeed touched him and was helping him exactly as he claimed. She knew this because inexplicably, Julie could now neither speak nor move, although she remained conscious and alert. Like everyone else in Judge Grove's courtroom, she was going to watch the "video," like it or not.

As the playback progressed, there she was, larger than life, first trying to bribe Peter and then threatening him. It was so vivid, so real, she thought, not like a videotape or a film, but rather something more. Julie swore that if her invisible restraints were removed, she could get up and walk right into the image being shown and sit down on the grass. When it was over the lights came back on and the monitor returned to black.

"Mrs. Morgan, I will ask you once more, would you like the chance to change your testimony?" Gabriel's tone was somber now, and his statement was made in the form of a warning, not a plea.

"Do not answer that question, Mrs. Morgan." Judge Grove, along with everyone else present, was now free from the shackles of the invisible force. "Mr. Gabriel, you will explain yourself, sir. Just exactly how did you come by this recording? Who made the film? This court wants answers and until it gets them, the machine stays off and the witness will answer no more questions."

"Harmon Grove, do you believe that God sees and knows all?" Gabriel asked. "That nothing one does escapes the attention of the Almighty?"

Harry was in no mood for any more surprises. He could have sworn that he had somehow been temporarily muted and immobilized during the five minute or so "video" of Mrs. Morgan and Mr. Carson, but how could that be? It was obviously some trick, some mental slight of hand. On an instinctual level Harry knew that what he had just witnessed was very real, but who shows a tape without a tape player? Now this clown wants to know if I believe in an omniscient God? Harry had seen and heard more than enough and he was only slightly more incensed than he was scared to death.

"This hearing is over. I will see counsel in my chambers immediately!" Judge Grove boomed, hoping to sound authoritative despite feeling inside like a bug headed straight for a windshield.

"No, Harmon Grove. This hearing is not over. It's just begun," Gabriel said matter-of-factly, as if he were the one running the proceedings, which of course he was.

"Well, you brazen son of a bitch! I'll be damned if you'll come into my courtroom and tell me what's what. I find you in contempt, sir. Bailiff, I want you to ..."

"Enough," Gabriel said, and as he did, the Judge fell silent. The courtroom wide paralysis returned. Only Gabriel, Peter, Gail, and Kevin were unaffected by it.

"Judge Grove, the time has come for you to be held accountable. How many men have come before you seeking justice only to be given unmerciful abuse? Who are you to judge another anyway, Harmon Duke Grove? Your sins are so numerous and vile, words cannot express the revulsion God has toward them."

When the lights dimmed this time and the picture returned, the subject matter had nothing at all to do with Peter's fitness to be a parent, or Julie's lying. It was the Judge's life that was now on display.

Harry was forced to watch helplessly as his carefully concealed double life was exposed. On the screen for all to see were images of him having sex with children and doing drugs. Dates and times of each event were noted on the bottom of the display. One by one, encounters rolled by which were both pornographic and disgusting. Later, Kevin said that he had neither seen nor heard any of this, a blessing for which Peter was very grateful.

Then, as the sexual images stopped, there was Walter and Harry, relaxed and sipping bourbon on the back porch of the Morgan estate, cutting the financial deal for Harry's protection of P.R. Morgan Distillers. This was followed immediately by clips from a victory party celebrating Judge Grove's dismissal of a wrongful death suit against the company less than a year before.

Then the lights came back on. Although now free to do so, everyone present was too shocked to say or do anything.

In the confusion, just before Judge Grove's "video" began playing, three men slipped into the courtroom unnoticed and took seats in the back. One was the United States Attorney for the State of Georgia, another was the FBI's Special Agent in Charge.

The day before each had received a package in the mail. In it was evidence, sworn statements from "Little D," and Harry's pimps and drug dealers, and still photos of some of the images Gabriel had shown in court, along with an invitation to be present at Peter's hearing. While neither of the men knew who A.A. Gabriel was, or why he had sent them this information, it didn't take them long to figure out that what they had been given was on the level.

After a minute or so of sitting in his chair red faced and dazed, the only command Harry's brain could come up with was "flee." *Forget where you are, forget you are a judge, stand up and run for your life.*

The last in a long line of the "Honorable Groves" took a deep breath and decided to follow this primitive flight instinct, albeit in as orderly a manner as was possible. He looked up and saw that everyone else was as stupefied as he was, no one knew what to do. This, he thought, might buy me some time to make a discrete exit.

But right then Harry caught sight of the Feds sitting in the back row, both of whom he recognized. As Harry watched, the FBI Special Agent in Charge spoke into his cell phone, whispered something to the prosecutor, stood and reached for his handcuffs.

My God, Harry realized. He's coming for me. I'm being arrested.

It was too late for arguments, too late for explanations, or legal maneuvers. No amount of money, social status, or family pedigree was going to save poor Harry Grove now and he knew it. There was only one way out.

Harry kept a pistol hidden in the top drawer of his bench desk, carefully concealed inside a hollowed-out legal text. While he did not ever envision having to use it as a means of escape from his own courtroom, when Harry opened the book he was very thankful that it was still there, a dull black six shooter loaded and at the ready.

As the Special Agent in Charge approached the bench, Harry was set to pull out his pistol and get the drop on him.

But before he could, five more of the FBI brethren entered the courtroom, weapons drawn.

With a fatalistic sense of calm, Harry immediately realized that he couldn't shoot all of them. His escape plan had been nullified, he was trapped.

The demons that had haunted Harry for so long, and had tempted him into living a godless life of depravity and conceit, were now ready to finish their work. The trauma of having his sins revealed caused Harry's mind to become like a dry sponge, and on to it the servants of hell splashed images of brutal prison rapes and beatings, isolation, humiliation, and despair; that even someone as lost as H.D. Grove could repent and be made clean again was a truth the demons buried under layers of shock and terror.

In one smooth motion, Georgia Superior Court Judge Grove pulled out his pistol, cocked it, placed the barrel in his mouth, and pulled the trigger. A few seconds later Harry awoke to his eternal reward amidst the dull grey ruins and the agony of the black mist.

Since just before the Judge's portion of the "tape" started "playing," Kevin had been sitting on his father's lap, arms wrapped around his neck in the hope that he might never have to let go. Julie, so close to the action in the witness chair that her dress was splattered with bits of Harry's blood and brain, now leaped out of her seat and into Peter and Kevin's embrace. Overwhelmed, all Julie was able to say was "I'm sorry, I'm so sorry."

"Julie Morgan," Gabriel said, as he bent down to wipe away the tears that were streaming down her cheeks, "Peter will tell you who I am. Woman, God has given you another chance and spared your life today. Do not be deceived, God is not mocked.

Obey His commandments and live, Julie Morgan. Repent and be a mother to your son."

Then for only a split second everything stopped, time stood still. It was just long enough for Gabriel to raise his hands upward and vanish into a sparkling shower of thousands of points of brilliant white light.

"Tell me you saw that too, Peter." Julie said, needing to be reassured that her senses were still functioning properly.

"Wow, Dad, that man just disappeared! How'd he do that?" Thankfully, Kevin seemed untraumatized by everything he had seen, no doubt by the grace of God alone.

"If you guys liked the show today, come on out to Parkersboro. We see this kind of thing all the time," Gail answered. She was standing right behind Peter, a position she assumed after the Feds rushed into the courtroom. Had Harry done anything else with his gun besides put it in his mouth, in the blink of an eye, Peter would have been tackled and covered by one very protective prison warden.

It took a couple of hours for the small army of FBI agents and Atlanta police to secure and process the crime scene that was Georgia Superior Court, Atlanta Division, Courtroom B. The former fiefdom of Judge Harmon Duke Grove was suddenly thrust into the national spotlight as the main stage of a bizarre sex and suicide scandal. All of the major news organizations sent someone to cover the story. One reporter, though, had a huge head start on the competition.

Alex Anderson was the third man who slipped into the courtroom before the lights dimmed. He'd received the same package as the Feds did in the mail the day before. However, Alex's knowledge and interest went far beyond today's events alone.

Several times during the past year, Alex Anderson, a world renowned freelance investigative journalist, had been approached by a man who identified himself only as Gabriel, who told him that he had been "selected by God to witness to the world that His messenger has arrived." Being a devout atheist and a skeptic of all things, especially claims of faith in an invisible God, Alex Anderson at first scoffed at the whole idea, dismissing it as the ravings of a lunatic, or perhaps even a practical joke. That is until Gabriel got his attention through more than one supernatural act, the last one of which was being transported to a Federal prison to witness, as he floated unseen thirty feet above the action, Peter Carson raise a man from the dead.

Gabriel's instructions to Alex were clear; he was to say nothing about his knowledge and the revelation to anyone until he was told to do so. This was less than no problem for Alex. He could wait. He was not at all looking forward to becoming an outcast among the men who had praised him so much for so long.

While he certainly needed no more convincing that Gabriel was real (and, therefore, so must be God), Alex was not grounded in the Word. In his case, the proof came before the faith, but unlike Peter, Alex was not motivated to learn more about His ways and laws, to become part of His Holy priesthood.

If there was ever a man saved by fear alone, it was Alex. He viewed himself not as a saint, but rather as "God's reporter," an intimate yet still objective observer of the most significant human event in the last two thousand years.

Through his extensive broadcast television news experience with the networks, and later as an independent writer and producer of award winning documentaries and investigative reports, Alex Anderson was known worldwide as the face and voice of truth and quality journalism. The words "credibility" and "integrity" were synonymous with him and his work. Alex's reputation was unblemished by even the hint of scandal.

Though deceived through his pride into denying the reality of the Living God, Alex nonetheless lived a life of exemplary character and devotion to his craft. Without him being aware of it, the Lord had strengthened and protected him so that someday he might fulfill His purpose.

That time had finally arrived.

"Mr. Carson, I'm Alex Anderson. Do you know who I am?" Alex waited to approach Peter until the buzz of activity in the courtroom died down and the authorities had finished their work.

It took him a second to respond, but of course Peter knew who Alex was. Anyone over thirty who owned a television set had seen Alex Anderson's face at least a thousand times.

"Yes sir. I know who you are," Peter replied.

"Do you know why I am here?"

To Peter, this seemed like a lame question, unworthy of someone of Alex Anderson's stature. He was exhausted and in no mood for foolishness.

"You're here, I suppose, to cover what happened today. Well, let me save you some effort. I have no comment and neither does my son, Mrs. Morgan, or Miss McCorkle."

"That's not why I'm here, Panos Kallistos."

It was the way Alex pronounced it, slowly and expressively. Panos Kallistos. The name rolled off his tongue as if he'd been saying it everyday for years. Peter's spirit received the message, he knew what was happening.

"Lord have mercy," Peter sighed. "It must be time, isn't it Mr. Anderson?"

"Yes it is, Peter, and please, call me Alex. The Lord says you must now begin speaking to the world."

Twelve

For Peter Carson, the two weeks following the spectacle of Judge Grove's flamboyant suicide were busy ones. His life was taking another dramatic turn, and Peter was doing his best to keep up, to walk the path the Lord had set for him.

Through the miracle of paperwork, and by manipulating the Byzantine Bureau of Prisons bureaucracy, Gail McCorkle managed to create the illusion that Federal prisoner number BP-7617R4, Mr. Peter Carson, had been temporarily reassigned to an Atlanta area facility for "administrative purposes." This was a deliberate deception, but one made in accordance with His will. Gail knew that the procedural shuffle created by this fictitious relocation would take fourteen to twenty days to unravel. By then, Peter needed to be back at Parkersboro anyway.

Alex Anderson's estate sits on forty bucolic acres to the west of Atlanta. Nestled in the green rolling hills of Georgia, Alex's "gentleman's farm," as he calls it, was the ideal setting for Alex and Peter to discuss both the future and the past.

Julie and Kevin had driven with Alex, Peter, and Gail straight from the courthouse to the estate. With help from the Spirit, they were able to do so surreptitiously, and once on Alex's grounds, they were safely tucked away from the world's prying eyes, at least for awhile.

The lurid story of the double life of Harmon Duke Grove had some staying power, especially since several of the more fantastic aspects of the affair could not be credibly confirmed, nor were they being denied, by any of the witnesses.

Mr.'s Palmer and Kemp, transformed overnight from bush league lawyers to minor media celebrities, swore on national television that they were "paralyzed and muted" by an "invisible force" in Judge Grove's courtroom. Also, they would not back off their assertion that Peter Carson's lawyer, a mysterious Mr. A.A. Gabriel, had shown a "tape" of Judge Grove's indiscretions without the use of a VHS, DVD, or any other electronic playback device.

Adding fuel to the speculative fire was the U.S. Attorney in Atlanta who, despite refusing to publicly say anything about what he personally experienced, off the record confirmed his office had in its possession "prints of images" of Judge Grove engaging in illicit sex. Also, he would not deny Kemp and Palmer's contention that everyone in the courtroom was somehow mysteriously "frozen."

Perhaps the biggest mystery was the existence, or rather the lack thereof, of Mr. A.A. Gabriel, Esq. Astoundingly, in the middle of a sealed and guarded crime scene, the man had simply disappeared. No record of an "A.A. Gabriel" could be found with the Georgia Bar, or any other State Bar Association, or the American Bar Association.

The press was in a fever-pitch to interview Peter Carson and Julie Morgan. Warden McCorkle's paper shuffle, and God's grace, kept them away from Peter. Julie simply left word with her mother that she and Kevin were alive and well, but did not want to be found. Their unavailability only added to the intrigue.

There was no way Alex Anderson's presence in the courtroom could be disguised or denied, nor did he want it to be. Alex issued a brief statement to his professional colleagues saying that "after further research and review" he would be "reporting on the tragic events witnessed."

In the days following their arrival at the estate, Alex helped Julie find a quality family law attorney, who both formally ended her pursuit of the parental rights case against Peter, and filed the necessary paperwork for her to begin the process of divorcing Walter Morgan.

A week after the "Tragedy in Courtroom B," as the press had now labeled the episode, Walter Morgan received notice through his attorneys that he was facing an indictment on Federal corruption charges. Shortly thereafter, Julie's plea for divorce was served on him. In response, Walter retreated into alcohol and isolation. He made no attempt to either find or to communicate with his wife and stepson.

No doubt the happiest and most content person on the Anderson compound was Kevin Carson. He refused to let his father out of his sight without protest, fearing that if he did, someone might take him away from him again. Kevin was much more interested in spending time with his dad than he was in explanations of what happened, or what might happen next. Taking his cue from his father, Kevin was making progress in forgiving his mother for lying to him, although that wound would take a very long time to fully heal.

Peter did his best to comfort and encourage his ex-wife, who alternated between states of shame and recalcitrance. One minute the damage she had caused by her selfish pride and greed would weigh on her soul and awakening conscience, the next her "old woman" would try and rationalize what happened, to minimize her sin, or make excuses for it. With a gentle hand, Peter guided her through the process, which to one degree or another is common to all. He taught Julie how to pray, and they petitioned the Lord as one for the well being of their son.

What was no longer a factor for Julie was any doubt that God had a plan for their lives. She was beginning the process of learning how to follow His lead.

Perhaps the most difficult part of her spiritual awakening was for Julie to come to grips with the fact that she and Peter would never be together again as husband and wife. When Gabriel touched Julie in Judge Grove's courtroom and wiped away her tears, the hard shell that had covered her heart vanished. Her true feelings, the most profound being a deep and everlasting love for Peter, could no longer be masked by evil.

Julie knew now what a selfish fool she had been to abuse Peter, to inflame his weaknesses, and then to abandon him. But what was done was done, and though one can be cleansed, one cannot change the past. Hours of discussion with Peter about how repentance and forgiveness restores the soul helped her to grasp the concepts, but deep wounds do not heal quickly. Nor, as Peter explained, should they.

Alex was anxious to share with Peter what he knew, to compare notes, and to strategize; but he pursued this agenda slowly, understanding that the family he was hosting needed some time to put itself back together before they could move on.

By the morning of their seventh day together, it seemed right to everyone that they should begin to discuss the future. Gail had returned from Parkersboro the night before, bringing with her the prayers and best wishes of Saul, Malik, Kenny, and Larry.

"You guys wouldn't believe it. I mean really, if you thought Parkersboro was a zoo before, brothers you ain't seen nothin' yet," Gail said, in between delicious bites of eggs benedict and lox and cream cheese prepared by Alex's full-time gourmet chef.

The press was probing Parkersboro, and while none of the disciples were talking, plenty of the other inmates were. Reports of a paralyzed man walking away from a wheelchair and a dead man rising only served to pique the interest of the media throng. Gail could only do so much to keep them in check. She restricted access to the inmates, but she could not turn off the phones or stop the mail.

"That's not a problem, Gail," Alex Anderson explained. "Let the rumor mill generate what it will for now. It will only serve to increase interest in what we have to say when we choose to say it."

"Alex, we're all curious," Peter asked, as he devoured his marvelous breakfast as quickly as good manners would allow. "What exactly is it that you have in mind?"

Alex Anderson had thought of little else other than this subject for the past few weeks. How does one go about announcing a revelation from God? He considered many possible scenarios before arriving at the one plan that sat well with him, and therefore, by extension, with the Lord.

"Panos, for some reason Christ chose me for this job. Why He did I'll never know, not while I'm still breathing anyway. I was the most committed secular humanist and atheist around. Who was it that repeatedly trashed men of faith? Me, it was me. Christians, Jews, Muslims, it didn't matter, I went after them all. I would look for flaws and weaknesses in spiritual people and then I'd pounce.

"Did I spend even a minute trying to balance my reporting, like pointing out the millions of young men the Roman Catholic Church has spiritually and physically saved over the centuries for every one that was abused by some demon-possessed, pedophile priest? No, I didn't, but it would be a lie to say that it never occurred to me to do so. It did.

"As you know better than I, Peter, you can tell the truth and still be a liar. I did my best always not to fabricate or even to stretch the facts in my reporting. I took great pride in that, as if somehow my limited virtue set me apart, made me better than everyone else."

"The sad reality of it is I wasn't interested in seeking the real truth, the nature of God. Stories of faith, miraculous healings, lives lived for others, selfless acts of courage attributed to an invisible God's grace, those were stories I could have cared less about. Not sexy enough. I let someone else cover those, but I sure was willing and able to tell the world all about the pastor who stole from his flock, or the priest who raped the nun, or the imam who fronted for Al-Qaeda.

"Denying the existence of the Living God and His son Jesus Christ is the biggest and worst lie a human being can ever tell. I know that now, I should have known it then. God has chosen you, Peter, to bring this message to the world and the hope that comes with it. I will see that you succeed in this mission, or I will die trying."

"It's that 'die trying' part that I'm worried about," Julie said. "My son just got his father back, and I'd like Peter to be around to see Kevin grow up."

"I agree," added Gail. "If the sorts that are showing up at Parkersboro are any indication of who we're going to be dealing with, it's obvious that most of them would like nothing more than to see Peter discredited, or worse."

Everyone was looking to Alex for some reassurance, for him to put a positive spin on the dangers of the trials to come.

"What can I tell you that I haven't already said? If it was the 'old me' on this story, I'd be doing my best to expose everyone involved as a fraud or a crook. That's the tale most of the media wants to tell."

"They are all frauds and crooks," Gail said, drawing a smile from Alex. "Or rather, they used to be."

"My friends," Peter had remained silent until now, allowing everyone the opportunity to express their thoughts and emotions before he brought them back on course. "Let none of us forget why we are here. We can talk about the dangers and the problems, I think that's healthy and helpful, but God is with us. Like Paul, we are stewards of the mysteries of God and it is required of stewards to be faithful. We shouldn't worry about what might happen to us, we should do what must be done and trust God."

"I know that's right," Gail agreed, "but still, my brother, I'm not interested in any one of us, including and especially you, Peter, standing in harm's way if it can be avoided."

"Is that what you have in mind, Alex? Having us tease the bull, so to speak?" Peter asked.

"You might think so once we've done it," Alex replied. "There is a very short list of journalists who have the power and the access to secure an hour of prime network television time based solely on their reputation and on the promise of delivering something spectacular. I'm one of them."

"Go on," Peter said.

"What I have in mind is a partially taped, partially live event. Peter, you are the Executive Producer. You determine the content; I'll help to fit your ideas into a broadcast format."

Everyone's wheels started turning. They all knew that in order to reach the masses, the media had to be employed, but creating their own television program? Other than Alex, no one had considered that possibility.

After a few minutes of quiet contemplation, ideas were shared. Gail worried about how she was going to get BOP approval for a live broadcast from Parkersboro. Julie argued that coming out so boldly was like "putting a target on Peter's back." Alex asked Gail to sketch out a rough diagram of the camp for him, so that he could better visualize the filming location.

With the others busy talking amongst themselves, Peter slipped away and walked outside onto Alex's spectacular patio. It was overwhelming, befitting the estate. Half of the patio's two thousand square feet were enclosed, the other open, and all of it looked out upon the verdant Georgia countryside, the stables and the farm.

Peter thought the terrace was more like a dream than a real place, a representation of an artist's ideal setting, somehow willed into being. He relished the peace he was granted here, the contentment he felt simply by being with Julie and Kevin. As fleeting as it was, or perhaps because it was so impermanent, Peter's soul was at ease. For the first time in what seemed like forever, he felt normal.

For Peter Carson, "normal" was a temptation. He knew this and he felt the pull of a possible life with Julie and his son trying to divert him from the path God had set for him.

As humbly as he could, Peter asked God if He would allow him ever to live such a simple life. To worry only about how

Kevin was doing at school, to hold down a regular job, to have a mortgage, a sedan, and a dog.

The answer came clearly and instantly. No.

Peter knew that what he was asking for was not evil for other men, but it was for him. God must come first, he told himself, and in my case, there can be nothing second. He was reminded that God had saved him from eternal destruction, and whatever He asked was nothing more than reasonable service.

As he knelt on Alex's patio in prayer, what Peter was given was not permission from God to retreat into a worldly life, but rather the inspiration and instructions required to implement Alex's plan. After a few minutes of blessed solitude, Peter went back inside and rejoined the others.

"Well, what did the Boss have to say?" Gail asked. They all knew what Peter was doing out on the veranda.

"Alex, you want to tell our story, don't you? Have us bear our testimony to the world?"

"Yes, Peter, I do. That seems right to me. Do you agree?"

"For sure, but there is more, isn't there. You want more."

"The audience loves a show. To attract the maximum amount of attention, it would help if we could do something, uh, how can I say this? Biblical?"

"Would you like to fly over to Egypt and have Peter part the Red Sea?" Julie said sarcastically.

"Can we do that?" Alex asked, more than half seriously.

"No, well not no, but that's not what the Lord has in mind."

Peter spent the next hour going over his ideas, or rather God's ideas, as expressed through him. Alex took notes and silently concentrated, envisioning how best to implement the concepts. Despite her objections, Gail mostly nodded. She knew by now that once God had given His instructions, it was wiser to listen than to argue. Julie had not yet reached this level of spiritual maturity.

"I know I'm new to all of this and don't think I don't believe. I do," Julie testified. "But Peter, what you're talking about is insane. Plain crazy. Do you realize what will happen? Do you even give a damn about Kevin and me? I know you're not my husband anymore, you can't be because of God, whatever. I have to live with that. But you say you love me and I know you love Kevin. What am I supposed to tell him after they kill you?"

"Whether they kill me or not, Jules, is not a consideration. I must obey."

"Peter, I can sure understand what Julie is saying. How can we protect you if you do this? Every nut from the tree will fall off and come running after you, not to mention the men who rule this planet. Remember them? They have all the money and the guns."

"What do you want me to do, Gail?" Peter argued. "Disobey? Tell the Master no? I am His servant, He is not mine."

"Ask Him again. Tell Him it's too hard. Tell God you have a family," Julie pleaded.

"Neither you nor I can bargain with God, Jules. Please, learn this lesson. He knows what is best for us. You must open your heart to Him, Julie. It's tough, but you've got to stop thinking about yourself. Let God take care of you, He's far better at it than you could ever be."

In response all Julie could do was cry. Between sobs she said, "Excuse me," and left to find Kevin, who had been sent to the stables for the morning so the adults could be alone.

"Give her some time, Peter," Gail suggested. "She is still trying to sort all of this out. You know, Peter, despite her many sins, that woman never stopped loving you. Now that the Lord has touched her heart, all she wants to do is be with you. None of this is easy for her, she's been through hell."

"I know, Gail, I know. Seeing Julie like this, vulnerable and open and even a bit humble, how do you think I feel? More than a small part of me wants to run after her, tell her I'll be her husband again, and find the nearest bedroom where we could spend the next three days naked and alone.

"I've asked, Gail. It is His will that must be done, not ours. Don't think I'm not hurting too."

"Not to change the subject, but..." Alex interjected.

"No, please Alex. Change the subject," Peter begged.

"Are you sure about this? I mean the first part of the strategy, telling your story, how the men all came to be in one place, God's revelations, I was expecting that. But Peter, I'm sorry if I sound skeptical, but..."

"How did you put it, Alex? You wanted something 'Biblical'? Isn't that what you said?" Peter asked.

"Yes, that's what I said, but I guess I wasn't expecting you to take my suggestion so literally."

"Why not?" Peter replied. "When it comes to God, the closer you get to Him, the more careful you have to be. If what you want is what He wills, you're likely to get much more than you asked for."

Thirteen

"I thought this would be easier the second time around. I was wrong. It's much harder."

Fifteen days after the adventure in Judge Grove's courtroom, Peter and Gail were driving back to Parkersboro. They were almost "home."

"Shall I pull over and let you out, dear?" Gail teased.

"Very funny. You know what I mean. The last couple of weeks have been awesome. Even Julie was coming around by the end. Did you notice that too, Gail?"

"I did. A couple of mornings ago I got up early and had my coffee out on the terrace. Wasn't much past six thirty. I heard some mumbling and looked over at the fountain and there was Julie, still in her nightgown and robe, on her knees praying. She saw me and then I joined her."

"My Jules praying. Trying to be obedient and righteous. That's a miracle, Gail…"

"But?"

"But it's so unfair. When we both finally get it right, we aren't allowed to be together. I've really been fighting my flesh, Gail. You have no idea."

"Desiring a little horizontal recreation are we, Mr. Carson?"

"Like you wouldn't believe, but that is only part of it."

"I know, well I think I understand at least. I've never had a husband, much less an ex."

"Consider yourself blessed. I hope the water is still cold in the dorm. Boy, do I need a long run and a brisk shower."

Neither Gail McCorkle nor Peter Carson had much time now for any personal distractions. They had been put on a tight schedule. For Peter especially, this was a blessing. Preaching the Word and living it were two different things, Peter knew that, but the level and intensity of his passions had both humbled and frightened him.

Panos Kallistos discovered that he still loved his ex-wife, and not in a purely agape manner. He had thought that all of those feelings, those deep yearnings that in so many ways had led him into sin were dead and gone, buried along with his "old man." Peter's emotional revelation was anything but trivial. God's plan for his life, for the first time since his awakening in the prison library, now had some competition.

Kevin didn't make it any easier. Like any child of divorced parents, it was his heart's desire to see his father and mother reunited. Peter did his best to explain why this wasn't possible, at the same time reassuring Kev that never again would his parents fight or be bitter and ugly toward each other.

It was during one of these father and son sessions that Peter's flesh reared up and asked, *Why? Why must you say no to your son? After all he's been through, doesn't he deserve better?* This opened the door for a demon to suggest to him that the God Peter served was a cruel one for not allowing him to have a family. For longer than he would ever admit to anyone, Peter actually considered these thoughts, weighed his alternatives.

Julie, whose heart had been opened, but who was still so new to Christ that her spiritual weapons had not yet developed, was determined to change Peter's mind. She believed that the right thing for him to do was to be with her and Kevin. Why he couldn't do that and also serve the Lord she didn't understand, or more accurately, she was not willing to understand.

It was the little things she did that made Peter's pulse race, and Julie knew it. Walking into his bedroom naked with a bottle of wine at midnight was probably not the right approach, she correctly reasoned, but brushing up against him coyly when Peter wasn't expecting it, touching his hand while they talked, spending as much time together with Peter and Kevin as possible, these were among her most effective tactics. For two weeks at Alex's estate, she pursued this strategy, relentlessly.

More than once Peter had almost talked himself into the idea that sleeping with Julie was the right thing to do. "We've earned it," he told himself. "She's my wife in spirit," he rationalized. "We need the release. It will help us both to heal," he lied.

But Peter Carson was not new to Christ. He was keenly aware of the dangers of going off course. Every time his resistance to Julie weakened to virtually nothing, his response was to get on his knees and ask for help. When he did so, always he was strengthened, but the war against his flesh was ongoing and would not be won with a single victory.

Peter was considering all of this as Gail's sedan pulled up to the camp.

As promised, Alex Anderson was there waiting for them. So was his film crew and van load of equipment that Gail had "approved" to be on BOP property, although more than her approval alone was required. When it comes to dealing with the Federal bureaucracy, Gail knew that it was often easier to ask for forgiveness than permission.

Being one of the most recognizable men in America, Alex had drawn considerable attention to himself already in the hour or so he'd been at Parkersboro. Malik had been briefed by Peter on the phone and was providing as much security as was necessary. The only real threat to Alex at the moment was being pestered to death by curious inmates.

"Told you I'd beat you two here," Alex boasted, as he greeted Peter and Gail in the prison lobby.

"Any problems?" Gail asked.

"None. Malik and your staff have been very accommodating. We've already shot about half an hour of B roll. I know where things are, what to do, and when to do it. How are you two?"

"We were just talking about how nice it was to be 'home,'" Peter answered snidely. "To tell you the truth, Alex, I prefer the estate."

"Pay him no mind, Mr. Anderson," Gail said. "He gets snippy when he's frustrated. You wouldn't believe the nonsense we have to put up with from him around here at times."

Before Peter could offer an equally pithy comment in return, his spirit was quickened by the sight of his men. Malik, Saul, Kenny, and Larry had missed their friend and leader terribly, and worried for his safety every minute that he was away. Handshakes and hugs were exchanged all around.

"We've got a surprise for you, Peter," Larry said, obviously pleased with himself.

"And I didn't bring you guys back a thing," Peter joked.

Standing off in the corner were two men Peter had never seen before. Neither were dressed in prison khakis and tees, both wore street clothes. As Peter glanced over, they each waved demurely to him.

"Thought we might get the last two in about now, Larry. What, they just got here, is that why they're not dressed out?" Peter was feeling happier and more confident with each passing second. Being together with his men settled him and reminded him of his love for God, and the importance of his calling.

"No sir. They are not Federal prisoners. These men, well, let them tell you themselves. They've come a long way, Peter, and like all of us, they knew who you were, and who we were, by revelation long before they arrived," Larry explained.

"I thought for sure ..." Peter didn't finish his sentence.

"You thought what for sure, Panos?" Larry asked.

"I guess I had it in my head that we would all be prisoners. Let that be a lesson for us, Larry. Never presume. Never get ahead of God."

"We are all prisoners, Panos," Larry answered. "As long as we walk this world, we're all prisoners. Besides, if you think they are a couple of innocents, then that will be twice today that you will have been surprised."

All Peter could do was smile and say, "Thank you Lord." He was truly "home." Home is where your brothers are, he told himself. While it was not the life he would have pursued, recognizing it as the one God had chosen for him and freely submitting to His will returned Peter's joy and peace to him; the kind of joy and peace that no earthly intimacy could bring.

It was a beautiful afternoon. Wonderfully temperate, both the chill of winter and the swelter of the Carolina summer were absent. The leaves had returned to the deciduous trees that surrounded the camp, green was everywhere. The air was fresh and pure. The songbirds were plentiful and making themselves known.

The perfect day and, strange as it would seem to anyone but them, the ideal setting for the completion of the circle, the fulfillment of a promise. Those present all knew what it meant for the seven all to be together in one place and of one accord.

They met on the outdoor library porch, which by now had become their temple, their holy ground. The other inmates, both God fearing and not, moved away on command, allowing them a measure of privacy.

But it was anything but a private setting, since Alex and his crew were filming everything, and had placed microphones on the porch to capture the audio. Peter instructed his men to ignore the cameras and the equipment as best they could. Before they got started they rose to their feet, held hands, and prayed.

Peter was then introduced to Jose Enrique Vargas and Timothy Austin. They were the two new "arrivals," if that label could be accurately applied to free men at Parkersboro. Jose and Tim were renting a by-the-week apartment in Georgetown, and had been driving into the camp in the morning and out at night for the past few days. Now that Gail was back, their plan was to grab a bunk and spend all of their time at Parkersboro.

As Jose started to share his testimony, Peter realized that Larry was indeed right, he was very surprised.

Until two weeks ago Jose Vargas had been General Jose Vargas, the number three officer in the command structure of the United States Marine Corps. Alex had recognized him on the spot, but remained silent, keeping to his self-appointed role of being more of an observer than a participant.

"Where should I begin, Panos?" Jose asked.

"Let the Spirit lead, share with us your heart and your history, brother," Peter answered.

Jose laughed at himself.

"Gentlemen. I am accustomed to formalities. Chain of command, duties, rigid authority. It is not at all familiar for me to simply begin anything spontaneously. Forgive me."

Jose Vargas spoke in a solid, even locution. His appearance, he was five-foot-ten-inches of muscles, capped off with a flat top, completing his aura of authority. He was a man who both gave and commanded respect, who believed in discipline, a patriot who loved America, drank beer, smoked cigars, idolized John Wayne, and most certainly obeyed the law.

In sum, the exact opposite of most of the men who now surrounded him.

Yet as he began to speak, it quickly became apparent that the Lord had touched Jose, and from an early age. Despite all of their differences, the common bond of the calling of God united Jose with his brothers, bridging all worldly gaps. None of the disciples doubted Vargas' sincerity or legitimacy, but all were very curious to learn how and why the Lord had called such a man to be one of them. Until now, Jose had related only bits and pieces of his testimony, waiting for Peter to arrive to tell all.

"I was born in Bakersfield, California," Jose began, "the son of illegal immigrants. Both of my parents were migrant farm workers and day laborers, who slowly killed themselves for starvation pay. My folks lived for me and my brother Ramon. Every spare penny they had went to improving their children's lives.

"Unlike almost everyone else I knew in the barrio, my brother and I did not work in the fields or at a sweat shop. We went to school. Because she had to work, my mother could not be home with us when class ended in the afternoon. My brother and I tended to ourselves from first grade on, and kept our noses clean when we were little. As small children, neither of us would risk disappointing our mother or invoking the wrath of our father. I don't think many families are like that anymore. Built on pure respect, I mean."

"I grew up in the same house in Brooklyn, respect-wise at least," Saul offered. "How old are you Jose, fifty-five or so?"

"Fifty-seven, sir."

"Well, I understand what you're saying. Your father was king and your mom was queen. You were at best the regent, and you were expected to return the love and the respect given to you through obedience."

"Have you done a stretch in the military, Mr. Cohen? Sounds like we have much in common." Jose had no way of knowing how absurd his question was.

When he, and everyone else, stopped laughing, Saul answered.

"No, my friend, no. I am about as far away from being a military man as one could possibly be. I'm afraid that all of my parent's best efforts to instill discipline in me largely went for naught."

"Just like Ramon," Jose said softly. "Just like Ramon." There was sadness in his voice whenever Jose spoke of his beloved older brother.

"Where is Ramon now, Jose? Does he know you're here? Is he a God fearing man?" Larry asked.

"Ramon is scattered across a rice patty in Vietnam, Mr. Coleman. He couldn't stay off heroin long enough to keep his wits about him during combat. He was probably hallucinating when he walked out into the open for no apparent reason. The VC cut him to shreds."

"Lord have mercy," Peter prayed. "That must have been a tough time for you and your family. Were you also in the military when Ramon was killed?"

"Yes sir, I was."

"Horrible, simply horrible," Kenny empathized. "How did it make you feel?"

"Not so good, sir, not so good. I was standing fifty yards away from Ramon when he bought it."

General Vargas was the only one of the seven with any military background. Try as they might to be understanding, only Malik could directly relate to Jose's experience.

"Seen men die too, General, sir," Malik said. "Tears your insides out. Especially when it be your own family or when you're the one doin' the killin'."

Malik Graham had become such a mellow soul, full of love and compassion for all of God's creation, that his brothers had almost forgotten that he once was, not so long ago, a violent predator with little respect for any life other than his own.

"I agree, Mr. Graham, violent death is never pretty. In fact, in God's eyes, there isn't anything much uglier. There is no excuse, no justification for it, other than self-defense."

As Jose spoke, the disciples all marveled at how a career military officer could say such a thing, much less believe it.

"Jose," Peter asked. "I thought brothers weren't supposed to serve in the same units in wartime, to prevent what you went through."

"True enough, sir. We were in different units. He was Army, I was a Marine. By pure coincidence we ended up in that nasty little valley at the same time."

"There are no coincidences, General Vargas," Peter said.

"I know that now, Panos. Didn't at the time, didn't at the time." The General seemed to drift back to 1969 for a moment, as if just talking about Ramon forced him to relive his brother's death, to endure images stored in his mind better left dormant.

"About a week before he died, I received a letter from Ramon. When I first arrived in country we would write each other every two weeks or so, but his letters came less frequently over time. Found out later that's when he started using heavily."

"I was aware from his letter that his unit might be in the same general area as mine. It was my plan to find him that very evening and to finagle a ride to wherever he was bivouacked and surprise him."

"So he had no idea you were there?" Kenny asked.

"None. Couldn't have. My platoon was supposed to be at least five clicks west. God put me there for a reason, but at the time, well, let's just say I didn't understand."

"I recognized Ramon's voice when he started yelling. Never have been quite sure what he was saying. His buddies claim he was singing some Stones song. I'll never know. What I do know is that it got him killed."

"Like you, Saul, Ramon was a rebel. By the time he turned eighteen, Ramon was no longer the obedient child. In fact, he was damn near uncontrollable. Back in the sixties, LSD and heroin were easy to find in Bakersfield, and Ramon had no problem getting the money he needed to buy drugs through stealing.

"The police caught him several times, but it became serious for him in '68. Ramon was looking at doing some hard time."

"Unless he enlisted," Saul surmised.

"Yes, you got it. It was Vietnam or jail for Ramon. That was the choice he was given, that he forced himself into really. His draft number was so high, he might never have been called otherwise.

"As for myself, I wanted nothing more than to enlist. In my room at home, I had a calendar, on it I marked the days left until I turned eighteen. I knew on that day I'd be in the Marine recruiter's office signing my enlistment papers.

"Ramon thought our country was a hypocritical society whose basic purpose was to take advantage of the weak, like blacks and Chicanos, so that the rich could get richer. As with many other men I've met during my lifetime, gentlemen, Ramon used America's flaws as an excuse to act like a fool, to ruin his life, and to discredit himself and his family."

This was a reality many of the disciples had lived and no one argued with Jose's premise or his conclusion.

"As for me, I loved America and the Corps. Everything about the military life fit my personality; the training, the discipline, the teamwork. While I'm not a violent man by nature, I learned to fight and kill and to do both highly effectively on command. My specialty was sniping. In my prime I could knock a hair off a fly's butt at a thousand yards with the proper scope and rifle."

"After Ramon was killed, I kind of fell apart for awhile. I was already headed downhill. Seeing Ramon get shredded stripped away my last layer of humanity. The Corps offered me a discharge, even encouraged it, saying my parents deserved to have one son make it out of 'Nam alive. They were right, of course they were right. But I wasn't right.

"Only nineteen at the time, I figured the best way to deal with my problems was to kill as many Vietnamese as possible, as if by doing so I could somehow get justice or payback for Ramon, or find happiness for myself. I refused the discharge. Instead, I became a predator, a murder machine without any conscience, a true servant of hell. After a while, my feelings about Ramon were irrelevant. I came to enjoy hunting and killing human beings, gentlemen. I got off on war."

"Know all about all those feelin's too, Mr. Jose," Malik related. "Been so mad and lost at times the only thin' seemed to make any sense at all was hurtin' somebody else. I thank the Lord everyday that He delivered me from that evil."

Jose nodded, glad that at least one of his brothers had shared some of his same struggles. Then he continued.

"For the next nine months I unleashed hell on any Vietnamese that crossed my path, VC or friendly. Earned a couple of commendations, damn near got nominated for the CMH. I was wounded twice, once seriously."

Jose Vargas lifted his shirt. His left side, from armpit to waist, was one giant scar.

"Took a glancing blow from an anti-personnel mine there, gentlemen. Ripped me all to hell, but didn't clip any vital organs. I should be dead, but now I know the Lord had other plans for my life."

"It was after those first few months following Ramon's death, February 1970 as I recall, that I first met him. I was on leave in Saigon, drinking heavily and whoring, trying my best to numb the pain. Me and a couple of buddies had just shared a Vietnamese girl, she couldn't have been much older than fourteen, and then we beat the hell out of her for her trouble. In fact, we were laughing about it in the bar when he approached me."

General Vargas paused for a moment, while he remained calm and in control, his trembling hands revealed his inner turmoil.

"My Lord," Jose prayed, eyes now moist. "I know you have forgiven me, Lord, but bless those who I have made to suffer. Show them mercy Father, grant them peace."

Although they could not have known it at the time, Jose was sharing events and emotions with his brothers he had never fully revealed to another living soul. It was obvious that Jose deeply regretted many of the things he had done in his life, which was a condition common to all present.

"I'm almost positive I know who you met, Jose," Peter said, reassuringly touching Vargas's shoulder, trying to offer some comfort. "But we are always amazed by the variety of roles he assumes."

Vargas gathered himself, straightened his posture, and sat at attention. His main defense against evil was self-discipline. He knew that he must focus and ignore his pain and fear if he was going to be able to finish bearing his testimony.

"Back in '70 I wasn't even an officer yet, so when a full-bird Colonel walks up to you, whether you are in a bar, on base, or on the moon, you are supposed to stand and salute. I was so drunk I didn't even realize he was there until I saw my buddies all standing chest out, shoulders back."

"The Colonel, who looked to be thirty something, with light brown, curly hair, dismisses the other men and sits down by me. He had this look about him, this vibe; somehow I knew right off this was no ordinary officer. Of course he wasn't even a human being, much less an officer."

"Colonel Gabriel says to me 'Rico,' that's a nickname only my mother called me, 'you need to let God handle your pain. Give your problems to Him, let Him take vengeance. Rico,' he says to me, 'the wrath of man does not produce the righteousness of God.'

"Now, drunk or not, by instinct I defer to all higher ranking officers. So while I have no idea why this serious marine was preaching a sermon, I say 'yes sir,' nod and look him straight in the eye.

'Rico,' then he says, 'do not patronize the Lord or His servant. Your orders come from God, not the Corps. I know you were paying attention when Carmela told you to put your faith in God, not in man.'

"Carmela was my mother. This was something she said often to me. She was always worried that the world would use my strength to lead me astray.

"I was sobering up fast. I asked myself, how in the hell did this Colonel know who my mother was? Had I told anyone else alive about her admonition to me?

"Before I had the chance to ask him how he knew my mother and a secret only she and I shared, he spoke something in a foreign tongue and then touched my hand.

"Suddenly she was sitting there right in front of me."

"Who, Jose?" Kenny asked.

"My mother. She looked ghastly; all sick and pallid. Life had been very hard on mom, and the years of backbreaking work and exposure to toxic chemicals had broken down her body. I didn't know it then, but she was dying of liver cancer. She had been diagnosed with it right about when Ramon was killed, and she didn't want to burden me with her suffering while I was in Nam, so she didn't tell me.

"I'm freaking out. 'Mom! Mom!' I shout. 'How did you get here? What's going on?' She reaches over and touches my cheek like she always did, and smiles, and then puts her finger to her lips asking me to be quiet.

"Then she says, 'Rico, God loves you. He has a plan and a purpose for your life. Come to Him when He calls, Rico. Put your faith in God and not in man.' Then she disappears. So does Gabriel. I'm left sitting there stupefied, wondering if I was losing my mind or maybe if someone had slipped me LSD or something.

"A few hours later I'm finally able to get through to my family in Cali. My dad is just out of his mind with grief. 'Your mom died this morning,' he tells me.

"Then he says he wants me to know that her last words were directed specifically to me. 'It was like you were right here in the room with her, son,' he says. Reading from the notes he took of mom's dying declaration, he then repeats the exact statement, word for word, my mother made to me in the bar. It also wasn't hard to figure out that I saw mom at the exact same time she died in California."

If Jose was expecting some awestruck reaction to his story he didn't get it. Each of the disciples silently contemplated what they had heard and believed it without reservation. By now, nothing God did surprised them.

"You know what, gentlemen, I never told my father about seeing mom in the bar or about Gabriel."

"For heaven's sake, why not?" Peter asked.

"I was afraid. Scared he might think I was crazy, or worse, weak. I have always believed in God, my mom and dad were devout Catholics, but I never really believed, 'believed.' You know, accepted as fact that the miracles and supernatural events in the New Testament were actually real, not just p.r."

"Don't feel alone, Jose. I preached the word for a couple of decades, sure that it was all superstitious nonsense," Kenny confessed.

"I am so ashamed, gentlemen. I should have changed my life right then and there, repented and gotten right with the Lord. I mean I was given a miracle for hell's sake, and still I was too proud, too hard headed, to believe."

"Reminds me of eleven other men, Mr. Vargas," Peter said.

"Who were they, sir?" Jose asked.

"A few fellows from Galilee, saints all. They watched Christ raise the dead, exorcise demons, walk on water, disappear into the midst of crowds, and still when the Romans came to arrest Him, they fled. The man upon whom the Lord built His church, the rock, Cephas, he denied Him three times."

"What is it you're trying to tell me, Panos? I'm to have an excuse for my sin? Comparing me to an Apostle seems, well, forgive me sir, a bit extreme."

Peter was beginning to understand that while General Jose Vargas had great faith and the calling, otherwise he would not be sitting with him now, he was still stuck in his sin, not yet ready or able to completely accept the cleansing power of God, to fully submit.

"Whether you know it or not, Jose, you are no different than the Apostles. No better, certainly no worse. Nothing is troubling you that is not common to all men, and no, there is no excuse for sin, but there is forgiveness if you seek it."

"But Panos, you don't know what I've done." As Jose said this he looked down and slumped, at last losing his military posture. He sounded like a man defeated, not a warrior.

Peter then also understood that they were listening to a confession that also happened to be a testimony. His newest disciple was desperate to unburden his soul, but his "old man" was dying hard.

"You never confessed your sins to a priest, did you, Jose?" Peter surmised.

"No," was the answer. "I was too ashamed."

"Well, then now is the time, brother. I suspect it is well past the time," Peter said, hoping for Jose's sake that he would not waste the opportunity.

Vargas stood, stretched, and looked around. His brothers knew, they could all sense and see it. A war was raging in Jose's soul. At that very moment the devil was doing all he could to keep Jose from fully committing to the Lord.

"Part of you wants to run?" Saul asked.

"Honestly? Yes," Jose answered.

"Wondering how in the world you ended up here in a Federal prison camp with a bunch of convicts?" Kenny asked.

"Yes."

"Considering the idea that we're all a bunch of con men who have somehow tricked you into being a fool?" Larry asked.

This time Jose did not answer.

Saul then fell to his knees in silent prayer. The attention briefly shifted to him. When he was finished he opened his eyes, sat back down, and spoke.

"The Lord has granted my request, Jose," Saul told his struggling new friend. "For the next few minutes He has blessed you with my gift."

"What gift would that be, Mr. Cohen?"

"The ability to see for yourself who is putting all these doubts and heresies in your mind."

Saul reached over and touched Jose's arm. That's when Peter and the disciples saw something that the Vietcong, the Iraqi insurgency, or any of the thousands of men Jose Enrique Vargas had commanded over his lifetime ever saw. The unconquerable General Vargas was suddenly paralyzed with fear.

Jose's main antagonist was an especially large and vile looking demon. He was surrounded by imps, too numerous to count, who were all chewing on something. Exactly what, Jose could not tell.

Vargas was in shock. He had never seen such creatures, or truly believed they could exist, imagining demons to be the fantasies of overzealous or delusional men. This beast, though, was very real. He could also speak.

"So, you stupid son of a b****, you can finally see me. Think you can beat me now? You are only a worthless ape, Vargas, a toy for me to play with and dump on when I'm through."

In the beast's hands were weapons: automatic rifles, grenades, spears, and clubs. The assortment was endless and kept changing by the second. His image seemed to flux, to get weaker, then stronger, pulsing like a strobe.

"Who are you?" Jose asked, trembling so violently he thought he might shake himself apart.

"Why, I'm you. What a stupid question, Vargas. You made me. Aren't you proud?"

"How could I make you?"

"Damn you, you blind fool! Look at my servants all around me. They're eating the bones of your victims, Vargas. You've killed enough people to feed them forever.

"I'm your beast. Every time you hate, or even better, ignore the suffering you create, I get stronger. Death, pain, killing, it's what you do, Vargas. It's you. I'm you."

Enlightenment is always best experienced gradually. If the harsh reality, the naked truth of the horror of the monsters and demons created by a lifetime of sin is thrust on a man without warning, chaos can be the result.

Jose had his epiphany, but the consequences of it were unresolved. The demon was telling him the truth, but like all evil, he

Solomon's Porch

193

only told him part of the truth, the condemnation side of the equation.

Feeling forsaken and unworthy, believing the lie that he was no better than the demon who tortured him, Jose Vargas was standing on a precipice, ready to jump into the abyss. Try as he might, he could muster no argument against Satan, because he hated what he'd done, and thought it made him every bit as vile and ugly as the disgusting nightmare from the pit of hell who was trying to steal his soul.

From afar, outside of his evil narrowed field of vision, Jose heard his brothers praying for him. So did the demon.

"You think they can help you? Those losers? What a stinking pile of garbage they are. Worthless thieves, con men and killers, all of them weak. You call that undisciplined collection of filth brothers? They're not worthy of bathing in your piss."

"Lord have mercy on me a sinner," chanted the voices in unison.

"Christ was a wimp, Vargas. You worship Him? That limp wristed queer died on the cross like a piece of spoiled meat. We laughed at Him then and we are still laughing now."

"Lord have mercy on me a sinner!" The chant grew louder, stronger.

"Don't listen to them. Stay with me. You've seen me now, you know what's real. Accept what you are, Vargas. You can't change it, so revel in it! If you will forget all of this stupid, childish bull**** about God and Christ and righteousness, all your suffering will be over. I offer you the peace that comes from acknowledging your true nature. We can have so much more fun, monkey boy! We haven't even gotten started yet."

Despite the pain, the crushing weight of his unrepented sin, which was urging him to abandon Christ, somehow Carmela got through.

In his agony, Jose saw her standing close by, along with another woman. They called to him.

"Rico, put your faith in God, son, not in man. Confess, repent, and live. I love you and so does the Lord."

"Lord have mercy on me a sinner!" The call from his brethren was now almost deafening.

Seeing his mother urged Jose's spirit to accept his gift, to realize that he was being given yet another opportunity to turn to the Lord. That this was by no means his second chance, or even his hundredth was unimportant, irrelevant. Carmela was here now, along with her angelic host, which meant to Jose that Christ was with him also. He was strengthened and ready to do battle.

"Lord have mercy on me a sinner," Jose prayed. While his heart was in it, he sounded reedy and weak.

"Please," the demon baited. "Who do you think you are talking to? I know you, Vargas. You don't love God. Look at all the pain and misery He's allowed in your life, in everyone's lives. He's a joke, not a God. Don't be a damned fool."

"Lord have mercy on me a sinner. Jesus forgive me for the lives I've taken and the pain I've caused. Heal me Christ, lead me away from this vision of sin and death."

Sensing Jose's resistance to him growing, the demon spread his arms, which looked like giant deformed bat wings with undersized claws. The demon then called to his attending imps, who responded by opening their mouths. Images, rather than voices, came pouring out.

Jose saw the six children in that little village south of Hue, the ones who had ignored his lieutenant's evacuation order and stayed behind. Vargas' platoon burned them alive, they had come out of one of the disintegrating huts aflame, four foot high human candles.

Then he saw himself that very night back at the base getting drunk on Jack and beer and laughing about it, as if it wasn't somehow children he'd tortured and destroyed, but rather some subhuman vermin deserving of extermination.

Next, another imp showed him the five civilians he'd casually killed less than a week after the children simply because they were in the wrong place at the wrong time. Then one after another came a rapid succession of death and mayhem, scenes of violence from his life in Nam and elsewhere, some of which he'd actually been able to forget.

But General Vargas could never forget Aziz.

Above and beyond every other callous act of cruelty he'd ever directly committed or ordered another man to commit, what happened to Aziz was by far the most troubling to Jose's soul.

Back in 2004, Vargas was in command of a Marine division taking part in the battle of Fallujah in Iraq. While American casualties were light, the hand to hand, house to house fighting to rid the town of Sunni insurgents and terrorists was bloody and at times intense. During the Iraqi campaign the enemy used women and children to carry out their vicious suicide attacks. This was nothing new to Jose Vargas. As a grunt marine in Nam, he'd seen the VC use this same tactic, and use it very effectively.

Division commanders were supposed to remain at headquarters, but leading from the rear was unacceptable to General Vargas. Among his faults were neither cowardice nor a lack of concern for his men, so barely a week after the fighting in Fallujah started in earnest, he called for a driver and a platoon escort and headed straight into the action to see for himself how the battle was progressing.

The U.S. air strikes and subsequent occupation left the once prosperous and bustling city of Fallujah nearly deserted and selectively reduced to rubble. Precision munitions targeting allowed the Americans to hit one block where they believed the insurgents were entrenched and leave the next virtually unscathed. Jose found this brand of twenty-first century warfare both disingenuous and naïve, for like rats, his enemy fled when the light shone on them and melded into the background to avoid capture or destruction. As in Vietnam, political considerations took precedence over the most effective military strategy, which Vargas at the time honestly believed, was to use all available means to root out and kill his adversaries.

There weren't many children left in Fallujah, so when Vargas' marine escort came upon a small group of them, they were immediately suspicious. Aziz and ten other kids, the oldest fifteen and the youngest no more than five, were playing in an empty lot, kicking around something brown and half flat that at one time could have been a soccer ball.

Despite having to endure the hardships of being born in an oppressive society and in a war zone, Aziz was a beautiful child, full of love and hope. Barely twelve, he was already almost manly handsome with bright eyes and a mind to match. Aziz knew who the Americans were. They were his heroes. He loved them because they were getting rid of the men who had taken over his town, the evil monsters who had killed his father and his brother. Aziz had on a light sweater that was three sizes too big for him. Because the raggedy ball was his most prized possession he tucked it under his sweater for safekeeping before he ran toward the American convoy that was slowly pulling up behind his makeshift football field.

That's when the mortar rounds hit, five in rapid succession. All missed the marines, but it put them on the defensive. They were under attack.

Running out of the smoke was when Jose first saw him, or rather when he first saw an indistinct but obviously human shape, and it was moving straight for his vehicles and his men. Just as he caught sight of Aziz, the platoon started taking rifle fire from the opposite direction. Two of Vargas' soldiers were quickly wounded.

The American platoon, and by every military protocol quite properly, opened up. They sprayed the surrounding buildings with round after round, hoping to destroy or at least silence the source of the incoming fire.

Aziz was petrified. When the mortars hit at first he stopped. He knew what to do, drop to the ground and lie flat until the fighting was over. But these were the Americans, he told himself, not the cruel gangsters who terrorized his family and his town. To be with them was to be safe. He began to run in the direction of his heroes.

Satan was forcing Jose not only to watch, but to virtually relive his worst nightmare.

When Aziz ran toward the American platoon's position, so did the other children. Only Vargas and one very raw and frightened young marine private were focusing on Aziz and his buddies, the rest of the men were fully occupied with the wounded and the firefight.

"Please, no." Jose begged for the vision to stop. He was back there again, smelling the same smells, feeling the same fear, feeding the same hate.

"What's wrong, Vargas," the demon heckled. "Big bad marine doesn't have the stomach to witness his finest hour? You f***ing coward, you worthless pile of s***! You're a baby killer, that's what you are, Vargas. You're scum, not a marine. You're not even a man."

Jose watched himself, as large as life and right in front of him, make the same mistake twice. The young marine private could see now that it was children who were thirty feet away from their position and closing fast. He hesitated, couldn't bring himself to fire despite knowing full well that one or all of them might be carrying enough explosives to send them all to hell.

Jose did not hesitate. He was a professional soldier, a highly trained and disciplined combat veteran in the employ of the United States government. Given the situation, his men were taking rifle and mortar fire, they were pinned down and at least two of them were wounded, there was no time to do anything but react.

General Vargas saw that the lead kid coming at them had something stuffed under his shirt. His hand was also inside his shirt, holding on to something. Detonator! Jose concluded.

Vargas then unleashed his automatic weapon on Aziz and his friends. When he fired so did his young marine escort, who, of course, followed his General's lead. Seconds later all of the children were dead, their small bodies desecrated by hot lead.

At that point the skirmish ended. Chaos was replaced by order.

"Dear God, no," Jose pleaded. "No, no. Lord have mercy on me a sinner. Please Christ, forgive me. Forgive me, Aziz."

"You murdered innocent boys, Vargas," the demon accused. "Put them down like rabid dogs. But it was nothing new to you, was it! We'll just put it on your account."

The vision continued as Jose and the rest of his platoon carefully moved out from behind the cover of their vehicles to investigate the situation. They were cautious, "frosty" was their term, alert with weapons at the ready. The remaining unwounded marines led the way, very conscious that they had a General behind them to protect.

"F****n' A, Sarge," said the young corporal. "These kids were clean. Nothin' on em."

The words cut through Jose's soul like a hot dagger once more, exactly as they had on that day.

Gunnery Sergeant Williams also did not hesitate. He'd been through this before and knew exactly what had to be done.

"Look again, Corporal," Gunny ordered.

The Corporal did, searching each small corpse thoroughly.

"Like I said, Gunny, nothin' on em," the Corporal repeated.

The Sergeant then walked over to investigate for himself. The General was a few feet behind him, watching closely and listening to every word.

"I see an undetonated explosives package right here under this one's shirt, Corporal! What, are you blind? Do your job soldier!"

The Corporal looked for a third time. All he saw was a deflated and shredded ball stained almost completely red by blood under the boy's sweater.

"Gunny, I mean come on, Gunny. That's not a …" The Corporal's comments were cut short by his Sergeant's rifle butt not so gently poking him in the ribs.

"Who is that standing over there, Corporal?" Gunny shouted.

Short of breath from the blow to his chest, the Corporal answered weakly, "General Vargas, Gunny."

"Damn right it's General Vargas. Now get off your a** and double time it in the Humvee over to that position about a click south of here where those Army punks have a pile of captured munitions. Get me a proper insurgent explosive device and bring it back here. You read me, Corporal?"

Jose watched as both the Sergeant and the Corporal looked at him, both waiting to see if the General would put a stop to the Sergeant's plan.

Vargas watched himself look at his men, then silently turn away and walk back to the Humvee to search for his canteen.

"Corporal, if you expect to make it out of here today without my boot permanently shoved up your a** I suggest you get moving!" Gunny yelled.

"They covered for you, Vargas. Your men concealed your crime, made it look all neat and tidy. A nice clean little killing, all right and proper." The demon was playing his hand now.

"My men loved me," Vargas explained. "They knew I'd do anything for them, so they did something for me. What they did was wrong, but well motivated. You are a liar if you say that makes them evil."

"Did I say they were evil? No, I said you were evil. Come on Vargas! Enough of this! We don't have to see and deal with all this pain. I can take you anywhere you want to go. How about you come with me and we'll go back to Saigon in '70 and sample some of those fresh young Vietnamese delicacies you like so much! Or would you rather stay here with the convicts and pray yourself to death?"

Jose could see Carmela and her angel again and could hear who he swore was Peter exhorting him to command the devil to flee.

Jose prayed once more, this time silently. The demon and his imps were shimmering in the foreground of his vision, fading in and out.

"You beast, you servant of hell, all my life you've been with me, tempting me, feeding my weaknesses. It's over, I'm through, and so are you." Jose sounded confident now, like a man who was certain of an outcome before a conflict began.

"Vargas, you worthless piece of trash. You can't get rid of me that easily," the demon responded.

"Oh yes, he can."

Entering Jose's vision now was another angel, brilliant white with large, stately wings. Despite his angelic form, his basic structure was undeniably human; he looked like a white man, about thirty, with light brown, curly hair.

"Gabriel. My old friend! Why must you always intervene to help these wretched creatures? You are more pathetic than they are."

"Humans are made in God's likeness and image. Do not mock the Lord, your God and Creator, by torturing them. Away with you."

Gabriel spread his beautiful wings, and as he did Jose saw a fountain of Light stream from them, a Light more powerful and intense than looking directly into the sun. Before he was forced to look away he saw the Light, the very Uncreated Energy of God, envelope and disintegrate the demon and his imps.

Jose returned to the reality of the world back on the porch, still seated on the folding chair with his brothers now standing over him in a circle, each with a hand on his head or his shoulder.

"My God," Jose whispered. "My Lord God. What happened? Did you men see what happened?"

"We saw, Jose, we saw," Peter said, as he knelt down and put his arm around his disciple.

"Then it was real?" Jose asked.

"Very real, General. All of us here saw everything you did," Saul reassured.

"The demon, he's ..." Jose looked to Peter for confirmation.

"Gone, brother. You and Gabriel sent him back to hell."

For the first time since Ramon's death, Jose Vargas wept. The tears were mixed, some were shed in the godly sorrow he now felt for his sins, and some were shed in joy for the blessing of being liberated and at peace with God. For almost half an hour, one of the toughest and proudest soldiers ever to put on the uniform of the United States Marine Corps cried like a child.

When he was finished, he experienced an emotion heretofore unfamiliar to him; settledness. Jose was "perfected," to use St. Peter's term. He had now become the man he needed to be to fulfill God's purpose for his life.

"I need to tell you men the rest," Jose said to his brothers. "After that day when the Iraqi children were killed, I made it my business to find out everything I could about them. Two of the older ones were probably insurgents, as if that mattered. But Aziz, he was special."

"How so General?" Larry asked.

"Aziz was loved by everyone. He was always friendly, looking to help anyone in need. He was also touched by God. Everyone who knew him was better for it."

"Some months later, after I had quit active combat command and was kicked upstairs, I was back in the states. Someone knocked on my door at Parris Island in the middle of the night. I thought it was an aide with urgent news, but it wasn't."

"When I opened the door, there they stood. Aziz and Gabriel glowing in the night air."

"My God in heaven," Saul exclaimed.

"I fell to my knees, shamed. I thought for sure they were coming to take me away, to send me to hell where, gentlemen, without Christ, I most certainly belong."

"Aziz says to me, 'General, don't be afraid. I'm in a better place now. I forgive you.' Gabriel says, 'The time has come, Jose. What will it be? Will you put your faith in God and become His servant?' I told him yes. I was then given the same vision all of you men have had, the one of us standing on the porch and fire shooting from the tops of our heads. Then I passed out. Hours later a quite worried corporal had me transported to the infirmary; I woke up there.

"Can you believe it, though? Until now, gentlemen, I still had some doubts. God forgive me. At times I thought I might be losing my mind, even considered the idea that I had been poisoned by some chemical back in Nam and again in Iraq. As you all now know, I'm a very stubborn man."

"How did you find us?" Peter asked.

"That would involve me, Mr. Kallistos," Tim Austin interjected. "Gabriel sent me to get him and bring him here." The men had heard nothing as yet from the seventh disciple.

"That's right," Vargas confirmed. "Tim found me fishing in a trout stream out in western North Carolina. He knew things that no one else could possibly know. I'm so thankful God did not give up on me and that He has given me the chance to help put an end to the senseless violence of war."

"Once more, General?" Kenny asked, puzzled.

"When Gabriel and Aziz came to see me that night, they told me that it was my job to show God's people that 'the wrath of man does not produce the righteousness of God.'"

"And how exactly do we accomplish that, General?" Larry wanted to know.

Jose smiled. He was beginning to understand how all of the shapes were arranging themselves to form the picture.

"Why, through you gentlemen, of course. The Lord intends to use us as His tool to demonstrate the futility and evil of national organized murder. I believe, brothers, that very soon we will make believers of millions and enemies of millions more."

Fourteen

"Do any of the other inmates know?" Peter asked.

"No sir, Mr. Pete. We kep' it 'tween us. Not the type of thing one should be broadcastin'," Malik explained.

"Good, good. Lord have mercy, brother. Who is God going to bring us next? I'm half expecting the Pope himself to stroll in here."

The seven took a dinner break after hearing General Vargas' testimony. That's when Malik pulled Peter aside and told him that Mr. Austin had an "issue" he should be aware of.

Timothy James Austin was just as surprised as his brothers were about his being in a Federal prison facility, although he'd been to many over the past twenty years, from Leavenworth to Lompoc. The difference this time was he didn't have to check his gun and credentials at the door.

Tim Austin was a career FBI man, and not some run-of-the-mill agent either. He had enjoyed a spectacular tenure, notching his belt with everything from high profile narcotics busts in Texas to white collar fraud prosecutions on Wall Street. He'd been the Special Agent in Charge of some of the most important districts in America. Austin's peers honored him regularly, so much so that every square inch of his office wall was filled with awards and accolades. The FBI Academy at Quantico held up his professional accomplishments as the prototype for its most ambitious cadets.

Alex had already contacted his research consultants in New York. A literal mountain of background information was quickly made available to him on Timothy James Austin, including varying accounts of his abrupt and unexpected departure from the FBI five months previous.

Alex was juggling these new facts in his mind, trying to coalesce the diverse elements into his common theme, when the chief stagehand said that the lights, camera, and the audio were all set. Alex gestured to Peter signaling that they could now begin.

"Brothers," Peter said, "as has become our custom, we welcome Tim into our circle through the bearing of his testimony, but before he speaks, let me offer a word of caution. For the moment, we must be prudent. Soon enough the world will know all about us, but until then, for his safety at Parkersboro, brother Austin's former profession should remain known only to us. Are we all in agreement?"

Five heads nodded. Then six sets of eyes turned and focused on the sharp featured, athletic, and impeccably groomed man who very much looked the part of the policeman amongst the thieves.

Tim Austin intentionally dressed down for the occasion. Normally he wouldn't be seen in public without a suit and a tie on, with shoes freshly polished. He had always believed in projecting an image, creating an aura of power and worldly righteousness through his speech, mannerisms, and appearance.

Those habits held little value for him now and he knew it but, regardless, they died hard. He managed to allow himself to be present this night in khakis and a crimson shirt and was even so bold as to put on loafers with no socks.

"Gentlemen," Tim Austin always addressed any group of men as gentlemen or sirs, "Our Lord Jesus Christ has blessed me to be here. It may seem odd to you that a man who has dedicated his life to imprisoning lawbreakers is now amongst the repentant, but remember the Lord is no respecter of persons. We may hail from different strata, but the divine protocol unites us in our common crusade. I'm proud to be a part of God's action plan."

Genuinely confused, Malik asked, "Mr. Pete, what the heck did brother Tim just say?"

Everyone appreciated the innocent humor in Malik's question and laughed. Except for Tim. His face turned as red as his neatly pressed, open-collar knit shirt.

Peter understood the problem.

"Are you nervous, Mr. Austin?" Peter asked.

"Very much so," was the honest response.

"I'll bet you are," Peter said. "Brother, we, by choice, lack formality. Other than General Vargas and yourself, none of us are accustomed to much structure. We are not laughing at you, Tim, honest."

"No sir, Mr. Pete. Sorry, Mr. Tim," Malik apologized.

"Why don't you try and tone down the Bureau speak a little, Tim. Be yourself, but consider your audience as well. God knows what is in your heart, brother, and whether you believe it yet or not, you have never been among better friends."

"Thanks, Peter," Austin said, staring contritely down at his shoes. "I've found it hard to unlearn the lessons of a lifetime. I ask for your patience."

"You've got that, Mr. Austin," Peter said reassuringly, "and don't think that most of your lessons need to necessarily be unlearned. All of us here have respect for God's command that we are to live righteously and at peace with others. We do not defend sin, Mr. Austin, and you need never apologize to us for living a life free from shameful misconduct."

"Is that what you all think?" Tim asked.

"Be more specific, Mr. Austin."

"That I've lived a life free from shameful misconduct?"

"Well," Peter hesitated, caught unawares, "we just assumed that ..."

"Don't assume anything, men," Tim interrupted. "Don't assume anything."

In the cool, late spring night air, made only a bit warmer by the large stage lights Alex's crew employed, Tim began to testify. While too formal and a bit pompous in his presentation, Tim was also brief. He spoke like a report and shared his personal history as if he was reading from one of his case files.

Born in Kansas City. Lettered in three sports in high school. Turned down a West Point admission to play football at Nebraska where he was the starting free safety, and All-Conference, for three years. Only a devastating, career-ending knee injury in his last regular season game against Oklahoma kept him out of the NFL.

Always wanted to be a cop if he couldn't play football, just like his dad, who made it all the way to the Chief's office in the Kansas City department. Went to the FBI academy right after college. Became an instant star, an up-and-comer from the start.

Never drank, not once. Never used drugs. Can't even recall stealing a candy bar as a kid. Mr. Clean.

"For many, many years," Tim confessed to his brothers, "I looked at my job as being impersonal, an almost sterile thing.

Congress wrote the laws, the FBI enforced them. Simple as that. Logical, patterned behavior and response. I became a voluntary robot, little more than a computer with a pulse."

"So much the opposite of most of us here," Saul broke in. "I was trying to see how little I could conform, how much I could get away with."

"I laughed at guys like you," Kenny added. "Thought you were all a bunch of ridiculous fools. Look at where my attitude got me. I'd be dead and in hell if it were not for the mercy of Christ."

"Can't say I've ever had much use for the police," Malik said in his completely open, disarmingly blunt manner. "Never gave a second thought to what ya'll were thinkin'. Always just counted you as the enemy. Knew for sure all cops hated black folks anyway. Ain't that a shame?"

Tim looked around and now he was the one who laughed, not in response to a joke, but rather to the irony.

"James, chapter two, verse thirteen," Tim said, as he made revolving eye contact with each of the other six.

"For judgment is without mercy to the one who has shown no mercy. Mercy triumphs over judgment," Kenny recited.

"Matthew, chapter seven, verse two," Tim said, now focusing his gaze solely upon Peter.

"For with what judgment you judge, you will be judged, and with what measure you use, it will be measured back to you," Peter quoted.

"Those were two of the verses he impressed upon my mind six months ago, gentlemen. And then, God help me, he interpreted them for me, applying their principles to my works." As Tim said this his stiffness lessened a bit, as if just listening to the passages being spoken soothed his spirit.

"Let me guess," Larry said. "He came to you as someone you arrested?"

"No."

"A supervisor then? A man you respected, an authority figure?"

"Wrong again, Larry."

"Well then I'm all out of guesses."

"The Angel of the Lord came to me as a beggar, a homeless bum who reeked of alcohol," Tim testified. "I was never very sympathetic to the plight of the homeless. Thought they were mostly lazy and shiftless, of no value. A drain on our society."

"How unfortunate," Larry said. "I've fought that prejudice all my life. We are all God's children, brother Tim."

"Gabriel made that and much more very apparent to me once he got my attention."

"How did he manage to do that?" Saul asked.

"As you might imagine a drunken beggar would. Passing by him on the street, he blew chunks on my shoes."

"That's a new one," Peter said, grinning. "Can't imagine you were too happy about your shoes getting soiled."

"I'll never, ever forget that day," Tim said, looking up into the clear, black moonless sky filled with stars. "Not one thing about it, not the slightest detail.

"I was in mid-town Manhattan, there to receive an award from the newly formed Federal-State Law Enforcement Project. Exactly for what I wasn't sure and neither were they. I was the honored one; they were a neophyte lobbying body trying to build clout, so they gave me an award. In their estimation, association with my name could help them to secure more Federal funds, put them "on the map," if you will.

"Now, I knew very well it was all just political masturbation, but I was quite full of myself at the time. I remember walking down that street thinking how far I'd come, how high I'd reached. Important people fawned over me, colleagues respected and even feared me."

"As clear as if it was happening today I recall telling myself, 'I have arrived.' Within a few years I was certain that I'd be taking the leap to the consulting and lobbying position all of my fame and reputation was building for me. Then, I told myself, it's goodbye to Chevys and condos and hello to BMWs and beach houses.

"Worse still, I believed the lie that I had earned these privileges by being better than others; smarter, tougher, more skilled at the game. My busts, the people I sent to prison, they weren't even human in my eyes. At best, they were numbers on a page, statistics upon which I fed my ego and built my success."

"And then Gabriel heaved on your shoes," Larry said.

"He did. A rather rank mix of beer, Southern Comfort, and hot dogs with beans."

"You weren't kidding about recalling every detail," Peter said.

"I don't miss much, Panos, ever, but I could even tell you what was playing at the Cineplex across the street from where Gabriel was sitting, so much is every detail of that day burned into my soul."

"My initial reaction to being soiled was disgust and indignation. With all of the proud thoughts I was having at the time, such a gross affront really, well, really ticked me off."

"What did you do?" Larry asked.

"I picked him up off the sidewalk and, as I did, I immediately noticed that he was a solid man with sharp eyes and a healthy body. Not your typical wasted away bum. I stood him up against the wall and said, 'Those are two hundred dollar shoes, scumbag, and you're going to clean them up.'

"I began searching on the ground for a rag to give this man. I was fully intent on forcing him to clean my shoes to my satisfaction or else I had no compunction at all about jacking him up, right then and there."

"As I was looking around for a suitable cleaning tool, holding him up against the wall with my right arm, he did it again."

"Did what again?" Peter asked.

"Threw up. This time all over my suit. He covered me in vomit. I felt insulted, sullied to even have to be on the same planet with such a pathetic waste of air and food."

"A picture is forming for me here, brother Tim," Peter said. "You seemed to be awfully proud of yourself. I take it you were not a believer when this happened?"

"Once, maybe twice, in my life prior to that time I'd attended church services and then only because some girl I was dating dragged me there. My folks taught me right from wrong in man's terms, but the subject of God was ignored in my house. The Almighty was an irrelevancy."

"I understand," Peter related. "We cannot learn what we are not taught."

"Let me put it this way, Panos," as he spoke, Austin was once again looking meekly at his feet, "Gabriel made up for lost time."

"After he barfed on me again, I reared back on my heels, shoved Gabriel up against the wall and prepared to throttle him. As my first right cross was on its way he moved, quicker than any human being could, and avoided the blow. He was sort of crouched down and from that position he reached up and grabbed my face with both hands."

"Immediately I became as weak as a rag doll, not paralyzed exactly, but without strength. He looked at me with those crystal clear blue eyes of his and said, 'As filthy as this vomit is, so are your works before the Lord.'

"Then he spun me around. By my ears. Now I'm the one backed up against the wall. For the first time in my life I'm the man in the vulnerable position. In the space of a minute, I went from being enraged to scared to death."

"Huntin' ain't so fun when the rabbit's got the gun," Malik rhymed.

"My friend, truer words were never spoken," Tim admitted. "I experienced helplessness for the first time that day. It was but the first of my many humility lessons.

"Gabriel has me firmly in his grip and from that position he twists my face to the left and says, 'See the fruits of your labors.'

"Before me flowed a stream of images, places, and people from my past. Most of the scenes were familiar to me. I was somehow made aware of how what I didn't recognize fit into the overall scheme of things.

"Carl Taylor. His life was put before me first. Just a kid of twenty-three when one of our Kentucky meth stings took him down. His father and two brothers were already doing time, his mother long since dead. Carl had a girlfriend who was involved in it too. Liz."

"Now they were not the all-American couple, but neither were they Bonnie and Clyde. They helped run a methamphetamine lab, a rather large one. As part of the conspiracy, they were criminally liable for the lab's entire production which amounted to a life's sentence for Carl, twenty years for Liz."

"Gabriel showed me images of them together, holding hands and feeding ducks in a park, going to the movies, cuddling in bed. They were planning a future, one without drugs or a criminal lifestyle. Both had stopped using. They wanted to, and were, changing.

"But to me they were nothing more than fodder for my cannon, disposable objects to be used to maximize the size and strength of our case. I justified this thinking always by saying 'they're criminals' and 'they get what they deserve.'

"Carl plea bargained down to twenty-five years, Liz to probation. I considered this merciful, as if by destroying their lives I was somehow being kind."

"Mr. Tim, meth is the devil's own tool. Seen it ruin people quick. What we supposed to do, let people make the trash and sell it with no penalty? Ice is pure poison, Mr. Tim, just like that nasty crack." That Malik Graham was expressing anti-drug, pro law enforcement sentiments would have floored anyone who knew him before Parkersboro.

"I could not agree with you more, Mr. Graham," Tim responded, "but recognizing that truth leads us to miss a far greater one if we are not careful."

"Mercy combined with chastening," Peter said. "God commands us to be merciful, as the Scriptures you had us quote confirm. That does not mean sin, or specifically crime, is or should be consequence free."

"Well put, Panos. Let me apply this principle to Carl and Liz. All of us on the prosecution team knew what and who we were dealing with. In fact, a new agent, a female, brought this to our attention during a strategy session. Amanda, that was the agent's name, said 'Carl and Liz have had a rough life. They've come clean. Why don't we consider dropping her and recommending two years for Carl? Let's give them a chance.'"

"What was your response?" Peter asked.

"When Amanda said this everyone looked to me, of course. I was the lead agent and the man with the rep. Rather than thinking and listening, I set out to embarrass my young FBI associate and gave her a boorish and cruel recital of sterile stats on criminal behavior and drug trafficking recidivism. Made her look naïve, like a fool for even bringing up the suggestion."

"Did you believe in what you were saying?" Larry asked.

"Yes and no. Yes, in the general sense that I wasn't lying about the facts or even my spin on them. No, in as much as I could also see what Amanda saw, that it would not be unjustified to cut Carl and Liz a break."

"But I didn't give a damn about Carl and Liz, or Amanda either. My reputation was built on seeing the maximum possible penalties applied in all cases. Super Agent Tim Austin does not cut you a deal unless you earn it by informing on your friends and family, and in this case, what help Carl gave did not merit further prison time reduction consideration."

"What happened to them?" Saul wanted to know.

"Gabriel showed me. Once Carl realized his life was over for the next twenty years, and that he and Liz would never be together again, he gave up. Carl did not know Christ, he did not draw on God's strength for help, so he hung himself in his cell by his shoelaces. Gabriel made me watch him die. Liz took a handful of pills and never woke up once she heard about Carl."

"Lord have mercy," Peter prayed.

"There were many, many more 'Carls,'" Tim confessed. "For every unrepentant, violent, and predatory man I helped send away for a decade or more, two or three lives that could have been redeemed were needlessly destroyed for no other reason than mine, and my FBI colleagues, cold evil hearts and selfish career ambitions.

"A prison chaplain once asked me if I ever considered the fact that the men I sent to the penitentiary all had lives and families too, and that everyone, including myself, was a sinful, struggling human being."

"He was trying to open your heart to the wisdom of God's mercy," Peter said.

"Yes, he was," Tim acknowledged, "but I was not interested. My self-righteousness was always at the ready to respond to such assaults. I told him, "I enforce the law, chaplain. You can save their souls after I've made sure they are no longer a menace to society.""

"Well, Gabriel finished what that chaplain at least tried to start. He held me there against that wall for no more than a minute, but it seemed like hours to me. One after another I was made to see, to somehow experience, the unnecessary suffering I caused hundreds of my fellow men and women through my unmerciful judgments."

"You got a crash course in perspective and empathy," Kenny related. "Been through that myself."

"What about the victims of crime?" Larry asked. "Where do they fit in? Many of my homeless brothers and sisters are cruelly abused by others just because they are weak. Don't they deserve justice?"

"What is justice?" Tim asked.

"That's a profound question, brother," Peter answered. He was now better understanding the direction the Lord had taken

Tim and its inevitable conclusion. "Man defines it one way, God another."

"That is the heart of the matter, Panos, at least for me. I never realized that I was accountable to a code of conduct that supersedes any human legal standards. Thank Christ, Gabriel showed me. Otherwise I had surely punched my ticket for hell."

"The victims of crime," Austin expounded, "are called upon to both hold the one who wronged them accountable and to be merciful and to forgive their transgressor. People think that these goals are mutually exclusive. Thanks to the Lord's mercy I know now that they are not."

Tim paused for a minute and stood, reflecting on his experiences and how they helped shape the "new man" he'd become.

"Before God touched my heart, gentlemen, I never stopped to consider the awesome and simple majesty of His creation," Tim admitted, arms folded behind his back as he slowly paced between the concrete boundaries of the porch as he spoke. "He gave us a beautiful home and everything we need to prosper. What does the Scripture say?"

"Every good and perfect gift is from above, and comes from the Father of lights, with whom there is no variation or shadow of turning," Kenny quoted.

"I'm not at all surprised you chose that passage, brother," Austin said, as he stopped walking and touched Kenny on the shoulder. "The truth found in St. James' words now guide my life, leading me toward the grace and mercy of the Savior.

"In that incredibly brief period of time Gabriel held me there against that wall, the Lord infused my mind and soul with the reality of His existence and His ever presence in the world. Literally in an instant He changed forever the way in which I think, view myself, and all of creation. It was like being plugged into a divine super computer and receiving a massive download. To tell you brothers the truth, I'm still trying to sort all of it out, but His purpose for my life was forever burned into my heart and spirit that day. That's why I'm here."

"I can directly relate to what you experienced, Tim. To say what happened to you was a life changing event doesn't begin to do it justice. I know how a direct link, however brief, to the Absolute Power can forever change a man, humble him, and force him to admit the error of his ways." As Peter said this he recalled his own vision in the library. His awakening seemed now to have happened a lifetime ago, yet less than a year had passed since God first touched him.

"When Gabriel released me, he was no longer a homeless drunk, but rather a glorified angel. His brightness was so intense, so purely white, it was blinding. I looked around and saw other people walking by not ten feet away. They were oblivious to us, as if Gabriel and I did not exist. I realized that no one else had shared my experience.

"Before Gabriel disappeared, he showed me this prison, this circle, and he told me about you, Panos. 'The Lord's Messenger,' he called you. Again it took me days, weeks really, to organize all of this in my mind. You should see it, gentlemen. I have note-books filled with Scriptures, ideas, comments."

"Sounds like at first you were confused," Larry observed.

"Again, yes and no. Gabriel 'flashed out,' disappeared into a dense cloud of bright points of light. I found myself standing there alone on that New York sidewalk a totally different man than I had been just moments before. After Gabriel left the vomit was gone too, I was completely clean. People could see me again. I was back in the world.

"But I knew, more certainly than I had ever known anything in my life, that God exists, that my vision was real, and that I must discern and follow His call. The details were incomplete, but my transformation was absolute."

"I had accumulated over six months worth of unused vacation time through my workaholic ways, so I told the FBI I needed a break, nothing more. Led by the Spirit, I drove up to Massachusetts to a small coastal village just north of Boston. It was quiet and serene. The town has a two-hundred-year-old Catholic parish. For days I walked, sat, prayed, and wrote, communicating only with the local priest who is an older and very spiritual man. While I did not share my vision with him, I told him that God had called me to His service and that at forty-seven years of age, I was quitting the FBI. He understood, he said, but he did not pry."

"God sends us help in many ways, Tim. He uses people to fulfill His purpose, much of the time without their conscious knowledge," Peter explained.

"As I prayed and walked and talked to Father Reilly, that's the priest's name, some of my confusion dissipated as my vision came into sharper focus. I'm here, brothers, first and foremost to be obedient to the Lord and through him to you, Panos, but I'm also here to try and put a stop to the unmerciful destruction of human life caused by our ungodly judicial system. The Lord has given me some profound inspiration as to how we, as a society, can vastly improve our efforts in these matters."

"No doubt those ideas involve unpopular concepts like bringing God's word to every inmate, pursuing compassion rather than revenge, and true efforts at rehabilitation," Jose said.

"Yes, General Vargas, just as we have discussed," Tim answered.

"I have to tell you, gentlemen," Alex said, as he walked out from behind the camera and on to the "stage" of the library porch, "what I'm hearing all of you say, collectively, is that you want nothing less than a radical transformation of our culture, a movement away from our materialistic, violent, and self-centered ways toward a world based more upon the values each of you espouse through your testimonies: honesty, generosity, forgiveness, tolerance, love, and cooperation."

"That is the essence of the revelation that the Lord gave me last summer, Alex, right over there in that library, not twenty paces from where you're standing now," Peter confirmed. "These men are the instruments of God's plan, His willing servants. I believe the Lord intends for us to bring His message to the world directly and boldly."

"To rid the world of hunger, disease, violence, prisons, and hate? You aren't trying to accomplish very much, are you, Mr. Carson." Alex was playing the role of on-camera interviewer.

"With God nothing is impossible, Mr. Anderson, as you and the rest of the world shall soon bear witness to. We are challenging mankind to realize its potential, to become all our Creator intended us to be. As the Lord said, 'I am the way, the truth and the life. No one comes to the Father except through Me.' It is through Him that we shall advance, for without Him, we shall surely fail.

"The Lord granted us free will, Mr. Anderson. He gave us this beautiful home and all its riches. We are being held accountable by Him to use these gifts for the betterment and salvation of all humanity."

"So that's what this is all about, Mr. Carson, the betterment of humanity?" Alex asked.

"Indirectly, yes," Peter answered. "But what this is all about is the Creator reminding the created that He is sovereign. Man is not above his Maker. We have become too proud, convinced that we reign supreme in the universe. But we are not gods, there is but one God."

"It's about humility then," Alex probed.

"Yes, and through true humility, the ability to use God's power in the ways He intended it to be used. We must stop wasting precious lives and time by indulging evil."

"We proclaim to the world a better way to live, one in accordance with man's true nature, one ordered by God."

Fifteen

"That does not surprise me," Peter said, as they walked around Parkersboro's track. He and Alex were enjoying the fresh morning air and the peace and quiet that can best be found at dawn.

"How so?" Alex asked.

"According to the Orthodox calendar, this year June nineteenth is the Pentecost, the day God gave the Holy Spirit to the Apostles," Peter replied.

"Interesting." Alex's inclination was still to offer explanations of events in worldly terms. "The network told me we could get June nineteenth from eight to nine p.m. because otherwise they would be rerunning some medical drama. That I promised them the show of their dreams, a 'unique and unforgettable event,' didn't hurt either."

"Worried?" Peter asked.

"Only that you'll do exactly what you've promised to, Panos, and then God help us all."

"We may need some of that help right about now," Peter said, pointing across the prison grounds.

Two hundred yards away from where Peter and Alex were enjoying their leisurely stroll, they watched a steady stream of vehicles fill the prison's small parking area. By the time the sun had fully risen, the lot was packed and cars were overflowing into the dirt field adjacent to the camp. A line formed outside the main entrance. The curious and the faithful had arrived, or at least some of them. If today was anything like the past few days, the human procession into Parkersboro would continue on well into the evening.

"Amazing, isn't it?" Alex said, as he and Peter continued to make their way very deliberately around the oval, sipping coffee as they walked. "All these people seeking the Almighty at a Federal prison. These folks are starting to believe that you're Moses, Jeremiah, and John the Baptist all rolled into one."

"Did you get a chance to interview Melissa and Britney yesterday, the mother and daughter who had driven all day and night from Ohio to get here?" Peter asked, ignoring Alex's reference to the prophets.

"Yes sir. They are on tape and they have lots of company. I'd say you've had more documented miracles occur here at Parkersboro during the past eleven months than the Catholic Church has recognized over the previous fifty years."

"Those two especially touched my heart, Alex," Peter continued. "Imagine being ten years old and getting melanoma, then being told you had maybe a year to live."

"But the mother, Melissa, refused to believe it," Alex added, recalling his mental notes from the interview. "She never believed that her child was going to die."

"No, she didn't," Peter agreed. "Then the Lord told her in a dream to come here. She hadn't seen any of the media coverage; Melissa had no way of knowing who I was or what was going on at Parkersboro."

"Faith," Alex said. "Like all the rest of them, they come by and in faith. They believe, they hope, and some, like Melissa, claim that they absolutely knew that their prayers would be answered here."

"Melissa had no doubts." As Peter spoke, they quickened their pace a bit, both aware that their few moments of stolen serenity would soon be over. "She walked right in and picked me out. I hadn't really even begun to pray over Britney, I don't think I'd gotten out a full sentence, when the child started laughing."

"What was it she said?" Alex asked.

"She said, 'Mommy, it tickles.'"

"People will most certainly allege that we doctored the film on that one, Peter." In fact, Alex Anderson was quite sure that all of his footage would be challenged by skeptics, religious and scientific alike.

"It was unbelievable. I stopped praying and opened my eyes when Britney spoke, and I could see her lesions disappearing, fading away to nothing. The cancer, the evil, could not survive the power of her mother's faith."

"Are you saying you didn't heal her, Panos?" Alex phrased his question in such a way as to deliberately rekindle their on-going debate.

"I don't heal anyone, Alex. You should know that by now. The power of the Living God heals them."

"Yes, Peter, I do know that, but..." Alex was not allowed to finish his thought.

"No 'buts,' Alex," Peter said, as he stopped walking and firmly took hold of Alex's arm. "Britney's healing, perhaps even more than some others, should have been a lesson for you. She was healed at Parkersboro and not in Ohio only because the Lord wants to use the miracle for His purposes, not because I was here. They didn't need me at all."

"Are you trying to tell me something, my friend?" Alex said, looking down at the firm grip Peter had on his bicep.

"Most definitely, Alex. It's what I asked of you back at the estate. Do not glorify me or the brothers, glorify God. We are nothing, convenient and willing servants only. We neither seek, nor want, any credit or fame."

"And like I told you, Panos," Alex replied, as he reached out and grabbed Peter's arm to demonstrate his own emphasis. "It's not that easy. Like it or not, God chose you as His prophet, and in that role you are highly visible."

"I prefer the term 'messenger' it's more accurate and less presumptuous."

"Just be glad Larry didn't get his way," Alex shot back, smiling broadly. "Otherwise we'd be calling you St. Peter."

"Lord have mercy." Peter did not have the strength to argue about this for the hundredth time with Alex. Besides, Gail had opened the prison to the masses. It was time to do the Lord's work.

"I've been keeping a log, Panos," Larry said. "Since you returned from Atlanta, we've had three thousand six hundred and twenty visitors, not counting today's group. I'll bet there are five hundred or more people out there right now."

"Five hundred and thirty-one, as of ten minutes ago," Gail confirmed, as she walked up behind Larry and Kenny who, perched in chairs and sitting behind a portable picnic table, had become the unofficial greeting committee for the Parkersboro Federal Prison Camp and Sanctuary. Peter and Alex were standing directly behind them, nodding and saying hello to the people making their way inside.

"Miss McCorkle," Alex asked, "how have you been able to handle all of this activity? More than a bit unusual for a federal prison facility, wouldn't you agree?"

"By 'handle' I'm sure you mean, Mr. Anderson, how have I been able to keep the BOP regional office in Raleigh off of our backs? You'll have to ask Peter about that. Everyday now, I'm thoroughly amazed when I come to work and I still have a job. No, check that. I'm amazed that I'm not yet under arrest."

"Peter?" Alex asked.

All Panos did was point up at the sky and smile.

"We've had no complaints, and no contact beyond the routine with Raleigh," Gail explained. "We answer the phone, try to sound normal. I guess they don't watch television up there or read the newspapers."

"What would happen if one of your supervisors saw what was going on here, all these people moving in and out, the lack of security, etc.?" Alex knew the answer before he asked the question, but he wanted to quote Warden McCorkle accurately when the time came.

"Like I said, I'd be fired and probably arrested," Gail admitted. "Now ask me if that worries me in the least."

"Well, does it?"

"Everyday I get to see people healed of physical disease, mental anguish, every type of human suffering imaginable. No one leaves here the same, Mr. Anderson, everyone's faith is strengthened and hope renewed. So, as far as I'm concerned, I could care less about the BOP. God's got my back, I serve Him without reservation. I'm very blessed."

And with that Gail stepped away from Alex and Peter to help a child of five or so, whose body was obviously wracked by sickness to come over and shake Peter's hand. Peter did more than that, he picked up the frail youngster and gave him a hug and a kiss and said "God bless you" before returning him to his mother's arms.

"What time do the services begin, Brother Peter?" the attractive young mother asked.

"In about twenty minutes," Peter told her. "Just follow the crowd outside. You'll see the chairs all set up on the lawn in front of the porch."

"And what, may I ask, is the topic of your sermon today, Brother Peter," Gail teased sarcastically, noticing the flirtatious glances the young mother flashed his way.

"Humility," Peter sighed, "our constant and never-ending battle against the sin of pride. It seems to be that..."

Peter was interrupted in mid-sentence by a blood curdling scream, followed shortly by another. The pitch of each was distinct; it was obvious that the cries came from two different people.

Malik ran into the lobby, Saul was right behind him.

"Mr. Pete, sir. Come quick, bro. We need you outside." The look on Malik's face conveyed imminent danger. Saul was white as a sheet.

In the few seconds it took for Peter to exit the administration building and scramble outside, the screams continued, as did other sounds of general distress. When Peter reached a vantage point from where he could see the stage, he gasped in horror at the scene laid out before him.

A prisoner no one had ever paid much attention to, Warren Sutton, was standing near the rostrum covered in blood. At his feet lay the bodies of two inmates, a pair that had neither embraced, nor were openly hostile to, the spiritual revival at Parkersboro. Both of the dead men had been horribly mutilated, no doubt by the very large and bloody knife Warren was holding in his right hand.

Warren's left arm was wrapped around a little girl of no more than three. She appeared to be too traumatized to scream, her eyes as big as saucers, and fixed on the blade Warren was dangling a few inches from her face.

"Saul?" Peter asked.

"Oh yeah. I'm sure it's our old pal Legion. He's brought company, too. They've come in force." Saul kept close to Peter, using him as a shield against that which frightened him to the depths of his soul.

"Panos Kallistos." Warren, or rather what used to be Warren, spoke in a low and guttural manner completely unlike Sutton's usual mid-range Southern twang.

"Put the child down. Now!" Peter ordered.

"Panos Kallistos. You have no idea what you are doing," the demon said. "You are a child playing with matches, and if you are not careful, you will burn the whole house down."

"I said in the name of Christ, release the child!" Peter's rage was evident; his righteous anger directed at his only true enemy, Satan.

Warren's face then began to change, to twist into a series of hideous, fleshly masks. He began to shake and drool. His skin turned an odd shade of dull purple as if his entire body had become one giant bruise. But he did not let go of the child.

The crowd, that to this point had backed off but had not yet fled, now became a herd of skittish sheep. Most of them scattered in all directions, but more than a few remained, their curiosity and fascination being greater than their fear.

"Kallistos, you are so green. Such a f***ing lap dog. Do you think Christ is the only power in this universe, or even on this pathetic little planet? You s*** eating monkeys are so proud of yourselves! How little you really know." Warren's face twisted in a series of bizarre distortions as he spoke.

"You cannot defy Christ, of that I am completely sure."

As Peter said this, he slowly approached the stage, moving directly toward the sickening, knife-wielding creature that had once been Warren Sutton. Before he reached the edge of the platform he was met by Malik and Gail, who both restrained him.

"Let me at him, Mr. Pete. I'll send him back to hell for sure." Malik's usual mild countenance was gone, murderous blood-lust now filled his eyes.

"If you go up there, you'll do it with me riding on your back, kicking and screaming." There was no way that Gail McCorkle was going to let Peter walk into that kind of peril. She'd die first, gladly.

The demon said nothing, but emerging from behind him, visible to all, arose a swarm of hundreds of indistinct, misty black shapes whose forms were surely not human. A stench like that from an open sewer now wafted from Warren as he danced the blade of his knife around the girl's head goading Peter, daring him to approach.

Peter took a step back and Malik and Gail released him. Then he put an arm around each of his beloved friends.

"Do you trust me?" Peter asked.

"That's not fair, Peter, I mean…" Peter cut Gail off.

"Do you both trust me?" Peter repeated. "Do you believe that I know what I'm doing, that God is leading me?"

As Peter spoke, the fury in Malik's eyes was replaced by his normal gentleness and he smiled. He understood.

"Yes sir, Mr. Pete. I trust you with my life and with my soul." Malik then stepped to his left and put Warden McCorkle in a tender, yet very firm, bear hug.

Gail could see what was happening and she panicked. Her thoughts were of her holy mission, of Gabriel's charge to her to lay down her life for her brother. She did her best to try and free herself from Malik, but that was an impossibility for anyone even twice her size.

"Mr. Pete, do what you gotta do," Malik said, tightening his delicate but unbreakable embrace around Gail McCorkle's waist.

Peter softly touched Gail's cheek and said to her, "Don't be afraid." Then he turned and faced the demon. He simultaneously began to speak and walk.

"In the name of Christ, I command you to put that child down. You cannot resist the power of the Living God." Peter repeated this phase three times before he reached a point about two feet away from his enemy, where he stopped.

Peter then closed his eyes and began to pray, audibly but not distinctly. He reached his hands upward summoning the Power.

Legion was in agony. The Force brought forward by Peter's prayer was tormenting him. Through the body of Warren Sutton, he let loose shouts and curses that sounded as if they came from a thousand different voices. Sutton's face, indeed his whole body, now pulsed and phased between horrible images of hellish creatures.

After a minute or so of this ghastly drama, Warren dropped both the knife and the child. When he did so his agony lessened. Malik then let go of Gail and swooped in, gathering up both the little girl and the knife in one motion and rushed them off the stage.

Peter continued to stand toe-to-toe with his adversary. They stared each other down like two warriors in a spiritual joust preparing to duel.

"Legion, leave that body you're in. It's not yours. Be gone and trouble us no more."

"You do not order me around like some pet, Kallistos. This human gave himself to me willingly. You do not control him."

Once more Peter offered a whispered plea and raised his arms toward heaven. Again the demon reacted as if he was being stretched and racked.

The mass of grey black mist creatures behind Legion then began to take the shape of a single organism, appearing as a deformed cross between an insect and a snake, a vision no doubt projected for the sole purpose of being ultimately nightmarish to the watching humans.

Warren was not really Warren anymore. His body had become a sickly bluish pupa with no limbs or other features other than the barest outline of a face on top of a throbbing cocoon of rank smelling, rotting flesh.

The black cloud then changed shape again. It became an evil, mutant cockroach as it engulfed what had been Warren, ingesting his remains, which by then were only a pus-filled, disgustingly grotesque bag of skin.

Peter did not move during Legion's spectacle. He neither cowered nor flinched, showing no fear.

"We will not let you open their eyes, Kallistos." Legion spoke now in a clear voice filled with rage. "You will be crushed along with your pathetic attempts to save your kind. Your God is nothing but a puffed up meddler, we control the destiny of this world. We are supreme."

Peter remained immovable, steadfast in the face of evil. He projected a sober confidence, a surety in the power of Christ to deliver him.

"Be Gone!" Peter demanded, his voice miraculously amplified ten fold.

Legion could no longer resist. The black cloud collapsed into itself, like filthy wash water pouring down the drain. As the last of the demons disappeared, a loud pop was heard, as if a jar had been resealed.

No trace of Warren remained. Neither was there any evidence of Warren's two stabbing victims. No audio, film, or still picture of any of these events survived. Every record was erased, right down to the BOP files, which now showed that Warren Sutton and the two dead inmates had never been assigned to Parkersboro, and had all died elsewhere. However, the memories of all those present were intact.

Once they were certain that Legion was gone, people began to reassemble around the porch. Peter conferred with the disciples and took stock of the situation.

After a few minutes, the crowd's collective conversations rose to a roar. Peter held up his hands, asking for quiet.

"Brothers and sisters," Peter began, "what you saw here today was the very face of our enemy. Take heed, friends! Satan is real and it is through his power alone that violence, hatred, sickness, indeed even death itself plagues our earthly home."

"We were put here by God to defeat evil, to triumph over the devil and his kind, and by doing so unite ourselves with our Creator."

"Rational men will tell you that what happened here today was some delusion or a trick. Do not be fooled! All of man's accumulated wisdom, scientific, social, economic, all of it, is without value if it is not placed in the context of spiritual warfare."

Those present were no longer afraid, they were captivated. Peter knew he had a rare opportunity in the aftermath of the confrontation with Legion to teach, to reach some souls who might otherwise be forever dead to the truth.

Alex got his cameras rolling again. The other journalists, who were sprinkled in amongst the crowd, now stopped trying to figure out why their equipment had malfunctioned and focused instead on recording Peter's sermon.

"Satan does not want Christ's message to reach you. We all heard the demon, he dares brag that he 'will not let us' open your eyes. My dear brothers and sisters, be certain of this; Satan cannot stop you from seeking and finding God, he cannot keep you from the loving arms of Christ! The devil is a liar and a coward. As our Lord said, Satan is indeed the father of all lies, and was a murderer from the beginning.

"So, let us now do the Master's work and not be distracted or deterred by the enemy. Those among you who believe and came in faith seeking deliverance from suffering, let you now receive according to your faith."

The seven disciples then formed a circle and began to pray. They gave thanks for their many blessings and for the privilege of being the human instruments guiding God's mighty hand on this glorious day.

It was then that the shouts of joy began erupting. "I can hear! Praise God, I can hear!" screamed a young boy as he hugged his mother. Alex's cameras quickly shifted their attention to the crowd and away from Peter and his men.

They filmed an older Asian gentleman, who was holding out his hands in front of him, turning them over left and right in fascination. He carefully examined his arms and fingers, his legs and his feet, as if he had never seen them before. Until a few seconds earlier he had not. The man looked up at Peter and wept in reverent thanksgiving.

More shouts came from the crowd. "I can walk!" "My pain is gone!" "I am healed!" Alex captured all of these miracles on film. No one present was expressing any disappointment; the Lord had turned no one away on this day. It was a gathering not witnessed for almost two thousand years, as God, for His purposes, poured out His healing grace in a very open and profound demonstration of His power and glory.

Gail came up from behind Peter, touched his arm and kissed him on the cheek.

"Thank you, brother," Gail said. "Thank you for letting me see this, to be a witness to something so perfect."

"My dear, sweet Gail," Peter responded, returning her kiss, "as Christ told Nathanael when He called him to His service, you will see greater things than these."

"It's just cool enough to enjoy a fire," Julie said, as she refilled Peter and Gail's wineglasses. "A Carolina beach on a June night is a beautiful thing."

"Brings back memories, Jules," Peter said, as he methodically stirred the flames with a skinny, green tree limb. "Great ones. Don't think I don't remember."

"Listen, if you two need to be alone I can just..."

"No, Gail. Stay. We're talking about history, not current events." As Peter spoke, Julie frowned and looked away.

By God's grace they had made it all the way to the eighteenth of June. Alex was incredulous. He simply could not believe that with all the media attention Peter and Parkersboro had received over the past few weeks that some governmental authority, Federal or State or whomever, hadn't shut them down.

For weeks now, Parkersboro had ceased to be a prison and had in effect become an outdoor cathedral. Gail's staff stopped doing head counts or taking roll calls, some officers didn't even bother to show up for work. Inmates came and went as they pleased. As of ten days ago, Warden McCorkle hadn't even bothered to file her required daily BOP reports. She quit doing so primarily because she could no longer in good conscience lie to her superiors, nor did she see any further need to do so.

"I've got it right here, Panos," Alex announced, as he stepped out of the blackness and into the firelight. "It's a pretty thick file for only a few weeks time."

Alex sat down on one of the portable beach chairs that were set up around the fire and Julie brought him a glass of Merlot.

"Everything at the camp is in order," Alex told them. "The remote truck pulled up an hour ago, so our satellite uplink is secure. The network crew just called me on the cell. They had a question I couldn't answer though."

"Which was?" Gail asked.

"Where are all the inmates?"

"We were just talking about that, Mr. Anderson," Gail said, flashing a sly grin at Peter. "Did they say how many are still there?"

"You mean you don't know, Warden McCorkle?" Alex was amazed by the total disregard Gail seemed to have for her soon to be former job responsibilities. "They said maybe a hundred, roughly."

"That's about right," Peter chimed in. "Something like half of the men have faith and would not miss tomorrow for anything."

"And the other half, Warden?" Alex asked.

"Escaped, gone, AWOL, whatever. Mr. Anderson, I could care less about them. If they could live through what we've all lived through, see what we've seen, and still not believe, which means they'd have to stay, then I say God bless them and I wish them well."

"You know, Warden, when the Feds up in Raleigh finally wake up, none of this will amuse them. Odds are you'll become an inmate yourself."

"That is probably true, Mr. Anderson," Gail agreed. "And if it comes to pass, then so be it. I can no longer be part of returning evil for evil anyway. No Christian can in good conscience run a human zoo."

"Can I quote you on that, Warden?" Alex prodded.

"Of course."

"If you two are quite finished chattering," Peter teased, "I'm interested in learning what the press has been saying about us."

"Like I said, Panos, it is a thick file. Maybe I should…"

"Maybe you should just read to us, Alex. I don't need a full briefing, a highlight reel is more than sufficient." Peter settled in next to Julie on the blanket and slowly sipped his wine.

"Fine by me. Let's take it by geographic location," Alex decided, as he shuffled through his folder.

"From the Atlanta paper, five days ago. 'This reporter has confirmed that three Atlanta area residents, who prefer to remain anonymous, all with confirmed terminal illness diagnoses traveled last week to the Parkersboro Federal Prison Camp facility near Georgetown, South Carolina, hopeful of realizing a miracle cure. This minimum security prison camp has attracted considerable attention recently, since an inmate there, Mr. Peter Carson, shook up the authorities with his role in the much publicized and bizarre outing and suicide of Georgia Superior Court Judge Harmon Grove. Subsequent to this incident, claims of miraculous medical cures have streamed out of Parkersboro, along with other incredible stories including demonic apparitions and even the raising of the dead."

"Let's see," Alex went on, "blah, blah, blah, okay. 'This paper has independently substantiated that the three people in question have indeed been completely freed of all traces and symptoms of their respective maladies, which in two cases were advanced stages of cancer (lung and liver) and in the other a rare and fatal congenital heart disorder. In each instance, the patient attributes the healing to Mr. Peter Carson and the prayers of him and his "disciples" at the camp. Both the patients' physicians and our own doctors hired to verify the claims have no explanation as to the cause of the symptom remissions.' Blah, blah, blah. The Atlanta paper has run five stories on us in the past five weeks, all pretty much the same as this one."

"What a dry account of such an extraordinary thing," Julie observed.

"True enough," Peter agreed, "but, regardless, the word is getting out."

"No doubt about that," Alex said, as he pulled another group of documents from his stack. "This one is interesting. It struck me as significant because it comes from a D.C. newspaper. I didn't know that anyone up there was paying much attention to us yet."

"Dateline June Second. The headline reads, *Finding Christ Amidst The Sinners?* The reporter's name is Art Davenport."

"I remember that dweeb," Gail recalled. "Smallish little mealy mouthed dude. Walked around with a major bad attitude and a tape recorder. Had to resist the urge to slap him across the face a couple of times."

"Gail," Peter chided. "I hope you're exaggerating."

"No, Panos, I'm not. The little punk deserves it, needs it in fact. Sorry if I sound un-Christian, brother, but I remain convinced that a serious butt whipping can do more good for some men than any prayer or church service ever could."

"Violence is never the answer, Gail," Peter admonished. "But I hear what you're saying. Some people invite retribution through their ignorance and rudeness."

"Anyway," Alex continued, "Mr. Davenport was not impressed by us or our claims. Blah, blah, blah. Let me start here. 'This reporter interviewed several inmates not associated with Mr. Carson's cadre. They hold firm to the belief that Peter Carson and his friends are running an elaborate con game at Parkersboro. While they could offer no direct proof to support their theory, two of these inmates reported seeing Mr. Carson and his associates receiving large envelopes full of cash from prospective miracle seekers. They also believe that some of these funds made their way to the prison staff, including to Warden Gail McCorkle.'"

"Why that little, lying piece of garbage. I ought to …"

"You ought to what, Gail?"

"I ought to forgive him and pray for him."

"That's more like it," Peter said. "Do not play the devil's game. Don't let these fools get the best of you, sister."

"Davenport wasn't finished," Alex said, as he continued his selective reading from the story. "Parkersboro is in fact a federal prison now in name only. Inmates are not restrained to the prison grounds, or even properly accounted for. The staff, with considerable help from Mr. Carson's dedicated group of 'disciples,' is entirely focused on the religious revival taking place there. Normal prison routines and functions are non-existent. For the entire two days this reporter spent at Parkersboro, I witnessed a corrections facility that has become an ad hoc spiritual festival with hundreds of attendees from various parts of the country mingling freely with the prisoners. Families who came to Parkersboro to see and hear Mr. Carson preach and had nowhere else to stay were given bunks in the prison dorms and fed meals in the cafeteria."

"Didn't know you did that, Gail," Peter said, breaking in. "What a wonderful act of charity. Well done."

"I couldn't just let them sleep in their cars. You saw some of them, Peter. More than a few of those families had no food, no money, no anything. Why it was…"

"Can I finish, please?" Alex asked impatiently.

"Sorry," Peter and Gail apologized, as one.

"It seems apparent to this reporter that by some method of persuasion, Mr. Carson has, in effect, as a federal inmate, taken complete control of Parkersboro prison. However benevolent his intentions for doing so may be, this is an unprecedented event and is perhaps the aspect of this story most deserving of attention by the public and the Federal Bureau of Prison authorities."

"Didn't Mr. Dweeb call the BOP region, or the D.C. office?" Gail asked.

"He did. According to the story they refused comment."

"So this is how it's going, one story sympathetic or at least open minded, the next skeptical or completely negative?" Peter wanted to be sure he had an accurate sense of the general media climate.

"I'd say that's a fair assessment, Panos," Alex confirmed. "Some of the articles in the small town papers are fantastic. No butt is covered or axe is ground in those pieces. The folks who came to Parkersboro were pretty much allowed to speak for themselves with no editorial filter. The large papers, Charlotte, Columbia, Raleigh, Richmond, are at best neutral, 'dry' as Julie put it, or openly hostile. Should I keep reading?"

"No, Alex," Peter said. "That's enough. Nothing you've said in any way comes as a surprise."

"Want to hear about the magazine articles or the local television coverage?"

"No, my friend, I leave those things in your most capable hands."

"What is all that commotion?" Gail wondered, nervously scanning the few yards of beach she could see in the darkness.

Soaking wet from the waist down Saul came stumbling up to the fire. Larry and Kenny were right behind him, also covered in salt water and sand and panting heavily. "Have you boys been playing in the mud again?" Gail mocked in her best "mad mommy" tone.

"Yes ma'am," Saul answered meekly, playing along. "And we got our school clothes all dirty too."

"Look out! Here he comes!" Kenny yelled.

Two hundred and seventy-five pounds of black muscle then lumbered up from the gloom and grabbed Saul and Larry. Using one arm for each, Malik hoisted his two brothers up by their heels, all the while giggling like a sixth grader.

"These little white boys think theys tough, Mr. Pete. Down there by the water they jumped me. Gonna teach 'em a lesson, for real." And with that Malik turned and carried his "victims" back down to the ocean, no doubt to be duly "punished" for their insolence.

"I better follow them, Panos," Kenny said. "Make sure no one gets hurt. Still got some sodas up here?"

Gail handed Kenny four cold bottles of pop from the cooler. Then he disappeared in the general direction of the surf, following after the laughter and the less than compelling cries for mercy.

"What about Jose and Tim? Where are they spending the night?" Alex wanted to know, making himself comfortable by the fire.

"They said that they had some things to do, calls to make," Peter said, as he continued to slowly stir the embers. "Those two are never very far apart, you know that. I have no doubt they'll join us here in the morning or sooner."

Then for a few minutes no one spoke. All that could be heard was the gentle roll of the surf, the popping of the fire as the green wood mildly exploded, and a few distant squeals of delight from the "boys" who, despite having been at it for over two hours, did not seem yet to be tired of their childlike games.

Peter broke the silence.

"Walk with me?" he asked Julie.

Julie didn't say a word, but rather stood and offered her hand. Peter took it and they made their way down to the water line and headed south, away from Malik and his playmates. After a couple of minutes worth of a casual stroll they were alone.

"Jules, I just wanted to make sure that you and Kevin are prepared. I know we haven't had a chance to talk much since you got here. All of this is so ... I don't know, Jules."

"Crazy?" Julie offered.

"I'll accept that. Did you get Walter's check? You guys set up?"

"Yes, but I feel guilty about taking his money, Peter. I don't believe I came by it honestly."

"He did sign the pre-nuptial agreement, didn't he?"

"Yes, yes he did. But Peter, you know I never loved that man. I used him. He was a convenient means of getting what I wanted, nothing more. God forgive me."

"And you think he was the only one in the relationship being used? Come on, Jules. You're many things, naïve isn't one of them."

"What else am I, Peter?" Julie asked. She stopped walking and took both of his hands and placed them gently on her shoulders. She looked up at Peter longingly, hoping to stir in him something near the burning desire she was feeling at that moment, indeed at every moment when she found herself alone with him.

Memories flooded back in both their minds, the remembrance of a physical relationship that was for both of them close to perfection. It was a powerful allure and impossible to ignore.

"You, my dear," Peter answered the only woman who would ever be his wife, "are the most beautiful creature God ever created."

They shared a deep and long kiss. It was an expression of affection and desire long overdue between two people so passionately in love.

For a few minutes kisses and cuddling sufficed. But Julie had much more on her mind and she was determined not to waste this rare opportunity.

She took a step away from Peter and slowly undid the buttons of her blouse and unclasped her bra. In an instant she was bare from the waist up.

Solomon's Porch

Peter was helpless. He could no longer resist. As he reached out his hand to touch his wife, to give her what they both wanted, a voice clear and strong rang out in his head.

"I did not save you for this."

On the eve of the biggest day of his life, God reminded Peter of the absolute necessity for focus and self-control. The message could not have been more unwelcome, but it was heeded nonetheless.

"Julie," Peter whispered, as he kissed his wife again and slowly rebuttoned her blouse. "I can't do this. Please believe me, I want nothing more. I love you, I'm on fire for you. There will never be another woman for me."

In the low light, Peter could see the tears start to cascade down Julie's cheeks.

"Why do you keep breaking my heart, Peter?" Julie sobbed. "We were meant for each other. Don't tell me this isn't right. I know it is."

"God does not want me thinking about you Julie, putting you ahead of Him. We are most certainly right, but the time is not."

"Why can't we both put Him first and still be together? You know I'd marry you again tonight, right here, right now, if you asked me."

It was time. He'd kept the truth from her for too long. She deserved better.

"Jules, I'm not getting out of this alive. There is absolutely no possibility of a future for us. I'm very sorry, but I've known this was going to happen for a long time."

"Peter, how do you know this?"

"Trust me, Jules, I know."

"I don't believe it. I won't believe it. God wants you dead? That does not sound like the Christ you preach, Peter."

"Through my death, many will come to Him. I am an example, Julie. He has a plan. I'm only an instrument in it."

"Do the others know?"

"No, and you must not tell them. They have to do their part, fulfill their roles. Knowing that I'm going to be killed would only be a distraction. Satan would use their feelings for me against them."

"As you must believe the devil is doing to me."

"It's not the same thing for you and me. We were once one flesh, Julie. In many ways we always will be, Kevin is proof enough of that. What you want, what I want, isn't wrong, Jules. The problem is it conflicts with His will. We serve God, He does not serve us."

"You're trying to tell me ..."

"I'm trying to tell you that if we made love and became one flesh again, God knows I might not be able to leave you and Kevin behind. I'm a human being, Jules, not a machine."

"Peter."

"Yes."

"I will never marry or make love to another man ever again."

"I know, Jules, I know. I'm so sorry."

"Don't be. I need to quit asking you to do something that can't be done. I'm so weak, Peter. Help me to learn how to trust, to believe like you do."

"After tomorrow, Jules, it should become easier for you."

"Do you believe that, I mean really believe that?"

"Yes. Once everything happens it will become impossible for any one of us to give as much thought to our own lives."

They held each other on the beach for an hour or more kissing, talking, watching the tide roll in. Both of them knew that this was very likely to be their last peaceful night together away from the crush of the waiting world's attention, for in less than twenty-four hours, both man and his institutions would be humbled by the power of the Living God. For a humanity that had become too proud of itself, too certain of its own preeminent place in the universe, too convinced of its own ability to understand and explain its existence apart from God, the lessons to come would not be well received. Especially by those with the most to lose, should mankind turn away from darkness and toward the Light.

Alone among the seven, Peter understood the totality of the consequences. His faith in God was unshakable, but he was also very aware that his fellow human beings had been given free will. Would the creatures God created in His "image and likeness" come together and transform the earth into the paradise it should be? Or would the evil one succeed in defeating them through their fear, greed, and pride?

Tomorrow the die would be forever cast. Nothing would ever be the same again.

Sixteen

For all but a few of the billions of people that call the earth home, this June nineteenth was like any other. An ordinary, midyear day; nothing special. The world continued to endure its miseries, the persistent plagues of greed, violence, hunger, and disease. In the developed countries, these problems were masked by social stability and economic prosperity, although even there, just under the surface, widespread need and desperation existed like dirt swept under the rug. Those souls unfortunate enough to be born in less affluent societies suffered more openly and severely.

Yet it could not be honestly said that the human race had remained in some stagnant backwater over time. Material life was improving; unevenly, but steadily. However skewed and at times chaotic, humanity appeared to be moving forward, judging progress by overall quality of life standards.

Why then was God so concerned? Why the need for such radical changes? Why act so boldly now, versus fifty years ago, or two hundred years in the future?

These were questions Peter had asked many times and in many different ways over the past year. Were we really doing such a poor job of governing ourselves? Had we strayed that far off of His course?

As Peter knelt and prayed alone in the trees behind the camp on this morning that would change all mornings he still found himself struggling with these issues. He knew better than to second guess God, he wasn't even remotely trying to do that, but he was very much aware that the course He was about to set was in many ways an extreme departure from the one that had yielded such widespread benefits for so many for so long.

He listened as he prayed. There was a stillness in the woods, and all Peter could hear in his secluded spot a few hundred yards away from Parkersboro was the sound of a trickling wind flowing through the trees. Peter indulged himself in the solitude, seeking to focus his mind and his spirit as much as possible. He knew that very soon any amount of peace would be a precious commodity.

It was during these times the Lord made Himself known to Peter, usually not audibly or visually, but rather through the influence of ideas and Scripture.

Part of the answer to Peter's question was simple, if not intellectually satisfying; God is omniscient and His ways are known only to Him. His will be done and by definition, His will is what's best for His creation. Man is not God, he cannot see the outcomes God can see, the results of a continuation of business-as-usual on planet earth.

Peter also knew that it was not his mission to debate the issues of the day with others on man's terms. He was not called to be another voice in the crowd, trying to be heard above the roar.

While few could see it, and fewer still would accept it, the future, if there was to be one, had to be ordered differently than the past. Incremental change over time, building slowly on successes, while suffering through painful mistakes, taking two steps forward and one back, this was no longer a viable option for the standard method of human progress.

The Spirit taught Peter that the dynamics of life on earth were changing. Self-centered materialism and violence as the primary means of political and economic control were rapidly reaching their limits as effective social systems. In many ways, as Peter knew by both reasoning and revelation, humanity was "pushing on a string," living in the reflected glow of its past achievements, not realizing the dangers lying directly ahead.

He wondered, if left to his own devices, how long would it be before man fell victim to his arrogance? Before a disciple of hell installed by Satan as a dictator in some small third world nation decided it was time to trigger a nuclear or a biological war? Horrific weapons of all kinds were becoming available to more and more societies, control by America and its allies over Armageddon was now only an illusion.

When would the strain on the planet's finite natural resources, sought after by millions more every year as their economic power increased, reach the breaking point? Would Europe and America eventually be forced to go to war to maintain their control over the world's energy and food supplies?

Peter thought about the ecosystem, the treasure of the earth over which man was made steward. If present trends continued, how much longer would it be before the sons of Adam trashed their home?

Why should most North Americans and Europeans be able to live comfortably with plenty of food, housing and medical care while in Africa, Asia, and South America millions died each year for want of the basic necessities of life? Peter asked himself, would resentment by the less fortunate eventually lead to global economic collapse or large scale destruction?

Peter did not pretend to have an encyclopedic knowledge of these issues. He knew that he was not called to be a political leader, a captain of industry, or a scientist. He grasped the fundamentals of worldly matters as God gave him the power to do so, more was not required.

What Peter Carson was most certainly called to do was to try and change the very nature of how man viewed himself and his place in the universe. From this change would eventually flow the solutions to every specific problem faced by humanity.

"Christ give me strength," Peter prayed. He'd been repeating this request, along with the Lord's Prayer, for over an hour when Gail found him standing in the woods, eyes closed, head bowed, body still.

"Peter," Gail whispered, as she slowly approached him. "Peter, it's time. Alex asked me to come and get you."

"Do you think anyone will listen, Gail?" Peter gently asked, his eyes still shut, head lowered.

Confused, Gail said, "Will who listen, Peter?"

"Our kind, the sea of souls breathing along with us right now. Will they listen? Will they open their hearts and minds to Him?"

"I don't know, Peter, I truly don't. People can be so stubborn and prideful. Getting them to show love to one another, to really do that, won't be easy."

"We have to make them see, Gail," Peter said, as he took her hand in his, "that we're running out of time. God is making Himself known now for a reason. He wants to save us, but we must come to Him."

Gail realized that she'd interrupted Peter as he was deep in thought and prayer. She did not want to intrude, knowing how valuable such moments were to him.

"Peter, let me go and tell Alex you need a few more minutes. Honestly, that man is in such a snit today! Ordering me and everyone else around like his very own slaves. I mean..."

"It's okay, Gail," Peter said, lovingly squeezing her hand. "Alex is only doing his job. For all of our sakes, pray I can do mine."

Beginning at noon Eastern Time, on June nineteenth, the network ran a series of promotional ads for a program it was airing that evening called "Miracles at Parkersboro." In the spots, Alex Anderson, proclaimed as "one of America's most respected journalists" promised to "bring to the world irrefutable evidence of the existence and power of the Living God." Doing a voice over on top of a tape of people receiving healing miracles at Parkersboro, Alex said, "Tonight the words of the prophet Isaiah will be fulfilled as the Lord will again do a marvelous work among the people, a marvelous work and a wonder: For the wisdom of their wise men shall perish, and the understanding of their prudent shall be hidden." The promos were not hyped by slick production, special effects, or a thumping soundtrack. Their spectacular claims were made without any added theatrics.

The executives at the network did not carefully review the proposed program content or the promotional material for "Miracles at Parkersboro." They were so accustomed to trusting both the instincts and the judgment of Alex Anderson, that they let the first few spots run without paying much attention.

It wasn't very long before they regretted that decision.

E-mails and phone calls began pouring into the network. Many asked if the whole thing was a joke, most thought it had to be. Some said if the program was an attempt at humor, it was done in "damn poor taste." An atheist group demanded equal

Solomon's Porch

251

time, even though the program had yet to air. An Episcopal bishop wanted an "accounting" for "this affront to our faith," for this "bombasity." Three quarters of the initial pre-show reactions received by the network in the afternoon were negative. A raw public nerve had been struck.

For another very special group of people, numbering in the millions and spread out across the globe, the announcement of the "Miracles at Parkersboro" program solved a mystery.

For months the Spirit had been planting seeds among the select, making them aware in various ways that God was about to speak and act in a very direct and dramatic fashion.

Some of the select were already Christians, although many were not. They were a cross section of the human race, diverse in every respect. A few held positions in a religious hierarchy, or were socially prominent in some way, but most were ordinary human beings living out their lives in seeming indistinction.

But the select were anything but typical, for without their tremendous faith and courage, the Lord's works done through Peter and the disciples would be in vain. They were God's army, His foot soldiers in the battle for the human soul. "Miracles" was their siren call.

Most of the select had the exact same dream as the disciples did. They clearly saw seven men standing in a circle and praying with "tongues" of fire emanating from their heads. Many could only remember parts of the dream. Others deciphered virtually all of the clues and were entirely convinced that what they were dreaming was a prophetic vision of what was certain to come.

Without exception, what all of the select did have in common was a knowledge, a complete and total surety, that they were chosen by God to undertake some as yet unknown mission. Each of them also knew that His purpose for their lives would be announced by the passage Alex quoted in the spots from the book of Isaiah, only they did not know this until they actually heard the verse being read. This was the trigger that set their new lives in motion.

Spread out across the earth in every country willing, but also anxious, souls who had been in a quandary for weeks or months, somehow positive that they were being sent a message from Above, but not at all sure what it meant and even less sure what to do about it, all of a sudden experienced clarity.

Within a few hours the word was being disseminated planet wide. Husbands told their wives, parents told their children, complete strangers recognized that "certain look" and stopped each other on the street and shared Isaiah's words.

The selects' reaction upon hearing the good news was always the same, "Thank you, God." They were both relieved and energized.

Those in North America and Europe had access to the "Miracles" program through satellite or cable television. Quickly and quite illegally, thousands of computer savvy select made plans to pirate the network signal through a variety of means and feed the broadcast on to the web. By the early evening of June the nineteenth, an internet search using the keywords "Parkersboro" or "Isaiah" resulted in hundreds of hits on websites set up to carry "Miracles" as a live web cast.

Neither Alex nor Peter had planned any of this, but both knew that God intended His message to be heard by all. As word reached them that thousands, or perhaps hundreds of thousands, or even millions of souls were somehow already primed to receive His word, they were greatly encouraged, but not very surprised.

"What exactly did they say?" Gail asked, as she continued to pack up the personal belongings in her office.

"If I can remember, Miss McCorkle, it was, 'What the hell is going on down there?' or something close to that," Larry answered.

"Did you tell them who you were?"

"Yes ma'am," Larry said. "The lady from Washington wanted to know my name and employee I.D. number. She got real upset when I said I only had a BOP inmate number. I think they're coming down here, Miss McCorkle, a whole bunch of them."

"Let them, Larry. Peter says we don't have to worry about the Feds or anyone else being able to stop the broadcast. Afterwards, well, it just doesn't matter now, does it?"

"No ma'am, I don't think it does."

By the early evening of the nineteenth, preparations were nearly complete. For the first time in weeks, Parkersboro was actually secure, albeit not in a manner prescribed by the authorities.

Malik's trusted group of young black Christian soldiers formed a human perimeter around the camp. Armed only with two way radios and cell phones, it was their job to turn away any uninvited guests using the power of persuasion only, not violence. Anyone approaching Parkersboro through the woods would be very intimidated when they reached this wall of large athletic men. Peter assured Malik that their presence alone would be enough to stave off any trouble or intruders, at least until it no longer mattered.

General Vargas and Agent Austin were in charge of gathering intelligence outside of Parkersboro and implementing any necessary delaying tactics. Inmates were posted in Georgetown at key intersections and around the public safety building. Local law enforcement channels were monitored. When the police came, as they surely would, this basic but effective system would give them at least some advance warning of their approach.

There is only one way in and out of Parkersboro: a five hundred yard long, two lane access road that branches off of South Carolina route sixteen and ends at the camp. On each side of this road are thick stands of trees that extend for a mile or more in each direction. General Vargas was quick to point out the potential effectiveness of a substantial barrier placed on the road fifty yards down from its intersection with the highway.

At eight p.m. sharp, this barrier went up, or rather went over. Three yellow school buses appropriated for the Lord's use from the local district transportation yard were tipped on to their sides creating a serious roadblock. Strategically placed cans of gasoline among the toppled buses threatened to turn the steel obstruction into a flaming one on command. Once lit, it would take a large force of men and machines considerable time to remove the obstacle and penetrate the camp.

Nature was cooperating too, as the night was both temperate and dry. A hint of a new moon peeked above the horizon after sunset. The air was tranquil and kept fresh by a light breeze.

As the time for the broadcast neared, a harried Alex Anderson was put even more under the gun. His crew of twenty had to do the work of forty. Production was being done on-site, and largely on the fly. He had thirty minutes of tape to fold into his live narration and the final segment. He was revising his script continuously, deleting this, adding that. Through it all, the fact that his journalistic career, and perhaps even his freedom or his life, would soon be over weighed heavily upon his mind.

Unlike Gail McCorkle, Alex did not have the option of turning off his phone and ignoring the outside world. Executives at the network were livid, they felt Alex had blindsided and personally betrayed them. In the late afternoon, the decision was made to kill the show, but then the cooler head of the Vice President in Charge of Programming, Dave Martz, stepped in and pointed out that the huge number of comments and complaints received by the network in response to the promotional spots indicated an enormous potential audience. Despite the risks, quite considerable all the network execs agreed, of running a program so openly controversial, Martz overrode the decision to cancel and actually increased the promotion for the show.

Alex knew where he stood. Martz pulled no punches when they briefly spoke around five p.m. Alex had "deliberately deceived" the network by using his stature to slide in the promos, and therefore, by extension, the broadcast, because he "knew damned well" that the "inflammatory nature of the content" would create a firestorm of debate. Martz made it clear that he intended to impale Alex on this two-edged sword; the network would blame Alex if "Miracles" was a catastrophe, and would take all of the credit if it were a hit.

"Either way," Martz told Alex, "you've ruined your reputation. I hope it was worth it." After Martz said this he hung up, not waiting for a reply.

Of course, it was beyond "worth it." Alex knew it was foolish to compare the loss of his career to the honor and privilege of delivering God's message to the world. Still, it was torturous for Alex Anderson to turn his back on his former life so abruptly and completely. He had worked very hard to become a preeminent journalist. Discarding a lifetime's worth of success in one night taught him the meaning of Christ's admonition that, "If anyone desires to come after Me let him deny himself, and take up his cross and follow Me."

As for Martz, he continued to feel the heat right up until airtime. Around eight forty-five p.m. an Assistant Attorney General from the Justice Department in Washington called him and threatened to prosecute the network if it aired the broadcast for "unauthorized use of a government facility," and "conspiracy to aid and abet a prison escape," and "anything else I can think of walking into the Grand Jury room." Martz countered by saying the network was a buyer of the program only, not the producer or the owner.

"Anderson Media Inc. is whom you should be bullying," he told the arrogant government lawyer. Martz came up through the ranks as a news reporter before he made it to the executive suite, so while he was angry as hell at Alex Anderson for manipulating him, never would he be a willing participant to any prior governmental restraint of a television broadcast. That such an affront to the Constitution was used as a threat only intensified Martz's determination to see the matter through, and further confirmed his gut instincts that Alex hadn't lost his mind, and therefore whatever he was planning had to be incredible.

As would later be much discussed, a series of unfortunate and unlikely coincidences from noon onward on the nineteenth delayed Federal police intervention. Everything from stalled vehicles to missing approvals, lost paperwork, misdirected communications; a virtual cornucopia of bureaucratic bungling got in the way. For whatever reasons, the rather straightforward task of sending in fifty or so heavily armed United States Marshals to restore order to a minimum security federal prison camp quickly became a debacle. In hindsight, no one could really say for sure just how it was possible that with nine hours advance notice, the most powerful government on earth was unable to secure a tiny piece of real estate in South Carolina.

"Good evening. My name is Alex Anderson. Tonight, those of us here at the Parkersboro Federal Prison Camp and all of you in the viewing audience shall witness history. For His reasons, and in His time, the Lord God through His son Jesus Christ has chosen this day to once again declare Himself to the world, to give hope to all of His creation."

"Since when is Anderson a Jesus freak?" Martz asked, as he monitored the broadcast from the network's main New York studios.

"Don't know, boss," a tech replied, "but if what his people are telling me is on the level, he might not be exaggerating."

"It was here, just over my right shoulder in fact, in a prison library less than one year ago, that a former stockbroker and convicted white collar felon, Mr. Peter Carson, was given a vision and called by Christ to lead a small group of disciples on a holy crusade. Through them, God has a message to deliver to each of us individually and to humanity as a whole. The men you will meet tonight have been chosen by the Lord to help us reach for the Light."

"What do you think, Peter?" Gail asked, looking over his shoulder at the video monitor. "Is Alex doing what you expected him to?"

"Everything is going according to plan," Peter answered. "The Spirit is strong here, Gail! Can you feel it? There is a Divine Energy all around us."

"I am not merely reporting on these events, I am a part of them. Jesus Christ has given me the great honor of being His spokesman, of sharing with you what I and many others have seen and heard. A prophet of the Lord has once again come among us, and like Moses before him, he will use His mighty power to perform signs and wonders in the sight of all men."

"What was that? I didn't catch that," the President said, as he reached for the remote control to turn up the television in the oval office.

"I think, sir," the aide replied, "that this Carson fellow is going to walk on some water."

The President and his two most senior advisors chuckled at the aide's quip. They were meeting tonight to discuss an energy bill that was stalled in the Senate. Someone in the group suggested that they "check out this wild program Alex Anderson was doing" as they ate a late dinner in between strategy sessions.

"That's your cue, Mr. Carson," the stage hand said. "Just walk on over and stand by Alex as we rehearsed."

Peter took a deep breath. His time had finally arrived. As soon as he stepped out in front of the cameras he knew that his fate was sealed. He rejoiced in the blessing of offering himself up as a sacrifice for Christ.

For a second, Peter glanced over his shoulder at the now dark prison library. A year ago his life had no meaning, he was broken and alone, a piece of garbage discarded by society with no hope. Then for some reason, the Power, the Force that created and sustains the universe, chose him to witness to the world. So much had happened since then. It was an impossible imagining that had become reality.

Peter felt the Holy Spirit move in him, quickening his mind and his physical senses. Like the original twelve of the Gospels, Peter Carson was now never alone; the Uncreated Energy that was God had become an inseparable part of his soul.

In a way difficult to precisely describe, Peter began to shine. Not like Gabriel did in his glorified state, but rather like a finely polished diamond reflecting sunlight. He was changed, not into a different person, but rather he became a more perfect version of himself.

Alex immediately noticed this transformation and was awed. As Peter walked toward him, he had trouble maintaining his composure, so overpowering was Peter's aura.

"Brothers and sisters," as Peter began to speak, many watching from in front of the porch fell to their knees in prayer, "my friends and I are here tonight for only one purpose, to witness to the world the power of the Living God, and through that witness to offer hope for the future, for without the Lord we shall have no future."

"What is it about this guy?" the President asked, in between bites of his sandwich and gulps of soda. "Is the TV on the fritz? He looks too bright or something."

The President's advisors and their aides agreed with grunts and nods. As political experts, the image on the screen had them transfixed, they sensed the ability of Peter Carson to grab and hold an audience. They were drawn to the Power like moths to a flame.

"Last July," Peter said, gesturing toward the library, "God blessed me with a vision. He made it clear that He has provided everything we need to prosper. Given His benevolence, the fact that millions suffer daily for lack of food, shelter, or medicine is inexcusable. That we continue to use violence and hatred as means of controlling ourselves is inexcusable. That most of us are only concerned with satisfying our own selfish passions and have no mercy for others is inexcusable. And, most of all, that after two thousand years few choose to truly embrace the Son of the Living God, to make him their Lord and Master, is inexcusable.

"But while this is true, it is also true that God loves us, all of us. He desires that we should succeed, that we should become the glorious images of Christ that he intended us to be. For this purpose, to help men see the Light, my brothers and I were called."

"I ask everyone who can hear and see me now to stop whatever it is that you are doing, take a minute and ask God to enlighten and strengthen you. Your prayers should be simple and short. If it helps, I'll get you started."

"Alright. Close your eyes and repeat after me: Lord have mercy on me a sinner. Help me to hear Your word and respond to Your call. Amen."

Martz looked over at his studio crew. More than half had bowed heads and closed eyes. "That's amazing," he mumbled, wondering if his small sample was indicative of a larger trend.

In the oval office the tone remained casual, but the pull from the television set was undeniable.

No one in the room was interested any longer in energy legislation or the remnants of dinner. The only thing that broke their attentive mood was a commercial.

"That's just not right," the aide said.

"What?" another one asked.

"Selling soap during this program. Seems almost blasphemous."

"That's America for ya. God bless Madison Avenue."

For the select, the vast majority of whom had managed through one means or another to tune into the broadcast, events were falling into place with unconscious expectations. The Divine seeds planted in them were germinating, breaking through the soil that had been their previous lives and reaching toward the Son.

Blessed to attend the broadcast at Parkersboro were around a hundred inmates and two hundred or so additional guests, some of whom were from the national and international media, others were people who had been healed or otherwise touched at Parkersboro during the past few weeks, and a few more were invited by God directly as part of His plan.

One of these invited guests was the powerful Roman Catholic Bishop of Boston, Cardinal Reardon. High officials from several mainline Protestant churches were also present, along with four Buddhist monks from Los Angeles, an Islamic Imam from Detroit, a conservative Jewish Rabbi from New York, and a Hindu Fakir from New Delhi.

Since the next twenty minutes of the program were tape with Alex doing voice-over narrations, Peter wasn't needed on the set, so he took this time to greet his religiously prominent guests.

"Mr. Carson, it's my pleasure to meet you sir," Cardinal Reardon said, extending his hand in friendship. "You are even more charismatic in the flesh than you were in my dreams."

"Cardinal?" Peter asked, looking for clarification.

"After talking with your Mr. Cohen and Mr. Graham, it appears that I had the same dream as they and many others did; the one where the seven of you are standing on a platform and are receiving the Holy Spirit."

"So you're here then because you've been called?"

"I'm here, Mr. Kallistos, to see my dream become a reality, to be a witness. I take it that you and the brothers will be praying in a circle right over there in a few minutes, or am I wrong?"

"Yes, your Excellency. You are not wrong."

"Praise God. These other gentlemen here with me have also shared this same dream."

Peter shook each man's hand in turn, humbly thanking them for honoring him by their presence.

"Mr. Carson," one of the Buddhist monks asked, in a pronounced Vietnamese accent, "I wonder, why did your God invite us? We are not Christians. This puzzles us, but we are most honored to be here with you and share in this experience."

"Unity, my brother," Peter answered. "God's flame, His eternal essence, burns in many spiritual men of various faiths. Your Buddha saw the Light through a tinted glass. God wishes to reveal Himself now to you directly, to add another spiritual layer to your knowledge, to make perfect your good works."

The monks said nothing as they slowly bowed. They believed Peter Carson was a Buddha, an "Enlightened One," and for now Peter would not dispel that or any other faith specific label given him by humble, God-seeking men. The Lord taught Peter to respect the spiritual traditions of others, and not to blindly discard all non-Christian theology as pagan or idolatrous. While, as Christ said, "salvation is of the Jews" because He came to the world through David's seed, God had not ignored the rest of non-Judeo-Christian humanity either before Jesus' birth and passion or since.

"Panos," the Cardinal said, as he gently touched Peter's arm, "permit me the honor of blessing and praying with you before you leave us."

"The honor is mine, Cardinal," Peter replied. "I know you are a righteous man."

After Reardon offered a short prayer in Latin, Peter looked over and saw Alex's stage crew motioning for him to return to the set.

"Acts, chapter two," the Cardinal said, as he gave Peter a holy kiss and sent him on his way.

The Rabbi looked curiously at Cardinal Reardon, asking him with his eyes to expound on his comment.

"Acts, chapter two, Rabbi Rosefielde. You are seeing another version of those momentous events here tonight."

"A second Pentecost?" the Rabbi asked.

"At least a type of one, my friend. I'm quite convinced that these gentlemen have already received the Holy Spirit."

"And Mr. Carson, you're saying he is like Cephas, Christ's Peter?"

"He is not St. Peter reincarnated, but rather a type of Peter, a new apostle."

"Then that stage up there, that must be Solomon's Porch. The area of our Temple where St. Peter gave his first sermon after the Pentecost."

"You know the New Testament well, Rabbi," the Cardinal complimented. "Yes, that's more than fitting. You've moved further along in Luke's narrative to Acts, chapter five, verse twelve, 'And through the hands of the apostles many signs and wonders were done among the people. And they were all with one accord on Solomon's Porch.'"

Two newspaper reporters from New York's biggest daily were not only listening to the Cardinal and the Rabbi's conversation, they were writing down every word.

"Solomon's Porch," one reporter said, reviewing his notes as he watched Cardinal Reardon and the others walk back toward the stage. "That has a certain ring to it, don't you think?"

"Yes, yes it does," the second reporter agreed as he continued to scribble. "Sounds Biblical, kind of ties the old and the new together."

"I never liked the constant prison references anyway, seemed clumsy, not really fitting."

"That's it then. From now on we'll tag our pieces as being from 'Solomon's Porch' and give credit for the name to Cardinal Reardon."

"Done."

As He intended, from then on the label stuck. After this night, the world would be confounded and amazed regarding the wonders done from Solomon's Porch.

Seventeen

"At least they're not all convicts," the President's first senior advisor whined. "How in the world Rico Vargas got mixed up in all of this is beyond me."

"General Vargas is one of the finest men I've ever had the privilege of knowing," the President responded. "If he's involved with Carson, well then ..."

"Well what, sir?" a young aide asked.

"Let me put it this way, son," the President said, as he slipped into his familiar light Virginia drawl, "if Marine Corps General Enrique Vargas tells you that a chicken dips snuff, you better go grab that bird and look up under his wing for a can."

"You take this seriously then, sir?" the second senior advisor asked.

"I do. We've had some dealings with Special Agent Austin as well. Remember, two years ago I believe, that ugly business down in Texas?"

"That's right," the first senior advisor agreed. "It was Austin who caught that guy, Barrigan, the one who was funneling all the illegal money into the Congressional races."

"Austin refused to be bullied or influenced by anyone," the President confirmed. "Letting the chips fall where they may could have cost him his career if the charges didn't stick. Austin's an honest man."

"And a gutsy guy," the first senior advisor added. "But sir, I mean come on, sir. All these claimed miracles and healings? Don't tell me you believe in demons too, Mr. President. And this business of bringing a dead man back to life. It's absurd."

"Is it? Is it really?" the President said, raising his eyebrows quizzically.

"Yes, Mr. President, it is. It must be."

"Could have sworn it was you and the Mrs. who went to church with Ellen and I what, at least two Sundays a month for the past five years? Maybe it was your long lost identical twin."

"Sir, of course sir. I believe in God. I believe in Christ. But if the Almighty had something to say to the planet, wouldn't He be a bit more choosey? Why use these amateur middlemen? Don't we have Popes and Bishops and Reverends for that?"

"I can see you need to brush up on the Scriptures, my friend," the President said as he held up a Bible. "This book is filled with prophets God chose to raise from among men of the lowliest stations in life. Joseph was a prisoner and a slave, King David was a young shepherd boy, a nobody, from nowhere, St. Matthew was a thief, and St. Paul hunted down and killed Christians like stray dogs before his conversion."

"But sir, I mean really, sir ..."

"Why don't we just see what Carson does next," the President said, turning back up the volume on the TV set. "All I'm saying is I don't smell a hoax here. Something very real may be going on at Parkersboro."

"Not for much longer," the second senior advisor muttered under his breath. Ten minutes earlier, at his direction, acting under the authority of the President, a contingent of federal officers was finally dispatched to Parkersboro to pull the plug on the whole affair.

"So now you know who they are," Alex said to the camera, as the taped portion of the broadcast ended and the program went live once again. "Seven men each with his own history, sufferings, and testimony of faith. Over the years I've interviewed Presidents, Kings, billionaires, even a Pope, but never have I met more righteous and extraordinary men. Regardless of their past sins, they are gentlemen of the highest character. I would gladly die to protect any one of them from harm."

Alex then turned and began slowly walking from his position just off stage left and on to the platform itself. He kept talking as he moved.

"But if I were one of you out there in the viewing audience, I would be skeptical, more than skeptical in fact, regarding the statements and claims made here tonight. After all, is it not an unfortunate daily occurrence that we are lied to? Even, sadly enough, by many so-called men of God whose only true interest is advancing themselves in some way, in getting rich or in promoting a secular political agenda. Perhaps the one thing most lacking in our common spiritual lives is credibility."

"So tonight, right here and right now, God is going to act. He wants to remove any doubts you may have that He is real and that these men serve Him. The Lord wants you to believe, to follow His lead. For His reasons, He has chosen this place and this time to make a bold and dramatic statement to the world."

"Say that again?" Martz asked the studio chief. The message was repeated.

"That's impossible. I mean come on, man. Lovely idea, I'll grant you that, but cut me a break. They really said that? They're going to look like damned fools and us along with them."

Martz chilled for a second and took a deep breath. Even a failed stunt delivers if it's big enough, he reassured himself, and if the initial ratings estimates for "Miracles" were anywhere near accurate, the network was looking at Super Bowl type audience numbers. Opportunity was knocking, Martz just hoped it didn't come crashing through the door.

Then he thought again about what his studio chief told him. "What the hell," he mumbled to himself.

"Audrey."

"Yes, Mr. Martz?"

"Is that security guard we have out front, you know the geezer everybody calls gramps, is he armed?"

"Armed, Mr. Martz?"

"Does the putz have a gun?"

Audrey thought about it, recalled what the guard looked like and said, "I think so, Mr. Martz."

"Bring him and his sidearm on in here then, will you please?"

"Sir?"

"Just do it, Audrey. Just do it." Martz had no desire to explain his request. The whole thing was ridiculous.

Peter and the disciples assembled in the center of the stage and formed a circle. For them, every detail of the experience; the clear, cool night, what everyone was wearing, the glare of the TV lights, the hum of the electronic equipment, even the placement of objects around the porch were parts of a familiar scene. They had stepped into their dream.

Peter began to pray. In the distance, the faint sounds of more than one approaching siren could be heard. As for the audience, they were supremely quiet. The tension of anticipation clenched all present.

"Lord," Peter prayed. "You delivered my brothers and I from Satan's power for Your purpose, to glorify Your name. We come before you now humbly tonight Lord asking only that you use us as willing vessels. Your will be done, Mighty God."

Then a sound like far off thunder began to roll toward Parkersboro, like a powerful storm popping up on a summer night. But the sky was completely clear.

In a few seconds the noise became more intense than any storm could ever be, it was like a hundred jet engines all revving up at once. The sound was felt as much as it was heard. Most of those present described it as "a wall of energy" or "an enormous pressure wave."

Then out of nowhere a bright plasma, looking like fire but without any heat, enveloped the porch and the men on it. Like a sheet of lightning, it surrounded them, dancing and sparking off each man like a Living Flame.

"Good God Almighty!" the President gasped, astonished. "What do you make of that?"

Trying not to show the fear that had seized him, the first senior advisor said, faking composure, "Sir, Hollywood can make anything seem real."

"But that is a live broadcast!" the President exclaimed. "Quite the trick, wouldn't you say?"

"What?" the second senior advisor said quietly into his cell phone. "It's on fire? Tell them to go over it, around it, through it, I don't care. These people have hijacked a federal prison to make some damned movie for hell's sake. What? Use of force? What the f*** do you call lighting a school bus on fire in the middle of an access road? Do your job."

The Living Flame then split into seven separate streams, one for each man in the prayer circle. From the top of their heads the

Holy Fire reached infinitely heavenward into the evening sky. The disciples did not outwardly react to what was happening. Whatever the Energy was doing to them was a mystery.

"I need a live shot of that, Randy. Not in a minute, now! Get a camera on that road!" Martz was in a panic. He was not at all convinced that what he was seeing from Parkersboro was real, his senses and his experience were screaming that it couldn't possibly be. Then he got word in his earpiece that a small army of Feds were invading the camp from the highway. When he heard a roadblock of flaming buses had been set up to stop them, he knew he had to get images of that on the air too.

For the select, seeing the Holy Spirit manifest itself in the form of a Flame was the final sequence of the combination that unlocked their stored instructions. God had opened His human vaults and the select were now ready to deliver His treasure to the world.

Two minutes after the Holy Flames appeared they vanished, accompanied by one last huge clap of thunder. Peter and the brothers remained standing in their circle in silence for a minute or so more. No one inside the compound made a sound, the only noise was coming from the access road in the woods a mile away; metal scraping against metal, diesels straining, and men shouting. The barrier was being breached.

Then Peter Carson spoke.

"God says the time has come for us to stop using violence against one another. We must spiritually evolve beyond our brutish nature. No longer should we approve of or condone physical force as a means to achieve any human goal, whether as individuals or as societies."

"We must freely choose to follow His will, to become peaceful. If we recognize that our only true enemy is Satan, and not each other, the Lord says this knowledge will help us to overcome our fears. God will strengthen us in our battle with evil if we reach out to Him and seek His love and wisdom."

"For the next three days, the Lord our God says He will not allow man to be violent. For this brief time, God is suspending our freedom to hurt one another. He says that we are to learn from this instruction, this gift, so that we will eventually be able to accomplish the same result through our faith, His love, and our free will."

"I'll be damned. What some people won't do for ratings," the President's first senior advisor caustically said. "What a load of crap."

But the President wasn't listening to his advisor. Seconds earlier a military officer assigned to the White House, the custodian of the President's portable nuclear command and control technology, commonly known as "the football," had rushed into the room and immediately pulled the President aside to give him an urgent message.

"Tell them," the President ordered the officer.

"Sir?"

"Go ahead, Captain."

"As of approximately two minutes ago all the command and control functions of our nuclear arsenal have been disabled," the officer reported.

"That's impossible," the second senior advisor said. "Those systems have triple, even quadruple redundancy. If one fails another kicks in. The backups are close to foolproof."

"Sir, we couldn't launch a bottle rocket right now," the Captain explained. "As we speak, I'm getting reports in my headset of weapon systems failures from, well, everywhere, sir."

That's when all hell broke loose.

Men and women, both in and out of uniform, streamed into the oval office barking orders into phones and sending out messages via various high tech communication devices. The answers they received back were all the same, everywhere on earth all forms of weaponry employed by the United States, from side arms to hydrogen bombs, simply no longer functioned.

The first senior advisor brought the President the bad news. "Sir, it appears that we are defenseless," he admitted. "We are trying to determine the cause of this phenomenon, Mr. President. It's been suggested that possibly some exotic, planet-wide electromagnetic pulse, or an until now unknown energy source, perhaps a wandering black hole, has us in its grip. We are speculating sir, but our best estimates are that this will all clear itself up in a matter of minutes. Sir, I have the Joint Chiefs standing by, we are rea..."

"Will you please be quiet!" the President demanded.

"Sir, I strongly suggest that we must take all necessary and proper..."

"Are you deaf? I said shut up!" the President yelled, as he maximized the volume on the television set.

Now several minutes into the next hour the network "chose," as if it had a choice, to continue to feed the world live images from Parkersboro.

"The American authorities will be here shortly to seize us," Peter said, pointing toward the vehicles and men approaching from the access road. "Do not worry for our safety, or indeed your own. For the first time in the history of man we are in no physical danger from each other. Pray for us, pray for yourselves, pray for the world. The Lord God loves you, each and every one of you. Rejoice! Ours is a chosen generation, blessed beyond measure! You will see and hear from us again very soon."

After Peter spoke these final words, for no apparent technical reason, the signal from Parkersboro went dead. The network desperately tried to reestablish the link, but their efforts were useless. The broadcast was over, God had spoken.

"I want those men in my office as soon as possible," the President ordered.

"Yes sir," the second senior advisor said. "The Marshal Service will arrest all of them, shut the whole circus down. You saw them entering the camp; we have a sizable force in place, Mr. President, more than sufficient to get the job done."

The President looked over at his advisor, a man whom he had trusted with the most important of matters for many years, a close friend whose intellect and expertise had been an invaluable part of his success, and all he could think of saying to him was, "Are you really that stupid?"

"Sir, I'm sorry, Mr. President. I guess, I mean ..."

"Get on that fancy phone of yours and tell those cowboys down there to treat Mr. Carson and his people with respect. They are to escort and protect, not arrest. Am I making myself clear enough?"

"Yes sir, I'll do that right away, sir."

"These men somehow disabled every weapons system we have and you're here trying to tell me a few policemen are going to subdue them? Honest to God, you people amaze me, honest to God ..." The President didn't finish his thought. He stopped talking, grabbed his Bible and started to make his way to the door to exit his office.

"Sir, where are you going?" the first senior advisor accusingly asked, astonished that the Chief Executive would abandon his post in a time of crisis.

"Where any sane man would go right now," the President answered. "To my private chapel to pray. To ask God to forgive me and to help me. It seems I'm about to meet His emissaries. I'd like to be prepared."

"Let me see that thing," Martz said, not so much asking as demanding. The guard handed him his weapon, a garden variety thirty-eight caliber pistol. Martz inspected it and returned the gun to the nervous guard.

"Does the bloody thing work?" Martz asked.

"Yes sir," the sixty-two year old retired policeman said. "Just fired it last week at the range. It's a beaut."

"Well then, make yourself useful and shoot that monitor out over there," Martz ordered.

"Mr. Martz, you want me to discharge my weapon in here, in the studio?"

"Hell yes. I'd rather you point the stupid thing at someone when you do it, but there are no suitable candidates for that job present, so the monitor will have to do."

"Well now," the guard hesitated. "I don't think I can do that, sir. I know you're the boss and all, but I would be violating…"

"Mr. Ames, isn't it?" Martz asked, interrupting.

"Yes, that's right. William K. Ames, Mr. Martz."

"Okay, Mr. William K. Ames, I'll give you a choice. Fire that gun at the monitor or pack your stuff and leave."

"You'd sack me over this, sir?"

"Damn right. Consider it done."

Ames did not waiver further. He pointed the pistol at the monitor and pulled the trigger.

Click, click. Nothing happened.

Ames was perturbed. He removed the weapon's six shells and replaced them with new rounds. He pulled the trigger again.

Click, click.

"I'm very sorry, sir," Ames said regretfully. "I guess you'll have to pink slip me. I don't understand it, I keep my sidearm in good condition at all times, I take my duties here most seriously, Mr. Martz, I..."

"Ames!" Martz yelled.

"...don't understand how this could have..."

"Ames!" Martz screamed again.

"Sir, yes sir."

"It's alright, Ames. You're not fired. Carry on."

"Sir, yes sir!" the old guard repeated and then immediately left to try and figure out what was wrong with his pistol.

Dave Martz, like millions of others, was simply stunned. Already he'd been told from his news staff that similar instant experiments with guns had yielded the same results. He wondered how far the phenomenon extended. Were people now incapable of stabbing each other, using clubs, or even landing a good left jab? He found it extremely difficult to grasp the possibility of the concept.

Then he looked over at one of the twenty or so monitors in the studio. The screen displayed a still shot of Alex Anderson's face from the broadcast.

"Alex, my old friend," Dave Martz said. "We really need to talk."

Eighteen

Peter was wrong. The American authorities, in the form of the United States Marshal Service, did not arrest or seize anyone at Parkersboro. Shortly after they breached the flaming bus barrier, but before they made it into the camp proper, their authorization to take any further action was revoked.

Per the direct orders of the President of the United States, Peter Carson, Alex Anderson, Warden McCorkle, and the six disciples were "asked to attend an urgent meeting with the President and his senior staff in Washington at their earliest convenience."

This Presidential invitation was delivered by the ranking officer of a company of Marines who arrived about half an hour after the Marshals were instructed to hold in place around the camp. The soldiers descended on Parkersboro in three separate helicopters, one of which was Marine Corps One, the President's own ship. Initially at least, rather than the stick, the government was offering the carrot.

Peter immediately agreed to the President's "request" and thanked the Marines for their courtesy. The soldiers deferred to Peter and, whether by order or of their own inclination, he was allowed to organize and time their departure. It was just after midnight when Peter told his escorts that they were ready to leave.

Julie made something of a scene after the broadcast. She begged Peter to allow her to go with him to Washington. He denied her as lovingly and as gently as he knew how, but for awhile it seemed as if she was refusing to take no for an answer. Julie was desperate to be by Peter's side, to protect him, to prevent what her husband had told her was inevitable.

"What happens in three days, Peter?" she kept asking him. "Do you think they'll still be so nice to you once God gives them their guns back?"

Julie Carson, Peter had given her permission to take back his name, did not accept the prophecy that Peter was predestined to be a martyr. She had been in a constant state of prayer since the night before on the beach, pleading with God to spare her husband's life, or at least to be kind enough to take her also when He called for Peter.

Knowing that it wouldn't satisfy her at the moment, but hoping that it would provide inspiration later, Peter reminded Julie that it was her first duty to be a mother to Kevin, to raise him up to be a man of God. "More than anything else, this is what the Lord wants you to do with your life," he told her.

Peter's tender counseling increased Julie's inner conflict. She loved her son and knew that her role as his mother was a holy commission, but so also, she believed, was her love and duty to Peter.

In the end, she deferred to her husband's wishes, quit arguing, and kissed him goodbye. What else could she do? Defy the man whom God so highly favored? As she watched the helicopters disappear into the northern night sky, Julie begged the Lord to return Peter to her, safe and sound. She couldn't help but wonder if her last image of him would be of Peter standing in the entrance of the chopper mouthing, "I love you, Jules" as the soldiers folded up the stairs. She prayed for God's comfort and mercy, but for now she was overwhelmed by sadness and fear.

"That is a fair statement," the President's first senior advisor agreed. "Without exception, weapons in any form in armed forces everywhere have simply ceased to be operative."

"So, you would agree that our threat assessment is valid?" the National Security Advisor asked.

"Yes, for the moment. But only for the moment."

"Elaborate, please," the President said.

"As of this minute, roughly one a.m. eastern time, on June twenty, the United States faces no external threats. Our ability to make war and the ability of any of our potential adversaries to do so has been, uh, suspended for lack of a better term," the first senior advisor explained.

"And?" the President prodded.

"Well, sir, when this restriction or paralysis is over, what then? Will everything be just as it was before it started? Our command and control functions are highly integrated, ultra sophisticated computer systems. Conceivably, there could be a significant delay window between when the switch, if you will, is thrown and when we are able to bring our strategic nuclear and non-nuclear weapons back on-line."

"So what? Isn't everyone else facing the same problem?" the President asked.

"They are, Mr. President," the first senior advisor continued, "but not all weapons systems are alike. For example, the typical Russian or Chinese ICBM is far less complex in terms of electronic guidance and computer technology than our own. Given this fact, they may recover their ability to launch quicker than we can."

"How much quicker?" the President needed to know.

"We estimate that the Russians might be able to launch a full, or nearly full, nuclear first strike anywhere from fifteen minutes to an hour before we could respond, sir. As for the Chinese, we don't have enough information to make an educated prediction."

"And this analysis is based upon?"

"It is based upon the time required to power up our systems versus theirs, to reboot and reconfigure digital files, to reestablish command and control capabilities, to ..."

"Wait a minute," the President said, breaking in.

"Sir," the first senior advisor asked.

"Didn't you just tell me a few minutes ago that lack of power was not a problem?"

"I did sir, that appears to be true Mr ..."

"In fact, as far as our experts, or anyone else's I'm willing to bet, can tell there is absolutely nothing wrong with any of our weapons or command systems. Isn't that true?"

"Yes sir."

"And let's not forget how far this suspension, as you call it, extends. Still no reports of any homicides or assaults or any type of violence anywhere?"

"No sir, Mr. President," the National Security Advisor confirmed. "We are monitoring a large sampling of police bands from across the globe. Since Mr. Carson's pronouncement, not a single incident of violence has been reported anywhere."

"I still find it impossible to get my mind around that," the President admitted, as he stood and began to slowly pace around his couches, "but I'd be a fool to ignore the facts. And gentlemen, as my pappy always said, I might be a fool, but I'm not a damned fool."

"Call the list," the President ordered his National Security Advisor.

"All of them, sir?"

"Yes, all of them! They're up and about anyway doing what we are, trying to make some sense of this. I want the Russians, the Chinese, the Brits, the Indians, hell I want the Prince of Monaco to know that the United States of America is in the same boat as they are and that we intend to fully report any change in our defense status the instant it occurs. I want commitments from all of them to do the same."

"Forget healings or visions, that right there is absolute proof of the existence of the Living God," Saul Cohen said, as he smiled and pointed at Malik Graham. "I was certain we'd never be able to get him in here."

It took ten minutes of prayer and fifteen more of persuasion by Saul and Peter to get Malik to step into the helicopter. He had never flown on a commercial aircraft, much less agreed to ride in some contraption that looked to him like a flying death-trap. Malik was in the very same position he assumed when they departed Parkersboro; double strapped in his seat, muscles flexed, eyes closed, his huge hands squeezing a Bible so hard it seemed certain to be flattened by the time they reached Washington.

"Panos," General Vargas said. "Mr. Austin and I would like to speak with you, sir. Alone."

Peter walked to the back of the spacious Marine Corps One cabin with Vargas and Austin after strongly advising Saul against his prankster inclination to undue Malik's seat belt "just to see what happens."

"Both Tim and I know the President," Enrique Vargas told Peter, "at least to some degree. I've been in several top military conferences with him. Austin was part of the prosecution team that briefed him on some sensitive matters in Texas."

"And?" Peter asked.

"He's a good man," Tim told Peter, "and I believe he fears God. He's highly intelligent, both street smart and book wise. As politicians go, he's basically honest."

"The Lord has allowed him to be President right now for a reason, I'm sure," Peter added. "What you're telling me is reassuring."

"The issue isn't the President," Enrique Vargas said, lowering his voice as he spoke. "It's some of the men he keeps close, Panos. Two in particular concern us."

"Go on."

"The President's two most senior advisors are ruthless men, Peter," the General said. "Evil. Rotten to the core."

"You're sure of this?" Peter asked.

"One hundred percent," Tim Austin corroborated. "In the Bureau we've known for years that both of these guys have and would do anything required to advance their own interest."

"Such as?"

"Such as destroying good men and their careers on a whim, fabricating evidence in criminal trials, finding ways to funnel billions in inflated government contract money to their cronies, and committing murder. And that's just for starters."

"Murder?" Peter wasn't shocked by corruption, but accusing two of the most powerful men in the government of such a high crime seemed extreme.

"I'm absolutely sure of it," Tim said unflinchingly, "but I cannot prove it in a court of law. These men are very clever and experienced, the best of the best. And know this, Peter, they haven't killed once or twice, it's a routine tool for them, part of their everyday arsenal."

"Does the President know?" Peter wondered.

"We don't think so," Enrique Vargas guessed. "At least, all the evidence would suggest otherwise. To protect themselves they keep everything away from the President. To them he is just someone else they need to manipulate. Very few people know what we've just told you, Panos, less than twenty men total that we're aware of, and none of us felt it was prudent to challenge these bastards without having the kind of evidence that would stand up in court."

"Forgive me, brothers, but this sounds farfetched. I mean, even I know that the worst possible place to try and keep any secret is Washington, D.C. Sooner or later it would ..." Peter stopped talking because the answer to his question at once became obvious.

"Panos?" Tim asked.

"Of course, it must be."

"What?" Vargas said, confused.

"Legion and his friends. These two advisors are his servants, they're under his protection."

Tim Austin and Enrique Vargas looked at each other. At the same time, each wondered, is it really that simple?

"Are you telling us, Panos, that these men are demons?" Tim asked.

"No, probably not. They're almost surely flesh and blood. I'll bet they don't have a clue that Satan is running their lives. Remember that the devil feeds off of our own desires and our willingness to break God's commandments in order to get what we want. I doubt very seriously that either one of these gentlemen has a Satanic chapel in his basement or draws pentagrams. Unless they can be made to see the Light before they die, they'd undoubtedly be quite shocked to pass on and wake up in hell. They probably don't believe that anything greater than their own egos exists in the universe."

"Hmm. I always thought..."

"Always thought what, Tim?" Peter asked.

"I always thought those two jokers needed to be prosecuted and jailed, but it turns out what they really needed was an exorcism."

Even in the low moonlight the crew and passengers of Marine Corps One could tell something unusual was going on at the White House. At least five hundred soldiers were busying themselves around the President's residence. They were putting into place a large concrete barrier topped with razor wire as fast as they were able. This makeshift fence was nearly complete by the time Peter's helicopter arrived shortly after two a.m.

"Could have sworn we just left a prison," Gail said. "Looks like we're flying into another one."

"What they're up to isn't hard to figure out," Alex said, as he continued to gather and organize his equipment.

"Okay, Alex, then explain it to me because I find it more than a bit odd, and unnerving," Kenny said, looking out across the White House lawn which was now a small army base.

"They are erecting a static defense," Alex explained. 'None of their weapons work and by now they've figured out that even punching someone in the nose is impossible. So..."

"So you put up a fence, as large and nasty as possible, to keep any enemies or uninvited guests away from the President and our seat of power," General Vargas said, finishing Alex's sentence for him.

"Exactly," Alex concurred. "What else can they do? God took away their power to hurt each other, but paranoia remains. They are afraid."

"Scared crapless," Vargas said. "I would be positively manic, trying to run every possible scenario through my mind, planning for all possible contingencies."

"That's what they're doing in there right now, General?" Peter asked. "Trying to figure out what to do next?"

"What should they be doing, Panos?"

"Praying, of course. They have been called to account by God. They need to seek His mercy."

Alex shook his head in disbelief. What a totally preposterous situation, he thought to himself; the President of the United States of America, the most powerful man on earth, humbled by a lowly prisoner. Many times during the past few months, Alex was forced to stop, take a deep breath, and get a grip, but this scene was over any imaginable top. Despite the rational part of his brain telling him that none of this could possibly be happening, Alex was compelled to accept that it was. The power of God cannot be denied, he reminded himself, and it seemed that no longer would He allow it to be ignored.

"Gentlemen and Miss McCorkle," the President said, as he stood and affably greeted his guests. "Welcome to the White House. It is an honor to meet all of you. Thank you for coming on such short notice and without complaint."

"Does he have to kiss their a** like that?" the first senior advisor whispered to his chief aide.

"It's degrading," the aide agreed, being careful to cover his mouth so that no one could read his lips.

"Sir, all of us are Americans. While my brothers and I serve God above all else, there should be no conflict between God's will and our country's best interest. We are humbled and honored to be here, Mr. President."

What is it about this man? the President asked himself silently as Peter spoke. *Is it his look? His manner of speech?* In a way that was impossible to articulate, the President found Peter not only to be credible, but also fascinating. Routinely in the presence of great men and women, the President was not easily impressed or awed, but Peter Carson had done both to him within seconds of entering the room.

"I really don't know where to begin, Mr. Carson. To say that you have us all at something of a loss would be the understatement of all time." The President was trying his best to be completely open and honest, to avoid all pretense and deception.

"You may, Mr. President, take us in all matters at our word, sir. None of us would ever try and lie to you, or to anyone else. We are messengers of God, appointed by Him for His purpose."

"Forgive me, Mr. Carson, for putting it so bluntly; is this real? I mean, I don't see how it couldn't be, or a coincidence either, as has been suggested. But Mr. Carson…"

"Please. Mr. Carson was my father. Call me Peter."

"Very well, Peter. Then I ask you straight out, man to man, is God really working through you as you say?"

"What do you think, sir?"

The President was afraid of this question, but not at all surprised that it was asked.

"I think nothing else could possibly explain what's happened over the past few hours. The other theories make even less sense."

"The other theories, sir?" Peter asked.

"That you're actually some form of alien life using our religious beliefs to manipulate us, or a mutant human being capable of extraordinary feats of psychic power by some unknown means, or that we've all gone mad and this is a mass delusion and you simply do not exist."

"You believe in God, don't you, Mr. President?"

"Yes, Peter. Yes, I do."

"Then behold His vision."

The President's head snapped back, his skin bleached and he fell in a heap in his chair. The Secret Service agents and the other staff in the room wanted desperately to come to his aid, but found themselves unable to move. After a few seconds it was apparent that the President had not been harmed, but it was also obvious that his attention was now totally focused elsewhere and not on his immediate surroundings. He was staring off into space, his head and body twitching in reaction to some unseen stimuli.

For almost five minutes, this eerie drama played itself out as the President was forced to endure whatever trial he was facing alone, unable to receive help in any form.

Then, as abruptly as it started, it was over. Men who could now move again rushed to the President's side. Two Secret Service agents had intentions of arresting Peter and his entourage on the spot, or at least forcibly removing them from the room, but of course their plan to use violence to accomplish these goals was, for now, an impossibility. Try as they might, the agents' minds could simply not order their bodies to follow instructions.

The President quickly regained his composure and after a couple of minutes his color returned. He was once again lucid and focused.

But he was not the same man that he was before the vision, nor would he ever be.

"Peter," the President said, as he shooed away the physician who was trying to examine him, "do you know what I saw?"

"Yes, Mr. President, I do. I know that the Lord has given you a glimpse of what the future will be for us if we fail to heed His call."

"I did more than glimpse things, Peter, I experienced them. I felt all types of physical sensations; pain, hunger, sickness, death, and emotions too. I know it sounds crazy, but I believe I could not only listen to the thoughts of the people I saw, I also somehow shared in their existence. It was like I was a part of them. Weird does not ..."

The President stopped talking. He realized through their stares and silence that everyone in the Oval Office not associated with Peter Carson was asking themselves the same question.

"Have I gone mad, Peter?"

"No sir. In fact, I believe you'll find that the more you pray about and reflect upon your vision, the greater your ability to make sense of the world, to truly grasp reality, will become."

"Leave now, get the Vice President on the phone," the first senior advisor whispered to his top aide. "I know he's returning from Europe and his plane isn't due in for two hours. Tell him I said we have a leadership crisis going on here." These instructions were given in the back of the room, as far away as possible from Peter and the President.

"Sir, what do I tell the V.P. when he asks for details?" the aide asked, speaking as softly as he could into his boss's ear.

"Tell him the President may no longer be mentally fit to hold office, that we may need to take extraordinary measures to protect the nation and the Presidency."

Confused and frightened the aide quickly left, saying nothing more.

"Peter, if I told you that I was exhausted, more tired than I have ever been in my whole life, would that make any sense to you?" the President asked.

"When I received my first vision I slept for more than twenty-four hours afterwards, sir," Peter acknowledged.

"Well, I don't have that kind of luxury, but by God if I don't get to bed right quick, I'm probably going to pass out in this chair."

The two attending doctors and the Secret Service men then bounced back to the President's side, called for a stretcher and an ambulance, and barked orders into their cell phones and radios.

"I swear, if you gentlemen don't take your hands off of me and back off right now, I'll fire the lot of you. I feel fine, maybe even tremendous, but I'm tired. Now leave me alone."

The President motioned for Peter to come to him.

"Peter, walk with me to my bedroom, will you please? I really don't have the patience for these dolts that I should right now."

"Yes sir, Mr. President."

If looks could kill, Peter Carson would have been murdered right then and there. The powerful men that surround the President had been rebuked and perhaps, in their minds at least, replaced by some low-life convict witchdoctor.

Men of such stature do not stand idly by and allow themselves to be reduced to irrelevancies. They take action. Every problem has a solution.

No one really noticed, but sometime during all of this commotion, Saul Cohen dropped to the floor in the back of the Oval Office. While the other disciples and Alex and Gail were busy talking to each other or trying to help Peter, Saul was hiding under the furniture. He was terrified, more so than he had ever been before in his life.

What Saul Cohen saw, no one else could see. It was a beast, a horrible and vicious image standing directly behind the President. Far beyond any image of hell or ghastly apparition he had ever endured before, this was something new, bigger, and more powerful.

Whatever it was, whatever its name, it knew Saul was watching him and the creature clearly did not like being observed.

The beast communicated only with Saul and only non-verbally, consciousness to consciousness.

"Shut up, ape boy," the beast thought and Saul heard. "Or I'll rip out your intestines and make you watch as I eat them."

It wasn't the threat itself that made Saul panic, other demons he'd battled had been just as vile and far more creative, it was the way the beast expressed himself, like it was a done deal. As if God and Christ had no authority over him. As if the beast feared nothing and had no need to.

Saul reacted to the monster's threat as any sane man might, he shut down. Saul's body and brain simply slipped into neutral. He sat cross-legged on the floor, eyes wide open, mouth agape and drooling, skin clammy and green, and was unable to think, speak, or move.

Nineteen

The twentieth of June was a day unlike all others that had come before it. A new version of reality was dawning along with the sun. No previous human experience could provide any context for what people everywhere would soon be calling "the restriction."

Homo sapiens are genetically designed to take for granted that their brain controls their body. Without any noticeable delay, because neurons fire and muscles and tendons react virtually simultaneously, we think *move left arm* and it moves. *Step* and our leg extends. For the most part, we don't consciously command ourselves at all, the directive and the action are one in the same. God indeed designed and built for us a magnificent physical machine in which to house our souls.

In order to teach His creation a lesson, to demonstrate for them His divine standards and expectations, and to make evident His power in a way never before seen on earth, the Lord God of Israel, who is above all natural laws and exists on a heavenly plane beyond our ability to understand, applied His will to our bodies and to our technology, and temporarily took away from us our ability to hurt each other.

But our hearts remained conflicted; good and evil were still at war within us because God did not further intervene and force anyone to think or feel differently about anything. People filled with hate and anger toward others, for any reason, could simply no longer act on their passions.

Battlefields in the several regional wars scattered across the globe fell silent. Criminals could no longer threaten people with harm in order to take advantage of them and the police were unable to offer their usual evil for evil in return. No abusive husband could beat his wife; no wayward father could pummel his children. For however long it was going to last, two and a half more days according to the American prophet Peter Carson, who overnight had become the world's most famous man, people were going to have to figure out how to get along peacefully. They simply had no other choice.

Other truly bizarre circumstances arose. Somehow, while no one could forcibly restrain them, across the globe some prisoners were simply unable to take advantage of the situation and walk away from whatever institution was confining them. Some could leave and did. It soon became obvious that those who could leave had, by whatever means, made the decision to obey God's commandment to be good citizens and respect righteous civil authority. The Lord, in effect, instantly pardoned a few million rehabilitated criminals. Christ knew their hearts and restored freedom to those capable of handling it.

Everyone was safe, as were their possessions. Minds corrupted by evil were still corrupted by evil, but the Lord simply would not allow anyone to take advantage of the restriction. No one could walk into a bank and walk out with stolen cash, or go to a car lot and drive away in a new automobile without paying for it. The restriction was anything but a bonanza for thieves; it temporarily put them out of business.

What was happening could not be understood or appreciated unless it was viewed from God's perspective. But, taken on the whole, considering the billions of souls alive on earth, initially at least God's perspective was not the foremost concern.

Fear was the most common first reaction to the restriction, followed by indignation. Whatever else it might have been, the restriction was most certainly a type of biological and cultural shock therapy. The primitive aspect of the human personality, that part of us most basic and animalistic, that arose when the world was nothing but flesh and teeth, no longer had an outlet.

God was making a bold statement. He was saying to His children that the time had come for us to take a huge step forward, to truly become more Christ-like, and to leave behind the aggressive and violent part of our natures, to spiritually evolve.

The other revolutionary and existence-altering aspect of the restriction was that it forced the created to acknowledge the Creator, or to put forward some other theory to explain what could not be denied. For many, this was a far more difficult thing to do than to live without violence. Until now, the subject of God could be dodged or dealt with circuitously, with each person picking and choosing what he chose to believe. This luxury was now gone. Direct evidence had superseded theory.

This was the new world that those in the White House faced on the twentieth of June, one in which the power of God had taken center stage above all else.

"Any change?" Peter asked the nurse.

"None, Mr. Carson. Mr. Cohen's vital signs are stable, but his brain is producing intermittent coma-type activity. It's really crazy; he seems to be alternating between deep but active sleep and a near total shutdown of all higher brain functioning. To be honest, I didn't think that was medically possible."

"He's fighting them."

"Fighting who, Mr. Carson?"

"Whatever servants of hell put him in this condition, ma'am." The young nurse looked at Peter as if he were speaking Latin. After briefly considering it, Peter thought better about the idea of trying to explain the workings and powers of demonic forces to the already bewildered and shaken nurse. He graciously dropped the subject so they could both move on. "Thank you so much for attending to our brother. We are in your debt," he told her.

After catching a few hours of much needed sleep, Peter's first task when he awoke was to check on Saul. Shortly after the President retired to his bedroom, Peter and Alex discovered Saul curled up and catatonic in the corner. Peter had no doubts as to the cause of his brother's affliction.

"The same?" Alex asked, as he came up from behind and put his hand on Peter's shoulder.

"Afraid so. Our prayers haven't pulled him out if it yet. We need to help Saul, Alex. Look at him. He's almost scared himself to death."

"And without Saul around we can't see what's coming at us, can we?"

"Perhaps that's best for now," Peter said, as he made the sign of the cross over Saul. "If we could, we might end up like him."

In a room adjacent to where Saul was being attended to, a television set was on. The five disciples and Gail were gathered around it watching the news.

"You guys get any sleep?" Alex asked, as he and Peter walked in and joined the others.

"No," came the response from all, nearly in unison.

"Men in dark suits keep walking in here periodically and handing this stuff to me," General Vargas said. "I've looked over some of it, but this is your department."

"The morning's press clippings?" Alex asked.

"Apparently," Vargas replied, "but I'm a hundred percent sure that you've never read accounts like these before."

The White House staff had been busy printing out selected newspaper articles from around the world as soon as they were electronically published. Write-ups from foreign countries had been translated into English.

Alex took the stack from Vargas. The General was correct, he'd never read headlines like these. But how could he have? This was the most important and unique event ever covered by modern journalism.

From New York the headline read, *Is God Real?*" in huge bold type that filled half the front page. Alex skimmed the text, which included the statements "the theory that a force more powerful than ourselves exists in the universe has been confirmed" and "this phenomenon, quickly becoming known as "the restriction," is without question both genuine and global."

The Los Angeles paper went with, *A Prophet of God?*" This story chose to focus on Peter and the details of the events over the past few months from "Solomon's Porch" and Atlanta. The reporter asked, "If Mr. Carson is to be believed, and certainly it is an undeniable fact that some very real power has boldly intervened in human affairs, then the Christian faith has been empirically validated. Those who remain skeptical of this conclusion find themselves unable yet to offer a reasonable competing hypothesis to explain the phenomenon people everywhere are calling 'the restriction.'"

In London, they seemed to be more interested in the effect than in the cause. *"Thou Shalt Not!"* was the banner of England's biggest daily. Fully half the newspaper was devoted to exploring and chronicling all aspects of the restriction.

Alex skimmed through the rest of the pile, but quickly lost interest. Peter had already told him that few would accept what was happening for what it was. Rather than a miracle God was using to help his people by example, most of the world was trying to explain the restriction some other way, or simply hoping to ignore it until it was over. Once everything returned to normal, it would be far easier to offer alternative hypotheses and spin the facts.

Denial and skepticism are rooted in fear. For most people acknowledging the restriction was neither welcome nor easy, because if Jesus is truly the Son of God and this is no longer a belief based on faith, but rather a reality as plain as the law of gravity, then the revelations of Yahweh both ancient and modern cannot be ignored. The "Great Debate" would be over. God is real, Christ is the risen Messiah, and all other spiritual systems and beliefs instantly become false mythology and obsolete.

Peter told Alex when they were together at the estate that even with direct and irrefutable evidence, most would still not believe. Some will simply refuse to abandon the false tenets of their previous faiths because, in their eyes, to admit a lifetime of error would be shameful and degrading. Rather than see the simple truth that, to some degree at least, God's grace and wisdom were present in all the major religions of the world, they will allow Satan to use their pride to keep them from accepting Christ. The atheists and the agnostics will hold out for a "rational" explanation. Even most Christian leaders will reject the God they profess to serve simply because His message to the world was not brought through them.

As Alex Anderson was thinking about Peter's predictions, hoping perhaps that his brother had been too pessimistic, all he had to do was watch the news on television to see that Peter's cynicism was valid.

"Turn that up, Mr. Simpson, won't you?" Alex asked.

"If you insist, Alex, but it's kind of depressing." Kenny increased the volume just as a new interview segment began.

"Do you go to church, Mrs. Wafer?" the reporter asked.

"Yes sir. Been a God-fearing Christian all my life. Southern Baptist, sir." Mrs. Wafer was a very large and unattractive white woman, perhaps fifty or so, and was clearly used to her spiritual views dominating any religious discussion within her earshot.

"What do you think about all this, Mrs. Wafer? Is God acting?"

"Well, let me tell you this, sir. I don't know about all this "restriction" business. Oh, it's true alright, can't nobody hurt another, but how is this really being done? I think it's the government."

"The government, Mrs. Wafer?"

"Oh, yes sir. In the last days before the rapture and the second coming, the anti-Christ will use the government to play tricks on all of us. A false prophet uses the devil to work miracles, sir. People should read their Bible. Otherwise this business just makes no sense."

"What makes no sense, Mrs. Wafer?"

"God using a bunch of no account criminals to tell us what to do. What nonsense! It's the devil, I tell you! Next Carson's going to say Mormons and Catholics are God's chosen, just you wait and see. It's nothing but the devil!"

"Poor lady," Peter said, reacting to the television. "Her spirit is polluted by her flawed theology and her prayers are blocked by her arrogance."

"She's got a lot of company, Panos," Gail said, pointing back at the screen.

"This is W. Monaghan coming to you live from Vatican City. For hours now we have been trying to get some sort of statement from the Pope, or perhaps from another Vatican official. Now we are told, yes, there he is, Cardinal Andretti will be addressing the crowd in Vatican Square, now estimated at over one hundred thousand. Is he? Yes? Okay, let's go to the Cardinal."

"As of this moment," the Cardinal began, speaking slowly and deliberately from his podium high above the crowd, "His Holiness cannot confirm that this condition, the restriction as it is being called, is indeed a genuine miracle or message from God. Our Holy Father is, as I speak, praying with and consulting the senior leadership of the church on this most serious and pressing issue. May God be with us all. Have faith in Christ. Be patient. Exercise caution in your affairs." The Cardinal moved away from the microphone and disappeared back into the Vatican without taking any questions.

"Did you see him?" Peter asked Alex.

"Who?"

"Reardon. He must have made it to an airport and caught a flight to Rome. He was standing right behind Andretti."

There was a digital recorder attached to the television. Kenny played back Andretti's brief speech. Cardinal Reardon was indeed there, standing a few feet behind Andretti on the podium.

"What does that mean, Peter?" Gail asked.

"It means that God has given the Romans a witness they cannot easily ignore. We should all pray for our brother Catholics. They are ... "

"Gentlemen, please excuse the intrusion," the young, well-dressed aide said as she entered the room. "The President is awake. He's asking to see all of you immediately."

Almost the same group of staff and advisors were gathered around the President as were the night before, but another senior official was now also present, the Vice President.

"Peter, gentlemen, and Miss McCorkle, please come in." The President was smiling as he greeted them and looked remarkably refreshed for someone carrying the weight of a nation on his shoulders on only a few hours of sleep.

"How are you feeling this morning, sir?" Peter asked.

"Very well, Peter. Maybe never better. But the folks around here, I'm sure, would disagree." As the President said this, he half scowled at his personal physician and the other medical personnel attending to him.

"That's not true, Mr. President," the physician responded defensively. "We are concerned, and with good reason, but we agree that you are in perfect health."

"Just nuts," the President added caustically.

"I didn't say that, sir. There is no doubt that you've been through a ... "

"Oh, please. I don't need a watch to tell me what time it is. The President of the United States has had a prophetic vision and furthermore he fully intends to act upon it." As he said this the President looked directly at Peter and nodded. "You professionals think that's crazy, that I've had a psychological breakdown or something. Well, you know what, like Grandma used to say, 'That's just hard cheese.'"

"Hard cheese, sir?" the physician repeated.

"Tough luck, too bad, or let me put this as indelicately as I can, I don't really care what you think."

"Mr. President, I strongly advise you to …" The doctor was not given the opportunity to finish his sentence.

"Leave me. Your presence here is no longer desired or required."

"But sir, I …"

"What part of get out didn't I make clear? I'm tired of being poked at and fussed over. You work for me, remember? Don't let the door hit ya where the Good Lord split ya, and take your friends with you."

The doctor and his attending staff did as they were told, gathered up their instruments and bags and left. As they did so, the President's two most senior advisors exchanged worried and disdainful expressions with the Vice President.

"Peter," the President said. "I need to discuss my vision. As horrible as it was I'm convinced, no, check that, I know beyond a shadow of a doubt God was speaking to me."

"Yes, Mr. President, He was," Peter confirmed. "That you realize it and are willing to act upon your belief only confirms my suspicion."

"Your suspicion, Peter?"

"Yes. My suspicion is that God chose well when he allowed you to become President."

"Can you believe this s*** ?" the second senior advisor whispered to the Vice President. "This is dangerous, nearly out-of-control. We must do something. Think of the nation. Remember your duty."

As is common in men who hold the office of Vice President of the United States, the current occupant was a personal and political lightweight. He was easily manipulated, and while he had a degree of loyalty to the President, his fear was far greater than his love or faith. For the master of all demons and his two willing and able servants, the Vice President was the right man in the right place at the right time.

"Peter, I saw civilization destroyed. Armageddon. Nuclear war and its aftermath, it had to be. But it wasn't just the bombs, Peter, it's what came after. The disease, the violence. People degenerated quickly into a savage, primitive state. It was as if…"

"It was as if all of the hard fought victories of the past two thousand years, the progress of mankind since the coming of Christ had been erased…"

"Yes, Peter, that's it. We fell back to being animals again. Worse than ever before, nasty, base creatures with no love, no grace…"

"And no God."

"Are you reading my mind, Peter?" the President asked in a most respectful manner.

"No sir. God showed me the same vision last July. It's beyond terrifying, I know. And if what happened to me happened to you…"

"I could feel their flesh rotting off of my bones," the President said, grimacing. "Their pain was my pain. And somehow I knew…"

"You knew that you had been given by God the charge to stop this from happening, to deny Satan his victory, to put an end to this foolish madness once and for all."

"My God," the President said, expressing his sense of wonder. Peter was finishing his thoughts, confirming his conclusions.

"Oh, yes sir, my God indeed. I share your burden, Mr. President. We are both messengers of His word, but you are much more. You are the instrument of his plan, the one put in place with the earthly power to overcome the evil."

"How much longer, Peter, before God ends the restriction?" the President asked.

"About sixty hours, sir," Peter replied.

"Then we have some time. I need to address the nation, meet with my cabinet, and the Congressional leadership. I have to make them understand, then go to work on the rest of the world."

"What do you have in mind, Mr. President?" the first senior advisor asked.

"Haven't you been paying attention? Unbelievable, do I have to hit you on the head with a bat?"

"Mr. President?"

"Do you wish to witness the destruction of the planet?"

"What? You cannot be serious, sir," the second senior advisor said.

"Never been more serious in my life. Life. That word has a new meaning now, doesn't it? Our lives, human survival is on the line here."

"Mr. President," the first senior advisor said sternly, as he stood and took up a position in front of the Vice President. "Do you intend to change the policies of this government based on your religious vision or on Mr. Carson's assertions of divine guidance and intervention?"

"I intend to do much more than that. I intend to use the power of the Presidency to tell the world that our God, our Creator, has a message for us, a warning, a revelation. Not only will I act swiftly and decisively to change the policies of this government, I will also use my office and personal influence to advance God's interests as Mr. Carson suggests I do so."

"Mr. President, that is a reckless course of action, one taken both in haste and against the advice of those closest to you." The style of the first senior advisor was grave, threatening.

"You don't even know what I'm specifically proposing to do and yet you're calling me reckless?"

"Yes, sir. You have elevated this man here, Mr. Carson, who may I remind you, Mr. President, is a convicted con artist and a federal inmate, to the status of some sort of prophet or sage or something. What did you just get through saying, sir? You're going to 'advance God's interests as Mr. Carson suggests?' Who elected Mr. Carson to public office?"

Unlike his running mate, the President was anything but a personal or political lightweight. He was being challenged on his own turf, called to account like some schoolboy who had botched his homework by those in his inner circle. Under normal circumstances, basically anything other than the situation he now found himself in, such a chastisement would serve as a reality check, a wake up call telling him that he might be dangerously off course.

However, in light of the events of the past twelve hours, all this tongue wagging did now was bring out the President's famous Irish temper.

"I see," the President said, as he walked over and faced his two most senior aides. "You both agree that I've lost it, gone off the deep end. Is that what I'm hearing?"

"Sir, with the utmost respect, the events of last night and this morning have taken their toll on all of us. It's more than understandable that your reaction to them might be a bit irrational." The first senior advisor quickly shifted gears from confrontation to condescension, hoping to exploit both the President and the situation.

"Maybe you're right," the President said, playing along. "What's going on is certainly well beyond bizarre, I'll grant you that."

"Yes, sir, I agree. Let's all take a little time and..."

"Or perhaps you and your evil twin," the President said, pointing at the second senior advisor. "Did you know that's what we call you two when you're not around, the evil twins? Probably not. Perhaps you and your evil twin are simply feeling threatened by all of this in general, and by Mr. Carson in particular. Perhaps you fear losing your personal power more than you truly wish to serve your country. Perhaps..." The President paused. He was struggling with the rest of what he wanted to say.

"Come on, Mr. President, speak what's on your mind, and mine," Peter whispered to Alex.

"Perhaps you two are nothing but worthless servants of hell, a couple of no good sons of bitches I should have given the boot to long ago."

"Mr. President! I must object to your comments. These gentlemen aren't your enemies, they're your allies. I believe we need to get a doctor back in here, maybe get you back in bed and after..."

"Patrick." The President had never before addressed the Vice President by his first name unless they were together alone. "Stop right there. Let me ask you something. Right now, at this very moment, I want nothing more than to pick up one of these scrawny scheming bastards by his ears and beat the living hell out of him. Part of the reason I want to do this should be obvious to you, they are directly challenging the authority placed in me by the American people. But the other part of my reason is less rational, intuitive perhaps, and most certainly brand new. Somehow I know that these two vermin are vicious, repugnant liars intent on doing me and our country great harm. They cannot deceive me any longer."

"Mr. President! Slow down, for God's sakes sir ..."

"Let me finish, Pat. As much as I want to, I cannot strike either one of them. I'm trying right now, visualizing my boot going right up one of their skinny little a***s, but I can't do anything. Do you understand, Pat? Please tell me the significance of this is not lost on you."

"Mr. President, yes, I do understand that some power has us all in its grip. But what are we really dealing with? God? Extraterrestrials? Mass hypnosis or psychosis? It is extremely unwise. No, let me rephrase. It is not a rational act to base decisions affecting billions of lives on a dream and the word of a con man."

"Why Patrick, you impress me. I've never seen this side of you before. It's almost like you've got some balls. And all this time I figured you for a coward." The President was feeling it now, his verbal wrath and his keen mind were both fully engaged.

"Mr. President, that was uncalled for. I mean really, such a comment is unlike and beneath you, further confirming our hypothesis ..."

"That's more like it, Pat. Go back to the weak suck-up mode, it suits you better. But do it somewhere else. And take my two former advisors with you."

"You do not have the power to fire me, sir. I was elected along with yourself to the office I hold."

"Sure enough, but hold your office somewhere else. I've got work to do in here right now. Part of what I'll be doing today, Patrick, is drafting your letter of resignation. I'll bet you'll be signing it damn quick once I get through destroying you in the press. Now, listen to me carefully. Get out."

Sensing the value of an orderly retreat, the Vice President and the two suddenly former most senior aides on the President's staff decided to walk away without further comment. They also had work to do.

"Peter, I need you to assist me today. General Vargas and Agent Austin, I need both of you here as well. Miss McCorkle, Mr. Simpson, Mr. Graham and Mr. Coleman, you are all welcome to stay or leave as you, and Peter, please."

"I'm welcome to go, sir?" Malik asked. The President had said it so casually, so matter of fact. More so than for any of his brothers, freedom for Malik Graham had been a distant dream, a hope perhaps too unlikely to pursue under any circumstances.

"Mr. Graham, I doubt anyone could stop you if they tried, but they'd be breaking the law if they did."

"Sir?" Malik's heart leapt with joy.

"First thing this morning I issued full Presidential pardons to all of you. You are a free man, Mr. Graham. No one will ever put you in a cell or shackle you again."

"Glory to God! Lord have mercy! I'm free! Don't have no record? Jesus be praised! Jesus be praised!" Malik hugged and kissed everybody in the room in turn, including the President.

The only being in the oval office not sharing in the revelry was the devil. He felt weaker, diminished after the President's charitable act of mercy and redemption. Such outpourings of love sickened him, decreased his powers and inflamed his eternal hatred of humanity.

Satan decided to vent his frustration on Saul.

Twenty

"Saul."

"Yes, I'm here."

"Saul, you must fight the beast. He is a coward and a liar, but he is not without powers. He will use your fear against you, Saul."

"Where are you? I can't see anything." Saul's mind was projecting only blackness.

"I'm fighting for you, Saul. I'm right here."

"Gabriel?" Saul could see the angel now, but he was far off and small, almost inconsequential given the depth of the void in Saul's mind.

How long have I been in this dark place? Saul asked himself in his thoughts. Time for him had become an elusive concept. What seemed like five minutes could well be five years for all Saul knew. He had been taken against his will, made a pawn in a battle that has raged since the most ancient of days.

It was Saul's gift that frightened and enraged the beast. Satan works best as an invisible mastermind, using the weaknesses of the flesh against his mortal prey. The devil is pure hatred, as opposed to God who is pure love. Unless it is cleverly disguised, human beings will always flee hatred and embrace love. Saul Cohen was dangerous because he exposed the devil for what he

Solomon's Porch

307

truly was, the very essence of all that is vile, destructive, dishonest, and diseased.

The contest for human souls, the arena in which Light and darkness engage in their perpetual warfare, had reached a critical juncture. Satan did not accept God's claim that the victory was His. The devil thought himself equal to God and believed he could defeat Him. Satan wanted Saul Cohen out of the way, and by accomplishing this, he hoped, he would also destroy Saul's gift, thereby denying it to God's faithful.

Saul's black peace was shattered as it had been ten or twenty (or was it a hundred or two hundred?) times before. His mind was suddenly flooded with stark images of hell, desperate loneliness, and the threatened absence of God. Saul fought back with his faith and his love, but he was weakening. Evil was winning.

While the demons feared Saul, they were also drawn to him because his gift connected them to the world and to the Light they so desperately craved. He was an attractor, and in his current vulnerable state demons latched on to Saul like iron shavings to a magnet. They now completely enveloped him. Their presence was overwhelming, draining Saul of what little energy he had left.

The beast is unlike his demons. He does not seek the Light, he's trying to extinguish it. Saul could sense the purity of the evil that was tormenting him, the raw ugliness of it, the absoluteness of its anti-God and anti-human qualities.

The attending nurse saw only the physical effects, not their spiritual cause. Saul's body temperature rose and fell ten to fifteen degrees within a minute, his skin instantly went from corpse clammy to red hot. Horrible sores erupted and then disappeared on his face and chest, his eyes filled with blood and then returned to normal. He moaned and flailed about, nearly reaching consciousness before suddenly falling back into a near vegetative state.

All she could do was keep Saul hydrated and as comfortable as possible. Peter had forbidden her to give him drugs, or to call in an attending physician, or to transfer Saul to a hospital. The President had made it clear that Peter's orders regarding Saul were to be carried out without exception.

As much as he yearned to, Peter did not have the luxury of being able to devote his energies solely to Saul. That honor fell to Malik Graham, who refused to leave his friend's side despite his near irresistible urge to simply go outside and take a walk around Washington as a free man.

"Mr. Pete, why ain't Saul gettin' no better?" Malik asked, as he cooled his brother's burning forehead with an ice pack. "Are we prayin' wrong? Is God mad at us?"

"Patience, brother. Have faith. God is with us and He is with Saul. It is not our place to say which trials we must face or how long they will last. We serve the Lord, He does not serve us, but His love and His grace are ours abundantly." Peter projected strength, but this genuine front masked grave concern.

While Peter Carson accepted the inevitability of his own martyrdom, he had no such similar attitude about the lives of his brothers. They were his soul mates, his charges, closer to him in many ways than Julie or Kevin could ever be. He continually petitioned God for their protection. Their safety and well being was far more important to him than his own fate.

It was not for Peter to know which of his brothers would die at the hands of the enemy and which would pass on peacefully in their old age. Peter accepted this lack of knowledge as God's will and took it as a sign that he was to do everything possible to keep his brothers safe.

But now the entire world was beckoning him. Peter could only do so much to protect Saul and the other disciples. God saved each of them for a purpose and that purpose most certainly involved sacrificing everything for others if that was required to accomplish His goals.

"The President wants to see you now, Peter," Rico Vargas said, as he emerged from the hallway and into Saul's makeshift hospital room. "Is he getting any better?"

"No. Worse, I'm afraid," Peter answered.

"What do you want me to do, Panos? I mean if you need to be here I certainly understand that, maybe ... "

"No, General. My duty lies elsewhere. Malik will stay with Saul. We must trust God."

It was early evening on the twentieth of June. By now every living soul on the planet was aware of the restriction and its unprecedented impact on human life. People spoke of little else. Issues considered vital and urgent only twenty-four hours earlier were now irrelevant.

In every society, the select were showing themselves and using their faith for the advancement of the Kingdom. Peter was miraculously blessed with millions of new witnesses to his claim of being God's messenger.

Whether they originated in China, Tibet, India, Pakistan, Vietnam, Israel, Greece, France, Brazil, or the United States, it didn't matter. The stories were the same; the assertions made identical. No one could rightly question the plain fact that something had touched a staggering number of people with nothing previously in common other than that they were alive, blessing each of them with the same spiritual experience.

Reports of phenomenal works began streaming in from everywhere. As might be expected, some of these claims were bogus, but most were not. The power of the Holy Spirit was pouring out like never before, abundantly manifesting itself on those who believed.

But despite this massive demonstration of God's power, most people only directly experienced the effects of the restriction. The select were a few million amidst billions. By no means did the majority of the world run to embrace the idea that God was speaking to them through His son Jesus Christ.

The President desperately wanted to further God's cause. He now believed, quite correctly, that for this purpose he was elected to his office.

Peter was the key. Everyone wanted to see him, to talk with him, to size him up, to determine for themselves whether he was a prophet or a fraud. He could not stay under wraps in the White House for much longer. The problem was controlling Peter's coming out process, how best to engage the masses without being trampled by them.

After an hour spent in solitude and prayer, the President emerged from his private chapel with an answer.

"It was actually Mr. Anderson's idea," the President admitted. "I just expanded on it."

"Alex?" Peter asked.

"I can't really take credit for it either, Dave Martz was the one who basically thought this thing..."

"Alex, please. Be direct." Peter was in no mood for long winded explanations or beating around the bush. Try as he might, the thought of Saul's suffering was a serious distraction for him.

"Yes, sorry, Panos." Alex took a sip of water and got right to the point. "Between the network and the President, we have over a thousand requests for interviews with you. And we're just counting those that cannot be ignored. Even if we wanted to, we could not accommodate all of them, at least not near term."

"We talked about this, Alex," Peter reminded his friend. "As I recall, our plan was to avoid the one-on-one stuff and focus on reaching the people."

"We can do both, Peter," the President suggested.

"I'm listening," Peter said.

"Dave Martz had the idea of a roundtable discussion format with a small and influential group of participants. And by influential I mean incredibly influential, Peter. The cream of the crop of our society." Alex lit up as he discussed the idea. He knew that the Spirit was leading him in the right direction.

"We sit around a table and ask each other questions?" Peter guessed.

"They'll be the ones asking the questions, Peter. Look at it this way, this set up allows you not only to interact with the world's elite, but also to bring the message to billions of people very personally. There will be time for the stadiums and the crowds after, let's establish your credibility first."

"By responding to questions?" Peter asked skeptically. "Alex, you know by now that I'm not some genius with an answer for every riddle. It wouldn't be too hard to make me look stupid if I was expected to solve every human problem from bed-wetting to lung cancer."

"You got me," the President said, "just by walking into my office. Tell them exactly who and what you are, Peter. 'I don't know' is an acceptable response when it's honest. You'll do fine, much more than fine, I'll bet. Let the Spirit lead you."

The President's confidence was infectious. Peter was warming to the concept, Alex was bordering on ecstatic.

"Who did you gentlemen have in mind for the panel?" Peter asked.

"Myself, for one," the President answered. "The public would expect no less, plus I can be right by your side through it all, offering any assistance as needed."

Peter had expected this. "Who else?" he asked.

"Cardinal Reardon, Sam Harwell, Reverend Tommy Peterson…"

"Peterson? Lord have mercy. Why him Alex?" Peter was very familiar with Reverend Peterson's particular brand of radical right wing evangelism. He found both it and Reverend Peterson misguided and distasteful.

"Because Peterson represents about fifty million plus American born-again Protestant believers, Panos," Alex answered. "By ignoring or excluding the good Reverend, we would only be giving him and the most rabid of his followers ammunition to use against us."

"My head hurts just thinking about him," Peter said, "but I hear what you're saying. Harwell, he's the owner of Harsoft, right? The multi-billionaire."

"Right." Alex knew Peter would not enjoy facing off with Peterson. But he was also sure that sooner or later such a confrontation was inevitable. "Five more, Peter. Rabbi Rosefielde from New York, UN Secretary General Carlos Benes from Brazil, and Roger Stone."

"Who the heck is Roger Stone?" Peter asked.

"Nobody. Just one of the millions of people calling themselves the select who shared the Pentecostal dream. He's an accountant from Wisconsin. Roger has two kids, a collie, and a mortgage. Middle America personified. Not much to look at either. Bright guy, but not what you'd call real smart."

"You're begging the question, Alex."

"Why Mr. Stone? Because he was invited."

"Okay. And?"

"Peter, I've had dreams about this guy. Remember I told you about him. The face that keeps popping up in my head."

"How did you put the name with the face?"

"Strangest thing. For some reason out of the tens of thousands of e-mails I've gotten since yesterday, his was the first on the list. I was going to simply dump them all to a disk and have someone else look at them later when I accidentally opened his message."

"Uh oh."

"He had attached his photo to the message. I recognized him right off. Guess what his message said."

"Wouldn't even try. Tell me."

"Stone wrote, 'Mr. Anderson, the Lord says I need to be in some group you are putting together. I'm honored, but hardly qualified or deserving. I think I'm supposed to ask Mr. Carson questions, but I don't know why. Yours in Christ, R. Stone.'"

"That would just about seal it for me, Alex."

"Yep, me too. God is good."

"All the time."

"Peter, we were thinking about doing this tomorrow night," the President broke in.

"Why so soon?"

"I believe it is important to move forward while the restriction is still an ongoing event rather than when it's history," the President explained. "You might be at the height of your potential influence right now, Peter. Once things return to normal, urgency is diminished, attention less focused. Strike while the iron is hot, so to speak."

"Makes sense, sir," Peter agreed. "Where are we doing it?"

"Right here in the White House. We can accommodate a fairly large audience in the East Room. Important people from all over the world will want to come. We'll have to do a lottery or something to see who gets in."

"Okay. Who are the last two on the panel, Alex?" Peter asked.

"Dr. Carl Fuchs, a Nobel Prize winner in physics and widely regarded as the world's top physical scientist, and Dr. Howard Simms of Harvard."

"Simms, Simms. I know that name," Peter recalled.

"H. Simms is an astrophysicist and an anthropologist. Reportedly he has an I.Q. over two hundred. He's known as much for his integrity as he is for his intelligence."

"And there's me."

"That's right, Peter, and you." Alex looked Panos directly in the eye as he said this, trying to convey some of the absolute confidence he had in the efficacy of his plan to Peter.

"Like I said and me, Peter Carson. I know God will be with me, Alex, but are you sure this is the way to go? Couldn't it backfire on us? God forbid I embarrass Him."

"Peter." The President stood, walked over to where Peter was sitting and put his arm around his shoulder. "In my chapel a short time ago I was drawn through prayer to a passage of Scripture. Led right to it in fact. Can I read it?"

"Please, sir. All that we do should be grounded in the Word."

"It comes from Paul's first letter to the Corinthians, starting at chapter one verse twenty-five."

Peter relaxed and smiled. He knew these particular verses well, and if the President was drawn to them it could only be confirmation of the correctness of their course.

"Because the foolishness of God is wiser than men, and the weakness of God is stronger than men. For you see your calling, brethren, that not many wise according to the flesh, not many mighty, not many noble are called. But God has chosen the foolish things of the world to put to shame the wise, and God has chosen the weak things of the world to put to shame the things which are mighty and the base things of the world and the things which are despised God has chosen, and the things which are not, to bring to nothing the things that are ... "

"That no flesh should glory in His presence," Peter said, finishing the quote. "Mr. President, it is the height of foolishness to assume that a base man such as myself, a weak former convict with no formal training in either religious studies, politics, or science could possibly hold his own with such an elite group."

"Exactly, Peter. Makes about as much sense as me not being able to punch those two no good former aides of mine in the teeth last night. What do you guys say to each other? God is good?"

"Always," Peter acknowledged.

At the exact same time that the President was holding his meeting in the White House, another group of powerful men were huddled down the street in the offices of a United States Senator. Darkness was formulating its plan to defeat the Light.

The Vice President of the United States was in attendance for only a brief portion of the meeting, the part where three of the most respected psychiatrists in America and five of the most senior members of the Senate decided that the President had become "dangerous and psychologically unstable." The term "desperate national crisis" was used to describe the blessing of the restriction, and "congenital liar and possible foreign agent" was the label applied to Peter Carson.

The Vice President needed plausible deniability, so he left after plotting the elaborate smoke screen that the conspirators hoped would obscure their actual intentions.

The two former senior advisors to the President wanted their jobs back, but with a twist; they also needed a new boss. They were intelligent and cunning men of the world, and because the evil one was now controlling them almost directly, they had become ruthless and amoral to the extreme. Nothing mattered to them other than their lust for power. They knew if their plan succeeded that they would become more than they ever were before. The new President would basically serve as their lap dog, a mere puppet that they and their master could control at will.

The beast attended the meeting in the Senator's office, encouraging lies and treachery. As was always the case, the evil one marveled at how easy it was to turn most men against their own kind. But a righteous few were not so easily swayed. Satan's most intense hatred was reserved for those blessed people who recognized evil and refused to acknowledge Satan's falsely claimed supremacy in the universe; vile, worthless monkey trash like Saul Cohen and all of his friends.

"Saul!"

"What do you want from me? If you think I'm going to bow down to you, you're wrong. You are nothing but a loser, damned for all time for your pride. I think you're pathetic, actually."

"If God is so good and powerful and loving, why does He let me hurt you, Saul?"

Into Saul's mind Satan implanted thoughts of searing flesh. Saul felt as if he was being burned alive. But God only allowed so much agony, within a minute of its commencement the torture stopped.

The nurse watched on in horror as the skin on Saul's legs charred and bubbled. Then, as quickly as it started, the bizarre effect ended and Saul's skin returned to normal.

By now she had seen more than enough. Convinced someone had slipped her some LSD or other powerful hallucinogen and not wanting to go mad permanently, the traumatized nurse stood and told Malik, "I can't do this," then ran screaming out of the room.

Malik did not flinch. His mind was completely focused on Saul. If it were possible to pray his friend out of his desperate condition, he was determined to do so.

Malik asked God if He would be kind enough to allow him to suffer for his friend. "I'm stronger, Father," Malik prayed aloud. "Saul has been through enough. Let me carry his load, Lord. I lay down my life for my friend."

For the first time, Malik Graham audibly heard His voice in answer to a prayer.

"Are you sure, son? What you seek is a difficult path full of sacrifice and suffering. Are you truly ready to serve?"

Malik didn't need Peter or anyone else to confirm the genuineness of His message. He knew with every fiber of his being that the Lord was calling to him.

"I'm ready God. Let Saul be, let him rest."

Into the blackness that had once again been projected into Saul's mind now entered a Light, bright and blazing like a white hot star. Saul immediately sensed that the evil one had fled, unable to withstand the power of His glory.

The Being now with Saul had hair as white as snow, eyes like flames of fire, and feet like fine brass. Saul knew he was in Christ's presence. He marveled at how accurately both the prophet Daniel and St. John had described Him.

"Well done my good and faithful servant," Christ said. "It is time for you to come home, Saul."

Overwhelmed by love, happy beyond any human standard of bliss, totally at peace and fulfilled, Saul Cohen gave up his earthly existence.

Back in the small room at the White House, Malik felt Saul's hand go limp in his and saw his brother's breathing stop. He smiled and cried a tear of joy for his friend. He knew Saul was safely in the bosom of his Father.

Malik looked up. Now he could see the beast in the corner, hovering about like a jackal, hoping to enjoy a moment of triumph over the creatures he so despised.

"Guess what, you filthy son of a bitch," Malik said boldly. "Now I can see ya! Oh, how I been waitin' for this day. All the hell you done put me through you sick, evil monster. I'm comin' to get you, devil! Praise God and Jesus Christ, I'm comin' to get you!"

For the first time in nearly two millennia Satan experienced an unwelcome, almost human emotion. It was the same one he felt as he watched Christ rise out of His tomb.

Fear.

Twenty-One

"Are you sure, Alex?" Peter asked. "I know we've talked about the possibility, but now it is a reality. This is your home we're dealing with here."

"Whatever I have is yours, Peter," Alex Anderson replied. "The estate is owned by a foreign trust that I control. Not even the IRS can touch it. As far as I'm concerned, the place belongs to all of us. It's our sanctuary. God owns it all anyway, brother. I know you don't need me to explain that to you."

Alex didn't need to explain, but regardless Peter was deeply moved. It was very comforting for him to know where he would be laid to rest. He and Saul Cohen.

"We'll ship the body down to Georgia tomorrow, Peter," Alex said. "Turns out along with everything else they have here at the White House, they've got a makeshift morgue. What plans do you have for the funeral, Panos?"

"There won't be time for that now, Alex. We can celebrate and pray for Saul here tomorrow. Julie will see that Saul gets buried properly. Later you and the brothers can pay the proper respects at his grave."

"Letting the dead bury the dead?"

"Like everything else the Master taught us, there is a time and place for its proper application."

"Where will you be, Peter?"

"Alex?"

"When we're all down at the farm mourning Saul, where will you be?"

Peter hadn't realized that he'd let his guard down and slipped. He castigated himself knowing that shortly millions would be hanging on his every word. There was no room for error.

"Who knows, Alex?" Peter said, as dismissively and casually as possible. "I guess I find it difficult to make any plans. God has set my path and He's left little room for any personal choice."

Alex Anderson wanted to pursue Peter's comment further, he could sense a benevolent ruse, but Malik had been patiently waiting to speak with Alex and Peter for over two hours. It had taken them longer than they expected to make the necessary arrangements for Saul.

"Sorry we were delayed," Peter apologized, as he and Alex and Malik found a small empty office for a private talk. "Alex and I know how much you loved Saul. It was good you were with him at the end. It must have been difficult for you to watch him go."

"I'm not sorry for Saul, Mr. Pete," Malik said, as he sat down and quickly scanned the room, making sure that they were alone. "I know where he is. He's restin'. 'Bout now he's speakin' to Jesus, I suspect."

"Of course he is," Peter agreed. "But I know how much you will miss him. We all will. Saul was not replaceable. We are weaker with his loss."

"Ah, Mr. Pete. Don't be so sure about all that 'weaker' stuff. I kinda know part of the reason why the Lord called Saul home."

"Please, Malik. Tell us. Praise God."

"Ah, yes sir, Mr. Pete. Glory to Christ. Well, sir, I don't think we're no weaker with Saul gone because now I can see, Mr. Pete."

"You can see? The demons?"

"That's right, Mr. Pete."

"Well I'll be." Peter hadn't considered the possibility that the Lord would keep the gift alive after Saul's death.

"Mr. Pete, I think you needs to know two things. First of all, I ain't afraid of no devil. Ah, I know I need to watch my language and all, brother, but alls I got to say is screw him. He can bring it on, I don't care. Now Saul, he was afraid of Satan. Not me. I'm gonna lick him. Me and God."

Peter was well aware that Malik Graham's entire life had been filled with violence and conflict. Surviving, indeed thriving as Malik had, under such circumstances breeds confidence and courage. Christ had taken Malik's fearlessness, the very quality that when abused had allowed Malik to succeed as a violent criminal, and employed it for the benefit of the Kingdom. Peter took Malik at his word that Satan did not scare him. He understood his brother's gifts and admired his abilities.

"The second thing is?" Peter asked.

"Sorry to tell you this, Mr. Pete, but the head man himself, Satan, he's here tryin' to do us in."

"You're sure? Legion is very powerful, Malik. Do you know the difference between the devil and his servants?"

"Mr. Pete," Malik answered coolly. "Trust me. This thing is the devil himself. He ain't like Legion. Don't look like him, act like him, don't even so much as smell like him. Oh, it's Satan for sure. He's the one who scared poor Saul to death."

So, Peter thought, *the battle is on. No more proxies, no more second stringers.* Peter prayed silently for wisdom and strength.

Unlike Malik he was not fearless, but like his brother he had the ultimate confidence in Christ.

"My friend, you've become our eyes and ears," Peter said. "As I counseled Saul, be cautious. Stay humble. Do not underestimate the evil one. Remember the source of your power, Malik; Christ, the cross, the resurrection. Despite your courage you must always remain meek."

"Meek, Mr. Pete? What's that mean?"

"It means that Satan will try and tempt you to use evil against him, to let your confidence get the best of you, to step out of God's power and protection. You can beat the devil, Malik, but only with love, not with hate."

"I cannot love the devil, Mr. Pete."

"No, of course not. But to overcome him we must pour out God's mercy and love when he brings hatred and pain."

"I get it, Mr. Pete. Like you been tellin' me since I met ya, don't play the devil's game."

"Exactly. And Malik, something else. Don't tell anyone but the brothers about your new gift. Understood?"

"Yes sir, Mr. Pete."

"Mr. Carson," said the voice that called out after the sharp knock on the door. "Your wife is trying to reach you. She says it's urgent. I'll send the call through to the phone on the desk."

Julie, Peter thought. *What now?* Reluctantly, he picked up the handset.

"Peter, honey, I know we planned to talk later on tonight, but I thought this couldn't wait," Julie said. "Something told me you needed to get this message now."

"Go ahead, Jules," Peter responded, a bit condescendingly. His mind was occupied by a thousand different thoughts, all competing for his attention. Focusing on the moment was becoming more and more difficult for him. The last thing he needed was another distraction.

"An hour ago I got a call from overseas, Peter, from Greece. I could barely understand the guy. His accent is real thick and his English is limited."

She's calling me about some man in Greece? Now? Peter thought, but did not say. *Lord have mercy,* he silently prayed.

"Jules, honey. Millions of people would call you if they…" Peter caught himself. "How did this man get your number? I thought no one had it but Alex and me. We better get on this right now, Jules. I mean if this person…"

"Peter, baby, relax. No one told him how to find me. He lives in a small village about forty minutes north of Athens. The last thing he is is a threat, to me or to anyone else. God gave him my number."

Suddenly Julie had Peter's total attention.

"His name is Gregory Kallistos. According to him, he's your uncle. He's a priest, Peter. An Orthodox priest. He says he needs to speak with you as soon as possible."

Instantly the Spirit confirmed to Peter that what Julie was saying was true. But he wondered, why hadn't the Carsons told me that I had an uncle in Greece? Why lie and say that my only close living blood relative was Marie Carson, my mother's first cousin? Peter had never met anyone from Greece, or anyone named Kallistos, and had always assumed that his direct family heritage would forever remain shrouded in mystery.

"Peter? You still there?" Julie was reacting to the silence on the other end of the line.

"Yes, sorry Jules. This is a bit of a shock. What should I do?"

"Call him." Julie gave Peter Father Kallistos' number in Greece. "He's a wonderful, gentle man, Peter. I can tell that just by the way he talks. I get the feeling he's been waiting for the right time to reach out to you, honey. And Peter…"

"Yes?"

"I love you. Kevin is taking a bath before bed. Can I tell him you'll call him tomorrow?"

"Of course, Jules. I love you too. Sorry if I was short with you. Please take care of Saul."

"I will. Alex and I got it all straight, love. Bye."

Peter gave the number to the White House operator. He heard the whines and clicks as the international telephone network processed the call. He felt an anxious but wonderful anticipation as he listened to the dull short blasts of the foreign ring tone.

"Hello."

"Father Gregory Kallistos, please," Peter said.

"My son?"

Peter heard the voice, but it registered more in his heart than in his brain.

"Father? Father Kallistos?"

"Panos! Praise Christ! My boy, Panos! You must think this very strange. I've been waiting so long my son, how you say? Since you very little."

Peter was dazed. He vacillated for a second, not quite sure what he should say. Then he asked, "How much do you know, about what's happened, I mean."

"Oh, Panos, my boy, I know everything. Known forever. Your papa, my brother, he and I knew your, how you say, fate since before you born. But much you do not know, Panos."

"Father, I…"

"Say no more, Panos. The evil one, he hears too much. Send me ride, how in English, airplane ride to Athens. I come to see you, must come to you. Do it now, son, do not wait."

Peter did not hesitate. With his uncle on hold he told the President's aide what he needed. An Air Force transport happened to be already manned, fueled, and ready for departure in Athens. It was immediately redirected and converted into the private jet of Father Gregory Kallistos.

"Father," Peter said, jumping back on the line.

"I still here, my son."

"Go to the airport in Athens. There is a section of the facility the U.S. military uses. They say there are signs that will direct you to it."

"Been to airport many times, Panos, know it well. I be fine."

"Tell the U.S. soldier at the gate who you are. They will fly you to me, to Washington, D.C."

"Panos."

"Yes, Father."

"I am very proud of you, my son. Nicholas is watching you from heaven, praying for you. You are very special man, Panos. You have big family here in Greece. We love you very much. I must go now."

The line went dead. Frustratingly, the millions of questions Peter had for his uncle would have to wait.

Alex and Malik had listened to the entire conversation from Peter's end.

"Panos, this is wonderful news! You have a family. I know how much this ..."

"Alex, Malik, could you brothers give me a moment or two alone?"

Without saying another word, Alex and Malik got up and left, but Malik didn't go far. He stood outside the office door as a sentry, ready to sound the alarm if the evil one appeared.

There was a sofa in the office. Peter felt weak and light-headed and decided to lie down and gather his thoughts.

Peter closed his eyes and tried to recall everything Thomas and Marie Carson had told him about his biological parents.

At one point he remembered seeing pictures of them, the last time was when he was in junior high, if he had his dates right, but every photo the Carsons had was destroyed in a house fire in Peter's freshman year of high school. The impressions he retained were that his mother was a beautiful woman, a blonde with classic Greek features; his father was a large man, strong and virile. Marie Carson always told Peter that he took after his mother. When he was a boy, Peter had often fantasized about her and what she looked like, and how it would feel to be hugged by her.

Peter had always known that he was born in Athens; in the Greek Orthodox Church priests are not only allowed, but encouraged to marry. He was told that his father and mother had been together since they were teenagers, long before Nicholas Kallistos went off to the seminary to become a priest. Peter was their only child. They wanted to have a large family, according to Marie Carson, but their plans were cut short by tragedy.

The Carsons told Peter the story many times over the years. When it happened, Peter was barely two years old. He was a "perfect baby," never cried or fussed or got sick; smiled at everyone, lit up any room his parents brought him into. Peter had always believed that these descriptions of him were exaggerations made to make him feel good about himself. Now he wasn't so sure. He needed to reevaluate all he knew about his parents' deaths in the context of God's revelations.

On that fateful March morning that changed so many lives, about a half an hour before the proud young Kallistos family was set to depart for a picnic with friends in the country, unexpectedly young Panos started to fuss, to cough, and to run a fever. It wasn't considered serious, but Panos' symptoms were sufficient to keep him at home that day in the care of a nun who acted as a part-time nanny for the popular parish priest.

"Funny thing was," Marie Carson always said as she got to this part of the narrative, as soon as Nicholas and Neitha drove away from the house, Peter was fine. No more fever, coughing, or complaining.

"You weren't meant to be in that car, Peter," Marie told him. She dwelled on the fact that it was very unlike her cousin Neitha to let Peter out of her sight for even a few minutes, nanny or no nanny. "Fate," she called it.

"Not fate, mom, grace," Peter said softly to himself as he stretched out a bit more on the couch. "It was God's grace."

He wondered why he hadn't thought much about this whole subject for years until today. It hadn't seemed too important, for whatever reason.

As the Carsons told it, several eyewitnesses described how a large black car of indeterminate make and model approached and then rammed the Kallistos' vehicle on a narrow and winding mountain road, sending it tumbling five hundred feet down into a ravine. Peter's parents died on impact.

No one was ever charged with a crime in the incident. Neither the black car not its occupants were ever identified. It was also uncertain whether the collision was an accident or a deliberate act.

For whatever reason, now increasingly more mysterious to Peter after learning that he had a living uncle on his father's side, following the death of his parents he was immediately shipped off to America to be raised by his deceased aunt's daughter, Marie Carson.

"There are no accidents," the Voice gently whispered in Peter's ear. "God has always had a plan and a purpose for your life."

Peter smiled. He knew the Voice well. It was his Comforter, his Friend, his Constant Companion.

Aloud but softly he asked, "Why did my parents have to die? Couldn't they have just been told to move to America? Why all the pain and suffering?" He stopped for a moment, reflected, and began to whisper again.

"Why did I have to make so many stupid mistakes? Did you know I would, Lord? Why did I have to lose everything in order to gain You?"

The Voice did not provide any more answers, nor did Peter expect It to. Trying to unravel the ways of God, to apply human logic and wisdom to divine events, he knew was a totally pointless exercise. God requires faith and obedience and an open heart. He does not necessarily provide the knowledge of His ways in return.

Another knock came from the door. This one was quiet and respectful, as was the voice that followed it.

"Mr. Carson," the young female aide said demurely. "They told me to find you. You are needed, sir. Sorry to disturb you."

"That's really what it comes down to," Peter said to himself. "I'm needed. Glory to God, what else can a man ask for."

"Coming," he said loud enough to be heard through the door. Peter was indeed coming, moving inexorably toward the destiny planned for him since time began.

"Well, Peter, let me put it this way," the President reported. "Pretty much everyone in this government thinks I've lost it, gone screwy. They do not have an explanation for the restriction, mind you, other than to say it's an 'amazing phenomenon that needs to be studied.' They're blind, which somehow makes me insane. To tell you the truth, I expected better from some of them, from most of them."

"Mr. President, if I may, sir, let me remind you what St. Paul told us. We battle not against 'flesh and blood, but against powers and principalities.' Sir, Satan is blinding them. That's why they refuse to see."

"The invisible controlling the visible concept again, Peter?"

Peter thought about Malik and Saul. Not so invisible to them, he reminded himself. "Exactly. If I can ask, sir, what happened?"

"I called an emergency meeting of our government a couple of hours ago, Peter," the President said. "Congressional leaders, cabinet members, the Chief Justice, the top military brass, all the major players. Like I told you I would, I brought Mr. Austin and General Vargas along with me."

Tim and Rico were in the President's office, along with Peter, Alex, and a small group of aides.

"I laid it out for them. Didn't hold anything back. Told them about my vision, described it in great detail in fact. I could not have been plainer with them, Peter. I said God made it abundantly clear to me that either we change our ways or we will die; maybe not all of us, but certainly most of us. We're facing Armageddon, total annihilation.

"As the President of the United States, my first and foremost duty is to protect this country. I said in order for me to do that now, I must work with my fellow world leaders to eliminate not only all types of weapons, but more importantly to once and for all end war as an acceptable human institution. Violent conflict between nations in all its forms must end, and end quickly. I told them I was prepared to take whatever action was required to accomplish this goal, unilateral or otherwise."

"And they said?" Peter prodded.

"That I was moving too fast, making decisions without enough information, panicking in response to the unknown. They didn't even consider what I had to say. It was obvious that they had their own agenda."

"Their own agenda, sir?" Peter asked.

"The Vice President, no doubt with considerable help from my former top two advisors, has convinced our leadership that you are the problem and that I am your lackey. They intend to try and remove me from office. God knows what they have planned for you."

Peter was well aware of what the world was going to do to him.

"Can they do that, sir? Remove you from office, I mean?"

"If they can convince the Senate I'm nuts, you bet they can impeach me. Or, and I know this is what they're thinking, they believe they can pressure me into resigning."

"Would you consider doing that, sir, resigning I mean?"

"Peter, my friend, the answer to that question is not no, but hell no. If they want to create a Constitutional crisis I say bring it on. The Lord is with me. I'm not afraid of them or what they think they can do."

"How soon will they come after you, sir? I mean, are they trying to impeach you today?"

"It's not that easy, Peter. The process takes time. Besides, no one can do anything until the restriction ends, and that's not until around ten p.m. on the twenty-second, right?"

Peter looked at his watch. "Yes sir, something like fifty hours from right now."

"Let those damn fools do what they will, Peter. What's happening in the world interests me far more than their shenanigans. Have you been keeping up? On the news, I mean?"

"No sir, not really. With Saul's death and everything else that's going on I haven't looked at much since this morning."

"Mr. Edwards," the President said to the suit nearest to him, "play the video you fellas made. The one we watched a few minutes ago."

"Yes sir, Mr. President," Edwards said as he cued up the disc.

The White House staff had compiled and edited a series of news reports from around the world. English dubbing had been added as required.

"Here in Germany an unbelievable scene is unfolding in Berlin," the excited British accented commentator reported. "Upwards of one hundred thousand people have jammed into the city's largest football stadium. But for what purpose? No one has organized this rally. Yet somehow the public address system and the physical plant of the arena have been activated. A rotating group of people, it's almost as if the members of the crowd were all taking orderly turns at the podium, is leading the throng in hymns and prayers. Shouts arise periodically as miracles are claimed. We're being told of families reconciling after years of bitter fighting, paralytics walking away from wheelchairs, deaf and blind people having their senses restored, clinical depressions lifted. We are doing our best to try and verify these claims."

"No church or denomination is sponsoring this event or has taken control of it. I've seen Catholic priests, Lutheran pastors, Anglicans, even some Muslims and Buddhists on the stage addressing the crowd."

"What could be chaos is rather a passionate but controlled celebration of what everyone here believes to be the announcement of a new Christian apostle to the world. Those gathered here are convinced that the restriction is the divine will of Christ. In between prayers and hymns the crowd can be heard to chant 'Peter, Peter,' calling out to their American prophet who is still, to the best of our knowledge, holed up in the White House with President..."

"In London today churches and public areas have been filled to capacity with faithful people who seem to be, more than anything else, seeking each other. Colin Stuart is one such man. We interviewed him just outside the Westminster cathedral."

"Mr. Stuart, why are you here at the Abbey?"

"I dunno exactly, mostly to give thanks to the Lord. Been waitin' all my life for this, I imagine."

"Waiting, Mr. Stuart?"

"Yea waitin'. I'm a simple man. The wife's passed on, kids are all grown. I live on a pension, do my best to scrape by. I'm nobody. But Christ, he chooses me for a vision. Why, I wonder?"

"You had the Pentecostal dream, Mr. Stuart?"

"The one with Peter and the brothers and the Holy fire comin' out their heads? Yeah, I did. Like I said, I'm here to ask God why."

"Got any answers yet, Mr. Stuart?"

"Yea, think so. I think God's sick of us all not doin' what we should. We should be showin' love to one another, not hatin' and killin'. He wants us to stop this nonsense, to start bein' more like Christ. I believe I've been asked to help Him, to be part of His team."

"We've spoken to twenty other people gathered here outside Westminster over the past hour, their stories are essentially the…"

"Japan is in the midst of a spiritual upheaval unprecedented in its history," the dry, monotone Japanese commentator said in perfect, unaccented English. "It is estimated that over ten million citizens have chosen to visit a shrine, church, or other spiritual center over the past twenty hours. Most come to meditate or pray, to reflect on the condition known worldwide as the restriction. Some have a more specific purpose in mind, namely to spread the Christian Gospel.

"These individuals call themselves 'the select' and profess to have had a common prophetic dream about the American Peter Carson and his disciples. Reports from around Japan of miracles of various kinds attributed to "the select" range from medical healings to divine apparitions. These supernatural claims cannot be verified. Members of 'the select' say they intend to 'evangelize' Japan and turn it into a 'Christian nation.' The government has had no further comment since…"

"The Communist Party of China," the English speaking Hong Kong reporter said, "is doing its best to ignore the restriction and its implications. Even in this enlightened era of modern communism, China remains officially atheist. The security apparatus of the Party is obviously unable to maintain order at present by use of force.

"This has allowed what is being estimated at more than fifty million people across China to gather and pray and worship openly. In the capital of Beijing a crowd of over two hundred thousand has filled Tiananmen Square, invoking memories of the 1989 democracy movement. Now, unlike then, those gathered on the square seem unconcerned about political issues. They are demanding nothing from the state. Their interest lies in one issue only, 'promoting the Kingdom of God,' as many of their banners proclaim."

"Reports of miracles are common among the assemblies. So much so that..."

"The central government is taking a cautious approach to the restriction and its implications," the Russian female news anchor said. "From the Kremlin comes word that the President has been in close consultation with his American counterpart. We have confirmed the fact that all Russian military weapons from rifles to missiles are presently non-functional."

"Perhaps half a million people here in Moscow and a like number in St. Petersburg have taken to the streets in a show of support..."

"That's enough, Edwards," the President said. "Shut it off. Peter can watch the whole thing later, if he wants to. Let's all take a walk."

The President, Peter, Alex, Vargas, and Austin got up and moved out on to a veranda that faces Pennsylvania Avenue. It was a beautiful, clear evening. The moon was bright and nearly full.

As they emerged from the building and came into view, the massive crowd gathered around the White House stirred and began to clap and cheer.

"My Lord in heaven!" Peter exclaimed. "How many people are out here, Mr. President?"

"We estimate the crowd at over a quarter of a million and it's growing rapidly. The vast majority of them you can't see from our position. They're backed up on the mall all the way to the Capitol."

"Peter, Peter, Peter." The chant was becoming louder and more organized.

"See that ugly fence and barbed wire monstrosity the Army put up?" the President asked. "Might as well be kite string. God is keeping them out, not the soldiers. Without our permission no one can set foot on the White House lawn. As much as they want to, they cannot make their bodies respond to their minds. Unbelievable, this restriction."

"Peter, Peter." The thousands of faithful surrounding the White House were now shouting louder and in unison.

"They want you, Panos," Alex said, marveling at the demonstration. "I'm not sure if that gives me hope or scares me to death. Probably both."

It was impossible for Peter to address the crowd since he was three hundred yards away from its leading edge and no public address system had been set up. So he waved and smiled and then grabbed the President's hand and raised it together with his own in a show of unity and triumph.

"Peter, my friend, I couldn't be more pleased about the restriction than I am right now," the President said, as he and Peter stood as one, arms held high.

"Sir?" Peter said, not sure if even his one word question could be heard above the tumultuous cacophony erupting from the crowd.

"Because if there was no restriction in place," the President said, leaning over and shouting directly into Peter's ear, "then this would be a great opportunity for a sniper to take me out."

Peter felt a pressure, like something was trying to get his attention. Then for a few seconds his mind was taken far from the White House. The vision was quick, but it was also unambiguous.

"Peter, you okay? You look weak, brother," the President said, as he and Alex turned Peter around and guided him off of the veranda.

"I'm fine, Mr. President. Maybe a bit woozy, but I'm straight."

Peter quickly recovered his senses, but now he had even more on his mind. He looked at the President, a man in his mid-fifties who was well known for his top physical condition and excellent health. A man who in a very short period of time Peter had come to love and admire.

"Lord have mercy," Peter whispered as they made it back inside. *Why Lord, why?* he asked God in his mind, for now he knew that this powerful and faithful man who had so quickly and easily befriended him did not have much longer to live.

Twenty-Two

"And I won't ever forget you, Saul, how brave you was and how you teached me how to fight back like a godly man should. It was you who schooled me that even though I was born black and poor and had did so much wrong that God still loved me, that He had a plan for me. You was and will always be my best homey. Bye bro, I love you."

Malik's eulogy was brief and powerful, much like his relationship with Saul Cohen. Only Christ could throw together a hard black gangster from the hood like Malik Graham and a white, fifty-something wayward Jew from New York and bind them tighter than the closest of blood brothers.

Malik was deeply wounded by Saul's death, more so than he would admit, Peter knew. It was difficult for Peter to even consider Saul without Malik, so inseparable had they become.

Peter thought back to the previous September, to the awkward sight of Saul and Malik approaching him on the yard after they got off the BOP bus from Atlanta. Malik still had that nasty "gangsta" edge back then, the look and cocky stride that communicated dominance and threatened violence. Hard to believe it was the same Malik Graham who was now unashamedly sobbing in grief as Peter gently squeezed his shoulder.

How much we've all changed, Peter thought, *and in such an amazingly short period of time. A year ago none of us understood what it meant to dedicate our lives to Christ and to our fellow man. Then we were still outcasts, misfits, in one way or another. The "off scouring" of society as St. Paul called himself. But by the grace of God alone, today we mourn the loss of one of our own in the White House, under the care and protection of the most powerful politician on earth and we do so as free men.* At times, even Peter found it hard to believe the unbelievable.

Peter was not at all sure that what he had to say about Saul was very important or even appropriate after Malik's passionate eulogy, but he knew it was expected that he speak.

"Without a shadow of a doubt I know that Saul, or rather Saint Cohen, is right now looking down on us and smiling. I'm also sure that he is constantly interceding with the Father on our behalf. We mourn today our loss, but we know it is indeed our loss, not Saul's. Saul is in Paradise, at rest and at peace and with God. No demon will be allowed to frighten or torture Saul ever again. I rejoice in our victory over Satan through our Lord Jesus and anticipate with great joy my reunion with my brother Saul when Christ calls me home. In the name of the Father, Son, and the Holy Spirit, Amen."

With a confirming "Amen" from those assembled the short service concluded. The President insisted on using his private chapel for the celebration. Until now, very few outside of the President's inner circle of family and close friends had been allowed into his sanctuary.

"Peter, I'm very sorry for your loss," the President said. "I regret that I did not have the opportunity to get to know Mr. Cohen. I'm sure that he was an extraordinary man, as all of you are."

"Yes, sir, he was. We will continue to honor him by our faith and through our obedience to the cause of Christ."

"Regarding that, Peter, my staff and I have a few more ideas about tonight's ... "

"Are you sure we can't be traced to this lunatic, Khan, or whatever his name is?" the President's former first senior advisor asked.

"Completely positive. Khan is a ghost. He is not on any U.S. or European terrorist watch list and his prints aren't in anybody's database. He's pure, pristine. This robot was hatched and grown in Iran in obscurity by the crazies awaiting the day when Allah orders him to become his 'avenging angel.'" The President's second former senior advisor had supreme confidence in their plan. Every detail had been checked, then checked again.

"So it's the twenty-third, then?" the former first senior advisor asked.

"Yes. We can be flexible with the date if need be. Circumstances will dictate the proper setting and timing," answered the second evil twin.

"The more public the better."

"Exactly."

"Peter, if that is how you want to proceed I will, of course, be obedient, but I must go on record saying I think your plan is unreasonably dangerous." General Vargas was reacting to Peter's instructions as to how their mission was to unfold after the restriction ended. The disciples, Alex and Gail had gathered together to discuss strategy after Saul's service.

"I can appreciate your concerns, General," Peter acknowledged, "but it's simply not feasible for us all to remain together.

The world is a big place, Rico, and the Lord would have us reach as many souls as we can as quickly as possible."

Peter's plan was simple. Vargas and Austin were to go to Europe and Kenny and Larry to Asia. Peter, Malik, Gail and Alex would remain in the Americas and "float" as needed and as led by the Spirit.

"We must remember why we are here," Peter continued. "It is not to be defensive or to seek safety. It is to boldly proclaim to our brothers and sisters everywhere on earth the good news that God loves them and wants His creation to prosper. All of the power that we have been given, the blessings, the miracles, everything has been done for this single purpose."

"Praise God, Peter," Tim Austin said, "but don't we have an obligation to do all we can to protect ourselves or, more to the point, brother, to protect you? Do we not serve Christ best as living souls?"

"I'm not saying we shouldn't be prudent," Peter responded, "but we are to trust the Lord, Tim, not necessarily in our own judgment. He wants us to disperse, just as he wanted the twelve to go their separate ways two thousand years ago."

"Panos, it's being 'prudent' that concerns me," General Vargas interjected. "I don't understand why you refuse to organize a professional guard detail, especially for yourself. It would not be difficult to do and the protection could be deployed discreetly. No one would notice them; they would in no way detract from the message."

No, Peter thought, they wouldn't. But they might very well unwittingly thwart God's will.

"I'll keep an open mind, General," Peter said, trying his best to sound diplomatic, "but let me be clear on my instructions. If you and Tim feel that a body guard detail would be a benefit to your ministry, then please feel free to assemble one. Same goes for Kenny and Larry."

Vargas wasn't buying the argument. "Panos, that just makes no sense, brother. Forgive me for sounding so harsh, I'm saying everything out of love, but don't you care about your own life? After all, it's you Satan wants most to kill."

Peter recalled the words of St. James, "For what is your life? It is even a vapor that appears for a little time and then vanishes away." Peter was certain that his brothers meant well, but he also knew that even the best of motives can be used for evil if what is trying to be accomplished is contrary to God's divine plan.

"Brothers and Gail, I know that all of you trust me and believe me when I say I am asking nothing of you other than that which God has ordained. We must always be obedient to Him or our efforts are in vain."

Silence followed. Peter had played the trump card and the debate was over. While only Rico Vargas had any previous military experience to draw from, all of the disciples viewed themselves as soldiers in the army of God. A good soldier obeys his orders, perhaps especially so when his personal desires conflict with them.

Gail McCorkle had her own orders. She'd had them for some time. Lately she had been obsessively diligent in asking the Lord to forgive her of her sins, sometimes asking for this two or three times a day. The Spirit was quickening Gail, prompting her to get ready to keep the promise she made to Gabriel. When the time came she did not want to die without being in right standing with God.

"Those sons of b******," the President cursed. "Those miserable, no-good, lying sons of b******."

"Mr. President," Peter chided.

"I'm sorry, Peter, forgive my language," the President apologized. "I do not yet have your ability to deal with the pathetic rotten scum of this earth kindly."

Early in the afternoon of the twenty-first of June, a skillfully planned political campaign was launched whose goal was to discredit the President and Peter Carson. The smoke screen was being deployed. Peter and the President were discussing what, if anything, they should do about it.

Through various means such as television ads and radio spots, public statements and appearances, and the selected lobbying of influential people, the argument was methodically advanced that the President of the United States was "emotionally unstable," "experiencing delusions," and was "out of touch with reality." These were not opinions, but rather "facts unfortunately substantiated by impartial experts." The President had become "a danger to himself and to the country."

The enemies of God labeled Peter "the American Rasputin." He was the cause of the President's psychological breakdown and apparent "inability to effectively lead the nation during a time of crisis." They attributed to Peter Svengali-like powers of mind control and illusion, and suggested that the restriction was just such an event on a massive scale. Senior U.S. Senators from both parties went on record saying they "feared that Mr. Carson has completed a bloodless coup d'etat and taken defacto control of the Executive branch of the United States government."

The Reverend Tommy Peterson led an impressive, in worldly terms, cast of clergy and theologians from many denominations who vehemently argued that Peter Carson, the disciples, and the restriction were not "products of the mind and love of our Creator" but rather "false prophets with evil delusions seeking to lead us to our collective doom." They offered nothing specific to substantiate these allegations other than their own self-pro-claimed status as religious authorities and "dedicated, lifelong servants of God."

Fear is evil's most effective weapon.

Addressing a filled-to-capacity crowd at a football stadium in Oklahoma, the Reverend Peterson boomed, "Who is Peter Carson? He is a man who claims to be God's apostle, someone who can heal the sick and even raise the dead. But, brothers and sisters, do not be fooled! In reality he is a con man, a person of such low moral character that he stole from his best friends. Carson is a manipulative liar who is playing out the ultimate scam. I believe without a doubt he is the most dangerous and ungodly man alive."

Other clergy denounced the inclusion of Buddhists, Muslims, and other non-Christians among the select. A group of Anglican Bishops issued a terse statement asking the question, "Why would Christ not seek His own? A large percentage of these so called 'select' are brand new to the Christian faith. By no means are the 'select' from among our own congregations in any way outstanding in character or reputation."

While as yet there was no official word from the Vatican, several small groups of Catholic Bishops joined together to denounce the "heresy being proclaimed in the name of our blessed Lord."

The central theme of all of these religious objectors was the same; Peter Carson was not who he professed to be, but rather he was a twisted, evil man or mutant intent on destroying America first, then the rest of the world.

On the political front, former high officials from previous administrations and current cabinet members and department heads being quoted as "anonymous sources" said that the President of the United States intends to "unilaterally disarm, or reduce our nation's ability to defend itself to a dangerously low level within a matter of hours or days." The President's vision, an unexplained and mysterious event, was used as exhibit A in his public lynching.

"The damn fool means to blow up the world," a former Defense Secretary opined. "He must, because if America drops its shield of armor, every two bit dictator and nutjob, and maybe more than a few of our so called friends, will seek to do us in."

Who stepped up to defend the President? Not many. The "rulers of this age" were overwhelmingly against him. A rational evaluation of the situation could only yield one conclusion; the President's sanity had been compromised. He was no longer fit to perform his Constitutional duties. Either this thesis was true or the finest psychiatrists in the world, virtually every influential current and former member of the American government and the vast majority of the established religious hierarchy were in error.

During this chaos, the select continued steadfast in their efforts, gathering people together to proclaim the truth, to defend Peter, and to perform miracles. They were noticed. Millions of spiritually destitute people, sick at heart from years of accepting the unsatisfying lies and false promises of happiness and glory spoon fed to them from those who advance the living of a selfish, hedonistic life, found peace and comfort through these impromptu ministries.

But millions more saw the select and their activities as a pernicious effort to eat away at their values system. To discredit vain materialism, to challenge blind ambition untempered by true mercy, to zealously proclaim a duty for every man to be his brother's keeper was not only taking a good idea too far, it was heresy. The select were blaspheming their god, who these ignorant and unfortunate souls thought was capitalism, social order, individual responsibility, stability, and progress; but who in reality was a fallen angel, a liar, a thief, and a murderer, and most of all, an eternal hater of humanity.

"Do you ever wonder, Peter, if the people who you are trying to save are really worth saving?" The President was dismayed by the depth and intensity of the hatred allied against him.

"Sir, I know how difficult this must be for you," Peter empathized, "but, if it's any comfort, not so long ago I was more confused than any of our critics. Don't forget that what these servants of hell are saying about me used to be true. If Christ can save me, turn me away from sin and toward the Light, I'm convinced, sir, He can do it for anybody."

"Lord, give me your faith, Peter!" the President shouted. "I've been in this world for too long, I'm afraid. There is no part of me any longer that even approaches innocence. Believe for me, will you, Peter? Reassure me that we are not wasting our lives and our time."

"Long ago, Mr. President, another ruler of men asked God the very same question you are. His name was David. What a marvelous and faithful King he was, sir, yet David fought his demons and had his doubts."

"One day he prayed, sir, 'Vindicate me, O Lord my God, according to Your righteousness; and let them not rejoice over me. Let them not say in their hearts, "Ah, so we would have it!" Let them not say "We have swallowed him up."

"That's it, Peter. You've nailed it. I do feel swallowed up by these damn fools," the President said.

"Let them be ashamed and brought to mutual confusion who rejoice at my hurt; Let them be clothed with shame and dishonor who exalt themselves against me."

"Amen, Peter," the President agreed. "What happened to David? I mean, I remember some of his story, but not all of it."

"God never left him, sir. Whether it was the lion or the bear or Goliath or King Saul or even his own children, no one could defeat him. His progeny includes Christ Himself. Despite all his doubts and faults, the Lord loved King David and prospered him in all of his ways."

"But I'm not David, Peter. America is not Israel. I fear our circumstances differ greatly from those facing the ancient Jews."

"Hebrews chapter thirteen, verse eight, sir."

The President grabbed his Bible and quickly looked up the quote. He then returned his full attention to Peter.

"Jesus Christ is the same yesterday, today, and forever," Peter recited. "No sir, you are not David and I am not St. Paul, but we serve the same God as they did. If we remain obedient, evil can never prevail against us. Remember, Mr. President, "the righteous cry out, and the Lord hears and delivers them out of all their troubles."

For Peter it was like looking into a mirror and seeing himself forty years hence. His blonde hair was streaked with grey and thinner on his uncle. His athletic, wiry frame was also recognizable, softened but not destroyed by age. Father Gregory's sharp, nearly perfect nose, his high cheekbones, and most of all, his penetrating blue eyes were striking features shared by both men.

"Panos! Praise the Lord for His mercy, son!" the old priest yelled. The excited Greek held nothing back. From the second he arrived at the White House and first saw him, Father Gregory showered affection on his nephew, inundating Peter with enthusiastic hugs and kisses.

For Gregory Kallistos, a lifetime's worth of patient and faithful waiting had finally been rewarded. Decades of separation and anxiety had come to an end.

Peter was profoundly drawn to his uncle, as if just by being near him he became more complete. He fell in love with the man instantly and knew that he could trust him. Everything about Father Gregory was soothing and reassuring to Peter. A sense of peace radiated from him, and peace was the blessing Peter needed now in most abundance.

The Kallistos family connected Peter to a legacy, to a tradition of men and women who have faithfully served the Lord since the church began. To Peter and the disciples so much of their experience seemed brand new, as if they had been cast into the world by God to do what no one had done before. Like everything else, this state of mind was by divine design, but so now was the context Father Gregory would provide.

"Panos, do we have place here son where, how you say, we can be alone short time?"

"Of course, Father, follow me," Peter instructed.

Gregory Kallistos brought with him from Greece one small suitcase and a leather satchel. The tote was plain and brown and quite typical, but the satchel was unique. Peter noticed that it was shaped much like an old western saddlebag. It had two separate pouches tied together with long straps. Every inch of the bag's ancient leather was covered with etchings, representations of men and women dressed in unfamiliar clothing.

The old priest picked up the satchel and took it along with him as he and Peter walked down the hall and found an empty office.

"If I embarrass you in front of friends, Panos, please forgive me, my son," Father Kallistos apologized. "My demonstration is, how you say, perhaps too much."

"No, Father. Please. I'm delighted that you're here." Peter found himself on the verge of tears. "You have touched my heart, Father, reached into my soul. But I suspect you knew I would react this way in your presence."

"My boy, you are so much like Nicholas when you speak," Father Gregory said as he opened one of the pouches. "Your words, your, how in English, voice manner is all Nicki. I loved your papa very much, Panos, he and I were close, more close than just brothers."

The priest handed Peter a small and very old photo album which contained twenty or so black and white snapshots.

"God save me! That's my father, isn't it!" Peter felt like a child on Christmas morning. "And that must be you, Father Gregory, standing behind him. Where was this picture taken?"

"In village north part of Greece, Panos. We was so young then, Nicki and I. Your father was, I search for phrase, most handsome man. Women always after Nicki, but he never know any of them other than your mother. He love Neitha since they were small children together in village. No doubt they would marry, all people knew this."

Peter took his time and absorbed the photographs, reveling in every detail. He saw that his mother was indeed a most beautiful woman, strikingly so, in fact. He wished Julie and Kevin were with him to share in his happiness.

Father Gregory was bringing Peter's parents back to life for him. The last two photos in the album were of Nicholas, Neitha, and a baby.

"That's you, Panos," the old priest explained. "This picture taken maybe day or two before the murders. Seems like, how you say, last yesterday my son."

"Murders, Father? The Carsons always said that no one was sure if my parent's deaths were accidental or not."

"Oh, we always sure, Panos. Your parents killed by the evil one. Satan been after you since you born, my boy. Poor idiots that killed my Nicki and Neitha they, what is word, weak in mind, easy to deceive."

"You know who did it, Father? Were they ever brought to justice?"

"My son, yes, my son. Not in human court. God took His vengeance upon them. Horrible what happened. Burned alive in fire, roasted like pigs. No doubt still burning in hell also."

"Father, why were my parents killed? How did I end up in America? Why didn't you raise me, I mean I would ..."

"Panos, son. How you say? Take slow. Give me opportunity to explain, but first we pray."

Gregory took his nephew's hands in his. Peter immediately felt the Power, a magnificent gentleness was conveyed to him, a strength through humility that was without limits. Peter could sense his uncle's incredible spiritual discipline, as if nothing on heaven or earth could possibly disrupt the connection between Father Kallistos and the Lord.

It was the first time Peter had heard the Lord's Prayer recited in Greek. Father Gregory said the few words of the prayer slowly and with a rhythmic elegance Peter found hypnotic.

"Panos, listen very carefully. My English not so good, but I try. Most important you understand clearly what I say. You cannot make fool mistake. Evil one, he will try and deceive you."

"Yes, Father, go ahead. If I don't understand I'll stop you and ask a question."

The priest then reached into the open satchel and removed a small wooden box which was covered by a velvet bag. Father Kallistos held it gingerly, treating the object as his most precious possession, which it was.

"Panos, I know that you are expert at Holy Scriptures so we, how you say, skip step or two. You remember where St. Paul founded first European Christian Church?"

"Philippi."

"Yes, my son. St. Paul wrote many letters to the churches he established in Asia and Greece; Philippi, Colosse, Thessalonica, Corinth, you know. Some of letters are in New Testament."

"Yes, Father."

"Some of his other letters mentioned in New Testament but not been, what is word, preserved for study."

"Yes, uncle."

"Panos, one of Paul's lost letters not really lost. Has been kept safe for almost two thousand years, but shown to few people. Not even Holy Synod knows about this letter. Romans don't know. But Panos I know and your father, he know. We part of, how you say, chain long of priests from church in Philippi given sacred duty to keep letter safe and secret."

The Spirit confirmed for Peter that his uncle was not only being honest with him about what he knew, but also that the letter in the old Greek's box was indeed authored by St. Paul.

"Panos, you know what I say is true, do you not?"

"Yes, Father, I know."

"Good. We must read together then, Panos. Month ago had young priest translate into English. I read from first original in Greek, make sure no mistakes made in English language."

Carefully, as if he was handling a most delicate and priceless object of art, Father Kallistos removed the letter from the box. It consisted of two pages of yellowish, thick paper, or what Peter guessed was paper. The writing on the sheets was in a foreign language, Greek, Peter assumed.

But something was strange. While he was as far from being an expert in ancient manuscripts as anyone could be, he noticed that the letter had a peculiar quality about it.

"Father, that letter. It looks…"

"Like written hour ago, I know. For almost two thousand years document does not age. But Panos, how you say, need not worry. Expert in field verify age by science, of this I do not doubt."

Father Gregory then produced a plain white envelope from his satchel. He handed it to Peter.

"This English translation, son. You read, I follow along." Peter opened the envelope and removed the letter. The first thing he noticed about it was its odd salutation. He had to read it twice to himself to be sure he wasn't making a mistake.

"Father, I mean how can this be?" Peter asked.

"My son?"

"The salutation, Father."

The old priest smiled and let out an odd sounding chuckle.

"Well, my boy, what you, I search for phrase, should expect it say?"

"You mean this salutation was written by St. Paul!" Peter had assumed that Father Gregory or the translator had added it to the English language version.

Then it hit him. Peter's heart began to race. He sat back in his chair, took a deep breath and tried his best to stay composed. He was beginning to more fully understand and appreciate God's magnificent plan.

The letter began;

Paul, an apostle of Jesus Christ by the will of God, To my beloved son in our common faith Panos Kallistos, heir by grace to the gifts freely given to the elders, who in the last days shall come forth from a new land, to proclaim to the Jew and the Gentiles the righteous judgment of God, and upon whom rests His glory, His trust and our fervent hope. Grace to you and peace from God our Father and the Lord Jesus Christ."

Twenty-Three

"Read on, my son. You must learn what Paul, how you say, intention for your life."

Peter flinched, momentarily overwhelmed by the impact of the letter's revelations. All that he'd been through should have prepared him to confront anything; but this, this was a radical twist in the midst of the bizarre. The Apostle to the Gentiles, witness to the risen Christ on the road to Damascus, the great Saul of Tarsus had written him a personal message and "mailed it" to him through the hands of generations of priests from the ancient town of Philippi. One of whom happened to be his uncle, a pure and gentle soul in this holy chain of custodians, who was right now staring at him, anxiously waiting for Peter to read the epistle and by doing so bring St. Paul's vision to life in the twenty-first century.

"Panos, you have problem my boy?"

Peter was doing his best to maintain, to stay on task. He prayed silently for strength.

"Uncle, I guess it's just too incredible. I'm not worthy of such an honor. God expects much of me, Father, sometimes I feel…"

"Like you are big sinner and who you are to say things God tells you?"

"Yes, Father. Why didn't God pick someone like you for this job? I'll bet you've been a pious man all your life, always dutiful in your service to the Lord. Why me? I'm not at all like you. Until last year I couldn't have cared less about God."

"You want answer to question?"

"Lord forgive me, I do, Father. I need some answers."

"Then, my son," Father Kallistos said, as he reached over and gently touched Peter's hand, "you must read. Paul address all concerns for you."

Calling on help from Above, Peter was able to steady himself. He picked up the English translation and began to read it aloud.

Paul, an apostle of Jesus Christ by the will of God, To my beloved son in our common faith Panos Kallistos heir by grace to the gifts freely given to the elders, who in the last days shall come forth from a new land, to proclaim to the Jew and the Gentiles the righteous judgment of God, and upon whom rests His glory, His trust and our fervent hope, Grace to you and peace from God our Father and the Lord Jesus Christ.

"Wow," Peter gasped. "Reading that salutation again stirs me up, Father, like someone's lighting a fire in my belly."

"Angels want your attention, that's all," the old priest told his nephew. "Go on Panos, do not stop."

My son, I commit this charge to you under the authority given me by Christ Jesus, who through His mercy has enabled me to prophecy concerning you and your brothers. The Spirit says that in your days men will become exceedingly violent and unfaithful, speaking lies in hypocrisy, openly mocking God without shame. They will be proud in their own opinions, revilers of all things holy, seeking false righteousness through vanity and covetousness. God's own will be scattered, pulled away from each other by foolish and ignorant disputes. Men will consider the Lord a nuisance to be ignored, such will be the depth of their evil. But you, my son, are empowered and entrusted by Christ Jesus and God the Father to show men in this dark age the magnificence of His being, the power and majesty of the Father of Lights, the glory of His Kingdom, the mercy of His love. To this holy mission commit your life, Panos, never doubting that the Lord your God is with you, as am I, giving you strength and courage to endure to the end. Value highly the Ethiopian and the Jew, the officer and the soldier, the master of tongues and the humble. The Lord has given them each a pure heart, a good conscience and a sincere faith. They are your willing bondservants in Christ, treasures who for love's sake will be bold in proclaiming the Gospel of our Lord.

"Uncle!" Peter shouted, amazed. "Paul knew my men! Glory to God, it's beyond belief, Father."

"Not too much to believe, Panos," Gregory Kallistos reasoned. "Look at what has happened and what must still happen. Paul receive, what is word, his map of road from same God as you. Keep on reading, my boy."

Panos, you were once profane, a worshipper of idols, unholy, proud, unloving, and deceitful. Let not your heart be troubled by what is past, my son, for as you once were so also were many others before the Spirit touched them. But you have since become rich in the fruits of the Spirit, filled with love, joy, peace, long suffering, kindness, gentleness, and self control.

God saved you for a purpose, Panos, that you may be an example to the world, to both the Jew and the Gentile, a living

testimony to the power of God. You shall give hope to all who are
dying in sin that they also may be lifted up by Him to glory.

"You see, Panos," Father Gregory said, interrupting Peter's recital of the letter. "God did not call priest, bishop, or Pope, he call sinners. No surprise. First twelve Apostles were, how you say, no bargains, Panos. They were worldly men, like you and brothers. That is why people come to believe them, Panos. Apostles not special, God is special."

"So why then do we have a Holy Synod or a Pope or Patriarchs, Father? Does God not honor His church?"

"Of course, my son. He honors church but church not, I search for phrase, honor always Him."

"I'm lost again."

"No lost, just not finished. Read rest of letter."

In your days, Panos, the simplicity of the Gospel shall be violated, the agreement of the Bishops held in contempt, the excellence of the knowledge of Christ Jesus distorted and defiled by schism, greed, and all manner of self-seeking. Turn away from the proud who are obsessed with disputes and arguments over words from which come envy, strife, suspicions, and all manners of evil. Embrace the power of the Living God and lead others to the Light. Reject the church of Satan and all its wickedness, bring forth Christ's true church into the Light, take it away from the profane and the ungodly.

"Father, help me to understand what St. Paul is saying here," Peter asked.

"You not see? Not so hard to understand, my boy. The Bishop's agreement I sure is Nicea Creed, simple statement of faith.

Schism, greed, all that easy too, Panos. How many Christian sects we have today? Thousands, yes?"

"For sure, Father."

"Creates big problems, no?"

"Yes. I do not understand quite how or why the church became so divided."

"Easy question also, Panos. Evil one, he do it. Divide and, how you say, conquer easier."

"So what does St. Paul want me to do about it? Unite the churches?"

"Yes, my son, and more still. You must take away power from profane and ungodly. Set things right. Prepare world for Christ's return."

"How am I supposed to do that, Father? Is your church, I guess I should say our church, the right one?"

"Not exactly, Panos. Read rest of letter, not much left."

My beloved Panos, to you our Lord commits His church. You must exhort the faithful to become likeminded, to be of one accord, of one mind. The House of God must no longer be divided. Vindicate the Apostles, press forward to the goal of victory through gentleness, conquer with the love of Christ and by faith.

Your blood shall pour out as a sacrifice for all to witness, your obedience shall terrify and defeat your adversaries. These things I commit to you, son Panos, according to the prophecy given me concerning you.

Do all things through love. Be not afraid. Listen to the Bishop. Follow Holy tradition. In all things seek His guidance and believe in Him who grants everlasting life. Grace be with you. Amen.

"I very sorry about sacrifice part, Panos," Father Gregory said. "If I had power to step in your shoes I would, son, what is word, in beat of heart."

Peter took a deep breath and put his copy of the letter down on the small coffee table in front of him and looked over at his uncle. He loved the old man's genuineness. Father Gregory's unfiltered honesty and open heart were beacons drawing Peter deeper into an understanding of God's will.

"Father, I've known about my destiny as a martyr for some time," Peter said reassuringly. "Don't be troubled by it."

"I not far behind you, my boy. I know someday soon we both stand in glory of Christ, together with my Nicki and Neitha."

Peter let himself contemplate that vision. He immediately knew without a doubt that what his uncle had just prophesied would come to pass.

"Father, help me. I'm still not clear on some of this."

"Yes son, go on. Ask, I try to help."

"The church. Which church, Father? My brothers and I have had no need for a denomination or label. We've just followed where the Spirit led."

"Exactly, Panos. You answer your own question."

"Father?"

"You have Eucharist, Peter, in your services?"

"Certainly. The Bible tells us to confess our sins and to then partake in the body and blood of Christ."

"Who you confess sins to?"

"Each other. We had a policy at Parkersboro. No secrets. We confessed to each other our sins and drew strength from our common weaknesses."

"Exactly like early church, Panos. They did same thing. Way God intended it. You will find that priest be necessary, though."

"Father, what about…"

"Panos, how in English, let's not get stuck in mud now. Leave church rituals on side for time being. Point is not style, my boy, but rather truth and basics of message."

"Keep going, please."

"Christian church must return to the Apostolic doctrines. No need for all this, what is word, diversion of activity. As Paul said to you such nonsense causes all kinds of evil result."

"So, I'm to tell the Romans, the Anglicans, the Lutherans, the Orthodox, the 'whoevers,' exactly what, Father? Shut down your churches? Come follow me?"

"You must tell them to start be one in Christ, to glorify the Lord as He meant to be worshipped, to stop making denomination schism, to become one body."

"I think it might be easier to raise the dead, Father."

The old priest laughed. "No doubt what you say is true. Nothing so stubborn as, how you say, mule with age. These pastors today, not only in America but also in Greece, Europe, all places, many like this mule. They stuck in ways, confuse ideas of man with God's commandments. But, you see these new faithful my son? English word is "select", I think, if I say right."

"Yes, Father, we've been watching them. God has clearly called them to His service."

"They your army, Panos. Oh, we should not be, what is word, too much pessimism about men already in church. Many, many will come to the Lord, change their ways, unite as brothers. But be not fool, Panos, the evil one have strong hold on many pastors' hearts, blind them with fear and pride."

"I've already seen that, Father."

"Many they hate you, Panos, for same reason Pharisee Jews hate Christ and twelve. Jealous of you, envy. Very deadly sin this envy."

"Father, who is the Bishop St. Paul is talking about?"

"My boy, me, of course."

"I thought you were a priest, uncle. Forgive me for not addressing you properly."

"Oh, Panos, you call me right name. I priest forever, bishop last few years. Church titles, how in English, little mean. Romans need to learn this lesson big way, you teach them."

"Holy traditions, Father," Peter asked, "what exactly are they?"

"Church from beginning have certain rituals not of men, but ordained by God. Baptism, Chrismation, Marriage, Healing, Eucharist, and some more. I teach you. Simple things, but required for Power."

Enthralled with his uncle and in a glorious haze since reading St. Paul's letter, Peter had lost track of time. A quick look at his watch reminded him that very soon he would be facing the world through a peculiar type of modern inquisition.

"Uncle, do you know what's going to take place tonight?"

"Yes, Panos. Men on plane tell me. Also I hear on radio news while in air."

"Do you think it's a good idea, Father? I'm not sure that I'm qualified to defend God. These men may make me look foolish."

"Who says you need defend God, my son?"

"Well uncle," Peter explained, "the way it's going to work is…"

"Oh I have, how you say, idea good on how it work, Panos. But do not fear. We use Scripture. Luke chapter twelve, verse eleven and also twelve."

Peter quoted from memory, "Now when they bring you to the synagogues and magistrates and authorities, do not worry about how or what you should answer, or what you should say, for the Holy Spirit will teach you in that very hour what you ought to say."

"Panos, you not believe God be with you? Why now would He abandon you?"

"I believe, Father. I do. Help me to be obedient."

"That's why I here my wonderful son, to help. When last time you confess and take Eucharist?"

"Last week we had Communion and I try to confess daily, Father. My brothers are patient with me. I can share anything with them."

"As should be, as should be. Now, my son, you share also with me."

Father Gregory reached into his satchel once more and removed the few items required to hear confession and give the Eucharist.

"Uncle, God bless you, but I don't know if we have time for that now. In a few minutes the President and his staff are expecting me ... "

"Make time, my son. Christ give time for your soul on cross, you give time for Him before battle. Panos, above all else, God must come first."

Peter required no further persuasion. Bishop Kallistos was absolutely right, he needed to cleanse himself through confession and strengthen himself through partaking of the body and blood of Christ. Every other form of preparation was secondary.

"Uncle, I cannot tell you how glad I am that you are here," Peter said, as he watched the priest get ready to minister to him. "I know the brothers will feel the same. Thank you."

"Oh, no thank me, son," Father Gregory said. "For two thousand years priests in my village live through wars, famines, plague, disaster, all manner of trouble just so I be here now to listen you say thank you. It is you, not me, who deserve honor."

Peter confessed his sins to his uncle, his priest. He admitted his fears and doubts and asked for forgiveness. As Peter partook of the Eucharist and he and Father Gregory held hands and prayed the peace of God came upon him. The comfort of the Holy Spirit replaced all of his anxieties.

For Satan, this could not have happened at a worse possible time.

Twenty-Four

"It's like this, dad. I just can't bat real good. I'm a good fielder, but it's tough for me to hit that dumb ball! Were you good at baseball, daddy?"

"So-so. You are probably much better at it than I was. I kinda liked football."

"Me too! Can I play Pop Warner, daddy? Mommy says no because she thinks I'll get hurt."

"I'll speak to her, son. No promises, but we'll see."

Peter relished any opportunity to simply be a father. When he and Kevin were together, even on the phone, everything else faded in importance.

Normal life, the powerful draw of simple, soul satisfying family pleasures. The fruits of living to a "quiet and peaceable" rhythm, as St. Paul suggested. For Peter Carson, this blissful version of reality was an illusion, or at best a very temporary island of tranquility in his sea of trials.

"When are you coming home, dad?" Kevin's question ripped out Peter's heart and brought to the surface all of the guilt he felt for being a very imperfect father. Only the Spirit saved him from falling into despair, from losing himself through mourning over lost chances and parental failures.

Of course, he could not say to his son what he said a few minutes earlier to Kevin's mother, that he may never get to come home again. To do so would only cruelly add to his only child's already considerable and underserved burdens.

"God has plans for me, Kevin," Peter said as bravely as he could. "I don't know when I'll see you again. Very soon, I hope. But you know what I'm doing tonight. Mom explained it, right?"

"You are going to be on TV dad, I know. Answer a bunch of questions from important people. Mom says I can watch you, but I wish you were here playing cards and eating popcorn with me. We need you too, you know? Tell God that, daddy, will you? Please?"

Whatever sliver of emotional self-control Peter Carson had left was dissipating rapidly.

"Kev," Peter said, choking back his raging emotions, "I wish I was there playing cards with you too. I love you, son. Remember that always. No matter what. Promise me."

"I promise, daddy."

"That's my boy. Now put your mom back on the phone, Kev. Pray for me, son. Don't forget."

"I won't forget, daddy. The angel, he won't let me. Here's mommy."

"Peter?"

"Jules, what was all that about an angel?"

"Gabriel has been talking to Kev, Peter. I'm sure of it. The way he describes his angel, it can only be Gabriel. You didn't know?"

"No. It's the first time Kev said anything to me about it. Jules, be sure to ..."

Peter was cut short by a gentle tap on his shoulder. He had asked for every spare second to talk with his wife and son. Reluctantly the President's communication staff had given it to him, they would have preferred a much more lengthy pre-panel prep, but now the clock was pushing seven thirty.

"Jules, I've got to go, honey. Remember everything we've discussed. From now on I'm just not sure when we might get the chance to talk again. Lord willing, I'll call you tomorrow."

"God help you, Peter, and God help me too." Julie barely got the words out in between her tears. She hung up the phone in frustration and fear, not sure whether to curse the Lord or to praise Him.

"Good evening. My name is David Martz. The gentleman to my right is Alex Anderson and the lady to my left is Doris Spence.

"Between the three of us we have over one hundred years of experience in television broadcasting and print journalism, four Emmys, and two Pulitzers. But such credentials mean little in this setting, at this most difficult and yet tremendously opportune moment in human affairs.

"We will be remaining largely in the background as our panel directs a series of questions and comments to Mr. Peter Carson, also known as Panos Kallistos, which is his Christian birth name. Our role is to facilitate the discussion, not to dominate it."

"While it seems to us impossible," Alex said, taking his turn as the narrator, "that anyone could not by now be well aware of who Mr. Carson is and of the events of the past forty-eight or so hours, let us briefly review."

"Unless a dramatic change occurs while I speak," Doris Spence said, chiming in right on cue, "no human being on this planet is capable of committing a violent act of any kind against another human being. Our mental processing of information seems unaffected by this 'restriction,' as it has come to be known. We can intend to be violent, but we are unable to act on our intentions."

"Nothing like the restriction has occurred before in the common memory or myth of our species," Dave Martz said, as the camera switched back to him. "Claimed miracles have been reported since man first started using language, but never anything on the scope and scale of the restriction."

"Peter Carson says he is an ambassador for God, a messenger as he describes himself. Since a purported divine vision almost a year ago, Mr. Carson has, in front of hundreds of independent witnesses, healed the sick, battled demons, and even raised the dead."

"The world is asking," Doris Spence said, in her somewhat stern and neutral newswoman manner, "is Peter Carson a genuine prophet of God? Millions are gathering to his cause across the globe, calling themselves the select. Is this phenomenon what Mr. Carson claims it is, or is it something else? Perhaps no other single question has ever been as important as this one."

"For if," Alex said enthusiastically, not at all trying to feign professional indifference, "Peter Carson is telling the truth, our choice is clear. We must, each one of us, embrace God and Jesus Christ His Son as our Savior or be left, spiritually speaking, on the outside looking in."

"Conversely, if another credible explanation for everything that has and is happening exists," Dave Martz said, as the camera backed off of a close face shot of him and went wide angle to capture the as yet unoccupied conference table, "then humanity will avoid being duped and perhaps brought to its collective knees through a dangerous and unprecedented manipulation."

"Tonight, in the historic East Room of the White House, a distinguished panel has been assembled to help a nervous world determine the truth." Doris Spence was clearly positioning herself as the most skeptical of the three moderators through her edgy attitude and stiff body language. "It is my honor to introduce them to you and to our live audience here in Washington."

"And what a live audience," Tim Austin whispered to Kenny. "Do you realize that within fifty feet of us are the chief political executives of every major country in Europe and the Americas? There is also enough money in the room to pay off the national debt twice over. Thank God we don't have to worry about security."

"I'm just trying to maintain, Tim," Kenny responded. "This scene is beyond any conceivable fantasy. Peter must be scared out of his mind."

"I know I am," Larry admitted.

"What about him?" Enrique Vargas asked, discreetly gesturing toward Malik. "He doesn't seem a bit rattled. If I'd been given a division of Maliks, I'm sure I could have conquered the world."

"Malik is on patrol, General," Gail quietly explained. "He's on the lookout for any uninvited guests. He and Peter have some signal worked out if the nasties get too thick in here."

" ... but before I bring in our panel," Doris Spence continued as she stood, pivoted, and gestured to her left, "let me introduce Mr. Carson's closest associates to our audience. Anyone watching the broadcast on the nineteenth already has a good sketch of each of their backgrounds."

"From left to right seated directly in front of me is ... "

As Doris Spence recited each disciple's name, Malik was busy surveying the room. His sudden head movements and wide eyes indicated the proximity of unseen activity.

"Talk to me," Tim Austin whispered to Malik, as he also smiled and nodded in response to Doris Spence's introduction of him.

"Bout twenty or so really ugly sons of b**** , sorry, demon things flittin' 'round, but they stayin' way back, Mr. Tim. They scart or somethin'. I can feel the rotten beasties fear. It's like they don't want to be here, but somethin' is makin' 'em be."

"Satan?" Tim asked.

"Be my guess, brother. Ain't no sign of him yet, thank you Jesus."

"Keep watching, Malik."

"Don't worry, Mr. Tim. I got Mr. Pete's back. No way I'm lettin' these fiends spoil this party."

" ... and Miss Gail McCorkle, formerly of the United States Bureau of Prisons," Doris Spence said, as she finished and deftly handed back the narration duties to Dave Martz.

"The first member of our panel is the President of the United States, Mr. ... "

"Mr. Tim, theys gettin' all twitchy 'bout somethin'. Can't tell if it's a general type of thing or if they mean to start up some nonsense in here."

"Keep alert, Malik. And pray."

"Been doin' that, bro. Non-stop."

" ... Cardinal Thomas Reardon of Boston, Massachusetts, Mr. Sam Harwell, entrepreneur and owner of Harsoft, the Reverend Thomas Peterson of the Cathedral of Christ Church in Oklahoma City, Rabbi David Rosefielde of the ... "

"Kind of weird how he's doing the intros, don't you think?" Kenny observed.

"How so?" Larry asked.

"It's like Martz is giving the starting lineup at a basketball game. For gosh sakes, I would..."

"Ssh!" Gail said, leaning over toward Kenny's chair. "They might be able to hear you up there."

"Sorry," Kenny mouthed.

"...United Nations Secretary General Carlos Benes from Brazil, Dr. Carl Fuchs, most recently from Princeton University, Dr. Howard Simms of Harvard, and Mr. Roger Stone of Madison, Wisconsin."

The panelists took their assigned seats as their names were announced. They appeared to be calm and poised, although Peterson was noticeably more intense than the rest with his disapproving scowl and pages of notes. The only exception to the common demeanor was Roger Stone, who took his seat with a huge smile on his face and an almost carefree countenance. He appeared neither worried nor tense, but rather joyous as if he had been invited to a friend's birthday party or a wedding.

The President saw both the humor and the significance in Roger Stone's well-worn polyester suit, his ten-year-old necktie, and oversized turtle shell glasses. While the rest of the panelists either glared at or ignored him, the President reached over and shook Mr. Stone's hand and wished him well.

Alex took over for the final introduction.

"And now it is my great honor and pleasure to present to you my friend, Mr. Peter Carson of Atlanta, Georgia."

"Lord have mercy," Peter prayed. He slowly walked out to the conference table and sat down.

"He's doing it again," Gail observed.

"Do you think it comes through on camera?" Kenny wondered.

"Hey, Chuck," the stage director barked into his headset. "We got a problem with camera three? Carson looks like he's glowing or something. What's all that residual shine?"

"Copy that," the studio chief acknowledged. "No malfunction. We were told by Martz to expect it. Same thing happened at Parkersboro."

"Mr. Carson," Doris Spence began, arranging her notes and laptop computer in front of her, "in order to give some initial structure to our discussion each panelist will be allotted five minutes to ask you whatever he wishes. After that time, there will be no order of engagement; good manners and respect will be our only guide."

"As you know, we have no preset time limit for our discussion. We shall continue on until you or the panel decides to conclude."

"Lots were drawn. First up is the Reverend Thomas Peterson of Oklahoma City. Reverend Peterson."

"My Lord in Heaven," Kenny complained very softly. "Why him?"

"Ssh!" Gail admonished. "I don't want to miss a word."

Thomas J. Peterson, all two hundred and seventy-five self-righteous pounds of him, was primed and ready to pounce. Blinded to the simple truth of God's plan by his pride and arrogance, he had become like those misguided Jews Christ described in the Gospel of John who believed they were "offering God a service" by persecuting Christians.

"Mr. Carson, sir," Peterson began in his puffed up and pretentious preacher's drone, "I want to acknowledge how impressed I am by your tactics. You have considerable skills, Mr. Carson, but let it be known that Thomas Peterson believes you to be a fraud and an imposter. I find you and your friends neither to be righteous men nor worthy of the acclaim being so hastily heaped upon you without just cause."

"May Christ bless you, sir," Peter responded matter-of-factly, clearly unshaken by Peterson's rude assault. "It is unfortunate that you have such a low opinion of myself and my friends. I hope that it will not always be so."

"Yes, well." Peterson was caught unawares by Peter's coolness under fire. "Be that as it may, sir, I have questions for you."

"Please, Reverend. I am your servant."

"What denomination are you, sir?"

"I was baptized as an Orthodox. Recently I have reestablished a connection with this church, but I do not consider myself to be a member of any one denomination."

"An Orthodox. Does your church claim you, sir?"

"By that I assume you're asking if an Orthodox hierarchy has declared a miracle or endorsed our efforts in some official capacity. I don't believe so and it's not important. Denominations and schisms are contrary to God's plan. Seeking validation from factions is irrelevant."

"See, there you go, Mr. Carson. You just insulted millions of Baptists in my denomination. We are not in any way 'contrary to God's plan,' we are God fearing followers of Christ Jesus, sir. Humility does not appear to be among your spiritual gifts, Mr. Carson."

"Reverend Peterson," Peter said calmly, trying not to allow himself to get caught up in a useless debate. "I did not say that your members were not Christians, nor did I say or imply that Baptists were not God fearing people. So are many Roman Catholics, Episcopalians, Methodists, Coptics, and so on.

"What I said was the division of Christ's church since 1054 into denominations has been counterproductive and has served only the goals of our enemy. We must return to the basic faith, Reverend, and ground ourselves in the Gospel and in Christ's love. I believe if we fail to do that we, we being humanity, may not survive."

"And who is to lead this new church of yours, Mr. Carson?" Peterson needled sarcastically. "You? An ex-con, a thief, an admitted liar, and embezzler? Do you realize how greatly you have insulted the religious hierarchy of all denominations, Mr. Carson? You and your mind tricks, your illusions. I'm not buying what you are selling, sir."

No, and you probably never will, Peter thought to himself. *Satan has prostituted you, used your passions to cheat you out of your heritage.* The Reverend Thomas J. Peterson was a fool trapped in his own ego and rhetoric. His prayers were blocked by his pride and the hardness of his heart. Peter felt bad for the man, pitied him more than anything.

"I'm selling nothing, Reverend Peterson. I'm sharing with you and the world what the Lord has revealed to me. I seek neither fame nor glory nor money. If left to my own devices I would gladly disappear and leave the earth to you, but I cannot do that. I must be obedient to the Lord."

"Two minutes, Reverend Peterson." Doris Spence was acting as the official timekeeper.

"Very well, let's move on. My 'misguided denomination' would like to know, Mr. Carson, is the Bible the literal word of God?"

Peter shook his head. Here comes the "born-again" litmus test. Such silliness. It was going to be a long night if the bellicose Reverend managed to dominate the agenda. Peter vowed to himself not to let that happen.

"If by saying that, Reverend, you mean to imply that every word or story in the Bible should be taken as being literal truth, as an inerrant recitation of historical fact, then no. However, the Bible is the word of God, His spiritual truth. It is our guide and our history and a most beautiful collaboration between God and man."

"That's what I thought. You mock the word of God, Mr. Carson. I'm not surprised, no, not at all. If I may, sir..."

"Do you know where this whole concept of Biblical inerrancy began, Reverend Peterson?" Peter was not trying to argue, but rather to educate the billions in the viewing audience.

"It has forever been so, Mr. Carson. True believers have always defended the faith and the Scriptures. I, for one, find..."

"The whole idea of Biblical inerrancy came about as a response to the Roman Catholic assertion that the Pope was infallible. Protestantism elevated the Bible to perfection to counter the Bishop of Rome's claims. Of course, neither the Protestants nor the Romans were right, and neither really cared about what God had to say on these subjects. Those men, like you, Reverend, were more interested in worldly power than in discerning the mind and will of God."

"Now hold on there, Mister Carson. Do not begin to believe that you can lecture to me on Biblical matters. I have been to seminary, taught at the finest univer..."

"The doctrine of Biblical inerrancy is directly related to the misguided notion that a person can be saved through faith alone; the idea that if one claims Christ as his Lord and Savior, then, regardless of his works, he will have eternal life with Him. This is not so and is in fact directly contrary to the Master's and the Apostle's teachings."

"Please, Mr. Carson. It's my time to ask questions. That you deny the most basic tenets of Protestant Christianity is a given. But rather than get into this, I'd much…"

"Read your Bible, Reverend. Matthew sixteen verse twenty-seven, Mark thirteen verse thirteen, Second Corinthians five verse ten, Revelations twenty verse twelve, Hebrews ten verse twenty-nine. You must live out your faith through your deeds in order to be saved."

"I can see that you have no interest in answering my questions, Mr. Carson. What are you afraid of? Scared I'll penetrate your flimsy fraud, expose your tricks?"

"Do you see how far we've come from the center, from Christ? You are jealous and worried about my status, my glory. You're embarrassed and angry that someone dares challenge your religious authority.

"Instead of being smug, Reverend, why don't you help? Work on your love, strive for His glory. The glory of God is not some sporting event or economic competition. It's about serving others, Reverend, it's about love, it's about Him."

"Why, you impudent a**! My ministry feeds thousands of needy people daily, helps to educate and clothe the poor in over thirty countries. While you were out stealing, sir, I was, and still am, healing. You are…"

"Reverend. I acknowledge your good works. They are considerable. Why then do you negate them by insisting on preaching a Gospel of exclusion rather than inclusion? The Master lived and died and rose again for all of us, Reverend, for the Jew, the Muslim, the Christian, even the atheist. God became man to bring true love into the world, not to win elections or to build personal fortunes."

"When this restriction farce is over, Carson, I will be the first person to …"

"Your time is up, Reverend." Doris Spence deadpanned like she was announcing the door prize winner at a charity bake sale.

"Yuk," Gail whispered.

"Double yuk. That man is a giant heap of slime," Kenny added.

"He's got friends too, Mr. Kenny. The nasty things seem to like him," Malik said. "Not a good sign."

Doris Spence announced, "Cardinal Reardon, you're next up, your Eminence."

In contrast to Reverend Peterson, Cardinal T. Farrell Reardon was anything but pretentious or antagonistic. He wore a simple priest's frock with a Roman collar, not his Bishop's robes. He had no desire to flaunt his status in the Catholic hierarchy. Reardon's gentleness directly contrasted Peterson's harshness.

"Peter, God bless you, son. How are you doing?"

"Fine, Bishop. God bless you too."

"I am very sorry about Mr. Cohen. His death was a loss to us all."

"Thank you, Bishop."

"Peter, so everyone knows, I am a part of this group that is being called "the select." I had the pentecostal dream. I was at Parkersboro two nights ago and I've been to Rome and back since. I believe you, Peter, I know God sent you to the world to help us all and for His glory."

"Damned useless Papist," Peterson muttered under his breath.

"Peter, please tell us why God is blessing us with the restriction. Understandably people everywhere speak of nothing else. Help the world make good use of this miracle."

"Bishop, eleven months ago I was blessed with a vision, or rather a series of visions. Part of that process was the Lord educating me about violence, its inherent ungodliness, and the danger we all face now as a species from our brutish tendencies."

"God is telling us that we must change, Bishop. We must spiritually evolve beyond the use of violence. Why is God acting now? The message is certainly not a new one, but we should all ask ourselves, since God chose today to bless us with the restriction, what does that say about our times? What does that say about the urgency of His message?"

"Bishop, as Christ is my witness, I declare to the world that the Lord our God is commanding us to change. He wants us to live because He loves us. He made us in His image and likeness. I pray constantly that we will heed His call, that my son will have a world to grow up in."

"What happens if we don't, Peter? What happens if we ignore God?"

"Then, Bishop, I believe that we are doomed. Disastrous consequences. Armageddon."

"Sorry to interrupt, please forgive me," the President said. "But I feel I must interject. I had a vision similar to Peter's less than forty-eight hours ago. The horror I witnessed was beyond any novelist's worst nightmare. God's message to me was clear; we must stop using violence as a tool for personal and social control.

"I apologize for intruding on your time, Cardinal. I felt it was important information given your question."

"And I suppose that means you are going to dismantle our military, disarm our police, and open our prisons. That about it, Mr. President? By Almighty God, sir, what they are saying about you is true. You've gone mad."

"Reverend Peterson!" Dave Martz shouted. "Please show respect for your fellow panelists. You've had your turn."

"But this is madness, Mr. Martz. This whole contrived circus. Someone has to speak up and..."

"Mr. Peterson!" Doris discarded the monotone and adopted her best school marm chastening. "That will be quite enough, sir. Please show the proper decorum."

For the moment Peterson kept his mouth shut, but only for the moment.

"Well, Peter, let's pursue the good Reverend's inquiry. Is that what God wants us to do, become as lambs amidst the wolves?"

"My sense of it, Bishop, is that God wants us to act, to take some immediate and meaningful steps in the right direction. But human nature being what it is, it seems obvious to me that violence will have to be worked out of our individual behavior and social systems gradually. We need leadership and wisdom to guide us thorough this process, Bishop, and I believe that the President will provide us with ample amounts of both."

"As far as what the immediate steps should be, I have one very strong admonition. War, armed conflict between nations, must be abolished. We are sitting on a powder keg and the devil is lighting a match."

Peter asked, "What about the Pope, your Excellency? Does he have a message for us?"

Cardinal Reardon frowned and shook his head.

"I'm sorry, Peter, but His Holiness remains silent. I pleaded with him to bring the church into the fold, but he is reluctant.

He is more hesitant than he is opposed, Peter. Under normal circumstances, whatever those might be, I would be sympathetic to his position. The church must be cautious in who and what it endorses. We are a conservative body, inherently slow to act.

"But I remain hopeful. Pray for the Pope, Peter. He is a good man, perhaps too timid, but a good man."

"I will pray for him, Bishop."

"At least the Pope still has some sense," Reverend Peterson grumbled loud enough for all to hear.

"Be assured of this much, Peter," Cardinal Reardon said, knowing that his allotted time had nearly run out, "groups of Bishops and large numbers of Roman Catholic laity are already with you. We Catholics are not united, not yet, but I believe in time the church will validate the miracles I have seen and fully endorse your efforts."

"Dr. Simms, your time begins now." With Peterson subdued, Doris Spence was her placid self once again.

Howard Simms was born to be a deep thinker, to use his mind to unravel the intricate secrets of nature. For as long as he could remember, the world, how it worked, and everything in it, had fascinated him. While the other kids in his small town Michigan neighborhood were out playing ball, Howard stayed in and built complex machines with his Erector Sets, or took it upon himself to dissect a frog or to read about Darwin or Einstein or Skinner until his eyes hurt.

He completed a doctorate program in Anthropology by age twenty and added a second PhD in Astrophysics by twenty-three. Thirty plus years had passed since these academic accomplishments, but Dr. Simms' childlike curiosity about his universe was undiminished by the passage of time.

Like many leaders of science, Simms did not formally practice any religion, but he definitely believed in God. The structured beauty of nature convinced Howard from an early age that the world was designed, not random. Howard Simms had always found bombastic men of the cloth like Thomas Peterson to be repulsive embarrassments, unworthy of his time or attention. But the gentle nature and subtle self-confidence of Cardinal Reardon instinctively captured him, reminding Howard that there was a good reason why he was not an atheist.

Though a deist, Howard Simms lacked faith. His greatest strength, pure objectivity, limited his intellectual options. Simms' lack of faith kept him from seeing beyond creation to the Creator, but he was an honest man who loved life and looked down upon no one. For someone blessed with great intelligence, he was extraordinarily humble.

"Mr. Carson," Simms began, "I'd like to …"

"It's Peter, sir, not Mr. Carson. Mr. Carson was my father."

"Certainly. Peter. Right. I've taken the liberty over the past twenty-four hours to detail the effects of this restriction of yours. A most interesting task. Have you been made aware of all of its ramifications, its various nuances?"

"I don't believe I have, Dr. Simms. Please, let me know what you have discovered."

"Yes, well. First of all, the restriction does not apply to animals, non-human animals that is. Violence toward them, among them, and from them continues, but most interestingly, seems to be reduced to a significant degree by the current event."

"The current event, Doctor?"

"Sorry. The restriction is the 'current event' in my lexicon." Simms stopped, rubbed the stubby grey whiskers on his chin, and then continued. "Forgive me, Peter. I can speak English. In this context, scientific jargon is simply needless blather."

"Accidents, violent ones, are still happening, Peter. Two cars collide, passengers are hurt, maimed, killed. People still fall down the stairs, curiously enough even when they are accidentally bumped by someone else.

"Our sporting activities continue on except for the martial arts. For instance, American football is still being played with all of its violent collisions. Of course, there are no after play fights, although tempers are not diminished."

"Many violent games, video games in particular, cannot be played. Some films will not show, but others with plenty of violent content are seemingly unaffected."

"I could go on for days, Peter, indeed I plan to record as much as possible about the restriction before it ends so that I might study it thoroughly, but the bottom line, as my business associates like to say, is that our behavior, and to a degree our stimuli, are being edited and controlled by some unseen force. To deny this is to deny reality. With all due respect to the good Reverend Peterson, the restriction is not some illusion or planet-wide hypnotic trick. It is a real event, one that can be detailed, catalogued, and studied."

"That's beautiful, Dr. Simms," Peter complimented.

"Beautiful?"

"Your description of God's works, His restriction. That was beautiful. From the vantage point of science no doubt you will be able to glean insights and provide a depth of meaning unavailable to other observers."

"So you're interested in applying a scientific method to the current ev. ., oh crap, so sorry, to the restriction?"

"For sure. God's speed, brother. We need your input and analysis. Science is every bit as much the Lord's work as is theology."

"That is an odd statement coming from a theologian, Peter," Simms said, suddenly sporting a tentative smile, "but a very welcome and interesting one."

"Dr. Simms, God gives us all sorts of tools to understand our world, His creation. How can knowledge gained through science be in any way ungodly, since it is by His will and His grace that we have curious minds, the ability to process information, and the desire to experiment?"

"Well said, sir. I admit to being both surprised and impressed by your attitudes."

"That is understandable. For too long a barrier, put there by the evil one, has created a rift between science and theology. Most of the problem comes from misunderstanding the Scriptures, greed, and pride."

"Please, Peter. Continue on this line of thinking."

"Alright. From the aspect of theology, misguided religious leaders have considered science a threat to God. From Copernicus and Galileo to Darwin and Einstein there has been this tension, this struggle for power between science and theology. It's nonsense for the most part."

"The Bible is not a science text. For one thing, God is above all physical laws, since He created them. For another, the Bible is a spiritual work. It deals with the meaning of life, our purpose in the universe, and our duties to each other and to God. Jesus did not come to the world to give us scientific knowledge; He came to show us how to use our gifts and blessings for the betterment of His creation. All knowledge comes from God, Doctor Simms."

"Until a couple of days ago, Peter, I would have been very skeptical about your theory that God is above all physical laws."

"But now, Dr. Simms?"

"I admit the very distinct possibility that an all powerful God is directly manipulating physical events. To deny that would be dishonest and foolish."

"Are you familiar with the Bible, Dr. Simms?"

"Only vaguely, Peter. My apologies."

"Permit me to quote a scripture for you. It's from the New Testament, the book of Colossians, chapter two, verse eight. It reads, 'Beware lest anyone cheat you through philosophy and empty deceit, according to the tradition of men, according to the basic principles of the world, and not according to Christ.

"What St. Paul said to the church at Colossae is the same thing I'm saying to you. Christ transcends all things, the institutions of man such as our government, enterprises, and technology, and also the "basic principles of the world," subjects like chemistry, biology, astronomy, and physics, which you scientists study and explain to us. As Christians we should not deny the 'basic principles of the world' for they were set by God. Science should not deny that God transcends these principles, that He reigns over all and is the ultimate source of everything our minds perceive."

"Your construct is not new, Peter, but now, given what we are all experiencing, a greater …"

"Mr. Harwell," Doris Spence broke in without apology, "your time begins now, sir."

"Oh my, that's too bad. I was really getting into that discussion," Tim Austin said.

"Me too," Enrique Vargas agreed. "Peter didn't flinch, did he? I had no idea he's so well versed in science."

"Neither did he, I'm sure," Kenny told his brothers. "The Spirit is moving through him, he's on autopilot."

"Peter, I consider it a great honor and privilege to be part of this panel. More than anything else, I suppose I was invited to plead for God's mercy on behalf of all of the world's crass capitalist pigs." Sam Harwell was famous for his self-deprecating humor and smart-aleck retorts.

"I've used your products for almost twenty years, Mr. Harwell. Harsoft has helped millions of people lead more productive lives. Your reputation for philanthropy is also well known. I'm sure that you are not a pig in any sense of the word."

"That's very kind of you, Peter, but probably not altogether true. I'm trying to confess here! Don't you Christian folk say that confession is good for the soul?"

"It is and we do."

"I am quite proud of Harsoft, Peter. On the whole, I believe we have been a positive force for humanity. But I'd be lying if I said I haven't stepped on more than a few toes on the road to success, cut some corners, acted ruthlessly, and maybe even broken a few laws. If I'm for sure going to hell, just stop me at any time and I'll slip off into my eternal doom quietly."

"Let's hold off on any judgments, Mr. Harwell. I think you might be making some progress toward your salvation." Peter was happy to play along with the less serious, tongue in cheek teasing.

"My question is, do the ends ever justify the means? If I do eight good things and two bad things and the net result of my efforts is one great big good thing, have I sinned?

"Let me be even more specific, Peter. In business, men and women like me have to make tough decisions daily. Sometimes it's a choice between the lesser of two evils. Modern capitalism, by its very nature, can be ruthless on its losers. Yet communism, state controlled anything, is far worse for everyone. Help me out here, Peter. You see where I'm going with this, don't you?"

Yes and no, Peter thought to himself. Harwell appeared to be seeking some form of absolution or excuse for his sin, but his question was profound and certainly could not be dodged.

"I will answer your question as best as I can, Mr. Harwell. First of all, are you so sure that it was necessary to do the bad things you did in order to ultimately succeed? Is it possible that you succeeded in spite of your sin?"

"At the time I can assure you, Peter, that every move I made was well-considered. Who knows what would have happened if I'd gone left instead of right to spare an economic injury to someone else."

"I do not believe, Mr. Harwell, that sin is required to be a success in business. That said, none of us is blameless before God. You know why I was sent to prison, Mr. Harwell, don't you?"

"Theft and embezzlement, if what I've been told is true."

"Oh, it's true, Mr. Harwell. I wasn't trying to create a new product or out compete a rival, I just wanted money. I have no excuse for what I did, but God has forgiven me for my mistakes. I no longer own them, to the Lord it is as if they never happened."

"So you're saying if my goal was legitimate I have an excuse?"

"Mr. Harwell, consider this. Christ makes it clear that it is a sin to kill. From the Ten Commandments to the Sermon on the Mount, God is consistent; He says we are to love our brothers and sisters as we love ourselves. Killing another human being is the ultimate form of hatred, evil, and ungodliness. What right have I to end the life God gave to another?"

"I detect a but coming on the horizon."

"But Mr. Harwell, what if the world hadn't stopped Hitler? What if the Jews had perished from the earth before it was Christ's time to appear as one of them?"

"So you're saying…"

"We must seek forgiveness for our sins, Mr. Harwell. Obviously, you know you've done some wrong on your journey of worldly success. Seek Christ, accept Him as your Savior, ask for His forgiveness. Atone for your sins as the Spirit leads you."

"You mean go back and find people I wronged twenty years ago, apologize to them, and compensate them?"

"What a marvelous example that would be to the world wouldn't it, Mr. Harwell? If you humbled yourself, others might follow your lead."

"I'm still not sure that you've answered my question."

"Christ is an absolute, Mr. Harwell, a mysterious and perfect combination of God and man. We are mortal beings, inherently flawed. In order to be righteous, to be in right standing with God, we must seek forgiveness and strive with our free will not to repeat our mistakes."

"Now I know better, that's what you're saying?"

"I'm sure that you knew better then too, Mr. Harwell. God is your judge, not me. I can only tell you how His word answers your question."

"Profit is not evil, is it Peter?"

"No, at least I do not believe that it is. To fail to use the wealth God gives you for the betterment of others, that is most certainly a sin."

"How much should I give? And to whom? I've never given a dime to a church, does that mean my gifts are ..."

"Thank you, Mr. Harwell. Rabbi Rosefielde, your time starts now."

"She's really beginning to annoy me," Larry moaned. "I believe Miss Spence is enjoying her referee duties a bit too much."

"She may not be real warm and fuzzy, brother," Kenny said, "but I understand the need for what she's doing."

"Peter, good evening."

"Good evening, Rabbi. Shalom."

"Shalom. I have so much to ask you, my friend, but there is so little time." Like Cardinal Reardon, Rabbi David Rosefielde was a humble man, honest and completely uninterested in pretense.

"Perhaps soon we can talk, you and me, privately and at length."

"I look forward to that, Peter. Of all of the questions I have one issue strikes me as being most important. If the world is to believe you, people must accept the concept of a reality greater than their senses, the existence of a Force of Uncreated Energy we label God."

"Yes, Rabbi. For less advanced societies acceptance through faith of the nature of God was easier, but today we suffer from excessive hubris, we believe man is all powerful, and we worship God's creation and ignore Him."

"I agree. Perhaps an important lesson of the restriction is to teach us that God is not only real, but also that He is omnipotent."

"As I see it, Rabbi, you are exactly right. God wants us to quit our violent ways, that is His message, but remember Christ's first commandment to us is that we are to love the Lord with all our heart, soul, strength, and mind. We are being blessed by a direct application of His power, this astounding restriction. We should respect the miracle with thanksgiving and obedience."

"Peter, what happens when the restriction ends? Like all miracles, the passage of time diminishes their impact. What else can we do to leave a lasting impression, if you will, of the true nature of the universe?"

What a spectacular question, Peter thought, so astute. To Peter the existence of God and the unseen spiritual dimension was a given, but not so to a skeptical world.

A direct answer to the Rabbi's question then presented itself.

"Good Lord!" Doris Spence shrieked. "How did that man get in here?"

Standing behind Peter, literally appearing out of nowhere was a man, about thirty, with light brown, curly hair. His white robe seemed to be emitting rather than reflecting light, his skin was a radiant bronze and his eyes sparkled like bright blue bolts of liquid flame.

"My name is Gabriel," the angel said, "and I am here to speak for the Lord."

Twenty-Five

"You getting all this, Chuck? Status, I need status." The Executive Director was unnerved, along with everyone else involved with the broadcast, but he was professional enough not to lose sight of his duties in the midst of a crisis.

"Copy that. Everything appears nominal. Transmission nominal, audio nominal, tape … hey, what the hell?"

"Chuck, talk to me, Chucky."

"Ah, transmission nominal, recording malfunctioning. Tape check shows new subject Gabriel not, well he's not coming through on tape. No image, no audio. All other systems nominal."

"Repeat that." The Executive Director heard what was said, but it made no sense, so it didn't register.

"This Gabriel character's image and voice is being transmitted live but, as far as we can tell, isn't being recorded."

"Chuck, I mean come on man that's nuts."

"Like any of the rest of this makes sense. Suggest we move on, keep monitoring."

"Mommy, that's my angel!" Kevin said, pointing at the screen. "What's he doing on the TV with daddy?"

"I'm sure that he's helping your father, Kev. That's a good thing."

"I guess so, mom. I'm gonna pray the angel brings daddy home."

"I'll join you in that prayer, son."

A few seconds after Gabriel appeared, four Secret Service agents rushed on to the stage. They were powerless to attack or otherwise subdue the intruder, but they surrounded the President and started shouting orders that the panel should disperse. Immediately.

But no one moved. An indecisive moment that felt like an hour passed by. The audience offered only a dull murmur, they all kept their seats.

"Please, I assure you that there is nothing to be frightened of," the President said, as he stood and moved away from his panicked security detail. "I know this man. Well, he's not a man, but I know him."

"Yes, please, you have no idea how blessed you are to be here tonight." Peter followed the President's lead. "This is the Archangel Gabriel. He is a holy messenger. No one in this room has anything to fear from him."

"Bravo, bravo," Thomas Peterson said, as he stood and mockingly applauded. "Best show I've seen in years, Carson. Last time I saw a trick that slick was in Vegas when a couple of homosexuals in tights made an elephant disappear."

"Thomas Peterson, we have no time for your stupidity. Sit down and keep quiet." Gabriel's voice was commanding and firm, but Peterson was not impressed.

"I'll do no such thing, Mr. Gabriel. Archangel of the Lord indeed, why when I ..."

Gabriel sighed and waved his arm across his body. In response, the rotund Reverend Peterson not only stopped talking, he floated up three feet in the air and ten feet away from the table. He hung there, suspended like a flabby side of beef. The look on his face was a mixture of horror and astonishment.

"My apologies, Peter. That was distasteful, but I'm afraid Thomas Peterson left me no choice. This is a unique opportunity. We must make the best possible use of our time."

"David, please tell me that you see Peterson floating above the table." Doris Spence, like the rest of the audience in the East Room, was dazed and unsure where reality ended and illusion began.

"We all see him, Doris, get a grip. We've got a job to do here. There are about a billion people watching this spectacle. Doris? Doris?"

"Right, David. Right. God, yes." Martz's admonitions pulled Doris out of her stupor and she tried to refocus.

"Peter," Alex Anderson said, realizing someone had to get things moving again, "what do you want us to do? Should we continue on as before?"

Peter looked up at Gabriel who said nothing, but he did keep his hand reassuringly resting on Peter's shoulder.

"Mr. Anderson, why don't we move forward. Gabriel can get involved as he wishes."

Evidently that was the right decision because Gabriel gave a confirming nod to Peter. The moderators took a minute to reorganize their notes.

Gabriel's appearance at the White House also answered a nagging question for many of the select. Somewhere around a quarter of them had seen Gabriel in their visions, including Rabbi Rosefielde, Cardinal Reardon, and the President.

"Uh, Rabbi, I suppose you are still up." Doris was holding her own, barely, but her former confident swagger was gone.

"Peter, you are truly taking us where no one has gone before." The Rabbi's skin was ashy and his hands were shaking as he reached for a glass of water. After taking a nervous sip he said, "May I ask Gabriel a question?"

The angel nodded, but said nothing.

"You knew the Biblical prophet Daniel? Spoke with him?"

"Yes," Gabriel replied.

"You appeared to the Holy Virgin, announcing Christ's birth?"

"Yes. I have been in many places over the ages. Those mentioned in the Book are but a few of tens of thousands."

"I don't know exactly why I'm asking this, Gabriel, but is it possible for you to show us some of what you've witnessed in your service to God?"

"You ask, Rabbi, because it is the will of the Lord."

Gabriel raised his arms in the air; reaching up toward heaven. He also chanted a few words in Hebrew that no one in the room other than Kenny understood.

"Watch yourself," Kenny warned after Gabriel spoke. "If I heard right, I believe we…"

There were exactly two-hundred-and-ten living souls in the East Room when Gabriel announced his blessing. They were all now frozen, unable to move or speak, except for Peter, Gail, and the disciples.

Afterward, every one of the two hundred and ten claimed to have seen the same vision.

It began on a lonely and desolate hill outside of ancient Jerusalem. Three men, bloodied and beaten, were being crucified. A small crowd was heckling the Man on the middle cross, calling him vile names and mocking Him as He suffered.

The blessed, as those present in the East Room would soon come to be called, would all later swear that they were more than spectators to scenes; they believed that they were actually present in the vision in a physical body and able to fully experience the five senses.

Some vividly described the putrid smell of sweat, excrement, blood, and death that permeated Golgotha. Others would never forget the jeering of the crowd and the cries of mourning from the small group of mostly women at the foot of the middle cross. A few recalled being pushed by soldiers and stumbling over the rocky ground.

As they watched, they heard Christ cry out in a language none of them understood and then die. They looked on as the Roman soldiers punctured His side with a spear and witnessed it gush forth blood and water.

Then the sky completely darkened, even though it had been a cloudless afternoon only a second before. Next a violent earthquake struck, causing a panic. As the crowd began to run, a torrential rain deluged the killing ground.

It was at this point that the blessed claim they were "transported" to Galilee. Although unable to articulate how they knew, they were all sure both of their new location and also that several days had passed since the crucifixion.

The Man who had been nailed to the middle cross was now standing by the shore of a lake. He was no longer bloody and beaten, but whole and fresh. Perhaps fifty or so men and women were gathered around Him. They were listening to the words of the risen Christ and sharing a meal with Him.

After a bright bluish flash the vision shifted to a battlefield, but not an earthly one. On alien plains with stark charcoal landscapes, vast hordes of hideous creatures were attacking other angelic beings that emitted an almost blinding white light.

None of the bright creatures had fallen, but thousands upon thousands of dismembered demon carcasses lay strewn in vast, grotesque heaps on the grey soil.

The blessed said the battlefield had an overpowering odor of sulfur, as if millions of paper matches had been struck all at once. The atmosphere was dense and charged, as much electric as it was gaseous. The demon creatures shrieked as the beings of light annihilated them, making high pitched wailing sounds like the cries of young animals being butchered.

One at a time or in groups the demons attacked, again and again, but the results were always the same. It was a slaughter. The outcome of the battle was never in doubt.

The carnage suddenly stopped when a bolt of energy, something like lightning but far more powerful, fell from the milky sky. When it hit the ground, the colliding stream of white plasma opened up a huge chasm. From out of nowhere hundreds of bright creatures converged on the opening and began filling it with material from the surrounding area. Literally everything within sight was pushed into the gash, demons both living and dead and all manner of debris. When they finished no trace of the battle remained, just dull grey fields covered with mist stretching into infinity.

Then another burst of blue took the blessed to a much more recent historical event. The scene was Parkersboro only a few months earlier.

Every person present in the East Room was able bodied, yet they would all later testify that during this part of the vision they were paralyzed from the waist down. Many remembered the rickety old wheelchair and its peculiar chirping squeak that announced its owner's arrivals and departures to the inmates at the prison camp.

The blessed were able to describe Solomon's Porch in great detail, from the rusty benches with wooden seats to the crumbling cement and gang graffiti found on its western corner. They also knew exactly who they were in this vision, a badly wounded and bitter black inmate named Alan Audry.

As Peter Carson recited the prayer of healing over Alan from the book of James chapter five, verse ten the blessed could feel a Force healing their broken body, restoring its wholeness. They experienced the euphoria of standing up and walking away from an incurable paralysis. The blessed felt Alan Audry's gratitude to God and the satisfaction he received from the validation of his faith. Then, with a final explosion of blue, the vision ended.

The technical crew working the studio in New York measured twenty seconds of dead air time from the raising to the lowering of Gabriel's arms. The blessed in the East Room believed that they'd been "somewhere else" for at least half an hour.

Although getting a precise count was impossible, over five million people who were watching on television also claimed to have seen the vision. It was believed that most of these claims were valid, since the vast majority of those making them were aware of details also known only by the blessed in the East Room audience.

"People? Say something. What's going on out there?" The Executive Director had been trying for about thirty seconds to get a response from any of his moderators. Alex Anderson was the first of the three to regain his senses, so he broke the silence.

"Everyone in the East Room has become a witness to the extraordinary power of the Living God," Alex said, without explaining exactly what he was talking about or how he knew it to be true. "Peter, I leave it to you to take it from here. I'm afraid those of us charged with the duty of managing this discussion are currently not up to the task." Dave Martz was leaning back in his chair, eyes closed. His lips were moving, but he made no sound. Doris Spence was curled up in a ball in her seat as if she was trying to reenter the womb.

"A vision as powerful as the one we all just experienced can drain and disorient you for a while," Peter explained. "Can we take a break? Let's give everyone a few minutes to collect themselves."

During the interlude Gabriel honored Peter's request and released the Reverend Peterson. He emerged from his stasis as a humbled man and said nothing other than "thank you" as he found his chair, sat down, and started to cry.

Alex Anderson used the interim to give the world a synopsis of what had just transpired. Assuming nothing, he walked the largest audience in the history of broadcasting through the content of the vision and told the viewers that, to the best of his knowledge, all souls present in the East Room had been blessed with the same experience.

As soon as the cameras were switched off, all of the important people gathered at the White House, the political, economic and scientific leaders from around the globe were attended to by a small army of aides. While it was quickly determined that everyone was in good health and in no apparent danger, the majority of the advisors to the great men and women argued that their superiors should run, not walk, to the nearest exit. The vision and Gabriel's continuing presence confused and frightened the counselors, but not a single invitee decided to leave, or even seriously considered doing so.

Gabriel did not move during the break, standing tall and still behind the conference table like a sentinel. He said nothing either, except to Malik Graham.

Malik was watching both the demonic activity and Gabriel very closely. He knew that Gabriel had the ability to see the spiritual world, because that was his natural plane of existence. He wanted to ask the angel what he thought about what he was seeing, to determine if his read of the situation was correct, so he approached Gabriel and spoke.

"You learn quickly, Malik. Yes, you are right, the demons do fear me. But their master does not." Gabriel moved nothing other than his lips as he answered Malik's question. "Make no mistake. Satan believes he is more powerful and more worthy than any other angel. He will not hesitate to strike at me if he believes he has an advantage."

Sitting in the back of the East Room, off by himself as much as that was possible in the crowd, was Bishop Kallistos. None of what he'd seen or heard surprised him. He knew what was coming, the terrible trials that lay directly ahead, so for him this spectacular event, while vitally important, was only part of a larger plan. What was happening was a necessary step toward an inevitable confrontation, not an end into itself.

Father Gregory felt a tremendous surge of pride as he watched his nephew more than hold his own with the worldly men. His satisfaction was both as an uncle and as a clergyman. St. Paul's prophecies made two millennia before were being fulfilled before his eyes. Bishop Kallistos thought about how pleased his brother Nicki would be to see his son so ably walk the path God had set for him and he marveled at God's grace as expressed through the love and dedication of the Phillipi brotherhood of priests, without whom the miracle of Peter Carson and Solomon's Porch could not have been brought to the world.

Carlos Benes was the least animated of the panelists. Somehow he remained nerveless throughout the chaos, keeping up the appearance of total confidence. He had always been very difficult to read and he used this trait to his advantage as he rose first in the Brazilian and then in the United Nations political hierarchies.

Benes publicly proclaimed himself to be a devout Catholic, but the truth was that he had harbored doubts about both God and church since childhood. As a politician, he was a dedicated, outspoken advocate for the poor and disenfranchised, a noble Christian pursuit if there ever was one. His championing of the masses had made him more than a few enemies during his illustrious career, especially among European and American conservatives, but no legitimate critic questioned either Benes' motives or his unblemished record of integrity.

The UN Secretary General came to the panel as a skeptic, quite certain that some rational explanation for the restriction would eventually present itself. But the East Room vision changed him. Benes was deeply moved by what he saw and needed no one to validate his experience. He was completely certain that he had been touched by God.

So when the panel reconvened, Benes was more than anxious to ask Him some tough questions. Issues that had weighed heavily on his mind since Carlos was a poor boy growing up in the slums of Sao Paulo were at the forefront of his thoughts.

"Peter, I want to begin by apologizing if I seem rude. Given our situation I feel the need to be direct. Have patience with me."

"Certainly, Mr. Benes, but please do not expect me to have all the answers that you seek."

True to his word, Benes got right to the point. "Why does God allow the rich to dominate the poor? I have never understood this. So many in our world have so little and so few have so much. Every time I read reports of children dying of hunger and disease I think of the economic elite and wonder why God does not punish them for their greed."

"Mr. Benes, do you believe in the doctrine of free will?" Peter asked.

"Yes."

"Then it is not God who allows selfishness and suffering to exist as much as it is we, His creation, who are responsible. God does not force righteousness on anyone."

"Yes, I understand. But if God is merciful and all powerful, why does He not act? Is there no limit to His patience? Will He ever provide justice on this earth for those who love Him the most?" Carlos Benes was thinking of his mother when he asked this question. Lily Benes lived her life as a pious Catholic and a virtuous woman, only to be rewarded with poverty, chronic illness, and an early grave. Benes had always resented God for letting that happen.

"Why are you so sure, Mr. Benes, that poverty and illness are always a curse? For some of us, life's problems are a blessing. Rejection of worldly comforts and deprivation can lead a soul to seek God. My brothers and I, some of whom were prisoners, can testify to this truth."

"That seems so unjust, Peter. Why must it be so? Didn't the Master teach us to share, to love our fellow man? Didn't He say that when you have mercy on the least you are showing mercy to Him?"

"Without suffering there could be no mercy. We are here to learn eternal lessons, Mr. Benes, what happens to us in this world is temporary, but also full of important spiritual meanings. Do you recall the parable of Lazarus from the Gospels? He who is last shall be first."

"So we must accept rampant poverty, starvation, and disease? Where is the love in that, Peter? Where is God?"

"Mr. Benes, I hope and pray that one of the outcomes of the Lord's blessing of the restriction is a new awareness by His people that God has standards and expectations of us individually and as nations. I have witnessed first hand how much it grieves God to see millions of His creation suffer everyday for lack of the basic necessities of life. I agree with you, we must not let these sad, shameful, and evil conditions continue to exist.

"So, Mr. Benes, I am anything but complacent. I say disband our war machines and bloated bureaucracies and fight evil directly on the true battlefields, the hearts and minds of all living souls. Make no mistake, Secretary General Benes, God hears the cries of every impoverished and abused man, woman, and child. Only Satan rejoices when our selfishness allows the suffering of so many. The evil one is betting that humanity will never get it right and move closer to God. I say the devil is wrong, Mr. Benes. I believe we can do better and become much more like Christ. That is why He called me to His service, to be an example of how an evil man can change and come to the Light."

"Carlos, my wonderful son. How proud I am of you. How much I love you, my beautiful boy." The words came from Gabriel's mouth, but the voice was not his own.

It had been close to forty years since he'd heard his mother call out to him, but Carlos Benes could never forget his mother's sweet, comforting voice.

"Min Ha?" It took only an instant to transform the Secretary General of the United Nations from one of the world's most powerful men back into a vulnerable ten-year-old boy who worshipped and adored his mother above all else. "Ma'e, is that you?"

"Carlos, do not grieve for me, son. I am with the Lord, happy and at peace. Listen to His messengers, learn from them and act. I love you forever my precious Morning Star. Use your gifts and blessings for the glory of God."

"Min Ha? Ma'e!" Benes did not have to think about what was happening, or carefully weigh all the possible alternatives before reaching a conclusion. He was positive that it was his mother who was speaking to him. Not only would it be impossible for someone to capture and exactly reproduce his mother's voice four decades after her death, no one, not even his siblings, knew that Lily Benes called her youngest son "my precious Morning Star."

"Your mother is free and rich and flourishing with Christ, Carlos," Gabriel said in his own voice. "She wanted you to know that and the Lord answered her prayer."

"I, I do not..." The most famous diplomat on earth, known for his ability to speak eloquently and succinctly under any circumstances, was at a total loss for words. He looked at Gabriel, then at Peter and whispered, "Obrigado." Carlos Benes was overcome with love and truly slain in the Spirit.

Carlos knelt and recited the Lord's Prayer in Latin, something his mother had taught him to do by the age of five. While he did not have all the answers he'd sought from God, he no longer needed them. When he finished his short prayer, he had only a few words left to say.

"Consider me a disciple, Peter. I commit the rest of my life to God's service. Please, help me to be of the most use to others."

Carlos Benes stood, approached Peter and they embraced. Tears of joy flowed freely from both men.

"Damn him, damn that man," the President's first former senior advisor said, as he threw a half eaten plate of food at the screen. "We don't need all of this f***ing drama! Benes is a weak fool, but the scum of the earth worship him. I tell you this whole thing could easily blow up in our faces. Have you considered that? This is not going well."

"Cool down. Let them have their moment of glory. I'm taking Carson at his word. Late tomorrow night this voodoo restriction psych job will be history. Then just wait and see. I know human nature, there will be a backlash." The President's second former senior advisor was doing his best to steady his wavering co-conspirator.

"So what if there is a backlash? If we get caught, you'll learn what a backlash is alright. I'm worried, no, not worried, f***ing panicked. You should be too."

"Why? Don't you see? This whole charade of Carson's is just that, a charade. These stunts he pulls are impressive, I've got to admit it, but we, my friend, we are the real deal. No phony god controls us. We are the princes of this world, not these two bit hustlers with their rinky dink magic show."

"I suppose it's my turn up to bat, Peter," Dr. Carl Fuchs said. If he sounded reluctant, it's because he was. Of all of the men on the panel, Carl Fuchs was the most out of his element.

It was during his senior undergraduate year at Yale when the future Dr. Fuchs decided he'd figured it all out. He chose to believe that the universe is governed exclusively by discernible rules; every action has a reaction, every cause an effect, every phenomenon an explanation. Nature is essentially orderly and any mysteries are only temporary, science will solve them all eventually.

Carl's mind processed mathematical information creatively and at near silicon chip speed. He solved complex equations no one else could and found correlations and connections unseen by other less brilliant minds. Through experience, Carl Fuchs developed an unabiding faith in himself. Given enough time, he believed he could always come up with the solution to any quantifiable problem and to Carl everything was, one way or another, a quantifiable problem.

For over fifty years Dr. Fuchs had no doubts, the certainty of his convictions forming his personal and professional bedrock. He was truly without peer as a physicist, or at least any living one. Carl was a toddler when the one man who had ever lived that could rival his intellectual abilities, Albert Einstein, died. Most of the scientific community believed that Carl Fuchs was the only human being yet born who was potentially capable of realizing Einstein's dream of constructing a valid unified field theory. This was Carl's greatest ambition.

Unless it could not be avoided, Carl Fuchs spoke only to other scientists. His lab at Princeton was off limits to all but a few faculty, because he trusted no one. He didn't concern himself with other people, what they thought, feared, cared about, or hoped for. Carl was not overtly evil, he was in fact by nature and practice basically benign, he just did not have any interest in pursuing human relationships. That's why he'd never married, had no children or friends, and did not maintain contact with his family. To Carl such things as love and mercy were a distraction, a superfluous drain of precious mental energy.

Then, out of the blue, a few weeks ago the strangest things began happening to Carl. First came the dreams. He had never dreamed before, at least he'd had no dreams he could really remember as being in any way significant. Now this "angel" was visiting him every night with some new admonition, imploring him to "humble himself before God." Carl had seen the pentecostal images from Parkersboro in his night visions and much, much more. He was now haunted, both day and night, by these all too realistic phantasms.

As if the dreams weren't bad enough, an ethereal voice was telling him that his blind faith in the scientific method as the path to all knowledge was in error. Damn that voice! It jabbed at him relentlessly, like a curse. Carl had come to despise it in a very short time. No one heard it but him, the voice that said he'd been wrong to value nothing other than objective knowledge. Carl seriously considered the possibility that he was going mad.

But now Dr. Fuchs was forced to conclude that he wasn't insane because the hated voice had been given a face and a name. Gabriel.

Carl did not want to be in the East Room tonight. He wanted nothing to do with the doubts that plagued his disciplined mind and his new sub-conscious awareness that somehow he'd over-reached for fifty years. Dr. Fuchs wanted things to go back to the way they were a few weeks ago, but he was too honest to succeed for long at denial.

"So, we finally meet," Dr. Fuchs said.

Before Peter could respond, Gabriel did. "Yes, Carl Fuchs, we are finally in the same place and time. But we have met elsewhere."

"Yes, I know. You come and see me every night and you pester me constantly with your tongue. Why? What do you want from me, Gabriel?"

"It's what God desires of you that is important. I want nothing from you."

"God? Why must we discuss God? What is God anyway, Gabriel?"

"He is your Creator, Carl Fuchs, your Lord and Master. He is the one who gave you your genius. You must begin to use your gifts for Him and become useful to the Kingdom."

"I do not believe you, Gabriel. These apparitions you force on us, these dreams and ideas are being generated by some technology we cannot see. I do not believe in God, especially the Christian God."

"You do not believe because your mind is so filled with knowledge you have lost the capacity for wisdom. You must repent, seek Christ, and fulfill your destiny."

"My destiny! What do you know about my destiny, Gabriel?"

"God knows everything."

"Prove it."

Gabriel smiled, something Peter tried to recall if he'd ever seen him do before. Moving for the first time since he appeared, Gabriel walked over to Carl Fuchs and gently tapped him on the forehead. The angel then walked back and reestablished his position behind Peter.

After Gabriel touched him Carl Fuchs had a puzzled expression on his face, like a person who couldn't quite figure out where he'd left something valuable. For a couple of minutes he sat at the conference table fidgeting, looking around, and drawing imaginary numbers in the air. Gabriel kept smiling. No one, including Peter, knew what was going on.

"Will someone please give me a piece of paper and a pencil. For the love of God!" Professor Fuchs abruptly ended his quizzical ticking and became very excited. The Reverend Peterson was sitting right next to him and hurriedly passed Fuchs a pad and a pen.

As if he was the only person in the room, Fuchs began to scribble frantically. Back and forth his hand went, flying across the paper, all the while he muttered to himself incoherently.

"My God," Fuchs finally said when he stopped writing.

"Yes. Your God and your destiny," Gabriel answered.

Carl grabbed Howard Simms and they began to mumble back and forth. Obviously the angel had given Carl some important information, but it remained a temporary mystery to everyone else.

"You must tell them," Gabriel said in a commanding tone, his smile now absent.

"No. What I need to do is get back to my lab. I'll take Howard with me. Who else should I call, I mean who do you call when…"

"Tell them." Gabriel's inflection was sterner still.

Carl Fuchs was unaccustomed to taking orders from anyone, even from supernatural beings. Until a few moments ago he didn't even believe in supernatural beings. But now everything had changed.

"They will not understand," Dr. Fuchs argued.

"Do not be so arrogant, of course they will understand," Gabriel replied.

Fuchs looked over at Howard Simms who was totally absorbed in the equations Carl had hastily written down on the pad. Aware he was being stared at, Simms raised his head, looked up at Dr. Fuchs and shrugged his shoulders.

"Gabriel, I believe. No, let me start over. Gabriel has somehow given me a very simple and straightforward series of equations which I have no doubt are a complete and perfect unified field theory. In only a few minutes these equations have taken my mind in directions I never would have considered otherwise in two lifetimes. The theory can and no doubt will be tested and validated by others. That may take years, but I do not need any proofs or experiments to know what it is. There is no doubt."

The men of science in the audience now reacted. They began to talk amongst themselves, loud enough to be heard by the panel at the conference table. Their comments ranged from rude to profound. All of them were dying to see the paper Howard Simms was intensely studying. None of the scientists would have given any credence to the outlandish claim that a unified field theory had been generated by divine osmosis, except that it was being made by Dr. Carl Fuchs, twice a Nobel winner and generally believed to be the smartest person alive.

"I did ask you to prove it, didn't I, Gabriel." Fuchs was truly humbled, which was a brand new state of mind for him.

"Yes, you put God to the test, Carl Fuchs. Now He says use this blessing for the benefit of His creation. See to it the miracle is not abused."

"Gabriel, I don't know what to do anymore. You have literally altered the way I think. What is next for me? How should I proceed?" The invulnerable Dr. Fuchs sounded more like a small child asking a parent for directions than the "Lion of Princeton," as his colleagues often called him.

"Seek the counsel of your brothers, Carl Fuchs. Peter and the disciples can open your mind to greater truths than these,"

Gabriel said, pointing at the paper full of equations Howard Simms was now jealously guarding.

"Greater truths than understanding how the universe was formed, how matter and energy are essentially the same, how to manipulate time?" Fuchs ran off just a few of the inevitable applications of a valid unified field theory.

"Unless your discovery results in the betterment of man and brings him closer to God, of what use is it? Love is the greatest power in any universe, Carl Fuchs. It is at the heart of any valid theory. Look for it in what God has given you. Find the Uncreated Energy and you will find the Lord, love, and all the answers you seek."

In a crazy, completely non-rational way Gabriel's statement made sense to Carl Fuchs. To everyone else it sounded like fantastical gibberish.

"Peter, I am at your service. That I have become a follower of Christ should be an amazement to you. I know it is to me."

The panel discussion generated an information blitzkrieg. It was impossible for the news media to keep up. "Slow down!" was the editors' most common response to the furious pace of electronic submissions. But they could not slow down because every White House reporter had lost his or her objectivity. Most were deathly afraid of missing the slightest detail. They knew how critical it was to get it right. The press had become part of the process, witnesses more than correspondents. Only a soulless robot would be immune to the influence of the Power in the East Room, and none of the reporters present fit that description.

Martz, Doris Spence, and Alex gave up trying to moderate the discussion. It was obvious that their help was no longer needed.

"Well, Mr. Stone, I guess that leaves just you and me," the President said, after Carl Fuchs finished his short speech. "I think I'll pass on my turn. Folks hear me drone on too much anyway. The world needs to hear from you, Roger Stone."

Despite Doris' earlier introduction, no one other than Peter, Alex, and the President really knew why Roger Stone was taking up space on the most prestigious panel in history. The concept that God had invited him explained little or nothing about why he was here to most observers. Weren't all the panelists invited? Who was this guy who could be a poster boy for Nerds 'R Us?

Ask Roger Stone why he was here and he'd tell you that he didn't have a clue. God wanted it to be so. End of story. But then the Lord had always been everything to Roger Stone. Nothing else really mattered to him other than to try and stay in right standing with God.

Roger was never the best or the brightest or the most handsome. As a child and as a young adult he showed a moderate interest in his education, but none in sports or socializing or arts or any of the thousand other things young people get caught up in as they grow up.

Roger Stone was, and always had been, interested in only one thing, God. And not so much through theology as through experience. Roger was a prayer warrior. He prayed for the neighbors when they got sick, asked God to find the resources to fill the food banks in his town, and pleaded with the Lord to restore love and kindness to broken marriages in his church.

But there was one thing Roger never did. He never prayed for himself, always for someone else's needs.

Other than his wife Elaine, no one really knew what Roger was praying for most of the time. He sought no recognition for his efforts, not even an "atta boy" or two from his pastor for selflessness. A couple of years into their marriage Elaine began to notice that, much more often than not, when Roger asked the Lord for something, He said yes. This actually frightened her a bit at first; it was almost eerie and too good to be true.

Roger did his best to explain to his wife the principles of effective prayer. God, he told her, is not some "magic genie" who grants requests like a divine vending machine. While in church once, the Stones are Methodists, Roger tried to explain to Elaine's best friend Louise how futile it was to ask God to give you this or that material possession. The Energy, as Roger often called God, could not be manipulated for personal gain. In order to succeed, a prayer's focus must be on asking Him to show mercy on another, or, if you are praying for yourself, your prayer should always be to give you the wisdom and strength to discern and follow God's will for your life. Louise did not want to hear the truth and quickly turned away, but Elaine listened and learned.

Roger Stone didn't really stand out in any way other than there was not a person in the world who could, or did, say anything bad about him. He had no vices, was kind, polite, humble, and pious. His basic personality had changed little since High School. The "salt of the earth," as his wife and daughters called him.

But as outstanding as Roger Stone was in his practice of the Christian virtues, it was his prayer life that set him apart. He was every bit as extraordinary in his field, intercessory prayer, as Carl Fuchs was in physics. He knew very well that it was his life's calling.

"Peter, please tell me," Roger asked, "what should I pray for? I want to help you and the brothers, but I need guidance."

"What is most on your heart, brother Stone?" Peter respected Roger perhaps more than anyone else on the panel other than the President. "I think it is you who should be guiding us."

"Well, if I could, I'd like to help people lead simpler lives, more focused on what's real than on the devil's worldly lies. I'm certain that if we could move in this direction, suffering would decrease and joy would increase."

"Do you fast, brother Stone?" Peter asked.

"Yes. I fast once during the week and also at Lent. But I could do better at it if I tried. I'm sure I like to eat a bit too much."

"Well, brother, I have an idea. Why don't we call for a world-wide day of fasting and prayer for the day after tomorrow. You can be the prayer leader. It would be a wonderful and productive thing to do the day after the restriction ends. It will keep our minds focused on God."

Within seconds the media disseminated Peter's proclamation, calling it "Holy Thursday."

"That is a great idea, Peter, but I am not qualified or worthy to lead such a prayer."

"Roger Stone, no one is more qualified than you. It is the Lord's will that you should do this."

"Then I accept," Roger said, without further hesitance and in total humility, "but I would appreciate your thoughts on topics for the prayers."

"Alright. Let's stay with your theme, brother Stone, helping people to lead simpler, more Christ-like lives. That is, in fact, exactly why God called me to His service, Roger. My scope is perhaps broader than yours, but our desired end result is the same."

"Yes, Peter. I've known that since I first read about what you were doing at Parkersboro. I wish I could have seen you preach from Solomon's Porch."

"Our goal can only be achieved through education, Roger. Everyone born on this planet, until the Lord returns, is subject to spiritual warfare. Light versus darkness, Good verses evil. If a person begins to see his life, and other's lives, in these terms, certain attitudes and conclusions inevitably result."

"I understand," Roger Stone said enthusiastically. "It took me many, many years, Peter, to separate the person from the sin. Hating people because they do bad things is not only against Christian theological and moral precepts, it is not even logical. If you believe in Christ's teachings, that is."

"But the world does not want to accept this, Roger. The evil wants us to stay at each other's throats. As individuals, we despise those that hurt us or act in sinful ways. I'm not talking just about criminal behavior here, but common, everyday human activity as well. We are quick to judge others, slow to shine the Light on ourselves."

"Few want to turn the other cheek, Peter, or welcome home the prodigal son. Where I'm from, many Christians will quickly and generously show mercy and kindness to total strangers whose lives have been wrecked by hurricanes and tornadoes, but some of these same 'Christians' will refuse to show love and compassion to their own children if they are gay or steal or will sit at home in front of the television set and cheer as the eleven o'clock news reports on another execution."

"Matthew, chapter five, verses forty-three through forty-eight."

"That's on the button, Peter. It is very hard to bless those that curse you and to pray for those who spitefully use you."

"You must help us, Roger. Pray to the Father on our behalf. The Lord is calling you to leadership, brother Stone."

"That's it, isn't it Peter."

"Brother Stone?"

"Why you're here, you and the brothers. To help us find true mercy, to find Christ in our daily lives, before it's too late."

"Time, Roger, is running out. I'm afraid we no longer have the luxury of half stepping His commandments. Our situation is critical, even if it appears perhaps not to be."

"Oh, it is critical, Mr. Pete," Malik Graham said, walking on to the East Room stage. "You need to get these folks on out of here and right now. I ain't never seen nothin' like this."

Peter could feel the disruption too, tremendous energies were being expended. At the same time both Peter and Malik looked up to see how Gabriel was reacting to the developing conflagration.

But he was gone.

Twenty-Six

M alik chose to directly intervene rather than to signal
Peter because what he was seeing wasn't merely a threat,
it seemed to him much more like the end of the world.

On the earthly plane of existence, Peter's nod to the President and the President's order to the Secret Service were all that
it took to clear the White House of its guests in less than fifteen
minutes. While no one could be physically compelled to leave,
the strong suggestion that forces beyond understanding now
posed a serious threat to human life was, after everything the
blessed had just experienced, more than enough incentive for the
audience to promptly evacuate.

When Gabriel disappeared he did not actually leave the
East Room, he simply switched dimensions. Through senses
indescribable in human language, the Archangel knew that his
ancient nemesis, Satan, was posturing, presenting himself in
such a way as to create the possibility of angelic conflict. This
was a very rare and dangerous development.

The true Power in the universe, the Uncreated Energy
that binds all things, exists primarily in a spiritual domain that
human beings can only occasionally glance. While dominated by
the Light, darkness also exists within the Energy and manifests
itself through hosts that have freely chosen to reject God.

Once, eons ago, the Uncreated Energy was one Force, pure Love, pure Light; then came Satan's rebellion, and the creation of creatures in the image and likeness of God, human beings. A battlefield was established on earth, a place where conflict could continue within limitations. Both Light and darkness knew that to bring their war back to their own dimension was to risk it all; the loser surely would be vaporized into nothingness.

The Light claims that ultimate victory over darkness is a foregone conclusion and expects its human creation to believe this on faith. St. John, the youngest apostle of Christ, was given a vision in the first century of what this final conflict between Good and evil would look like. John wrote down what he saw in the book of the Apocalypse, or Revelation as it is more commonly known.

All men are creatures of their times, St. John was no exception. He knew nothing of airplanes, missiles, spaceships, nuclear weapons, submarines, tanks, or lasers. His world was primitive by modern scientific and technological standards, so while John did his best, much of what he saw in his apocalyptic vision was inadequately described.

Malik Graham was a twenty-first century man. His limitations were far less than St. John's. It was not possible for him to diminish the horror of Armageddon through confusion or symbolism.

In a matter of seconds, the spiritual dimension Malik could see from his seat in the East Room expanded a thousand fold. Two armies were poised on either side of the "room," which now appeared to be miles, not yards, long.

On one side, Malik saw the beast in all of his repulsive ugliness. Around him were uncountable hordes of demons holding themselves back behind some invisible line of demarcation.

The forces of darkness radiated hate, a loathing of God and His favorite creation, man. Malik could sense the devil's unity of purpose, to destroy humanity and through the process of doing so become a god in his own right, to elevate evil above the Light, to vanquish the Lord.

The second army shone collectively like a blazing star. Its beings projected a reticence for fighting, a desire for peace, and a regret and disgust over being drawn into conflict. Malik absorbed the energy of the army of Light, it filled him with hope and joy and a confident assurance that victory over Satan was indeed inevitable. He was moved by a powerful desire to join them, to become one with them, but he knew that as long as he remained a mortal man he could not do so.

Then Satan extended one of his hideous claws and stretched out a vision from it that filled the space between the opposing forces. Malik was shown the destruction of human civilization, an all encompassing shredding of flesh, the unimaginable suffering caused by total global warfare. It was clear to him that Satan believed that this was the unalterable destiny of man, to destroy himself in a perverted orgasm of senseless brutality.

Then Gabriel appeared from amidst the beings of Light. With a wave of his hand, Satan's nightmare disappeared and was replaced by a vision of prosperity and peace. Malik saw gleaming metropolises with towers of shining glass and metal separated by open, green spaces. Within these magnificent cities, millions of people were working for their mutual benefit without strife or greed or hatred. Poverty was eliminated, disease tamed, crime abolished. God was established as the true ruler of man, Christ enthroned as an earthly king.

Then Gabriel's vision vanished and the empty space between the combatants was restored. As soon as this happened, the two armies began moving closer together, activity within each force increasing as they slowly crept toward each other.

That's when Malik decided it was time to get everyone out of the White House. Once the evacuation was complete Malik could no longer see the vision of the heavenly battlefield. Since he was still alive, Malik assumed that either the angels or the demons must have retreated.

"I'll never be afraid of the damn devil," Malik told Peter after he finished describing what he'd seen for him, "but I'm scared to death God and the evil one will battle it out. Don't think we'd make it through that. We don't amount to much stacked up 'gainst all their power. It's real humblin' to see that, Mr. Pete, to know how weak we humans really are."

"You made the right call getting the audience out of there, Malik," Peter told his brother. "I could feel it too, a sense of dread, foreboding. I felt like, well ... " Peter hesitated.

"Bro?"

"I felt like I was an insect lining up to get squashed."

The President did not delay action. At noon Eastern Time on the twenty-second of June, he announced a bold set of new federal government initiatives. He declared that "the moment in history has arrived when America must lead the way as a truly Christian country, we must put ourselves in accordance with the Lord's will for our national destiny and we must simply start doing more godly things and less evil ones."

Pledging that the United States would "act only in limited self defense" after the restriction ended, the President called for an immediate international summit of world leaders with the express purpose of forging an agreement to eliminate all armed forces and to forever abolish the practice of war. "Imagine the earth with no armies and no need for them," the President said in his globally televised speech. "All conflicts resolved peacefully through negotiation and compromise. A lunatic's fantasy, some say. But how can we ignore the fact of the restriction and the other miracles being reported from around the globe? Is it crazy to believe that warfare can be abandoned as a human institution, or is it insane to ignore the will of God? If we must choose between destruction or peace then I say the only rational option is to pick survival."

Professing his conviction that hunger and want for the basic necessities of life could be eliminated planet-wide in less than a decade, the President proposed an "effort of total commitment" to raise the standard of living for the "poorest and most vulnerable of our brothers and sisters." The problem of "systemic economic inequality should be attacked with all the vigor of a world war and on all fronts," he said, from the greater sharing of resources by the affluent, to the elimination of political and economic corruption in the Third World and through an "unprecedented outpouring of love and concern."

But the President did not stop with asking for the world, he added the moon and the stars. He called for the creation of a new American health care system, one based on "the maximum application of Christ's mercy, not upon material greed."

"The right to receive quality health care is a basic human right," the President said. "Anyone arguing that it is not should be ashamed of himself and fear his day of judgment before the Lord."

The President signed an Executive Order forbidding any U.S. law enforcement officer from "pursuing or apprehending" any of the estimated four hundred thousand inmates that were able to leave American prisons during the restriction. For the federal felons who walked off, he issued a blanket clemency. For state and local prisoners whom "God paroled," as he phrased it, he threatened states that refused to pardon them with "any and all monetary sanctions at my disposal as President." He called for a commission, to be jointly chaired by Tim Austin and Gail McCorkle, to "review all aspects of our current criminal justice system, from statutes to bureaucracies," and to offer "concrete proposals to the President for reducing the number of incarcerated persons, increasing educational, vocational and spiritual training options throughout the prison system and to provide practical ideas to bring our criminal justice system more in line with Christian values and by doing so, create conditions that will minimize criminal conduct and reduce recidivism."

"I know full well how these proposals will be received in some quarters," the President said, as he wrapped up his nearly hour long speech. "I will be called a madman, a dreamer, a threat to the social order. So be it then. I stand on the idea that the time has come for us to move closer to Christ, both as individuals and as a society. We must do so boldly and with faith. I ask you to pray for yourselves, to pray for your country and to pray for your President."

In a separate press release, not desiring to mix his positive message with an unpleasant task, the President called for the immediate resignation of his Vice President. He cited "not only serious personal and political differences brought to the surface by the restriction and related events" but also "significant ethical lapses by the Vice President better left unpursued in the interests of national harmony and Christian forgiveness."

Working together with the President and using the resources of the White House, Peter Carson announced that at six p.m. tomorrow, June the twenty-third, he, the President, and the disciples would be present at RFK stadium in Washington to "celebrate the Lord's miracles." The event was to be a culmination of Holy Thursday, and a rallying point for God's faithful. It would also serve as the beginning of a global ministry for Peter and the disciples. Solomon's Porch was coming to the four corners of the earth.

"It's almost too good to be true, my friend. Perhaps you were right, I am too pessimistic. Those fools are delusional to hold such a public spectacle right after the restriction. We could not ask for a more perfect scenario." Some sleep, tranquilizers, and an unhealthy dose of single malt scotch had calmed the President's former first advisor over the past eighteen hours.

"Everything is set. The assets are in place in Los Angeles and San Francisco. They slipped into the harbors last night completely undetected." As he spoke, the President's second former senior advisor was busy operating a small bank of computers set up in the conspirator's makeshift war room.

"And our assassin, he is ready too? No problems?"

"No problems. He's staying at the Watergate under the name of Mustapha al-Elyan. He's posing as a trade minister from Oman."

"And his assassin?"

"That's the least of your worries, my friend. He's guarding the President."

"My, my. Nice of you to tell me about that interesting wrinkle. Don't trust me?"

"Of course, I just thought you would enjoy the surprise."

"Not as much as the President will, I'm sure."

Twenty-Seven

There was no way to know precisely when the restriction would end. Some guessed ten p.m. sharp, others swore it would be ten o'two, o'three, or o'five. It was simply impossible to determine the exact moment the blessing began.

The ten o'clock sharp prediction proved to be accurate.

Dr. Howard Simms, now working through the Office of the President, coordinated an extensive network of resources whose purpose was to report on the immediate post restriction response of individuals and groups. In less than twenty-four hours, Simms put in place thousands of "special observers," as he called them, across the globe that had objective criteria they applied to record and categorize everything they measured and witnessed.

In a few months, Simms intended to publish "The Report," a massive tome detailing all the raw data collected about the restriction and its aftermath. He also planned to offer analyses and conclusions at that time, but certain post restriction activity was "significant" and "merited immediate comment," in Simms' view, so he issued a brief statement to the press shortly before noon on the twenty-third.

For about two hours after the restriction ended, a wave of "pent-up frustration," as Simms labeled it, was "released." Assaults, murders, fights, basically all categories of measurable personal violence, rose well above pre-restriction norms. Some in the media jumped on this early eruption of hate and predicted a widespread return to "worse than business as usual."

But they were wrong.

According to Dr. Simms, "the effect of being forcibly restrained from committing acts of violence caused many millions of persons across a variety of societies to reassess their personal values and their relationship with God." As the morning of the twenty-third of June progressed, less and less violence was being reported. Despite the initial violent surge, the "early post-restriction trend is clearly toward more, not less, peace."

Of course, all of Simms' data was preliminary. Extrapolating any long term trends from a few hours worth of activity would be foolhardy and Simms made no attempt to do so. He merely described and summarized what his small army of "special observers" reported to him.

Calling it "opinion and informed speculation," Simms was willing to climb out a little bit on a limb. He said "the restriction has altered attitudes and expectations, but for how long and to what ultimate degree remains uncertain. However, it seems undeniable that a significant step in the right direction has taken place. The social environment is not the same as it was seventy-two hours ago."

On the political front, about ninety percent of the invitations issued by the President to the global peace summit were accepted and confirmed by noon on the twenty-third. The impossible now seemed tantalizingly within reach. More and more people were beginning to believe that the President might actually pull off a miracle of his own.

The "Day of Fasting and Prayer" was also having an impact. In their homes and in public gatherings, hundreds of millions of souls fasted for all or part of the day and asked God to help Peter and their political leadership. Roger Stone led this effort from his home in Wisconsin, hourly conducting a prayer service that was televised worldwide.

Hope was rapidly supplanting fear. The belief that God had spoken, that the Creator of the universe had delivered a positive message of love for His children, was taking wide root, blossoming, and bearing fruit.

Then Satan struck back.

Two ships, both non-descript cargo vessels, exploded simultaneously in Los Angeles and San Francisco harbors. It was ten a.m. Pacific Time on June the twenty-third.

Each ship contained a nuclear warhead manufactured by the former Soviet Union and stolen from its Ukrainian owners by a radical Islamic group. The weapons had actually been missing for years, although they had supposedly been accounted for in one of the many desultory international weapons inspections of the Ukraine in the post-Soviet era.

In the blink of an eye, tens of thousands of people were vaporized, and hundreds of thousands more were subjected to lethal doses of radiation. Billions of dollars in property was destroyed and, far worse, two of the largest cities in America and their environs were contaminated and made uninhabitable for decades to come.

Those pursuing peace suddenly not only looked naïve, but recklessly dangerous as well.

Peter was sitting in a small office in the White House going over his sermon for the RFK event when he heard the terrible news. He watched as shocked faces hurried up and down the corridor. Many of them looked in angrily as they passed by, their eyes accusing him of somehow being responsible for bringing the unthinkable horror of a nuclear attack to American soil.

"Many will blame you," Bishop Kallistos said, as he strode into Peter's office and closed the door. "People, how you say, expect you can end all evil by yourself. Through lies like that and fear of death, Satan will tempt them. This is horrible tragedy, but as I told you, Panos, tragedy can be part of God's plan too. Are you ready? Time has come for you to face the enemy."

Peter was listening, but not responding. He was deep in prayer asking God to help those in California who were suffering and to give him the strength to do what must be done.

Twenty-Eight

"Peter, do you know how much I love you? How important you are not only to us, but to Julie and Kevin and to the millions who have heard you and believe?"

"Yes, Gail, I know these things."

"Then don't be a damned fool! I do not believe that God encourages suicide, and that's exactly what you'd be committing if you go to that stadium."

"Gail, my sister, please listen to me. I know that you mean well, I know that..."

"You heard those Secret Service guys. Do you think they're stupid? They are pros, Peter, they know what they are doing. How can you and the President just ignore them?"

"I'm not ignoring them, but I answer to God, not to man."

"Honestly, I don't get it. Aren't you the one who taught us that Satan has very real powers, that he is a most formidable adversary? Why are you making it so easy for him?"

Logically, Peter knew Gail McCorkle was right. As were the Secret Service agents, and the entire President's inner circle. Any sane man would cancel the RFK event, hunker down, and ride out the storm.

But men of God are not such men; once called, they can never turn back. They are required to keep their "hands on the plow," as Christ commanded.

"Gail, I know that I probably cannot convince you that we are doing the proper thing, but stop and listen to me. Just for a minute."

Reluctantly, Gail did.

"The President and I must not show any fear. We will stay the course and not back down, not one bit, from God's call to end violence. We have no choice but to be even stronger now in our convictions, more bold. Satan offers hate and fear, as messengers of God, we must meet this challenge with mercy and love."

"What are you going to do, forgive the psychotic bastards who nuked Cali?"

"Yes, that's it exactly. We intend to pray for them and to ask God to be merciful when He judges them."

"Peter, I hear what you are saying, God knows we all need more merciful hearts, but..."

"But what, Gail? If we do not show mercy to the worst of sinners, how can we claim to be God's messengers? Who do you think the Master died on the cross for? Just those who love Him?"

"Peter, brother, I hear you, but be sensible. We cannot just lie down and do nothing. Whoever did this committed an atrocity on a scale that's beyond..."

"Beyond what, Gail? Beyond God's unlimited grace?"

"You mean we have to let these evil monsters kill us all? We cannot fight back?"

"Of course we can fight back, Gail, but it's how we respond that defines us. What we must do is let God fight this battle for us. He says we can no longer return death for death, hate for hate. If we obey Him, how could you possibly believe He would let the evil one destroy us?"

"We win by giving up?"

"No, we win by refusing to play the devil's game. We say enough. We let God protect us."

"Which means?"

"Which means the President and I go forward as planned. We are obedient and ask for obedience from them. By now, sister, I really thought that you understood."

"Help me, Peter. Help me to understand this madness."

"I am nothing more than an example. So is the President. So were all the prophets and the saints. For that matter, Gail, so are you."

"Peter, brother, I do not have your strength. I know how useless it is to lie; God sees all, so He already knows what I think. If it were up to me, I'd hunt down the maniacs that did this and dismember them. Forgive me, but I do not have your ability to be so kind. Not now, not after all this slaughter."

"If they do not repent, Gail, you know very well what will happen to them. They will spend eternity in hell. You know what that looks like; you've heard Saul and Kenny testify. What could be worse?"

"I don't have a heaven or hell to put anyone in, Peter, that's for sure. But I'd take great satisfaction in sending those filthy scum to the devil for processing as quickly as possible."

"Gail, don't you see it? Isn't it obvious?"

"I see thousands upon thousands of dead people in California and the world turning against us."

"The devil wants us to hate, to lash out, to seek revenge. He's counting on it. Satan does not share God's faith in us, Gail. He thinks we are too weak, too stupid to realize it's a trap."

"If we fight back, launch a retaliatory strike or war, we're through. We will not get any more second chances. This is it. It's time for humanity to grow up or to be destroyed."

"But..."

"But nothing! God has spoken. Don't ask me why things are the way they are, or why God allowed the evil one to destroy those cities. I don't know, but I do know what must be done now. I need you, sister. I need all of you."

The President and the disciples had been listening to Gail and Peter argue for half an hour. No one had said a word. They knew love was working things out, binding them even closer together through the venting of fears, frustrations, and doubts. Gail wasn't only speaking for herself; everyone else in the room shared her sentiments to some degree.

"Peter, I have said my peace. I will do as you say, with a willing heart that would follow you anywhere. But do not ask me to lie down and watch you die. That is the one thing I will not do."

Gail could say no more. Her tears were flowing, hands shaking. She stood and said "please excuse me," walked out and went to the President's private chapel to try and work out her issues with the Lord.

"You know that I've seen this day coming, Peter," Larry said. "I'm not sure if my vision was an inevitability or only one possible future."

"All futures must be possible, Larry, from our perspective anyway, because we have free will," Peter reminded.

"Then, if we must go into the arena, Peter, we should go in knowing that all of us will not make it out alive. I'm totally sure of that much, brother."

Peter understood what Larry was asking him to do.

"Does anyone here wish to remain in the White House?" Peter asked. "Let the will of God be your guide, do not blindly follow me or anyone else."

"Death does not frighten me," Enrique Vargas said. "Lord knows I've seen more of it than any man here. As a soldier in the army of man, I respected it, feared it. As a soldier in the army of God, death has no power over me. God's will be done. I'm with you."

Every other head in the room nodded in agreement.

"Mr. President," said the voice over the intercom, "General Wagner is here to see you."

"Show him in," the President replied.

"Gentlemen, I too am willing to lay down my life for God and country, but we'll have eighty thousand plus other citizens in that stadium with us. I've asked the army to provide security for the event. Yes, I know that's not altogether kosher, using the military rather than civilian security forces, but I don't have time to be worried about details. A strong presence, a show of strength, may deter more violence."

"Mr. President, if I may, sir …" Peter was interrupted before he could finish his sentence.

"I know how you feel, Peter, but this is my responsibility. I'm with you a hundred percent, we will not back down an inch from our initiatives. But the troops will be deployed. It's my call and my decision is final."

All Peter could say was, "Yes sir." There was no more time for debate anyway. They had less than forty-five minutes to get to RFK and be ready to face their destiny.

Twenty-Nine

"Where is the damned fool? He needs to be tucked away in his official residence; saying nothing, doing less."

"Relax. He's on his way home. The President asked for his resignation, remember? To keep up appearances, he's been making the rounds, gauging sentiment. We can't be too obvious about this now can we?"

"You've got him under control, right?" He's not going to get some f***ing attack of righteousness on us, is he? Once he's in, he's in. We have only blackmail as leverage. Better be enough."

"You worry too much. I was wondering why you didn't go ape s*** over all the troops. There must be two thousand soldiers milling around RFK right now. That little wrinkle doesn't bother you?"

"You said the Secret Service remains in overall control of the security, yes?"

"That's correct."

"Then why should I be worried?"

"Well said, I think I'm rubbing off on you at last."

Evil had set its trap. The President's former senior advisors were confident and proud of themselves, congratulating each other on their cleverness and shrewd decision making. They believed that they were superior, the vanguard of a ruling elite poised to present itself as the only viable alternative to "the failed traditional American political system."

"Who will defend you?" they will shortly ask a paralyzed nation. "Who can you trust?" they will soon shout. Using the backdrop of the scorched and radioactive ruins of Los Angeles and San Francisco, they will petition Americans to abandon what's left of their liberties for a short time to fight and destroy the ruthless enemies of our society.

They will offer both security and revenge and all they will demand in exchange is a little leeway to get the job done.

The beast, who orchestrated all of this mayhem and hate, was at the ready. He was confident that his puppets would soon be in control of the most powerful nation on earth.

Then he would act and send all of the hated ape scum humans where they belonged, to hell. Satan would then assume his rightful place as their sole lord and master and use his dominion over man as the catalyst to achieve final victory in his ages old war against the Creator.

"What a stupid country," Mustapha said to himself, taking a position in a service duct behind the currently unused electronic display arrayed on the stadium's south side. "So rich, so vain. They are like overfed livestock, weak and good only for the butchering."

"Mustapha" could not believe how easy it was to get into RFK with his weapon and set up. A tall, dark haired man from the American Secret Service itself had walked him right in and tucked him safely into place.

"The Americans are a disgrace. Even their elite soldiers are traitors, no doubt for money." Mustapha had no one to talk with now except Allah, but that was sufficient. He was certain that very soon he would be in Paradise with the Prophet reaping his eternal reward. While he had an escape plan, he knew how futile and stupid it would be to try and run away. Besides, he was no coward. The assassin had spent his whole life preparing for this day, for this highest honor.

By killing the President of the United States and the false Christian prophet Carson, Mustapha knew he would be immortalized. He would become a martyr hero of Islam and put another nail in the coffin of Christendom's dying civilization.

He sighted and ranged his weapon. He was ready. All that was left to do was to wait and pray.

What should have been an orderly and joyous celebration was now a confused and frightened mix of people. The majority of the jittery crowd came to RFK seeking solace, to be reassured by Peter Carson and the President that the restriction was not a cruel deception gone hopelessly awry.

For the select, their faith was only strengthened by the California attacks. They came to the stadium to receive their marching orders, to be blessed by and to support their prophet.

Others showed to pin blame, to point fingers, to say "I told you so" and to clamor for a vengeful response. In other times and in different contexts, this group would have been correctly labeled patriots, righteous defenders of God, and country. They wanted to define the enemy, find him and kill him and then come home to the glory and the parades.

But the paradigm of using violent force as an effective national defense was no longer viable. From the time man first became civilized in the river valleys of Iraq until now, it had always been true that the first duty of any government was to protect its citizens against aggression. The enemy was always at the door; failure to provide an adequate armed defense sooner or later doomed your country, or your kingdom, or your city-state.

The relationship between the use of violence and national security was so ingrained in human experience that it seemed suicidal to abandon it, but the restriction shook this assumption of the need for organized savagery to its foundations. God exposed the myth, challenged the lie. Then the California bombings, coming when they did, reignited all of man's primal fears, and through terror caused people to run back to the all too comforting false security blanket of hate.

As Peter, the President, the disciples, and Gail approached the hastily set up stage through a tunnel of soldiers, they could hear the opposing chants coming from the frothy crowd, the conflicting calls for murder and mercy.

When they emerged into view, an eerie silence broke out, as if now the factions wanted to wait to hear something they could either cheer or deride before making any more noise.

Peter was about to walk up to the dais when Malik grabbed his arm.

"Mr. Pete, no. Don't go. Please, bro."

"Malik, we talked about this. I don't have a choice."

"Mr. Pete, it's the beast. He's waitin' for ya. I can see him. He's right there." Malik pointed to a platform about fifty feet off of the stage that held cameras and other electronic equipment. "He's goin' to kill you, Mr. Pete. I swear I know he is. For the love of God, Mr. Pete … Why you smilin'?"

"You know why, Malik."

"Because you've known all along this was goin' to happen?"

"Yes, brother. I have known."

"Jesus Christ wants you dead? How can that be?"

"There comes a point in the lives of certain men of God, brother, when they become of greater service to the Kingdom as martyrs than they can be as living men. I have reached that time, Malik. You may too someday, but you haven't yet."

None of the rest of the group could hear the conversation between Peter and Malik. They were standing fifteen feet away from them. The President, the disciples and Gail had also stopped approaching the dais when Malik halted Peter.

"Aren't you scared, bro? I've seen and caused more'n my share of death, Mr. Pete. It's brutal, ugly."

"Sure, I'm scared, but God is with me. Christ strengthens me, brother, as He does you. He will never leave us or forsake us."

"What if I just hit ya with one of these sledgehammers, Mr. Pete. I could lay you out so fast make your head spin."

"No doubt. Go ahead, friend," Peter said, as he took a step back and stuck out his chin. "But know that you would be betraying all you love, all we stand for. God didn't pull you out of hell so you could quit on Him now, brother. You must be strong."

Rather than hit him, Malik reached over and hugged Peter so hard he thought Malik might be trying to knock him out without throwing a punch. But Malik released Peter in a few seconds, gave him a kiss on the cheek and whispered in his ear.

"Don't worry about Mrs. Pete and little Kev. I swear to you no one will ever harm them. I will guard them with my life and soul."

"I was counting on that, Malik. God bless you."

Malik almost started sobbing, but he instantly sucked it up. If there was one thing he understood and admired, it was courage. He wiped his eyes on his sleeve and motioned for the rest of the group to move forward.

"You are the bravest person I know, Mr. Pete. I would follow you into hell."

"I think you're about to do just that."

Nothing Peter had been through or ever imagined could have adequately prepared him for the intimidating pressure of standing in front of almost a hundred thousand emotionally charged people in a stadium designed to hold no more than eighty. Every heart and mind was focused on him, anxiously waiting to see what he would say and do.

Peter suddenly felt hopelessly weak and small, even more overmatched and inadequate than he did before the roundtable. He knew that the only cure for his fear was prayer. One last time Peter Carson called on the Power to intervene on his behalf.

The disciples formed a circle. Someone handed Peter a microphone. He began to pray.

"Lord, we ask for Your mercy and favor today. Strengthen everyone here, Christ. Let no one act out of fear or hate, but rather seek Your power through love and mercy. Reach out Your marvelous hand, Lord, and pull us toward the Light and away from the darkness. We pray this in the name of the Father, Son, and the Holy Spirit, amen."

Something like sixty thousand voices boomed "Amen" after Peter finished, the rest of the crowd kept silent.

After the prayer, Peter could feel the Energy surging through him. Just that quickly God infused him with His grace, replacing the weakness of his flesh with the power of the Spirit.

Mustapha was unmoved by the Christian's impotent plea. He had finished praying minutes earlier, but unbeknownst to him, Allah, the Creator, wasn't listening to his prayers. The vile beast perched fifty yards below him on the equipment stand was

Mustapha's god, and he had done his job well. Satan made sure that Mustapha was completely focused on his "godly" task of committing bloody murder. Mustapha would not find out who had really been answering his prayers and how displeased Allah was with him until it was far too late to do him any good.

"Brothers and sisters," Peter began, "I ask you all to join me in another short prayer. If you would like to do so please stand, bow your head and take your neighbor's hand."

A little more than half the people in RFK did so.

"Lord, we ask for your mercy on all those who are suffering in California. Your will be done, Lord, but we ask that you spare as many as You will from death and disease. Especially, help and heal the innocent, Lord, and the faithful. Protect and keep them from further harm."

A few thousand discordant "amens" were given, but Peter's prayer was only half finished.

"Lord, we also ask for Your mercy on those who committed these terrible acts. Lead them to repentance, Lord, let them become sons of God and turn them away from the everlasting flames of hell. Hold not their sins against them. Christ, we ask you to forgive them. Amen."

Stunned, thousands repeated "Amen" simply because the prayer was over, not because they agreed with it. For others, Peter's amen was their cue to become belligerent and vocal.

"F*** you, Carson!" yelled a man who was standing directly behind a row of soldiers who had formed a human shield between the surging crowd and the stage.

"You filthy traitor!" came another shout. "Man of God my a**! Lunatic! Demon!" The cries of derision grew louder and more diverse. Peter let them holler unchallenged as he stood impassive at the dais. He showed no fear, or any other emotion.

After five minutes or so, the cursing attacks subsided and a far different set of chants were heard. "We love you, Peter!" "Praise God!" "Be strong, brother!" The supporters of Christ were just as vocal and persistent as the frightened and evil ones had been.

Once again, Peter said nothing. He stood stoically and waited.

"He wears no vest. Neither does the President. Allah be praised!" Mustapha had a clear line of sight and his targets were stationary and unprotected by body armor. But he held his fire, waiting for the perfect moment, all the while allowing part of his mind to drift to thoughts of his new life in Paradise.

Finally, when something close to calm was restored, Peter spoke.

"I am no one. Until last year I was hopelessly lost. I was a selfish, greedy thief cast aside by society in a federal prison."

"For His reasons and His purposes the God of all creation, our Heavenly Father, chose me to deliver a message to you. Why he picked me and not the Pope or a bishop or a famous evangelist I do not know, because I am only His servant."

"Over the past year I've come to understand many things, but I still wonder about many more. By no means do I have all the answers. I cannot waive a magic wand and solve all of our problems, because I am but a messenger."

"The message He gave me to proclaim to the world is this; we must do a far better job of being our brother's keeper. We need to focus our energies, talents, and wealth on helping each other, not on war or mindless competition or on satisfying our selfish desires. We must stop pretending that the will of God is a mystery, because it is not. He wants us to feed the hungry, clothe the naked, heal the sick, and show mercy to the prisoners. He gave us the blessing of the restriction to demonstrate the urgency of His call for us to forsake violence in all its forms.

"I know how you feel right now. Servants of hell, confused and lost souls, have murdered thousands of our countrymen. This makes us angry, fuels our fears and hate, but God made it plain to me that if we retaliate, try to attack or kill those who we believe destroyed Los Angeles and San Francisco, we will set off a chain of events that will lead to our final destruction. I know it is difficult to accept the call of mercy. We are used to seeking revenge, to exterminating our opponents and calling the result victory and peace.

"But, my brothers and sisters, stop and think. Has war ever really achieved peace? No. It has vanquished enemies, but new foes always appear. War itself has never been defeated. Until now."

"Let God fight this battle for us, my friends. Does anyone here still doubt His power? Have you forgotten the restriction already? Why would God abandon us now if we are faithful to Him? How much more will He protect and bless us if we are obedient?"

"I am not a political leader. The President will speak to you and explain how he will turn God's commands into American policy. But I ask everyone here to believe, to have faith, to 'seek peace and pursue it' as St. Paul said.

"God's way is strength through peace, victory through mercy, protection through forgiveness. Satan offers only to steal, kill and destroy, to fan the flames of violence to the level of Armageddon.

"If we become of one mind, with one purpose, which is to seek, obey, and glorify God, then each and every one of you will be blessed. We must take this next step in our spiritual evolution, brothers and sisters. Our only other choice is certain destruction."

The crowd was quiet when Peter finished speaking. People who moments earlier were shouting insults and obscenities hung their heads and were mute. The message of God was powerful, impossible to ignore and difficult to defy.

Peter stepped down from the speaker's platform and moved toward his friends. The President stood and greeted him with a hug and then walked toward the dais.

He made it about halfway.

No one heard the shots because the rifle was silenced, but the results were obvious. The President was hit multiple times in the chest and head. Blood and spilled brains oozed from his lifeless, but still twitching body.

Gail McCorkle was standing ten feet away from Peter when she saw that the President had been shot. She lunged at Peter, hit him full force like a linebacker on a running back, and knocked him down. She could hear the "tink-tink" sound of the bullets impacting the stage all around her.

Recovering quickly, Gail moved to throw her body on top of Peter's, who was struggling to get back on his feet. As she stood Mustapha put two slugs into her torso. Gail collapsed before she could reach Peter. She was dead before she hit the floor.

Then the soldiers opened up. They sprayed the electronic display array with sheets of fire, completely ignoring the significant collateral damage they were causing to innocent spectators.

The soldiers were shooting at a ghost. Mustapha was already dead. The Secret Service agent who had escorted him to his hiding place killed him the instant after he murdered Gail McCorkle.

RFK was in a state of pandemonium. Everyone feared the stadium was about to be bombed. A hundred thousand souls instantly became a spooked herd, shoving and trampling each other trying to reach the nearest exit.

Satan was well pleased. His plan was being executed to perfection. He had only one more objective to accomplish, and he chose to tend to the matter personally.

Mustapha's soul was already in hell, but his body was still warm. His assassin had put two bullets into his lungs, but Mustapha's head and limbs remained in tact. Satan jumped into the nearly bled out corpse, not requiring a whole man, just some of the parts.

The devil intensely disliked placing himself in a human body and had done so on only a few occasions over the ages. The last time was when he entered a man named Iscariot in Jerusalem. For Satan, whatever pleasure he was going to derive from the experience had to far outweigh the disgusting repulsion of joining himself with a filthy ape.

Satan picked up Mustapha's rifle. When he looked through the scope he saw Peter Carson kneeling over Gail McCorkle, praying for her soul. The devil could also see Peter's friends, especially Malik Graham, desperately trying to get to him and shelter him.

Mustapha fired three more shots and all of them found their mark. Peter's body exploded as the shells hit him.

Dead, he slumped over Gail McCorkle with his hand still clutching hers and a prayer for her salvation lingering on his lips.

Thirty

"Lord, you have led me down such a difficult path. Perhaps I live too long, sweet Jesus. I am your humble servant always; a loyal priest of Philippi, but Lord, my heart is troubled. Save me, Christ, help your sad and weary warrior."

Gregory Kallistos offered his prayer silently. He did not know the driver of the car Alex Anderson had provided for him and he was in no position to put any trust in strangers.

As they pulled up to the Anderson estate he saw them. Julie Carson was indeed a most beautiful woman, exactly as Peter had described. Standing silently and holding her hand was the focus of the Bishop's next, and perhaps final, mission for the Lord.

Fear and despair prevailed everywhere Kallistos had been over the past twenty-four hours. The losses were unimaginably severe; two large cities, a President, and a prophet of God all taken in the same tragic day. A state of shock gripped America and the world. Confusion was the predominant condition. Faith in the future, in any future, seemed reserved for a fortunate few.

Kallistos' special burden was that he'd known that all of this horror was coming. But knowing and being able to do anything to prevent it were two very different things. God would not allow Gregory to avert the trial, but He gave him the wisdom and the prophecy necessary for His children to endure and overcome it.

That's why Kallistos was here. Not to preside at Peter's funeral, or to comfort his widow, or to give counsel to Peter's disciples who must now go on without him. He would do all of those things and more, but that was not why he was here.

He was at the Anderson estate to deliver a letter. It was written almost two thousand years ago by St. Paul. The epistle was one of two prophetic messages entrusted by Paul to the Philippi priests.

"Lord, such pain and despair. Have mercy on them, Christ." As the limousine came to a stop, Bishop Kallistos looked out through the glass at Julie and Kevin Carson. Their expressions were dull, postures slumped, eyes red. He was sure that neither had slept over the past thirty-six hours. They had the vacant look of homeless refugees, shattered by loss and grief.

Julie considered the idea of not letting Kevin watch the event at RFK. But how could she keep her son from seeing his famous father speak to the nations? It was not possible to deny him something so important.

They held hands and watched together as Peter's speech calmed the agitated crowd to silence. Julie would never forget the relief she felt when she saw Peter descend from the platform unharmed.

Then the President was shot. The camera bored in on a close up of the slain leader. Kevin shrieked. For a few seconds they couldn't see Peter, they did not know what was happening to him.

Even amidst the confusion, the television reporter somehow managed to keep giving updates from his position on the stage.

"Carson's been shot! Carson's been shot!" They heard the voice before they saw any images.

An instant later a camera found Peter slumped over Gail. Blood covered both of them as they lay together in a final embrace.

Julie was in a state of shock, so for a second she forgot about Kevin. When she recovered her wits she saw her son staring at the screen crying and pleading "Daddy, no, Daddy, please, God, no."

That was almost twenty hours ago. Kevin had not slept, eaten, or spoken since. Julie was in slightly better shape, but not by much.

"My children," Bishop Kallistos said, as he left the limo and approached them. "I am here as your servant, to show you Christ's love in your most desperate hour."

"Papa?" Kevin said, looking up at the old priest. "Papa Kallistos? Where is my daddy?"

"He is with Christ, my son. Your father is in no pain, he is happy and free. His love for you will never die, never, how you say, fade out. He watches us now, trying his best to help you, my boy."

"Why, papa? Why did they kill my dad?"

"That will take many, many years for you to understand and accept, young Kevin. It is hard question for me to answer."

"Gabriel says it's because my dad was a prophet. The angel says no prophet is accepted in his own country."

"When did you talk to Gabriel?" Julie asked, thrilled that Kevin had suddenly come back to life upon Kallistos' arrival.

"In my room, mom, a few minutes ago. He told me Papa Kallistos was coming to help me and that daddy was okay. The angel loves me, mom. He loves you, too."

Julie didn't know what to say. She was battling her own conflicting emotions and ideas. God to her had become primarily a dispenser of cruelty. She struggled with the notion that He loved Peter or Kevin. How could a loving God allow such pain and suffering to be inflicted on them? Was such a God worth worshipping?

Yet, despite her doubts, Gregory Kallistos had an immediate soothing impact upon her. To some small degree at least, Julie's torment lessened just by being in his presence.

Julie, Kevin, and Bishop Kallistos spent the evening of June the twenty-fourth in seclusion. The disciples had all returned to Atlanta, as had Alex Anderson, but they kept their distance from Peter's uncle, widow, and son, allowing them some time to grieve as a family.

The world around the Anderson compound was in chaos. The Vice President of the United States had assumed the Presidency, but he did so under a cloud of suspicion and fear of imminent nuclear attacks. Several radical Islamic groups came forward and claimed credit for the California bombings. Unnamed American intelligence sources publicly tied these groups to several mid-east governments.

Rumors swirled, the most vicious and disturbing of which was that the California attacks and the assassination of the President and Peter Carson were part of a successful coup d'état. Even though "highly placed sources within the government" were making these outrageous allegations, not many considered them credible. Americans nuked their own country? It seemed insane to even entertain such wild speculation.

The new President called for an "immediate retaliation against any country that participated in the attack or in any way shields, supports, or condones the madmen who bombed California." The new Chief Executive also swore to "bring to justice swiftly the cowardly scum who murdered the President and Peter Carson, by whatever means necessary."

"We are at war," the President declared. "The might of America will be brought to bare against the enemies of civilization."

After Julie put her exhausted son to bed she joined Bishop Kallistos in Alex's study. He poured them each a brandy and asked her to sit with him.

"My dear, I'm afraid I don't bring you peace, but rather more tests. This is beginning of your struggles, Julie, not the end. God has chosen not only Peter, but Kevin as well."

"I don't understand, Father. Kevin is just a little boy. What can he do to help keep the world from destroying itself?"

"Maybe nothing, Julie Carson. Maybe everything. The future is not pre-determined. We must have faith and be obedient if God's promises are to be fulfilled. Trust Christ always."

"Speak plainly, Bishop. I'm in no mood for any more mysteries."

"Your son is also prophet of God. He was called before time began for this purpose. Peter came and he warned the world, hopefully they listen. We will help them to listen, but Kevin is, how you say, most important key to all God's plans."

"How do you know this, Father Gregory? What makes you so sure?"

Out of his ancient satchel and a second wooden box Gregory Kallistos produced another letter from the past and its English translation. They read it together.

"My husband and my son? God forgive me, Father, but I don't know if I'll let Him have them both."

"You must, my daughter. Much depends on you. Kevin cannot realize his destiny without your influence."

At that moment Julie Carson wasn't interested in considering divine prophecies. Her husband had been brutally murdered for doing nothing more than bringing peace and hope to the world, for encouraging people to love one another. She was angry and bitter, full of pain. Julie's only desire was to be left alone to raise her son, to give him some semblance of a normal life.

"Don't ask me to make commitments now, Father. God or not, letters from saints or not, I'm not sure I'll ever be willing to sacrifice Kevin, to place him at the mercy of the evil pieces of trash that call themselves human beings. I am not my husband. Throwing myself and Kevin to the mercy of the lions seems crazy to me. Good night."

As he watched Julie Carson get up and leave the study, Bishop Gregory's heart was breaking. He knew that Julie was a wonderful mother who would only get better at her role as the years went on. Her initial reaction to God's calling for her life was understandable.

But would the years go on? That was the question. Kevin was a big part of the answer, as was his mother.

"Lord have mercy on us all," Bishop Kallistos prayed. "Give us the strength to do Your will. It is a fearful thing that we have fallen into the hands of the Living God."